BLOODY HARVESTS

Richard Kunzmann is a native South African whose passion has always been African myths and mythologies, and their associated occultism. He majored in criminology, and has worked as a bookseller in London. This is his first novel.

RICHARD KUNZMANN

BLOODY HARVESTS

THOMAS DUNNE BOOKS | ST. MARTIN'S MINOTAUR
NEW YORK

THOMAS DUNNE BOOKS.
An imprint of St. Martin's Press.

www.thomasdunnebooks.com
www.minotaurbooks.com

ISBN-13: 978-0-312-36033-7
ISBN-10: 0-312-36033-9

First published in Great Britain by Pan Books,
an imprint of Pan Macmillan Ltd

First U.S. Edition: November 2006

10 9 8 7 6 5 4 3 2 1

This book is for

Berna and Sabine

*two wonderful women
who helped bring it all together
when it seemed just a dream*

Acknowledgements

Without well-informed people coming to the aid of a writer, he is nothing but a clever charlatan with his head in the clouds. A number of people helped with the creation of this book and to them I am deeply indebted.

Many thanks to Matthew Welz, Riaan Riekert and Aida Lingaseni Mahlamuza. This story merely touched on a complex range of issues. Whatever shortcomings may exist within these pages are entirely my own.

To my draft readers, Berna Buys, Sabine Bassler and my parents, I express immense gratitude for your positive criticism and advice.

Well done to the Pan Macmillan crews, both in South Africa and London. I dearly appreciate your enthusiasm and support.

Every fledgling needs a sheltering wing. From Peter Lavery and Mary Pachnos I not only received shelter and a chance, but patient guidance too. No words are eloquent enough for the dedication you have shown to this new author and his concept.

Prologue

The Yoruba does not feel safe here, but it has to do him for now.

A sour smell pervades the hot summer air, a stench that is not just stale urine. The building is rotten and the ammonia stench mixes with other stronger wisps of chemicals and garbage. In places plaster and crumbling brick have peeled away from the walls so extensively that the rusty veins of the dead building are showing through. Mosquitoes buzz endlessly in the air, breeding in stagnant pools that have accumulated inside the apartment. Flies shoot across the room like angry bullets, desperately looking for the meal that smells so good to them. Water is seeping through the ceiling in slow drops, plunging down from a large brown stain. A child is screaming loudly, its cries seeming to echo through the bowels of the building for hours; he cannot tell for exactly how long, because time has blurred for him. No one has yet bothered to attend to the infant, so he wonders whether everyone else there is dead or dying – or too scared to move, like he is.

Rats scrabble across the dirty floor in front of him, illuminated by the greenish light filtering through the black-painted windows. Cockroaches chatter around on naked grey concrete, also prospecting for food. He has noted well all these grimy details, because he has been waiting and hiding here so long. He knows every corner of this room better than his own hand.

He has made his toilet in the abandoned kitchen. The

1

smell occasionally overwhelms him, as gusts of wind punch some air back through the tattered cardboard fixed above the sink, where a window used to be. The bathroom itself is too foul to use, swamped in its own green porridge, and even if he wanted a bath, there is no running water. He is stranded in this filthy hole with no money and no hope, too terrified to ever think of going outside again.

The man has sores all over his arms and legs, but he cannot tell what has bitten him. He knows of nothing that bites like that.

The fetish?

He is sure it is his denunciation that has brought on this sickness. He should never have boasted so loudly to anyone ready to listen. His pride was his undoing.

This summer has been full of omens, bad ones. The signs were there, so why was he so reckless?

The worn mattress beneath him offers little comfort. He sits on it for hours, his thin legs drawn up so his elbows can rest on his knees, his hands clasped above his head as if in some kind of prayer. The skin hangs slack off his body, and he knows he is wasting away. He must look like a hibernating spider, he thinks, furled up here in his corner, something thin and spindly lurking in the darkness.

Food comes at intervals, wrapped in newspaper, and is shoved through a hole at the bottom of the door. It is dropped off, with a few whispers, by some unseen ally. The whispers have not offered much comfort yet, just urged him to be patient. He even wonders if the mysterious visitor is still his ally or has become his warder instead. The door is securely bolted and he cannot remember where the key is. In the beginning he tried to read the crumpled scraps of newspaper, but the light in the abandoned apartment was too poor. Nowadays his eyes pain him too much anyway, along with the rest of his decaying body. There is no electricity here, although he can hear civilization motoring past outside. He cannot even enjoy the benefit of light in this darkness.

He can smell Hillbrow beneath the stink of this solitary room of his; he can hear the ghetto humming just above the room's buzz of frenzied insects. Oozing through the painted glass, the light from the street outside looks sickly green.

What must it be like out there now?

He wishes he could reach up, throw those windows open, and enjoy another dawn's invigorating light, but that would be too dangerous. Death moves so fast and in far too many different ways, for him to do so safely. So he stares at the blackened glass instead, longing to taste the fresh air beyond.

Far below him, outside, he hears two voices suddenly begin to argue in Yoruba. He recognizes his native language and thinks of Nigeria and his family. He listens intently, his anxiety piqued, but the voices disappear under the next wave of traffic blasting down the city street.

A memory of swimming in the fresh, clean water of a river washes over him. He remembers squealing with pleasure, splashing around with his childhood friends in a country far, far away from here. That was a time of innocence.

A door slams loudly somewhere below him, and he feels the vibration snake up the walls. Next all he hears is the child's endless screaming, then somebody else suddenly yells up the stairwell.

Wanting to drown out the racket, he begins to croak a song, and clap an exhausted rhythm with his hands.

Suddenly there is the sound of wood splintering close

by. He ends his vocal attempts and looks up, eyes glittering. A woman screams, a child's voice joins hers moments later.

'Where is he?' demands a deep voice in Zulu. The voice resonates with violence.

'Who?' yells the woman. 'I am alone! I have only my child.'

The Yoruba freezes. Fear ruptures the senseless state he has lapsed into. He leaps to his feet, ears straining, eyes dilating.

'Oba,' growls that same voice. 'His name is Oba.'

'I don't know that name,' shouts the woman. Heavy steps cross a wooden floor. A scream, as sharp as broken glass, cuts through the thin walls.

'No? Does this little one know then?'

His name!

'No, I'm telling you! I don't know anyone like that. There is someone living next door, but I've never seen him. We hear him sometimes, moaning and singing, but I – No! Leave her alone!' Something heavy hits the floor, and the child begins to bawl in earnest.

Blood and fear rush through his tired muscles. He looks desperately around the room. For a brief moment he hopes he might find his long-forgotten keys. But the heavy feet are already on the move again, coming closer.

The window!

He throws himself at the window.

'Oba! We're here!' barks the voice outside his door. He manages to pull the window open. The dim orange light from the streetlights below startles him after the gloom. He stays confused a second too long.

There is a crash as old dry wood bursts into splinters. Something dark enters the room and Oba shrieks like a terrified five-year-old girl. The figure is moving far too fast for its size.

Oba is already trying to scrabble out the window, but he has grown too weak and too slow ever to get away. The creature that hurled itself through the door straightens up and approaches him.

Then it becomes a man, who grabs him, slivers of wood falling from his navy blue suit. His bulk is pure muscle; he has no neck to speak of. His head is shaven, the ridges of his eyebrows are prominent, while scars look like blackened petals tattooed on his face. This giant tears Oba away from the window and throws him to the floor. Oba feels a bone in his arm disintegrate as the man's force crushes it. He opens his mouth and exhales in one long howl of despair and pain.

Another person steps into the room. Splinters crunch under the heels of expensive leather shoes. Oba looks up at the second enforcer: a lean, short man, with violence and hatred rippling in the lines of his face. Dark scars run all the way from his brow to his chin. His head too is cleanly shaven, tapering to a sharp crown. Looking at him, Oba feels the last of his energy drain away, like the blood from a slaughtered pig. In the man's left hand is a panga, its blade barely gleaming in the orange gloom.

'Don't kill me,' whispers Oba, choking on his pain. 'Please, don't kill me.'

The lean man squats next to him and stares into his eyes. With a sneer he reaches out and strokes Oba's face, his hand savouring the cold sweat it finds there.

'Hello, Oba, I'm glad we found you alive.' It is the same growling voice he heard outside. He thinks of the object he was made to accept, and suddenly knows this must be Death who has come for him.

'You?' he asks.

The man glances at his accomplice, then back at Oba, a smile spreading over his face.

'Who did you think?'

Oba's breathing grows shallower as shock settles into his body. His teeth begin to chatter. He does not reply.

The enforcer stands up again and nods to his companion. The two intruders begin a chant that rumbles deep in their chests. The words are drawn out and threatening. The giant's hands slap an archaic rhythm on his thigh, while the wiry one pats his panga against his leg in unison.

Oba closes his eyes. Suddenly he feels very tired. The pain in his broken arm is overwhelming, but that is what he tries to concentrate on.

The lean enforcer hefts his panga over his head and pauses. As his partner's incantation rumbles to a close, he suddenly shrieks.

The hatchet comes down.

They leave the room and the body just as they are: a bloody and well-ordered message.

1

Believe, the man had said, and Ngubane believed. After all, there are men born with power, and there are those that seize power. Those born with power might have been born with the right skin colour or lineage. Others seize power by the rule of fear, by deception, even by wisdom.

Ngubane had already witnessed the man's miracles; he had witnessed the man's mastery of other people, of fear, of the spirit world. Ngubane had yearned to be part of that, too. Not only did he have faith in this man's power, he embraced it.

That had been seven years ago, back when Mandela was inaugurated as the first black president. Now Ngubane Maduna sits in a dark cell that stinks of disinfectant, with a bucket for a toilet, wondering about the turning point that led him here. Once he had seemed invisible, invincible, touched by the supernatural. Now his belt has been taken, as have his shoelaces. He has been stripped bare of his dignity, and nothing remains of what he had previously accepted as certainty. He cannot help but think there is a lesson to be learnt here.

Believe.

Ngubane sighs, running hands over his old and tired face. His hair is greying, but his fifty years of life have been kind to his chubby face. The shock of his capture has still not worn off, and fatigue is further clouding his thinking. He feels uncertain about what exactly he should believe.

His spirit feels drained. Was he too content with his life – docile even? Has he angered his ancestors? Was it his own jealousy that brought about his fall? He had been asked to have faith, but when he realized he himself was not believed in any more, his fortunes seemed to falter. Was that it? Was it his own fault? Or has he been too long infatuated with the man's ability to play a masterful deception?

Could it be that the man, who once seemed able to wield miracles, has himself now faltered?

What is there to believe in now?

The confusion makes him feel drunk. Anxious to understand, he whispers a desperate prayer to his ancestors. Will they intervene on his behalf tomorrow morning?

An hour later he wakes from his doze as a key rattles in the lock of his cell. He looks up to see his lawyer at the guard's side. The man's double-breasted suit is matt grey, his African curls are full and glistening with hair oil. His face is young and serious.

'Come,' the lawyer says in Zulu.

Ngubane gets up and follows him. The lawyer leads him to a small room furnished with a table and two chairs. A poster on the wall says 'No Smoking' and underneath that, someone has written '*nsangu*'.

'Sit down.'

While the lawyer pulls files out of his brown leather briefcase, Ngubane sits and waits. His mouth is dry and he cannot stop wringing his hands. In the next room, someone is quietly pleading with his lawyer. Ngubane is tired, having barely slept since his arrest. Tomorrow he will appeal in the High Court against the magistrate's bail refusal. It is his last chance to stay out of Sun City – the euphemism for Johannesburg's most notorious prison.

They discuss the particulars of his case, but Ngubane
is distracted, paying little attention. In many ways he fears
gaining his freedom as much as he fears staying in jail. His
distrust of the man might have grown, but he still fears
him deeply. The man might even want him dead. He does
not need faith or miracles to understand the threat.

'What?' The lawyer is irritated with his client, who is
staring vacantly into space.

'What will he do to me?'

'Mr Maduna, it's not for me to know what he will do,'
says the lawyer vaguely. 'I am merely paid to represent
him in the matters where he cannot take direct action.' He
slides a hand into his jacket and pulls out a small plastic
bag, tightly closed by an elastic band. 'Ask them for a few
pints of water tomorrow morning. Put this in the water
and stir it well. Drink all of it: it's a strong potion. He
wants you to know he's gone to great trouble to prepare
this for you. He says that once you've taken it, you will
speak with the voice of innocence and the heart of someone who knows nothing of the crimes the police accuse
you of. It was very difficult for him to acquire the ingredients, so think about that if you hesitate.

'You will vomit as a result of drinking this stuff. Do so
as frequently as you can. Make sure you are purified;
everything must come out. Also –' the man pulls out a
little pouch, tightly woven with beads – 'you will carry
this in your pocket. It's a blessing that will protect you
from bad judgement. With these things you'll have the
spirits on your side. This is going to be a very difficult
case for us to win, and your bail will probably be set very
high.'

For a brief moment Ngubane wonders whether this is
an elaborate ploy to poison him. The man has always

favoured vicious techniques to keep people quiet, or obe-
dient. Ngubane looks at the bag whose contents he has
been asked to trust in. The question, of course, still remains
whether the man would be better off with him dead.

Believe.

Ngubane exhales a nervous laugh. He is supposed to
take comfort in this hysterical reminder that the man still
wields power of some kind. But he cannot, because a seed
of doubt has rooted itself. Suddenly he is reminded of the
screaming terror of a young girl, the bloodstained miscar-
riage of her child, his own feelings of triumph. Has that
elaborate sacrifice come to naught?

'You'll be fine,' says the lawyer, though his face does
not endorse it. Not replying, Ngubane holds the bag of
smuggled muti up to the light and studies it.

2

Daniel is sitting in the back of the car as they drive into a
Shell petrol station. The stash of cut Thai White is under
his feet, an old pistol jammed into the front of his pants.
He is flushed with the prospect of money as he surveys the
mood outside their beige Nissan Maxima.

The forked road leading into Berea is a busy vein
feeding the city with traffic, but the station is a decrepit
oasis where no one – other than the minibus taxi drivers –
now stops. It is a place in the city where no business will
ever survive but where shops keep on opening in the hope
of attracting the hundreds of consumers that flit by on
their way to somewhere better.

It is a good corner for their kind of business, though.

The staircase leading into the dark block of flats across the street, called Egoli Mansions, is badly lit at night, and the petrol station acts like a drive-through takeaway for the white kids wanting to spend their parents' money. Park the car, buy some crisps, jog across the street and buy a bag of dreams. The pushers, meanwhile, can sit under the busted lights of the staircase, watch the cars and money pull in, smoking it up, without having to move a muscle. It is a spot not even Godfrey can resist.

'Here we go, brothers!' shouts Jim in Xhosa, over *Dr Dre* bursting his car's speakers. He smacks the steering wheel with anticipation, a big grin on his face. Jim's skin is a light brown colour, not as dark as the other two. He has peroxided his hair the colour of straw. When he talks his canines glisten with the same golden sheen his fingers have.

'You sure this is going to work?' asks Godfrey, sitting shotgun. 'Last time they nearly had us. After that, I can believe what they say about him.'

'Will you relax, Fries? *They* say a lot,' says Jim.

'Who you guys talking about?' asks Daniel. He is a lanky teenager with disproportionately long arms and legs. His prominent ears look like dried pears.

'Fries reckons this guy, the albino, is real,' says Jim.

'He *is* fucking real, man!' Godfrey thumps a fist on the dashboard. 'How come he knows when people are trying to push in on his turf? Why else do people shut up about him, like they do? Eh? No one's ever had a shot at him; he's like a ghost. It's like he's invulnerable or something. I'm telling you, he's real! You tell me how he corners people in their houses, how he fucking unlocks their doors at night and murders them in their beds. Themba saw him once, riding a baboon as white as any Boer's arse, here in the city, riding away from that guy Victor's place. Themba says they found the guy with his head cut off, man. He's bad, man, *bad*.'

'Themba smokes too much weed, man. You've seen him, Fries, you know he talks more shit than anything else.'

Godfrey cools off a bit, 'I'm just thinking, you know, he'll come after us when he finds out.' He looks at the other two, his face a billboard of uncertainty. 'You know, *if* he's real, he'll come after us wherever we go. They warned us last time.'

'Bullshit,' says Jim, 'Khuli says it's all bullshit. This guy who's in the paper, he's the one who made up the story of this albino. Those guys who warned us – they work for him, and he's gone down. Their money's gone, their H is gone; they're on the run, okay? Now *we* can start earning some real money. I'm telling you, it's all made up. You don't get powerful witches like that any more, and if you do, they won't be here in the city. If there was someone as powerful as they're saying he is, he'd own this city by now. But there's no one like that – that's why Maduna's gone to jail, man. We came all this way to make money, so don't get stupid now.'

'I don't know.' Godfrey shakes his head. 'I don't know.'

Daniel interrupts his elder brother, 'You know, I'm going to buy myself this leather jacket I saw. *Yo!* It's so nice and it's not a bad price. Maybe I'll get Lebo something, too – but I want that jacket.'

'You just want her to keep her hand in your pants,' sneers Godfrey.

'Look!' says Jim, pointing at the bland grey concrete staircase leading up to the entrance of the Mansions across the road. 'I'm right. See? There's no one there. They're usually sitting *there*, but they must be too worried now. They must be on the run.'

'*Ja*, Godfrey, I think Jim's right. If this albino was real, they would've already known we're here.'

'See,' says Jim, 'even Daniel's cool. You're cool, Daniel, right?'

'I'm OK,' says Daniel, one leg jigging up and down so his tracksuit pants are swishing against his ankle.

'Then get us something to drink.'

Daniel jumps out the car and awkwardly adjusts the gun hidden in his underwear. An assistant inside the garage shop gives him a startled look and hurriedly finishes his phone conversation. Daniel does not even notice his surprised reaction.

'Fries,' says Jim, 'you're too superstitious. How you going to make a good businessman one day, I ask you?'

'I want to do this, too, but, seriously, I don't know about this. Themba – just because he saw the albino – he still can't sleep properly. It's bad magic. He's gone to see a *sangoma* and everything. But this magic is just too strong. I don't want to mess with it.'

'I don't want to hear it, man. I say it's all bullshit; you're always talking about this magic and that magic: this thing you must wear, that thing you must shove up your bum, cut yourself here, burn yourself there.' Jim laughs. 'Stop this shit now. I just want to make money, simple. I can't hold your hand every time you see a cat, or your ear itches. You don't get people like that any more, so relax.'

An engine roars as someone shifts gears down badly. They both look up in time to see a black Mercedes speed into the station forecourt and loudly clip a speed bump.

Another Mercedes swerves broadside across the second entrance.

'What's this, now?' says Jim.

'It's them! They found us. We're fucking trapped in here!' Godfrey's eyes bulge as car doors spring open. He scrambles under the seat for his revolver. 'Where's my brother? Where's Daniel?'

Daniel stands frozen in the middle of the forecourt. He drops the bag of sweets and sodas he has bought, and goes for his pistol instead.

'Daniel! Get the fuck in the car *now*!' screams Godfrey.

Jim tries to start the car but floods the engine.

Shots crack. Slugs tear into the car's metal. Plaster spatters off a pillar. A tyre on a nearby car wheezes loudly as it is punctured.

Daniel cries out, spins and falls to the concrete as bullets tear into his shoulder and stomach.

'No!' screams Godfrey.

Bystanders drop on their bellies amid the dust and oil. Others run for safety, while an attendant has enough wits about him to shut the pumps down. There is a blur of movement as people scramble for their lives. The two in the beige Nissan look everywhere, trying to suss the confusion.

Men with handguns slip out of the two sedans and move forward quickly, crouching low, taking cover.

Jim swears and jams his pistol out the window. He has never actually used it and fires with his eyes closed. The gun bucks like a cobra striking in all directions.

Suddenly heavy automatic fire rattles through the air. The front of Jim's Maxima explodes into glassy slivers. A red splash appears on the driver's side of the car's smashed windscreen. In the brief moment of silence that follows, people stare in horror at the towering black man standing in front of the second Mercedes. In his hands is an AK-47, the barrel smoking like a fat cigar.

In the middle of the forecourt, Daniel, his eyes rolling with the pain, tries to get up. One of his shoes has come off, revealing a hole worn through the heel. He weakly lifts his weapon and fires, but his bullet buries itself in a concrete pillar.

'Godfrey,' he whispers, 'just go.'

A grey-bearded man in a cheap shiny suit walks up to Daniel and fires point blank. The round tears through his head, and red splatters over the oily ground.

Godfrey peers out of the mangled car and moans. He managed to evade the shower of automatic bullets by ducking down behind the dashboard. Splinters of glass hang in his hair and are sliding down his neck. Beside him, Jim is slumped against the steering wheel. The upholstery behind him is a mess of blood, torn sponge and wisps of white padding.

'Get out of the car!' yells someone in Zulu.

Godfrey begins to sob as the past sixty seconds sink in.

'Out, you little shit!'

Somewhere outside the vehicle, a woman blabbers with hysteria.

Godfrey opens the door a crack and throws his gun outside.

'Weren't you told not to come back here?' someone shouts.

'That wasn't us,' croaks Godfrey, his voice failing.

'Don't lie to us.'

Someone tears the door wide open. Another man pulls Godfrey out head first. A fist cracks into his face, once, twice. He is pistol-whipped in the neck before he collapses to the ground where feet crash into his ribs, his back, his kidneys. Instinctively, he tries to curl up into a ball, but it is not enough and he blacks out.

As he comes around they are dragging him across the concrete, towards a waiting, third Mercedes. With a thin electric whirr, the tinted rear-door window of the black vehicle slides open. They lift him up and jam his face into the opening so he cannot move his head. Godfrey looks up and notices a shadow in the cool, dark interior.

His face! His face!

It has the look of some creature that has not eaten in a while. As it smiles, its large mouth splits open like an old wound, its huge white teeth gleaming brilliant and white, predatory. In a voice that buzzes with a deep cracked bass, like an angry nest of hornets, the passenger asks, 'What were you thinking?'

'I'm so sorry,' wails Godfrey. 'I told them. I *told* them.'

The passenger broods over the boy's fear, before he says, 'I'm glad to see that you're one to understand what I am.'

'What?'

'You fear me, but do you fear me enough?'

'Yes, I do,' whimpers Godfrey. 'I do fear you. I told them we mustn't anger you, but they wouldn't listen.'

'Mm, it is better, I think, if I keep you alive. You will work for me and you will speak my will, won't you?'

Godfrey is still dazed. The taste of blood is strong in his mouth. He is finding it difficult to focus on the albino, so he lets his head hang.

'Yes, yes, just . . . I don't want to die.'

There is a sudden movement inside the car. Godfrey sees blood spill onto the cream upholstery before he even feels the pain. Then he screams and tries to reach for the side of his head, but he cannot get his hands into the window. He sees his own ear in the man's hand.

'Just so that we understand each other, just so that we *heard* each other properly, I'm taking this.'

The world around Godfrey turns hazy again. The hands supporting him suddenly let go, and he collapses to the ground. As if from a great distance, he hears people getting into the Mercedes and the car pulling away. His neck is slick with blood. People are shouting, but Godfrey cannot understand what they are saying. Someone pulls him up and orders him into a car, which sets off leaving the body of his brother sprawled on the oily and bloodied concrete in the midday sun.

3

The next day Ngubane is leaving the High Court on Pritchard Street. He wades into a pack of journalists waiting on the stairs, who begin flashing cameras and yelling questions. A few police officers watch the show without much enthusiasm. Ngubane's face is covered by a white pillowcase with a gauzy window sewn into it, made especially for the occasion. Six of his own men surround him: they are rough with the journalists, soon cutting a swathe through them.

Ngubane's ageing fingers are once more decorated with delicate gold. His cream suit, the elaborate gold tie and shiny beige shoes, complemented by his abundant stomach and ornate gold-and-ebony cane, give the impression that he is a circus ringmaster.

His mind is a whirlwind, because something has changed within him. Walking away free from the court house, he feels no elation. He feels nothing but uncertainty and a tense anticipation of how he is going to explain himself. His instincts tell him that the albino will want personally to deal with him.

A massive black Mercedes pulls up on the opposite side of the road. As soon as the car stops, a man jumps out and opens the rear door. A shadowy figure sits sunken deep into the back seat, his face hidden by a widespread newspaper.

As he starts to cross the busy street, the hood making it difficult for him to see, Ngubane is nearly struck by a taxi hurtling past. One of the men pulls him back, grabs his hand and leads him across. A photographer manages to snap this picture and the group of uniformed police officers merely laughs.

Pulling the pillowcase off his head, Ngubane gets into the car and sits down. He gulps for air and wipes a sheen of moisture from his flushed face. On the seat next to him is a wooden box inlaid with intricate designs of ivory. Beneath it lies a long butcher's knife sheathed in leather. The man who sits next to him is still reading and does not acknowledge him. The car slides deep into the passing traffic, and still there is only silence inside the car.

'I don't know how this happened,' begins Ngubane finally.

No response.

'This couldn't just happen by chance. Someone has cursed me.' He turns to the man next to him. Still he remains quiet and Ngubane feels his anxiety grow. He shifts nervously in his seat and tries discreetly to wipe his sweaty palms on his pants.

Eventually the albino turns the page of his newspaper and sighs. Without looking up from his reading, he says,

'My heroin is gone, and now the police are aware that you are not the respectable entrepreneur they thought.' His Zulu is tinged with an accent suggesting West Africa.

Ngubane has heard this particular tone of voice before, but he cannot bring himself to look at the unnatural-looking speaker. He stares out of the window and paws at his collar. 'But I am free again, sir. Is that not what matters? My contacts are still in place and our new project has not come to light.'

The other man's dry flaky skin is a splotched pink and brown all over, giving the impression that he's about to shed it like a snake. Thick lips are set in a gluttonously bulbous face. It is not his face nor his skin that frightens people most, but those abominable eyes. They seem swollen, and the whites are always bloodshot. The irises seem to glow a demonic red.

The albino finally turns to face him, his look hitting Ngubane with the impact of a sledgehammer. 'You took that stuff the lawyer brought you?'

Ngubane stares down at the albino's knee. 'Yes.' His voice breaks as he continues. 'The lawyer argued well for me. He is a powerful speaker.'

'You are free only because I myself willed it. Not because you spoke the truth to some judge, but because I saved you from your own stupidity.'

The albino is dressed in a traditional white *boubou*, a long flowing garment reaching down to his ankles. In his lap lies a fly whisk made from a buffalo's tail, its handle decorated with beads of white, red and black. Beaded adornments, with numerous little pouches woven into their lattice, criss-cross his chest and encircle his wrists. Thick black-rimmed glasses sit on his nose. His head is shaven.

He folds his newspaper away. 'My power gets stronger.

19

It's people like you who are weak.' He holds Ngubane's gaze. 'As for your contacts: how long do you think they will associate with you, knowing that you are now on trial? Your foolhardy actions are now threatening everything I have built up. Give me one reason why I should not kill you and deal with this crisis myself?'

Ngubane swallows hard. 'I am your voice to those people.'

The albino stares at him. 'You no longer convince me, Ngubane. You no longer sing my song.'

His lieutenant is forced to look away, unnerved as always by the man's abnormal gaze. 'They trust me,' he protests. 'They know very little about you.'

'Perhaps. But maybe it is time for them to get to know me.'

Ngubane's smart tie suddenly feels like a snake constricting his neck. It is then that he notices a splash of dark red on the cream leather upholstery. Tendrils of crimson have also trickled down the window's interior. He looks nervously at the sheathed knife resting beneath the ornamental box.

The albino unexpectedly barks commands at the driver in Yoruba, a language from up north that Ngubane recognizes but does not understand. The car speeds up in response to his request. Another two vehicles, one behind and one in front of them, simultaneously accelerate to keep pace with the Mercedes.

'Your indiscretions have nearly brought me to light,' the deep voice continues, sounding remorseless as a grindstone. The albino takes his glasses off and rubs his eyes, before reaching out a hand and tapping on the box between them. 'Already people think that, because *you've* been arrested, my organization is in trouble. Let me tell you, the only trouble I have is deciding what to do with you.'

'I—'

'You were the one who took that idiot in!' bellows the albino, thumping the door handle with his fist. 'You put him up in one of our safe houses. Who are *you* to decide who should work for me?'

'I thought you would be pleased.'

'*Pleased?*'

'He was a Yoruba like you, sir.'

'He is *nothing* like me!'

Ngubane looks confused. 'Forgive . . . forgive me.'

'I am *nothing* like him, and *nothing* like you. Of all, I am closest to the Great Spirit, closest to our ancestors. Do you understand that, you fool? Have you learnt nothing?'

The colour completely draining from his face, Ngubane says, 'I'm sorry, it was stupid—'

'Your stupidity is unforgivable. You have shown disrespect not only to me but to your forefathers as well. It seems you think yourself above them, and me.'

'No, it's not like that. I thought—'

'You thought what? Because I speak that language and come from the north, you thought that meant you knew *who* I am and *what* I need? Hah! Don't antagonize me even more. In Benin there's a saying, Ngubane: "He who has warned you has not killed you yet."' The albino spots the trace of blood still spattered on the door panel and a malicious grin spreads over his bulbous face. 'So consider yourself warned.'

The albino settles himself into a more comfortable position, shakes his head, then stares out the window.

Ngubane feels like a whipped child. He has lost both the albino's trust and his own privileged position. He suspects he should feel grateful for having been spared, but why should he now lose so much when he was promised much more? When will the albino answer for *his* failings? He stares at the blood smeared on the leather and wonders whether the albino left it there on purpose. Although he is badly shaken, he feels angry and betrayed. It should never have come to this, because this is the albino's fault, not Ngubane's.

With the albino totally ignoring him again, Ngubane's thoughts return to this morning's events. In hindsight he realizes he has been a fool. Lying awake, alone in his cell, he had held the sachet up for inspection and wondered again whether it was a poison or indeed a miracle potion. It must have been some other miracle that saved him, not the albino's doing.

As Ngubane had lain still in the early hours of that morning, he had spoken continually to his ancestors in a low murmur. Listening to the other prisoners coughing and whispering, he carefully explained himself to the dead. He had by then thrown both the plastic sachet and the beaded pouch into the cell toilet, because somehow he had felt reassured by his ancestors' voices. He had felt sure they would intervene for him during his ordeal.

4

The albino and his entourage finally head towards Ponte City, at the heart of Hillbrow, a hacked concrete building rising far above other neighbouring structures. Patched to its top floor is a gigantic Coca-Cola sign that flashes in harsh red neon, spraying its glow over downtown Johannesburg all night, every night.

BLOODY HARVESTS

Once the hub of bohemian life in Johannesburg, the building, anchored to the side of a hill, now watches over the city like a dark tyrant, steeped in urban myth. Constructed in the shape of a hollow cylinder, it comprises apartments around a central axis. It has become the city council's worst nightmare: an eyesore, a magnet for crime, and completely irremovable.

The poorest are drawn to it like insects lured in by light. The suicidal come from far and wide to climb its grim stairways to the roof before tossing their used-up lives down its central shaft. As they hit the garbage piled at the bottom, the thud of impact echoing up the internal walls is like the sound of souls fleeing a lifetime of misery. Prostitutes are packed together like cattle into tiny rooms, partitioned by towels hanging from the ceiling, and illegal immigrants congregate at the windows, hanging their rags out to dry and shouting gossip at each other over the black void below. Feral pigeons squat on every available ledge in the perpetual twilight of the building's inner axis, to breed there and mutate. On every level junkies wander the dark narrow corridors, slipping cash under battered doors in the hope of achieving that one last shot of heaven wrapped in knotted plastic. These lost souls, who toss their blunt needles down the same central shaft as the suicides toss their bodies, are never too far behind in climbing to the roof when that last narcotic kiss runs out and there is nowhere else to go. To many Ponte City represents the end; it is rock bottom for everyone except those who control it.

The albino sighs heavily and shakes his head. 'Your well-fed body, your pretty car, your lovely house, they all depend on me, you know.'

Ngubane does not feel he is in a position to say anything, so he keeps quiet and merely nods.

'You have become slow and old and heavy.'

He used to believe that to cross this man would be to cross the spirits. He really *believed* it. How did it ever come to this?

'Yes,' is all Ngubane says at last. His ears are flaming with the shame he feels. Never has he felt this weak and insignificant.

The cars lurch into the underground car park at Ponte City just as the sun turns to fire on the horizon, the day passing away. They step out into the gloom. The fluorescent lights in the abandoned parking lot are replaced only sporadically, and the ones that still function are covered in a muck composed of dust and cobwebs. Shadows appear from behind pillars and around corners, shouting vigorous greetings to grab the albino's attention. Their gaunt young faces are alight with fervour and the promised life they dream of.

Taiwo Ejiofer, the giant enforcer, gets out of the other Mercedes, while the wiry predator joins them from the dark stairwell.

'Adusa.' The albino greets him happily, holding out his hands.

Ngubane hangs his head at his own disgrace and the obvious affection being shown to another. He suddenly feels furious, because his circumstances should never have deteriorated to this extent. A pact had been made between them, after all.

'Has my guest arrived?' asks the albino, as Adusa Okechukwu clasps both his hands and kisses the strange-looking man's palms.

'Of course, he has, sir,' answers Adusa in Yoruba. The

albino hands over the decorated box and the knife from the back seat. Ngubane used to be the one privileged to carry the albino's personal possessions. 'He was drinking in the Hollywood Strip, complaining about his bad luck. His own brother took us there.' Adusa sneers at Ngubane with his eyes.

'Well done, well done,' says the albino paternally. 'Did we reward his brother?'

'Yes, of course,' says Adusa.

The three Nigerians laugh as they proceed upstairs. The albino flicks the whisk over his shoulders as he walks, his enforcers following him and now ignoring Ngubane, who follows a few steps behind them. They reach a lift foyer where graffiti and cigarette lighter burns scar the lino walls. A broken security camera dangles from its innards, and the brown industrial carpet is pocked with chewing gum. A stench of urine and beer hangs in the unventilated air.

The doors to the lift screech slowly shut. One of its small viewing windows has a spiderweb of cracks radiating from a bullet hole. The air inside is stuffy with the smell of beer and oil. Taiwo's bulk presses Ngubane against the wall. Ngubane stares up at him, trying to muster some of his old authority, only to find the big man grinning down at him sardonically.

The lift jerks to a halt and the doors slide open. They walk out into a shadowy corridor, its lights barely functioning, the walls covered in coarse brown carpeting material.

Three men guard the doors to the only occupied penthouse apartment in the building. They are dressed in worn-out clothes: one man's pants are far too short for him, while another's sandal straps are broken, and the youngest has a necklace dangling a bullet on his bare chest. The youth's eyes glimmer brightly in the dim light. The guards get up at once and move to greet the man they revere.

'Open the door,' commands the albino. The boy with the bullet scrambles to oblige.

The albino saunters through his apartment, lavishly decorated with African ornaments, to the study at its far end and throws the door open. Inside a man jumps up from where he has been sitting on the carpet, although there are chairs available. A plump blue bruise disfigures his left eye, and the skin has been raked off one arm which he holds close to his body. His dress is meagre, too: shorts and a T-shirt, no socks, and his crumpled shoes by the door.

'Oba!' cries the albino, spreading his arms wide, like a father welcoming home a long-lost son. 'Tell me, you dirty mutt, what have you done?'

5

With dusk approaching, the massive neon sign attached to the outside of the building came on. An eerie flicker filters into the room as the red glow scrolls around the summit of Ponte City, advertising its message over downtown Johannesburg.

A large, sturdy wooden cabinet stands by the curtained window. On top of it, a collection of bottles, boxes, jars and misshaped burning candles are arranged around a clay bowl that releases incense in slow smoky curls. That does nothing, however, to hide the odour of singed hair and meat hanging in the air. The cabinet's many drawers have black crosses painted over their locks. Feathers, bird skulls and the soft balloons of gallbladders are tied to the brass handles.

Ngubane looks at Oba and wonders whether the man is sweating because of the heat or because of the oppressive danger he is in.

Oba grips the albino's hands and kisses them urgently. 'Oh, Wise One, I am so glad to see you. It's an honour.'

'I am very glad to see you, too, especially after you've been hiding from me so long.'

'No, I haven't been hiding!'

'Don't lie to me.'

'Only because the police have been looking for us, boss.'

'Then why did I have to come looking for *you*? Why did you not come to *me*?'

There is a stunned silence, and Oba's fingers slip from the albino's hand slowly and drop into his lap.

'I . . . I didn't know . . . I . . . I didn't believe . . .' Oba strokes his own chest in a pathetic display of submissiveness. 'I was scared,' he whispers.

The albino laughs. 'You see, Ngubane? You brought a dog amongst us, and now it's rolling in the sand with a broken back. Spineless – just look at him!'

Ngubane looks at Oba and wonders what exactly the albino wants him to think.

'You were hired by this idiot over there?' continues the albino.

Oba looks at Ngubane, then drops his eyes. 'Yes.'

'All you needed to do was stay in that house and guard one special room, without ever going into it. You could drink my tea, eat my food, sleep on my mattress, make friends with my people, yes?'

Oba nods.

'But you couldn't do just that, could you? You had to go into that room and help yourself to something once in a while.' The albino looks smug and self-satisfied as he speaks.

Oba stays quiet and stares at the hands in his lap.

'All you were told was not to go into that room. But you still went into *my* room!'

Oba hesitates, then nods.

'I should kill you for that,' says the albino, and sighs. 'But that's not my main concern.'

He lays his whisk on the large desk that squats in front of the cabinet, walks around it and reaches into the incense smoke curling upwards from the clay bowl situated on top of the cabinet itself. He wafts fumes towards his face and murmurs something, before beckoning for Taiwo to fetch the ornamented box. He takes it from the man's massive hands and places it among the other items arranged on the cabinet's upper surface.

Ngubane's eyes are drawn to a large bundle lying on the desk, something tightly wrapped in a beige fleece blanket. Two animal skulls have been pushed aside to make space for it. Though the room is occasionally brightened by the glow of red neon rushing past on the outside of the building, Ngubane cannot make out what is tucked inside the bundle.

'After stealing from me for your own gratification, you decided to take things further.' The albino sits down in an elaborately carved ebony chair. 'First you sell to the children of the neighbourhood, then you start selling to the whites.'

Oba looks up, eyes glistening. 'No sir, I sold nothing. I took some, but I never sold it.' He reaches out his hands,

'Look at me, Wise One! Do I look like a man who has money?'

The albino gives Oba a cold, dead stare. He reaches out to run one hand over the mysterious bundle. 'Do not lie to me, Oba. I don't have to remind you of who I am, what I am privy to.'

Oba decides it might be best to stand up.

'Stay where you are!'

Oba sinks back to his knees, cradling his injured arm in his sound one.

Ngubane feels drowsy, as if waking from a long and restless sleep. Under such pressure, he has seen men ready to confess anything to the albino. It does not pay to anger a man so closely bound to the spirits, for to have the ear of the afterlife is to have the ear of Creation itself. One thing has become clear to Ngubane, however, since this morning he lay in his cell, praying to his forefathers. They are still with him – they have not rejected him for entertaining doubts about his Nigerian holy man.

Ngubane glances at the animal skulls arranged on the large desk: the mummified head of a baboon baring dirty brown teeth, its shrivelled skin pulled tight over the bone; and the white skull of a lion, featuring a broken fang. He then turns his attention to the sacrificial bowls standing in each corner, which produce the stench pervading the room. The ash they contain is mixed with coloured powders, herbs and seared and bloodstained chicken wings. Ngubane wipes at his nose.

Are they warning me? He glances at the two enforcers, both of whom are staring back at him. *Is this why the spirits are speaking to me?*

The long silence finally overwhelms Oba, who begins

to sob quietly. He looks up hopefully at the albino and notices his expression has not changed. The disgraced man casts his eyes down and nods resignedly.

Finally the albino continues. 'So you get high on my H, you sell it to the children living in our territory and then you peddle it to the whites. You cut what you steal from me and sell that inferior shit in my name. You go gambling with your friends, you get drunk and you pay *my* bitches with *my* money to fuck you.'

Adusa snorts with sudden laughter, while Taiwo does his best to quell a cruel smile. The albino is staring at Oba in mocking disbelief.

When Oba wipes his face on his sleeve Ngubane notices the large damp patch under the man's arm. 'Please . . . I am sorry, I did not mean to offend you. It's just I am so *happy* to work for you.' Unable to suppress his scorn any longer, Taiwo roars with laughter. 'I got carried away . . . maybe a bit greedy. But I swear I'll never offend you again.'

'So why did you go to the police?'

'What?' The colour drains from Oba's face. His eyes flick up towards Ngubane before returning to his hands again. 'I never sold you out to anyone, boss!' he whimpers. 'I'm not a mad man.'

'Of course, you couldn't sell me out. But what about my heroin? And what about him?' The albino points at Ngubane. 'He is the one that took you in, who put you in charge of the house. He is the fool who said, "Oba, you have been doing well for us," and, "Oba, you'll go far, because you speak Yoruba like the albino," and, "Oba, do a simple job for me. Look after my heroin!" Ha!' The albino leaps from his chair, looming his bulk over the table. The sudden impetus sends the baboon's skull flying and it hits the thick reed mat with a crack. The albino brings both his fists down on the table top, thudding onto the fleece-wrapped bundle. In Yoruba he bawls, 'You little shit, you would jeopardize my purpose? I can see your lies. I can see your betrayal. It was *you*!'

'I don't understand,' whimpers Oba in his mother tongue, his face now twisted with terror.

As he straightens up again, the albino lets his hands run slowly over the strange bundle. His tone softens as he resorts to Zulu again. 'Ah, but *I* understand, *I* can see. You have begun to doubt me. Once you start taking from me, that means you've stopped fearing me. Like a tick, you've feasted on me, and it seems you're now ready to drop off me and go lay your *own* eggs. Isn't that right, Oba? You're thinking of going into business for yourself?'

'I didn't do it,' the man whines.

The albino opens a cabinet drawer and extracts something, then begins to bellow a loud rhythmic chant. Taiwo and Adusa soon join him in chorus. Plunging several fingers into a jar, the albino sprinkles powder onto the candle flames, sparks fly outwards and the smoke releases a sweet musky smell.

'You not only betrayed me, you betrayed your ancestors and brought shame upon them. My anger is theirs, my revenge will be theirs, too.'

Oba tries to scramble to his feet, but Taiwo is faster, flapping an enormous hand across Oba's face. 'Sit down!' he yells.

The albino moves around the desk and raises cupped hands high, focusing his eyes now on a point on the ceiling. As he begins to jerk fitfully, Oba whimpers and pulls back. Suddenly the albino leaps forward, thrusting something in his hands towards Oba.

'Take this!' he snarls. 'If you are innocent you will survive. If you have lied to me, you will certainly die.'

Oba gapes at the thing in the albino's hand with anguish and horror. 'Please,' he snivels, 'don't ask me to do this.'

'I am not asking, I'm *ordering*. If you have nothing to hide from us, then it will not harm you.'

Oba wails and slumps to the floor in complete submission, burying his head protectively in his arms.

The albino nods and eyes Ngubane triumphantly. 'You see, I was right. This man has tried to deceive us. What will you do now, Ngubane – now you know he caused your arrest?'

Ngubane strokes his nose nervously, uncertain what to say. The enforcers are both staring at him again, and for a moment he fears he has been set up.

The albino turns back to Oba. 'All right, the spirits will decide.' He grabs Oba's hand roughly and squashes something into his fist. Red blood squirts from it, soaking the kneeling man's hand. Oba stares at it, horrified, then gags noisily.

The whole room seems to have darkened even further, although the red neon light still ripples past periodically. 'You will take this juju with you, and you'll do something special for me – as an apology for what you've already confessed to. And remember, you still have family living in one of my apartments. You don't want me dealing with them, too, for your mistakes?'

Oba shakes his head vigorously.

The albino smiles. 'You will now take what is lying here on my desk and dump it somewhere where no one will find it. If you do that right, who knows, perhaps the spirits might be appeased.'

Oba looks up, hope glittering in his eyes. 'Ah, yes, sure, I'll do that. Of course, I'll do it.'

The albino reaches his hands into the curl of smoking incense again. He snarls, 'Now get out.'

Oba has got to his feet and stumbled a few panicked steps towards the door before he remembers to retrieve his shoes. His subsequent exit through the door is fast enough to startle the guards outside.

Ngubane's mind is reeling with confusion. Things are moving too fast for him. The albino does not turn to watch him leave the room, too.

Adusa closes the door behind him and snickers. 'That man, he's falling apart!'

'Why do you even keep him on?' asks Taiwo.

'Sometimes the sharp tongue of a snake is advantageous. He can talk well and convince people in ways even I cannot.'

'Do we go after him?' asks Taiwo.

'No, he'll be back soon enough with his tail between his legs. That man likes the good life too much.' The albino picks up his whisk again. 'In the meantime, you need to find out who sold me out. Oba is clearly the weakest link, and answers will be with the people he knows. Start with his family – ' a deadly smile spreads over the albino's face – 'and do what you want with them.'

6

Streetlights flash past as Oba drives, panic washing over him in waves that make his teeth chatter. His hands are slick on the steering wheel of his grey Chevrolet, a vehicle dating back to the early eighties. All he can think about is that faint glimmer of hope, of finding forgiveness.

The bundle is now lying in the boot of the car. Oba briefly wondered about investigating what was in it but decided he has had enough of prying into the albino's business.

He halts the car on the shoulder of the highway, gets out and opens the bonnet to give the impression he has stopped to deal with a breakdown. The cool night air smells of rain and dust, lightning flickers over the hill-tops in the distance. Oba's feet crunch loudly on gravel as he heads around to the rear of the Chevrolet and opens the boot. Several cars speed past him without slowing down.

Oba suddenly gags as bile rises in his throat. The albino's death threat weighs heavily in his trouser pocket, but he knows he is obliged to carry it with him. He nearly drops the bundle as another car shoots past.

He peers into the gloom down below the steep embankment. He should be able to bury this bundle down there somewhere, but he cannot muster the courage to face the pitch darkness unarmed.

Returning the bundle to the boot, he heads back to open the passenger door and retrieves a battered .22 pistol from the glove box.

Oba again hefts the bundle onto his shoulder, before realizing he has neither a shovel nor a torch with him. What now? He cannot go back into the city to fetch them. He must get rid of this thing before he is caught with it – in case his family gets sucked into this, too. The storm is moving in fast and thunder booms close by.

He lays the bundle back in the boot. By the meagre

light available, he unties the knots to pull the blanket open.

He throws his head back in revulsion.

Minutes later, Oba unrolls the blanket again. The small body thuds to the ground. In the distance cars shimmer past his vehicle above him. He stares down at the naked child in the darkness. Her outlines are barely visible.

Is this how I'm going to end up too?

He rummages in his trouser pocket and pulls the hideous juju free. It is still damp with blood, and with sudden, violent, desperation he hurls the fetish away into the night. Then, retrieving only the blanket, he flees back up towards his car.

With the streetlights skipping past him again, he spots that distinctive red neon in the distance, spinning around the top of Ponte City and flashing him a grim reminder. He hopes that somehow he can manage to disappear. How long can Death pursue you? How long does a curse endure?

He does not know the answers.

7

'*Ten!*'

He hears Rodge's muffled yell echo through the trees. He needs to hurry, as his friend is almost finished with his count-down and he himself has not yet found a place to hide. He is nervous, too, as he skirts the eastern edge of the wood adjoining the land of the Morwarghs.

In the north-east of London, near Whipps Cross hospital,

stands Forest School, where his father is the principal and where they also live in a converted farm cottage. Behind the school is a narrow stretch of woodland, the beginnings of Epping Forest extending further north. Rodge and he visit there often. It is about the size of two football fields, filled with dishevelled old trees and bushes that make it a playground of endless possibilities for adventurous boys.

His father has warned them both about trespassing on the Morwarghs, although his father does not call them that. He has merely instructed them not to cross the muddy riding path – which seemed never to dry out, even in summer – that bisects this patch of woodland. This 'law' laid down by his father, concerning the muddy track and the mystery that lies beyond, has become a central theme for all the boys' games. For them some evil must exist on the other side, and occasionally, in braver moments, their games have tempted them over the line drawn by his father, that narrow line between obedience and boyish independence.

The air is heavy with the musty smell of a sweaty summer's afternoon. It has been raining a lot and this is the first time in days that they are allowed to play in the wood. Their parents worry too much; Rodge and he can cope with the bad weather and strangers and even the Morwarghs.

He wipes his nose with the back of his hand and scans the thicket for a suitable hiding spot. Most of the bushes are overgrown with holly, its coarse green leaves spiked with vicious thorns, but the undergrowth he has now found looks dark and promising.

'*Nine!*' yells Rodge shrilly.

It is proving difficult for him to find somewhere new to hide, since Rodge already knows all the best places on the other side of the trail. It is because of this disadvantage that he is heading further into forbidden Morwargh territory.

BLOODY HARVESTS

He forces his way deeper into an unfamiliar dense patch, branches plucking at his red shirt already covered in mud. He needs to be careful not to leave a trail of fallen greenery.

His father's limit lies far behind him now. The crucial border is the rotting fence, standing much deeper in Morwargh territory, encircling their homes at the other end of the park. He can see that if he squeezed all the way through the patch, he would probably end up at the fence itself.

All he can think about is impressing his friend with this new hideout, it being the only area that Rodge does not know like the back of his hand, perhaps because Rodge has always been uneasy about coming near the Morwargh fence.

They have only been as far as the fence a few times before. There is a path running along it, littered with garbage and Morwargh dog poop. Once he and Rodge witnessed an old Morwargh taking a shit in some bushes close by the fence. They smelt him even before they saw him. Hiding behind a big elm tree they watched, fascinated. The man kept talking to himself, straining and grunting. Rodge had burst out giggling loudly and bolted, but the Morwargh was so busy he did not even notice them crashing through the foliage.

On another occasion they stood there eyeing a humungous fat guy out in his backyard. The Morwargh carried a heavy plastic sack over to the fence and swung it over the top, as easily as if it was a pillow. It came flying over and got caught in some overhanging branches. The plastic tore open, pitching garbage everywhere below.

The next time they saw him, the same man was yelling drunkenly at his daughter. It seemed she had dropped a freshly washed bedspread on the dirty concrete of the backyard and now cowered before him, as he stood in his sagging yellow-stained underwear.

For a couple of moments he bellowed obscenities at her,

then, suddenly, whipped a massive hand across her face. She was spun right around, long blonde hair twirling, then collapsed howling in pain. The Morwargh had stomped back into his house, stopping only to grab an opened can of beer from the ledge by the kitchen door.

'*Eight!*'

Remembering this violent scene, he is vibrating with heebie-jeebies at getting this close to Morwargh. They had kept away from the fence since that day and never spoke about it to anyone, the memory of it almost forgotten until now.

Wondering if the same Morwargh and his daughter still live there, he goes on with his search for the ideal spot to hide. He pushes deeper amidst the wet shrubs, where the scent of compost fills his nostrils.

'*Seven!*' cries Rodge, sounding more distant.

Three oaks grow close together around his chosen hideout, their gnarled roots entwined like fingers digging into the earth. Thick bushes conveniently screen the spaces between them. He crawls forward on his knees.

'*Six!*' Rodge picks up the pace of counting. '*Five.*'

The boy flattens himself to the earth, peering underneath the leaves and branches; there always is more space to wriggle into a thicket close to the ground, where the older foliage has died and broken off.

Yes, there is a dark hollow in there, and it seems dry. Supported on his elbows he crawls in deeper, the deeper he gets the tighter the fit. Branches prick him in the back and snag his red T-shirt. He hopes that worms and bugs are not getting down the front of his trousers.

Squeezing through to the centre, he finds a bigger hollow space than he expected. It is dark but comfortable in there, wedged in between the three great trees.

'*Four. Three. Two, ONE!*' Rodge's cry sounds more like a

whisper from here among the tree roots. 'Ready or not, here I come!'

There is a rustle outside.

That can't be him already?

He holds his breath. Excitement tingles down his spine and makes him shiver. A twig snaps. This is what makes hide-and-seek the best game: when the seeker comes so close you can hear him blundering right past you. Branches and leaves continue snapping, as if the person outside is moving quickly. Either Rodge has located him immediately, or it is somebody else out there. The sound stops suddenly.

Is it a Morwargh?

At this thought, he suddenly feels very cold. He pulls his knees up under his chin in the near darkness of his hideout.

He is not going to call out to Rodge this early in the game – not from inside his best hideout yet. And he is definitely not going to let any Morwargh know he is here. The sound of movement comes again, but this time it is heading away.

Harry, however, decides not to act for now, because the noise he would make getting out would surely alert any Morwarghs on the prowl nearby. His stomach rumbles; now he is a *hungry* adventurer. Rubbing at his burning ankles, he waits.

8

Harry Mason is finding it difficult to focus, so he gets up, snaps a latex glove off his hand and fumbles for his cigarettes. He cups a hand against the slight breeze and his cigarette flares up. He sucks smoke deep into his lungs. The tobacco and the careful, rehearsed action of smoking lure his mind away from what lies at his feet.

Detective Inspector Mason is in his thirties with a rugged yet handsome build that his wife adores, although she frequently ribs him about his nascent paunch. His short blond hair approaches boyish disarray, a whorl at the crown of his head always finding a way to stand up. His face is a bronze colour, freckled lightly over the nose. The lines of approaching middle age, and the serious blue eyes, give an impression that this man has known sadness.

Again he digs into his pocket, and this time finds a handkerchief and wipes the summer sweat from his face. The white cotton comes away streaked brown. As he smokes he gazes at Johannesburg shimmering in the distance; its high-rises reach for a sky that is dusted red on the horizon.

Harry is standing in a broad dry riverbed which looks more like an uneven field crushed between two heaps of old gold-mine tailings stacked on either side. The soil underfoot is grey and hard, resembling concrete. All around him grow clumps of reeds and parched patches of long grass. Harry does not like the sound of the afternoon breeze stirring in those dry leaves; it makes him think of ghosts. Blowflies buzz around him and cars swish by constantly on the busy N1 highway. The stink of death is thick in the air, a cloud thicker and fuller than the cigarette smoke.

Finally he looks back down at the body. The little black girl is a crumpled mess at his feet. The sight of her works like a steel brush on his memory, cleaning away its rust and refreshing the sheen of his own past.

There is no blood left. Her chest gapes open where her heart should be. Her left arm is a mangled stump, the hand missing. Her eye sockets are raw holes. Like blind men, maggots tentatively pick their way over her decayed flesh, eager to feed. Dust and moisture have crusted on the side of her body she has been lying on. Her throat was slit.

She is naked and not much older than five.

9

Police pickups are parked on the highway's edge. Incident tape, spanning a massive area, snaps like gunshots in the wind. The scene is barren of spectators. Only the sandy heaps of yellow tailings, covered in scraps of dry grass, watch over the scene, casting deep cool shadows in the day's dying light.

Jacob Tshabalala halts his questioning of the man who found the body, and waits for the dog handlers to pass by. He has a friendly face: a big mouth with full lips, a large flattened nose, but small ears. His eyebrows, stranded far up his high forehead, give people the impression that he is always surprised at what they are saying.

The highway traffic is deafening, and Jacob finds it difficult to interview the unresponsive old man. His mind keeps wandering back to the lonely young corpse lying in the field far below them. The missing organs and the absence of blood have already convinced Jacob what they are dealing with. This is no ordinary killer, no ordinary murder. Jacob does not need a pathologist to tell him what she went through before her throat was finally slit.

The old man with him is dressed in an ancient thread-bare tweed jacket and thin faded blue trousers, a floppy old brown cap stuffed into his jacket pocket. His white stubble contrasts with black skin that looks like scarred leather. One eye is white, filmed by a cataract, and the old man's hands are arthritic knots perched on top of his cane.

So far he has made little eye contact, keeping his back resolutely turned to the murder scene. He had even refused to lead them down to the body when the detectives arrived; he just stood up on the embankment, pointing and trying to explain.

'I want to thank you again for your phone call and for waiting for us, *imkhulu*,' says Jacob in Zulu, addressing the elderly man in the polite form.

The old man grunts, his jaw working ceaselessly.

Jacob knows they have detained him much longer than the witness anticipated, because he has become increasingly hostile and agitated. Jacob shouts over the roar of a truck, 'Are you sure, grandfather, that you've told me everything?'

The man nods.

A dog yelps. Jacob squints down the embankment, over the aged man's shoulder. A chill spreads down his spine and into his stomach. Suddenly he understands what the old one must have sensed. He was so anxious to get away from here because he knew what was down there – that is why he has kept his back consistently turned to the murder scene. Jacob paws for the two-way radio tucked into his belt and presses the button. 'Harry? Harry? You must see this!'

In the riverbed the dogs have flown into a frenzy. Some of them are rearing up, madly snapping at the air and straining at their leashes. Others are yelping and crawling on the ground, licking their chops, tails lowered between their legs, eyes wide and white with fear.

For the first time the old man meets Jacob's eyes, and something unsaid passes between them.

10

Nina Reading's rented Hyundai coasts down the inclined road with its engine idling before she stutters to a stop outside a boarded-up bar. It is late morning, the air already throbbing with waves of heat rising from the soft tarmac. She is in her mid-twenties and has large Italian sunglasses perched on a bold but attractive nose. Her skin is a deep olive which, when she is not wearing her glasses, accentuates her penetrating eyes, irises so brown they seem like ink drops splashed on a pure white background. She whips her head around in quick, suspicious glances.

The grey concrete overpass of the De Villiers Graaff highway snakes overhead and the drone of its heavy afternoon traffic pierces the abandoned silence. The entire city block, in the old quarter of Johannesburg, has been condemned in preparation for a rejuvenation project that has been put on hold for years. There are ruined lots where buildings have been demolished, but the soot black rubble has never been cleared. Garbage clogs the gutters in the street. Shredded plastic bags dance in the wind, impaled on razor wire protecting the few buildings that still house businesses.

Seconds tick by, but no one seems to have noticed her. Satisfied that her arrival has drawn no attention, she kills the engine.

She is parked about a city block up from the beginnings of a slum street on the outskirts of Newtown. Further down the broken road shacks seem to bloom like fungus spilling into the street and up against the walls of a few ruined buildings, the pillars of the overpass providing support for some of the bigger structures.

Nina's heart is thumping in her chest, almost knocking the breath from her lungs.

She unclips her seat belt, reaches under the passenger seat and pulls out a camera. Its lens looks like the barrel of a howitzer. She pumps the window down and trains the Canon on her surroundings. She swings her camera slowly left and right, looking for the shack that Tumi described to her.

She finally locates it, its entrance covered with plastic sheeting and one side of it propped against a massive pillar supporting the overpass. As she repeatedly squeezes the camera's trigger, a plastic sunflower ring on her finger flashes in the sun.

Nina waits nervously, her tongue feeling like a swollen cork in her mouth. She yearns for a sweet cylinder of tobacco between her lips.

The camera is slippery in her sweating hands. Fearing she might drop it, she wraps its sling tightly around one hand. All that remains to be seen is whether the same people are still plying their trade inside. She waits impatiently in the hope of good pictures, *great* pictures, something to send home to London that will keep her editor interested.

By chance she notices a man eyeing her car through a haze of cheap blue tobacco smoke. One of his eyes is lazy and his wrinkled lips tremble continuously. She freezes, and a single thought flares up in her mind.

I am alone.

He looks away again, taking another lazy drag, and Nina sighs with relief.

Twenty minutes later, the sheeting spread over the front of the shack ripples aside. A man's shaven head pushes through it. His skin is black as night. He carefully surveys the area around him. Nina has to kill the urge to duck out of sight.

His eyes are hidden behind large reflective shades. She snaps a picture of him.

The man, however, seems happy that everything is clear. He worms his bulk free from the plastic cocoon and emerges. In his hands he is carrying a white-and-red cooler-box, the kind that families take to the park on weekends. The moment he is free from the plastic folds, Nina realizes he does not belong to this neighbourhood. He is not dressed like any of the other inhabitants of this derelict landscape, and he does not act like them either. This man walks with purpose and strength, not with hunched shoulders weighed down by poverty. He is wearing new green-coloured jeans, a white Nike T-shirt and clean white-and-silver trainers. His fingers and his neck are enwrapped with flash fake gold.

Nina's camera clicks and whirrs like a cicada grinding its wings.

Her target walks down the narrow road Nina is parked in, heading away from her. He glances momentarily over his shoulder in her direction, as if about to cross the street. That is when he suddenly stops.

Nina immediately snatches the lens back inside the car, convinced he has seen her. Panic washes over her. He puts down his cooler-box, sticks a hand into a pocket and pulls out his mobile. She huddles down behind the steering wheel and prays, until she realizes he is just answering a call.

A rumble separates itself from the roar of the overpass. Nina whips her head around.

'Shit!' she cries, throwing herself down across the passenger seat. The handbrake jabs her hard in the side, and Nina hisses in pain. The camera whacks the steering wheel hard as she pulls it down with her. She swears again. Outside in the street she hears the other car decelerate rapidly.

As the car smears past her, she sees only tinted windows and shiny red chrome, no passenger inside, although the vehicle passes close enough, and slow enough, for Nina to make out a greasy handprint on the passenger window.

She peeks over the dashboard in time to see the hulking red BMW draw up to the man with the cooler-box. He disappears from her sight as he bends over to talk to the driver.

She fidgets with the camera, uncertain what to do next. The thought of a passenger in the vehicle having spotted her sends her into a panic and, without even attempting to catch the BMW's licence plate on film, she decides she has already taken enough chances today. She turns the ignition key slowly, as if the car will start more quietly that way. The engine clatters to life.

She is about to reverse up the way she came, but then realizes that reversing uphill in the wrong lane is guaranteed to arouse suspicion. She shakes her head in frustration and shifts down into first instead. The only way out is to drive on past them.

The car lurches forward. As she passes the BMW she notices a mercurial glint out of the corner of her eye and wonders whether the passenger window is winding down. She does not turn to make sure; instead, she slams her foot down on the accelerator and the car squeals forward.

She spins the wheel this way and that, not thinking of slowing, as she races away from the scene. It takes another half an hour before she realizes she has driven deep into the industrial hinterland of Johannesburg and has completely lost her way.

11

Harry's radio lies, switched off, in a clump of grass. The detective hates to have the crackle of electrical voices interfere with his work. He squats down next to the corpse and checks it one last time for anything they might have missed, before he orders its transferral.

This could've been my little Jeanie.

There is a flash of pain through Harry's skull as he thinks of his daughter. Suddenly it *is* his Jeanie lying there: her curly red hair dishevelled in the grass, her body mutilated, her lovely green eyes raw cavities. This cold thought grips him hard and forces him to gasp.

Although his anxiety is growing, he reluctantly goes on working. This little child should never have been left unprotected. Where is her mother? And her father? Did they love her? Is his wife Amy properly looking after their own little treasure right now? He wishes, yet again, that he could spend more time at home with his child.

Gradually these thoughts of Jeanie mutate into something else that bubbles up from the murky depths of his mind. It rouses emotions he has not experienced in years, not since Amy and he finally settled down together and Jeanie came along. They surprise him, just as the headache had surprised him. It's been a while. He stops working, overwhelmed by sudden tides of panic threatening to drown him.

Does he still have some of those pills in the car?

Harry looks around him to check whether anyone has noticed him hyperventilating. He sits down, thrusts his head between his knees and tries to catch his breath. Gradually the terror subsides.

Harry pulls out his handkerchief and wipes at his face. Suddenly he feels old and spent.

Someone brushes through the reeds behind him, and Harry realizes who it is before the man speaks. He knows only one person who breathes with such difficulty, spluttering and popping with every breath.

'Harry,' gasps André, his lungs heaving with the exhaustion of perpetually lugging the man's excess weight around. Harry can smell him even above the surrounding putridity: the smell of an unwashed bachelor who loves rum and hates water.

'Yes, André, what is it?'

'It's the dogs.' André is dressed in the deep blue military-style uniform of the South African Police Service. With his blond crew cut and mean blue eyes sunk deep in his face, André looks as repulsive as he smells. Harry keeps silent, so André continues. 'I don't know. I think you must come see.' He speaks with a hesitant Afrikaans accent, his consonants drawn out like chewing gum.

'See what?' Harry looks up, hopeful. 'They find something?'

'Yes, but we haven't approached it yet. You must really come see it. The dogs, they're shitting themselves over something.'

'What do you mean?' Mason finally stands up. He looks over André's shoulder but he cannot see much of the riverbed from here where the body lies partly concealed in a patch of reeds. In the distance, higher up where the cars are parked, he spots Jacob suddenly grab the ancient witness and restrain him by the upper arms as the old man tries to back away in a hurry. The witness struggles, but Jacob holds firm. They seem to be arguing.

'Harry?'

Why is Jacob struggling with the witness?

'Harry, can't you hear them?' André insists, and Harry is astonished to recognize awe in his voice. When he looks at André again, he registers the bruiser's unnaturally pallid face and also the distant savage barking. He is amazed at the canine rage borne on the breeze rustling the leaves.

'Show me,' says Harry, now all attention. He brushes past the giant Afrikaner and pushes his way through the foliage.

'Really, I don't understand it,' grunts André, coming up behind him. 'They is good dogs. I don't know. They're fucked, man. I mean, it's just a little thingy lying there.'

The foliage thins out and Harry's first impulse is to laugh at the spectacle he sees in the orange light of dusk, but his instincts cause the hair on his neck to start crawling.

What the hell is this?

'See?'

In the broadest section of the riverbed, standing in a near perfect circle, the confused dog handlers are trying to restrain their German Shepherds. He has never before seen anything like this. The dogs are throwing themselves at something lying on the ground, nearly choking themselves on their leashes.

'What's that?' asks Harry, breaking into a fast stride, then a jog.

Behind him he hears André lurching into a quick

shamble. He sounds like a blocked gully gurgling with water, as his sinuses splutter with every movement. 'It's something funny-looking,' gasps André.

Harry reaches the other men, who gladly part before him. Their eyes look haunted and confused. They begin to babble all at once, everyone offering a different explanation of the dogs' behaviour.

'Get these animals away from here. Take them up to the vans. Call Jacob for me. Coetzee, please get me my things.'

The men obey, quickly dispersing the circle.

The object is about the size of a man's fist, partially hidden in a thick clump of veld grass. Ants are swarming over it.

The dogs do not go easily; the clamour they kick up is deafening.

'What is it, Harry?' asks André, suddenly so close behind Harry that he looks around, startled.

'Will you back off? I'm taking a look.'

Coetzee arrives with Harry's camera, some gloves and a plastic bag. He hands the stuff over and steps back, preferring to watch from a distance. Harry looks up and notices a group of his own team's African officers standing high on the embankment, debating this new discovery, their hands flying wildly as they emphasize their opinions. Harry can see Lubbe leaning against their car talking to Jacob, who must have ushered his interviewee inside it.

Harry circles the object and takes a picture, the forensic technicians busy elsewhere, and the coroner long gone, called off to a massacre in a jewellery store.

'I wonder why no one found this before the dogs were called in?'

'*Ja*, I don't know.' André keeps his distance. 'The dogs went straight for it.'

'Them going mad so close to this thing: it means they destroyed any other clues in the sand,' mutters Harry.

He hefts his camera to take another picture. In the failing light, even the zoom cannot quite detect what it is. He tosses a pen into the sand near the mysterious object, not quite sure yet whether he himself wants to get nearer to it. More pictures taken with the pen in place provide a useful size reference.

'They could've taken care of that for you, Harry. Sorry. They should've picked it up,' mumbles André.

'Why didn't you yourself pick it up – you know, take charge, if you felt they weren't doing things right?'

'Me? Ah, I just thought you wanted to see the reactions of the dogs first.'

'You're right,' says Harry, although the sight had disturbed him. He has often worked with dog teams and knows they get excited while hunting for things. It seems like it's a game for them. Not today, though. Today something scared them.

'Come on, André, get your picture taken.' Harry suddenly grins mischievously. 'If I can get a good shot of you, I'll stick it up in the locker room.'

'Ah, I don't have any gloves on.'

'Here are some gloves. Coetzee brought them along.'

'Don't you need them yourself?'

'No,' says Harry.

'Screw that, man,' André gestures dismissively as Harry smiles, sets the camera down and bends down towards the object.

As he leans closer, he catches a whiff of rotten meat.

The thing is a tangle of grey feathers bound around something inside it with strands of what looks like grass. Harry sticks out the pen and nudges it gingerly, as if expecting it suddenly to come alive and scamper away. Only the disturbed ants react, the object itself yielding like it is packed with jelly. It reminds him of a dead chick he once prodded with a stick as a child.

Harry hesitates further before picking it up. He finds it unnerving him more than it should. He remembers the angry dogs and their aversion. It will also be getting dark soon, so he decides to act.

'Har—'

He lunges, grabs it like he is pulling it from inside a crocodile's jaws and rises in one quick movement. He exhales with relief.

'Harry,' laughs André loudly behind him, 'I swear, you looked like you were picking up a scorpion.'

Coetzee is laughing as well. Harry grins at them, suddenly embarrassed. He holds the object up for inspection, pinched between his thumb and index finger. It is clearly some sort of fetish.

It is heavier than it looks, and Harry notices flecks of dried blood on the feathers. Slowly he unties the slipknot. He can feel something hard inside as he works it loose.

'Let's have a look?' André decides to come closer, more confident now that Harry has not fallen dead. The knot comes undone.

'God, I hate that smell!'

'Yes,' says Harry after a few moments, 'so do I.'

The covering of grey feathers turns out to be a pair of broken wings. Inside them is a severed rat's head caked with some ashen substance and coagulated blood. The rat's eyes are still open and glaring red.

12

Nina purses her lips in exasperation. The streets and buildings have all begun to look the same, familiar yet somehow not right at all. For the third time she heads down Hubert Street, looking for a way back onto the M1 that passed by overhead. In the height of a lunchtime traffic jam there is nowhere she feels safe enough to pull over in order to take a good look at her map, and she now feels too intimidated by the city to ask for help. There is no air conditioner in the car, and sweat is running into her eyes. She is close to tears.

Waiting at an intersection, Nina wonders what all this must have looked like to a child like Tumi who had never seen a city before she was abducted. The child had never watched TV, never seen more than a handful of cars, then suddenly she was plunged into the urban sprawl of Johannesburg.

'Your English has improved since I last saw you,' Nina remembers herself saying to Tumi.

Nina had been sitting in an uncomfortable chair that seemed designed by a Swede to maximize aesthetic value whilst minimizing comfort. The table in front of her looked fragile, its thin steel frame topped by an enormous slab of glass.

Outside, a deep orange twilight danced over the Thames flowing below them. Canary Wharf looked brilliant, awash with flames of light that burned on the water and in the glass of its countless windows.

'Yes.' The girl's reply was a soft whisper of defeat.

Tumi could still not look her straight in the eye. Nina

*thought her beautiful: smooth skin the colour of creamy
coffee, her eyes a perfect almond-shape above the high
cheekbones. The broad nose accentuated her African
origins – as did her habit of avoiding eye contact.*

'Your sponsors treating you well here?'

'Yes.' Again the minimum response.

'They have a lovely place here, don't they?'

'It's nice.'

*'It's really nice.' Nina mustered her best smile. Tumi's
mouth scrunched up in her own sad attempt to respond.*

*Nina looked out the window uncertainly and watched
the river burning in the day's last light, a ferry cruising by
looking like a lazy duck in a pond of flames. It was difficult
to keep watching the girl's face and the anguish branded
into it.*

A minibus taxi narrowly misses her as it suddenly swerves
in front of her car and slams on its brakes. She hits her
own brakes hard, stopping seconds short of a collision.

'Arsehole!' she cries.

She is leaning on the horn before she remembers she is
a stranger in an unfamiliar, violent land. Four people jump
out of the minibus, ignoring her, while others inside pass
out bundles of belongings. The cab driver jumps out, too,
comes around the back and gives Nina a baleful stare
before opening the hatch and pulling out more baggage,
mostly in black plastic bags and cardboard boxes. It looks
like another twenty people are still sandwiched inside the
vehicle.

The tide of passing traffic does not allow Nina back in,
and she still feels too much a newcomer on these roads to
shove her way in as she would in London. She consults her

map again, but that is futile – she does not even know what street she is in.

The minibus driver moves off, waving a hand briefly out the window. She is not sure if he is trying to aggravate her further or apologize for the inconvenience.

Cars behind her immediately start baying. She puts her own vehicle in gear and drives on.

Tumi had to be older than eighteen, but Nina could not help thinking of her as a little girl. Her behaviour, her way of describing things, seemed so innocent, so nervous, so undeveloped, as if she had become stranded in a younger period of her life.

'You OK, Tumi? Can you do this?' She noticed how the girl kept wringing her hands under the table.

'Yes,' Tumi replied briefly. These minimal responses worried Nina.

'Good. Thank you, Tumi. I'm going to record this. Is that OK?'

Tumi nodded.

'We can go slowly. We have all day, right?'

'Yes.'

'So if it gets too bad for you, we'll stop and make a cup of tea or something, OK?'

'OK.'

'Good.' Nina gave her a sympathetic smile and added, 'I'm ready when you are.'

Tumi brought her hands up onto the table, fingers still entwined. She inhaled, then sighed deeply.

Nina depressed the button of her recorder and picked up a pencil. There was a cup of hot coffee sitting in front of her, more of the black stuff ready nearby. She, too, felt fidgety.

'So how old are you again?'

'I am nineteen now, I think.'

'How old were you when you came to England?'

'I come to England six years ago. I was thirteen then.'

Tumi spoke slowly, as if still struggling with her English. Zulu was Nina's own mother's native tongue, a language she had tried teaching her daughter for a while, but her father had not been very supportive. When the two had first met, Tumi had responded immediately to being greeted in her own language. That small touch of something familiar had gone a long way in forging the relationship between them.

'Tell me, how did you get here?'

'My uncle bring me here.'

'Why?'

It was like a knife tearing into delicate membranes, as Tumi's story had unfolded, flooded with raw emotion and obfuscated by her uncertain accent.

'I come from Cullinan. I lived on a white man's farm. I had an uncle who worked there also. He was a bad man; he knew how to talk to people to get the things he wanted. He became a very rich man when I was still very young. He moved away to Johannesburg, but he still come back to the farm often. I think he make business with the white farmer. I think they were growing . . . cannabis?'

Nina smiled and nodded encouragingly.

'Yes, that. He come back to visit many times, and stay the weekend, but he did not stay with us, his family. No, he stay at the big house, behind the electric fence. I don't think anyone likes him, but my father had to welcome him whenever he come to us because my father believed in family.

'When I grow older, he began looking at me so much.

It was then the arguments, they start between him and my father. They argue about money, always the money.

'I was twelve when my uncle come to fetch me for the first time. At night, he come into the room where my sisters and me, we were sleeping. He woke me up, he put his hand over my mouth, and tell me to shut up and come with him.

'I was very scared. Outside, he grabbed me hard and put his mouth to mine. He smelt of sorghum beer. My father was nowhere; he must have gone to bed. When my uncle finished kissing me, he dragged me to the farmhouse.'

The signs Nina has been following are bringing her closer again to the overpass, but nothing resembling an on-ramp has yet appeared. At this point Nina cannot care less which direction she ends up heading in; all she wants is to get away from this inner-city basin.

She watches hopelessly as section after section of the overpass disappears over the roof of her car as she drives on. At times the road signs seem contradictory. She is increasingly nervous, because the route she is following is leading her inevitably back through Newtown, into the derelict area she was trying so hard to escape from in the first place.

Her heart thumps at the realization that she has probably been moving full circle.

'Afterwards, he say to me it was his right.' Tumi paused to stare angrily at Nina. 'His right because my father owe him such a lot of money.' Tumi shakes her head violently, her breath now coming in short hitches. 'No!' She glances away in an attempt to bring her anger under control.

'He tell me that if I tell anyone, he will slit my sisters'

throats. After that, he say, he will come for me and kill me, too. My uncle is a big man. He was crazy in his eyes – and I believed him.' Her hands, glistening with sweat, danced around the table top at breakneck speed.

'He come back to the farm more often then. He say business was good for him because he had the blessings of the spirits to guide him. But I knew he really come for me. *He started pushing my father for the money he owe him, saying my father must marry me off to someone he knew. But my father refused. All this time I want to tell my mother what is happening – but how could I do that?'*

As Tumi paused, the silence in the room rang in Nina's ears.

'Then my belly, it began to swell.

'I did not know what to do and I was very, very frightened. How do you tell your parents that? Everyone knew that something was wrong with me. They kept asking me what, but I couldn't talk. I keep it to myself. I was frightened my father would punish me. Maybe he would have gone after my uncle, but my father wasn't a strong man. My uncle was stronger and also he carried a gun. I wanted to run away, but the only person I could go to was my uncle himself.'

She stopped for a few moments and stared into space, seemingly overwhelmed by her memories. Eventually she continued. 'Stupid, stupid! I thought he would help me. I did not know enough about people like him, but I was so scared then. I did not want to talk to him – I hated him. But I thought maybe he would make things so my father would not find out. And then, maybe, he leave me alone.'

Tumi looked up, her eyes pleading for understanding. 'I had to ask him for a favour because of what he did to me!'

*Nina could only nod silently. Tumi's life had been so
different from her own, but she could understand what
had motivated the child's decisions. She had been a simple
country girl then, isolated by a predator who stalked her
on his own terms.*

*'I feared the anger of my parents even more than I did
my uncle. I thought they would blame me completely.'*

She is being followed, Nina is sure of it. They must have
picked up on the fact that she is lost.

The car has been hanging back, driving deliberately
slowly, but she has spotted the same light blue Datsun a
few times now. It is old enough to stick out in the traffic:
a square block of ugly metal and silver grilles from a
bygone era.

Nina decides to backtrack to the Engen petrol station
she stopped at a few blocks back. They could not help her
there – the mix-up in languages proving too much to
comprehend any clear directions – but at least there are
other people there so she will not be alone.

Turning into a short side street, she is forced to stop
by a red traffic light.

The blue car suddenly comes turning into the same
street. It rolls up close behind her and stops, too. She looks
up into her rear-view mirror.

Three men in the car; two of them wave at her.

'*Dumela*, my lovely!' yells the driver, leaning out the
window. Shirtless, he has massive gold-rimmed sunglasses
propped on his nose. She notices that several front teeth
are missing.

The man sitting next to him turns up the volume of
their massive sound system, suddenly belting out Kwaito

music whose slow rhythmic bass booms against the buildings either side of the narrow street.

As the lights change Nina slams her foot down on the accelerator and the car responds with tyres screaming. She tears the steering wheel over to the right and screeches out into a broad three-lane thoroughfare. The car thunders over a massive bump in the road and she is briefly airborne. She hits the tarmac and the car bounces a few times before she brings it back under control.

A few hundred yards up the seemingly desolate street she is suddenly surrounded by vehicles feeding in from her left. She looks at her watch: it is 16.30 and therefore people's going-home time.

Looking in her mirror, she no longer sees the blue Datsun. There is nothing else she can do but let the tide of vehicles box her in and drive her forward.

'The next time he come to the farm, he laughed at me when I tell him. He just laughed when he heard I'm pregnant. He was happy about it!'

Tears burst from Tumi's eyes, and she began chewing viciously on her bottom lip.

'He ... he ... he ...' she sobbed, 'he grabbed me by the shoulders with a big smile on his face, and he say, "What do you want me to do?"

'When I told him I could not have this child, he stare at me very long like I was a stupid girl to get myself like this. Then he say, "OK, I will take it away. But for that you must come with me to the city." When he say this, I felt frightened. I began to cry. He tell me I needed to go for an operation. That's when I ran away from him.

'But he knew I would go. When I come home that night, he already told my parents a story. He said he had

work for me. It would help pay my father's debt to him. My mother did not want me to go. I was too young, she said. But she knew we needed the money. Then I tell a lie, too. I say I wanted to do this thing. After a while, my parents, they say it is OK.

'It was the last time I ever see my family. The last time – and I lied to them. I walk away from them with this devil.'

13

'*Imkhulu*,' begins Jacob, sitting in the car with the elderly witness, 'I want you to stop thinking about those dogs and concentrate on what you are telling me.' The terrified man has agreed to sit inside the police car, but his constant nervous glances at the caged dogs are frustrating. 'It's not what you think,' says Jacob, by way of calming him.

'I think I'll go home now. I'm not staying here any longer.' The old man turns frightened eyes on Jacob.

'We are not finished yet.'

'I don't care. I've already told you how I found the body, so now you must let me go.'

'Grandfather, you must listen to me. This is important. Don't look at those dogs. They . . . they always act like that.'

The old man's one good eye lights up with anger and distrust.

'This is about a murdered child. Just think of that child,' pleads Jacob.

'I've told you all I know. Now leave me alone and let me go home to my family.'

'Will you really not help us catch the murderer?'

'I will go home now, boy.'

'You mustn't walk away from this. I don't want to have to remind you that I am a police officer. Instead, think of what people will say. What about the fears of the local community?'

'What are you talking about, boy?'

'You know, as well as I do, why she is dead. Look.' Jacob points across the highway to the shacks forming the outer ring of Soweto's suburbs. 'Because they fear witches who commit murders like this one, some residents over there have burnt totally innocent people before now. Until they, or we, catch the right killer, they might do so again and again. You live there, right? Are you going to make yourself part of that?' A minibus taxi booms past, spraying the car with dust. 'How many people will die before you come back to tell me everything you know? Remember, there are probably people watching us now, even if they don't show it.' Jacob stares at the black officers still excitedly discussing the behaviour of the dogs. The men do not dare proceed down the embankment for a closer look, their superstitions stemming their curiosity. 'Even those policemen,' he gestures at the officers now blocking their view, 'are watching us. People always talk, and if I need to arrest you now because you won't talk to me, what will they start saying? What will the rumours be? What will the newspapers say when we release you after questioning?'

The old man sags noticeably in his seat.

'You are old and you have one blind eye, which many people believe helps you see into the spirit world. Will you be the witch they hunt next, after you leave the police station and another child disappears?'

'*Aowa!*' exclaims the old man. 'I'm *not* a witch! I did *not* kill this girl.'

'Then stay here in the car with me and we will finish talking,' says Jacob.

'I . . . yes, I suppose I will.'

'Jacob?' The hiss of his two-way radio interrupts them. 'Come in, Jacob. Harry wants you down here right now.' It is Lubbe speaking.

Jacob ignores the call. Unlike the others chattering nearby, like sparrows in a tree, he is not scared of going down there, but he is scared of what it signifies.

'OK, please tell me your story again.'

'Aren't you going to answer that call?'

Two of the officers catch Jacob's eye as they glance over their shoulders furtively and look away again. The rumour mill has indeed begun to spin.

'No. Tell me everything again. Tell me right to the end.'

The old man tells his story again, compliant now that he realizes how his own interests are at stake. Jacob listens, carefully making notes.

There is a knock at the car window, which startles both men.

Jacob looks up and sees Lubbe. As he winds the window down he realizes how late it is getting, with the sun now dipping behind the yellow tailings. A cool breeze has struck up.

'*Ja?*'

'Tshabalala, Mason wants you down there with him.'

'I'm busy,' Jacob says.

'We found something strange.'

Jacob winces. Some of his fellow officers have the

sensitivity of a grindstone. He can almost feel the old man tense up at those words.

'I am busy here with this witness. But I'll be there just now.'

'*Ja*, all right.' Lubbe slaps the bonnet and walks off.

A large flock of sparrows, silhouetted by the dying sun, banks through the cooling air and descends into the reeds below, from where a cacophony of their screeching immediately erupts.

Their sudden appearance unsettles Jacob. When he turns back to the old man's sombre gaze, Jacob is reminded of his father. The old man had been right: Jacob could not find anything new in his story. He sighs and closes his notebook.

'OK, Mr Mbewu, you can go home now. Do you want someone to take you there?'

'No, I will go home by myself.'

'Thank you, then. You did the right thing to talk to me.'

'This thing will sit heavy in my heart.'

'In mine, too, *imkhulu*. In mine, too. You must be careful, for your sake, and do not speak of this. There are people ready to see witches everywhere.'

'The dogs are worrying you, too, aren't they?'

'What?' Jacob snaps out of his reverie.

'Yes,' says the man, 'I can see they do. We all know this is the work of evil. Even they can tell.' He waves a frail arthritic hand at the white police officers. 'But do *they* really understand what it means to us when a child is killed in this fashion?'

'I don't know,' says Jacob, his voice distant. He is still wondering what the screeching of the birds in the reeds might mean.

'You are listening to the birds, too, my friend?'

Jacob turns to the old man again, surprised.

The man chuckles. 'You seem to know a lot more than most of your generation does these days.'

'Yes,' says Jacob, but nothing else.

The old man nods. 'I must go home now.' He opens the passenger door, gets out and stretches, while listening to the dusk's familiar sounds. People are milling about them now, but Jacob has the odd feeling of them somehow receding, so that the old man and he are the only ones stuck in this moment. The old man groans with relief as his bones crack into place.

Jacob himself does not get out.

The old man moves around the car, after another truck has thundered past, and peers at Jacob with his one good eye. 'I can see something terrible is bothering you. You take care, boy. You know where to find me.'

He adjusts his threadbare tweed jacket and pulls his battered brown cap from his pocket. After securing the cap on his head and patting down his jacket – as if making sure everything is in place – he salutes Jacob and walks away, his cane clacking in the gravel alongside the road. A sudden rise in the angry cackle of myriad little beaks in the reeds distracts Jacob momentarily. When he looks again, the old man has vanished.

Harry is heading up the embankment as Jacob finally gets out of their car. Harry is carrying something in a large plastic bag. Twilight is now nothing but a purple streak on the horizon, and the police crew start to switch on their car lights. There is a sudden chill to the air and Jacob feels an intense urge to go home.

'What happened down there?' calls Jacob as Harry reaches the top of the embankment.

'I don't know yet,' his colleague says abruptly. He looks pale in the headlights, his eyes seem unfocused, his jaw is clenched.

'Harry?'

'Mm?'

'What now?'

'Oh,' replies Harry, with a puzzled expression. He holds the bag up as if he had been asked to show its contents.

'*Maie agwe!*' exclaims Jacob, shrinking back from it. 'Put that away!'

'What is it?' asks Harry. He feels disoriented, a migraine thundering in his skull.

'Just put it away,' says Jacob.

'You, too, Jacob?'

'What do you mean?'

'I asked the other guys about it, too. All they'd do was shake their heads and walk away.'

'You shouldn't wave that thing around like that, Harry. It's very bad luck.'

'Who else is going to carry it, then?' asks Harry, suddenly irritated. 'Will you?'

'Let's just finish up here and go home,' says Jacob coldly. He turns and walks off.

'What?' calls Harry after him.

Jacob's earlier fears have returned. The dogs could tell instantly, other police officers could tell. What was it with these white people – especially Harry?

Jacob oversees the removal of the body and watches the mortuary van make a U-turn on the highway. He issues a few more orders before he walks back to their police car. Harry sits smoking in the passenger seat, staring at the dashboard. Jacob has not seen him look this bad in a long time. Coming round to Harry's side of the car and leaning his elbow on the open door, he asks, 'Harry, is it your head again?'

His partner says nothing, just nods. In his lap lies the thing he picked up in the field below.

'Harry, give that thing to somebody else. I'm not getting in the car with it.'

'No.'

'Please, Harry.'

'Oh, for God's sake, Jacob! It's just a bunch of feathers and blood and a rat's head. I'm keeping it here with any other potential evidence we've found, all right?'

Jacob stares at him.

'Give me that.' Jacob grabs the bag but holds it at arm's length, as if he is carrying a bag of dog shit. He takes it over to André, who is about to climb into his City Golf.

'Here, take this with you.'

'What, are you crazy? I saw what happened to the dogs. I'm a religious man! I'm not touching that *kak*.'

'Take it,' spits Jacob, 'and keep it safe. It's evidence.'

André narrows his eyes. For a second he looks like he is about to say something else, but instead sticks his hand out.

Jacob drops the bag into the man's palm and says a cold 'thank you' before walking away.

Behind him, before he is out of earshot, he hears André muttering to Coetzee, who is sitting in the passenger seat, '*Hierdie fokken Kaffirs.*'

For a second he imagines going right back to André's car window and punching his face in, but somehow he manages to close his eyes, inhale deeply and walk away.

When Jacob climbs into the driver's seat, Harry has a fresh cigarette in his hand and pills in his lap. Jacob thought Harry had got rid of those when his migraines had stopped.

As Jacob turns on the ignition, Harry suddenly chuckles. 'You know, Jacob: what's done never stays done.'

'You are right, Harry, very right.'

Jacob makes a U-turn on the highway, and drives on into the darkness.

14

Nina flops down on the carpet of her Holiday Inn hotel room, relieved to be back and feeling relaxed after a shower. Sitting on the floor, she has her bathrobe on, hanging loosely on her body, and a fresh cup of coffee steams next to her.

A wide semicircle of news reports, photos and clippings is spread on the carpet in front of her. Her laptop sits on a chair to her right. She absentmindedly teases knots out of her damp curly hair as her eyes wander over the assembled information.

'My uncle give me food to eat in his car. We had been driving for a long time, so I was grateful. My eyes become heavy, even though I was scared and I wanted to watch where we were going. Then ... I don't even remember falling asleep.

BLOODY HARVESTS

'Someone slapped my face and I woke up. I was naked, lying on a cold concrete floor. There was thunder everywhere. Two men stood over me in a small room. One of them seemed as big as a house. The other man was thinner, he was the one kneeling over me. Again he slap me, hard enough to make my cheek swell up. He smile at me, but his teeth are sharp and his eyes very angry. The room had tin walls, patched together. There were no windows. The only light in the room came from behind the giant man. I realized the thunder all around me was the sound of cars – so many of them that I realize I must be in a big city. The walls shook with them. These men, they did not look like they would listen to me. If you ever see their faces, you will understand. I crawled away from them into a corner behind me. There was a dirty mattress there, so I pulled up my knees and hid my face behind them.

' "Good, good, my little thing," say the man in a very deep voice. "You learn your place."

'He spoke to the giant behind him, who hand him a plate. He hold it out to me. I didn't want it.

'He say, "Take it."

'I would not.

' "Take it!" he say again.

'He lean forward and smack me hard on my head. I stuck out my hand and he give the plate to me. They also give me water in a cup, and they put a bucket in the far corner. Then they leave me, locking the door behind them, leaving me all in the dark.

'I bang on the door; I yell for help; I beg them to open up; I ask them to take me home; I even cry for my uncle who brought me here. But it was like no one was there. No one even told me to keep quiet. After many hours I

69

lose my voice, so I listen hard for sounds outside, but I can only hear voices as if from far away.

'The food and water they gave me tasted funny. They put something in the food, so I first didn't want to eat it. But I was alone in the dark so long that I grew afraid that they left me there forever. In the end I pick up the food and I eat it. I drink from the cup. The water, it was bitter, and the food tasted very bad.'

Nina lights a cigarette, leans back against the bed and picks up a file of notes she has been collecting, searching for a specific article. It follows a British police investigation that has been prominent in the news over the last two months. The search for a five-year-old boy's identity and killer has led investigators from London over to South Africa and Nigeria. The wounds suffered by 'Adam', and the contents of his stomach, which held various minerals including traces of gold, animal fats and plant material, suggested to Scotland Yard's Serious Crimes Squad that the child had been deliberately prepared for ritual murder.

They had done that to Tumi – fed her porridge full of stuff that gritted in her teeth like sand. Soon she could not do much else except writhe around on her mattress, in pain. She could not sleep any more and began to hallucinate.

'One day the door open and my uncle come in. He was wearing his traditional clothes made of animal skins and coloured wraps. My uncle smiled at me and said, "Ah, Tumi, you and that child of yours will bless me today!"'

Another man had followed him into the room, barefoot and wearing the colours of a *sangoma*. From what Tumi told Nina, she gathered he had some kind of skin disease. The man chanted as he approached her, waving incense around the room. Tumi realized then what might happen to her, and she froze with panic.

'I was only thirteen,' she said, 'but the older folk often warn us of what *amathakhati* do to children that don't behave themselves.'

'*Amathakhati?*' Nina remembers asking.

'Yes, the ones who make bad magic.'

Up to that point, Nina had always suspected such things only happened in the remoter regions of Africa, not in a modern city like Johannesburg. After all, Tumi's uncle was a man who drove cars and wore suits.

The *umthakhati* had then unrolled a mat and sipped from a frothy brew, which he then spat onto the four corners of the mat. Tumi's uncle dragged her onto it and they smeared her body with oil before the *umthakhati* forced her legs apart and her uncle pinned her weakened arms behind her head.

'It felt as if they were cutting my organs out while I was still alive,' cried Tumi. 'But I couldn't do anything.'

When Tumi finished her story she sat staring at the table, tears running down her face. Nina found her hand sliding over the table to take hold of Tumi's arm and offer her comfort.

'Invisible forces raping women', read a headline from the *Sunday Tribune* of 1 September 2001. Several women claimed to have been raped at night by reportedly invisible assailants in a township north of Johannesburg called Alexandra. Nina is fascinated by two theories suggested: one proposed a *tokoloshe*, a small demon feared throughout southern Africa; the other that a *baloyi* had invaded their homes after smearing himself with the sap of some rare indigenous root that rendered him completely invisible. *Baloyi*, the Sotho word for the Zulu *umthakhati*, is easier for Nina to express. Both could mean wizard, witch or sorcerer, but she knows from her research that these Western terms fall short of describing these mysterious practitioners. Besides, when she thinks of a wizard, she cannot help visualizing old men in cloaks wielding spell books and wands. Their African counterparts seem much more ominous.

Nina gets up from the floor and looks out of her room's lofty window, seeing all the modern conveniences she is so used to: satellite dishes, mobile phone masts, the streets sparkling with modern cars. She is used to the potential dangers of London's streets, but out here in Africa it seems urban dangers are imbued with a darker undercurrent.

Her thoughts turn to her adventure earlier that morning, and the white-and-red cooler-box the man was carrying.

What was inside it?

She cannot repress a shudder.

15

Harry is late coming home, and Amy hates it when he does not phone to warn her. There is nothing worse than an empty spot at the dinner table where her husband should be sitting.

He is a cop, of course, so she must expect the odd hours. He is also a husband who still manages to phone her most of the time when he is running late. It is times like these when the natural worry digs in deep and a voice at the back of her head starts nagging.

Will he ever understand the visions she has of him lying in a hospital, or dead in the street? She will never forget that picture released to raise awareness for the police service's plight. It showed a police officer shot and wounded, lying in the dust and half concealed in grass, a colleague unsuccessfully trying to stem the blood. The caption read, '*We're dying to serve you.*'

She turns the oven off, leaving the lasagne inside, and absentmindedly tosses her gloves into the sink, full of tepid dishwater.

'Oh no,' she moans at her carelessness. She smoothes her brow and tucks her light brown hair behind her rather prominent ears. She fishes the gloves out and drums her fingers on the sink. Once that voice of worry starts, its nagging will not be stopped.

I love that man, she realizes, imagining Harry's rugged face and his crop of untidy hair which always looks like he has just woken up, no matter what he does to it. She wants to give him a phone call, but he is notorious for switching his mobile off while working.

Behind her, she hears their five-year-old daughter Jeanie humming a melody while dancing her purple Barney toy on her knee to the tune of a Barney video. Harry bought her that video; it is something they often watch together, Harry bouncing his daughter on his knee while he talks over his shoulder to his wife. Amy often wonders how any grown man, a policeman on top of that, can sit and watch Barney as if he genuinely enjoys it. Jeanie has already made her dad sit through hours of watching those same two videos. It is a strange sight, but Amy is not about to complain. It is great to have a husband who clearly loves his daughter so much. Amy herself needs to get away from her daughter sometimes, while Harry does not ever seem to get enough of her.

Just as she is about to call Jeanie in for dinner at the kitchen counter, Amy hears the garage door rattle open and the familiar deep hum of Harry's Nissan pickup drive in. With that sound comes a familiar flutter in her throat – even though they have known each other for so many years. Her mood softens instantly, but she decides to give him some stick anyway.

It takes her only seconds to realize that something is wrong. His usual timing is off: the habitual sounds are not coming from the garage. After eight years of marriage – five of them in this house – she has got used to the details of his routine. He usually steps into the kitchen even before the garage door has finished rolling down. Otherwise, when he has had a particularly stressful day, she can hear him scratching around aimlessly in his toolbox – it is something to do while he finishes a cigarette before coming into the house.

Amy pulls the lasagne out of the oven and puts it down on top of the stove, listening carefully for further sounds of Harry's movements. She has not even heard the car door slamming shut, now she thinks of it.

'Harry?' she calls, finally.

He does not answer. She glances at Jeanie, still playing in front of the television. She did not even hear her mother calling out, that is how engrossed she is in the Barney show, slamming her toy's head repeatedly on the floor in what looks like a mock-up of push-ups.

Amy wipes her hands on her apron, then opens the kitchen door accessing the garage. The car door is open and the internal light still on, revealing Harry slumped against the steering wheel. She hears the engine tick loudly and she steps through, closing the kitchen door behind her.

'Harry?' Amy calls again. She notices his shoulders hitch and realizes he must be sobbing. Her heart freezes, her own throat constricting in response.

How lonely he looks.

'What happened?' she pleads, her voice cracking as she struggles past her own Mazda to reach him. He looks up and blinks hard, his eyes looking bleary and red. Like a little boy caught crying at school by his friends, he clumsily tries to wipe the evidence away.

She opens the car door and seizes his head in both hands.

'Harry? Christ, you OK, baby?' She kneels down next to him, still cradling his face. He grips her sleeves tightly and buries his face deep in the comfort of his wife's soft body, her jasmine-scented clothes.

They huddle there for a few breaths more as she soothes him and strokes his spiky blond hair. Gradually he stops shaking and gently shrugs her away. He gives her a peck on the cheek – a silent thank you – and finally climbs out of his car.

'You OK, babe?' Amy persists.

'I'm OK.' He hoarsely clears his throat.

She hugs him again. 'You want to talk about it?'

'Nah, I'm all right.'

She stares at him.

Despite his emotional distress, Harry is glad to see the fierce concern in her green eyes. He forces a smile. 'I'm fine.'

'You want some dinner?' Harry nods. 'Go inside. I'll bring your things in,' she urges softly.

Jeanie's head whips around the moment she hears her father's familiar heavy tread. 'Duddy! Duddy!' she squeals, rejecting Barney like some dead animal. She bolts into the kitchen, her welcome-home charge aimed directly at his legs. She has clamped herself onto one thigh before she senses something is wrong. She glances up to catch sight of her father gazing down at her with puffy red eyes, barely managing a wan smile.

You're the second little girl I've had at my feet today.

His forced smile feels grotesque, and by the time he stoops to stroke her red hair, her happy grin is evaporating.

'Jeanie, it's OK,' he reassures her desperately.

Amy comes in and begins scooping out their meal. She watches Harry intently as she works, eager to bombard him with questions, but she knows Harry will never speak of his work in front of Jeanie.

By the time they sit down at the table Harry's spirits seem to have lifted and he and his daughter are soon chattering away, but the moment Jeanie's attention wanders Harry lapses into silence. Soon he is attacking his lasagne in a way that does not invite conversation.

Amy lets him be. She will wait until Jeanie is asleep.

'So what happened, Harry?' Amy asks later, lying in bed with a *Cosmopolitan* magazine's pages under her fidgeting fingers.

'Nothing,' Harry insists quietly, folding his clothes with unusual attention. It is an answer he has used often in the more distant past.

'*Nothing?* You know how it worries me when you say that.'

He shrugs and goes on tidying things away. The television set in the wall unit rumbles with more local news. She had switched it on in the hope of catching something that might give her a key to his current malaise. She turns her attention to another assassination reported in Hillbrow.

'Two youths were shot dead early this morning, in the staircase of their Hillbrow residential building,' says the broadcaster. 'Neighbours giving witness claim they were known to be involved in heroin trafficking. This incident may be related to the ongoing violence that erupted shortly after the arrest of Ngubane Maduna when he was charged in Johannesburg's largest ever heroin bust. He is still missing since leaving the High Court last week on Tuesday, following his successful appeal for bail.'

Harry briefly looks up on hearing the mention of two further murders, then climbs into bed beside his wife.

'Was it all about this?' She gestures with the remote.

'No,' he says, then turns his back, as if settling down to sleep.

'Oh, come on, Harry, talk to me!'

'There's nothing to talk about.'

She looks at him, not sure how to react. 'Don't you trust me, then?'

'It's not that.'

'What happened that was so bad you can't even talk to me? I don't need to be protected, Harry.'

He does not answer her.

'You've never let Jeanie see you in such a state before, Harry, and you've never cried about your work before either. In the fifteen years you've been doing that horrible job, you've never once cried in front of me.'

'Let it be, Amy, please,' he whispers, eyes closed.

'Harry, you really scared me tonight. I have a right to

know.' The moment she says it, she wonders whether she actually *does* want to know. 'Harry, please.' She tugs at his shoulder gently, and finally he turns around.

She puts the magazine aside and lies back next to him, staring deep into his blue eyes as if measuring him.

'I don't want to talk about it, Amy,' he whispers, his voice heavy with sleep, his eyes closing.

'Harry, you haven't been this evasive with me in a long time.'

He sits up suddenly and stares at her. 'Amanda, leave it alone. Not tonight.'

His angry glare soon turns into something softer and pleading. She looks away, dropping her voice, and says, 'OK.'

It is anything but OK.

How can he not trust her with his feelings after all these years together? She gets out of bed, goes into the en-suite bathroom and closes the door. She sits down on the toilet, about to bury her face in her hands, then notices the container of pills on the washbasin.

It has been five years since she has last seen it, not since Jeanie was born, and she assumed he had thrown those things away. But now his pain is back – and the past has finally caught up with them. Even having Jeanie around could not stem it forever.

She stares at the container for a minute, then blows her nose and walks back into the bedroom. Harry has switched off the television and the room is dark.

She slips under the duvet and tentatively touches his back. Instead of responding to this gesture, Harry shies away from it, pulling the duvet tighter around his body. Hurt, she rolls away from him and ends up staring at the dark wall. It is a long time before either of them falls asleep in the summer heat. The curtains dance high up into the room like apparitions waltzing to the music of cicadas and crickets rasping outside. Moths flutter against the glass of an outside light and, somewhere close by, Harry hears a dog baying to the moon.

16

The colour of the failing twilight resembles the red earth-and-dung huts of the compound extending beneath it. Birds have come raucously alive in the cooling air. The leaves of a giant paperbark thorn rasp in the same wind that is pushing white cloud tufts further north. A goat nuzzles the plastic buckets of water stored to one side of a hut, while chickens scratch in the red dirt that has been tightly packed with peach stones to provide a rough courtyard.

'Hurry, children!' yells an old black man, clapping his hands. 'My ancient bones won't carry me any more, once it's dark. So, in you go! I want to go to bed. Come now, Jacob, Landi, what have you got there? Bring it along, then. Stop fooling around, you lot, and let this old man get inside where it's warm.'

Cackling madly, he flaps his hands at them, sending the children squealing inside the hut. The old man, feeling uneasy, turns to gaze out over the long yellow grass growing beyond the compound, which is rustling in the strong breeze. He closes his eyes momentarily, trying to hear nature's song. After a few moments he sighs and follows the children inside.

Despite his advanced years, the old man looks extremely handsome, with a high, intelligent forehead, white hair and a well-tended grey beard. His eyes sparkle with humour and mischief.

Martha, his daughter-in-law, looks up as he steps inside. She is already undressing the children in turns and tucking them into bed. Of these five children, all aged under ten, only Jacob is her own. The older children and the rest of the family will be returning long after dark, their journey home a long and tiring one.

'Father, stop scaring the children, otherwise I'll never get them off to sleep.'

'Bah, I'll make sure they sleep.' And once all the children are in bed, he tells them their favourite story, about how Dog lost his tail. Martha leaves them to it, she knows the routine. At first there are wild bursts of laughter, then the yawns gradually begin. One by one, the children slowly drift off towards sleep.

The old man gets up and moves amongst them, touching their foreheads lightly as he offers a whispered prayer.

But when his turn comes, Jacob is staring alertly back up at his grandfather. The old man smiles at him. 'Aren't you tired yet?'

'What is that you always say to us whenever we go to bed?'

He strokes the boy's face. 'You are always so curious, Jacob.'

'I just want to know.'

'Don't you know already?'

'No.'

'Well, soon you won't need me to tell you. For you're going to become the kind of man who'll know what someone is going to say before he knows it himself.'

'Like you do, grandfather?'

The old man winks at him. 'Maybe.'

Jacob smiles up at his grandfather and makes himself more comfortable on the mat, tugging over him more of the blanket he shares with his cousins. The old man stops by the door to wave briefly at his grandson, before closing it behind him.

A woman is walking towards him in the evening's darkness, and Jacob can see insects and shadows pouring out of her hair, her wrap, her fingers. Although he can hear people talking close by, he knows he is standing all alone on the dirt track that leads to the little school attached to the farm. The woman's hair is braided, down to her knees, in thick dread-locks. Her face is obscured by the darkness enveloping her, but one red eye stares at him and her bottom lip seems to gleam with a green luminescence.

Suddenly she is right up against him, breathing foul air into his face. Her eyes are not red, but yellow, and her teeth are long and sharp.

Jacob wakes up, breathing in gasps and feeling cold. When he tries to pull the blanket up to his chin for protection, he becomes aware he cannot move. His breathing grows shallower, as if it is slowly giving up.

Rough hands suddenly pull him up from the bed. For some reason he cannot cry out, and his cousins do not wake. His whole body feels stiff and unbending.

The outer door that is always so carefully bolted at night now stands open. The moon glows brightly in the sky above and it seems to Jacob he is somehow now floating through the air, because the physical presence of the person carrying him is invisible. He can feel dry skin close to him and smell the sweet odour of old sweat, yet he sees no feet, no legs, no body.

His breathing grows weaker the more he struggles to inhale deeply and scream for help.

Whoever is holding him now crosses the courtyard. Just then the dogs begin to bark, and even the goat, tied up for the night under the paperbark tree, begins to bay.

Jacob feels like he is still floating towards the long grass bounding the other side of the compound. He realizes with terror that he might disappear, just like Frank Isondi did last year, and other children before that, but there is nothing Jacob can do except watch his own abduction and listen to himself moaning silently without the breath to protest.

'*Wena!*' a voice bellows suddenly behind him.

It is Jacob's grandfather, and the old man utters a string of words that seem to affect the person carrying the frightened boy. Abruptly Jacob is flung to the ground, where he begins to gag for breath and finally manages to draw some air deep into his lungs.

Looking up, he is confronted by staring white pupils in a face resembling a death mask. The witch's almost naked body is smeared all over with ash, covered only by his skimpy underwear and two thin straps of leather fastened around his biceps. The intruder, whose face is twisted in hatred, has lost interest in Jacob and is now staring at the old man. The boy shakes his head, convinced he is dreaming.

'Coward, you come and face me instead! Attack a grown man rather than a child.'

As Jacob looks up again, he catches a brief sight of something disappearing into the tall grass and the gloom beyond. He begins to sob, as life returns to his limbs.

'Jacob! Are you all right, Jacob?' Another shouting voice echoes through the compound, which had seemed so quiet only moments ago. Jacob's father, holding a torch, hurriedly crosses the forecourt. The boy's grandfather sinks to his knees and cradles him in his arms.

'Bantu, shine the light here. Quick, shine it here. What's this? Did he always have this? I don't remember it.'

'Yes, since he was born.'

His grandfather turns Jacob around under the beam of the

torch light, checking every part of his body for harm, before he stares the boy intently in the eye.

'Jacob, listen to me! Stop crying, my boy. Did he put anything in your mouth?'

The boy chokes out, 'No.'

'Are you sure? What about your ears, your nose – did he put anything anywhere?'

'No, nothing. I just . . . I couldn't breathe, grandfather. I couldn't move. And everyone else was sleeping.'

'I know, I know.' His grandfather hugs him tightly. 'That's how those cowards get away with brave little boys like you.'

Jacob continues to sob, his face pressed against his grandfather's shoulder, while the two adult men confer in whispers with each other.

'Did you actually see it?' asks his grandfather.

'No, what form did he take?'

'A hyena,' whispers the old man, in disgust.

Jacob is then handed over to his father, who clasps him more protectively than he has ever done before. This unexpected intimacy terrifies Jacob still further. Moments later, Martha joins her husband in the gloom and takes the boy from him.

An hour later, the two men have gathered up the things they need, having decided it best to alert the neighbouring compounds and the village before dawn, when the hunt itself would begin.

17

When he arrives at work on Tuesday morning, Harry feels in even worse shape than the day before. From the way he looks, he might have slept the night on a park bench. He barely greets anyone, heading straight for the office he shares with Jacob.

Harry falls into his chair and rubs at his face with both hands before reaching for his Rolodex and phoning the Child Protection Unit. A soft-spoken woman answers and puts him through to a Tienie Fourie.

'Good mornink, detective,' she says, her voice sounding shrill.

'Good morning, Inspector Fourie.'

'Call me Tienie, please.'

Harry's tired face at last cracks into a smile. 'All right, Tienie, I was wondering if you could please send me information on any missing black girls, aged between about four and eight years old, whose disappearance has been reported recently.'

'How recently do you mean?' Tienie asks.

'Say, the last six months?'

'That could mean a lot of work. We is almost six weeks behind, while we're logging everyfink onto computer. With two thousand childrens going missing every year, it could take me a really long time.' The inspector's pronunciations are notably harsh, each *th* and *k* sounding like she is swearing.

Harry is surprised. 'That many?' he says. 'What about just the West Rand, then?'

Ignoring his second question, Tienie continues, '*Ja*, detective, those are just the *reported* ones. In some cases these kids are not wanted by their own families and get thrown out, which means no one reports them missink, and then it becomes difficult or even impossible to trace the family either. Then there is all the kids that don't even have birf certificates. I'm not even going to get into *that*. It's bad sometimes, I'm telling you.'

84

'Are they all that young, though, the ones you're talking about?' asks Harry.

'The ones that leave on their own, they is usually older than ten, but, really, they can be younger than that. Haven't you seen them yourself on the streets in town? They're everywhere these days. Desperate single mothers, they throw these kids out of doors so the next man might marry them, but you know, they never do. If any child tells you she doesn't want to go home, even if she is looking like a dirty drowned rat, then you must realize how bad it can get at home.'

'I see,' says Harry. 'In that case, let's make it any young girls in just the last three months and focus on those who have disappeared in Soweto specifically. We're now looking for the family of one girl in particular. Can you do that for me?'

'Of *course*, I can,' she pipes up. 'But you got any other information for me?'

Harry thinks back to the small mutilated body and its nakedness, the identity it has totally lost in death, and decides that cheery-sounding Tienie Fourie does not need to know such gory details this early in the morning. 'Not much else to go on, sorry.'

'No clothes? Nothing at all? *Ach*, shame! The poor thing.'

Harry promises to phone Inspector Fourie if anything else crops up and then puts the phone down. He stares at it for a moment. *It just never gets any better, does it?* Fifteen years on the job, and lately it has felt like he is not getting anywhere and his vital organs are slowly burning out.

His old-fashioned office is barely separated from the bureaucratic madness that is the rest of the Murder and

Robbery Unit within the police station. On Harry's archaic wooden desk, clogged up with reports and an overflowing ashtray, stand his Father's Day mug ringed with coffee residue and a frame with twin photos of his wife and daughter. He directly faces Jacob's desk, which is situated on the other side of a small central space. In contrast, his partner's desk holds just a small pile of reports neatly arranged in correspondence trays and a desktop Ferrari calendar; all the rest of his stuff is hidden in drawers, which he tidies out regularly.

The walls are large perforated notice boards, broken in places by darkly lacquered pine fittings. One immediately to Harry's right has yellowing notes, office jokes and old Christmas cards pinned to it; to his other side are tacked details from unfinished cases. A set of photos there shows various shots of a murdered black male, a large panga wound bisecting his face, and the *shabeen* where he was killed, a large pool of blood caking the asphalt outside it. Another group of photos depicts a particularly gruesome hijacking attempt that Harry and Jacob are still trying to solve, where a man and his wife were shot repeatedly while still seated in their Pajero. The incident, occurring near Wits University, has left the couple's two young daughters orphans.

Harry looks up as someone steps into the office. It is Jacob carrying a cup of hot tea in one hand and the newspaper he has already finished reading in the other. Jacob always arrives at the office before Harry and the others and spends that time slowly getting a grasp on the day. He stops midway between their desks and looks at Harry with a worried frown.

'What is it now, then? You fighting with your wife?'

'Yeah, well.' Harry does not meet Jacob's probing stare

but wonders about his partner's unnatural ability to gauge what is bothering him. There had indeed not been any proper reconciliation between himself and Amy, either last night or this morning.

'How's your headache?' Jacob presses.

'I'm fine,' says Harry, nudging at some reports on his desk.

Jacob notes his grey pallor and the dark circles under his eyes. 'You don't *look* fine. Did you suffer bad dreams?'

'What's with all the questions? What do *you* care how I sleep?'

'I'd just like to know,' insists Jacob.

'Has this got something to do with the evidence we found yesterday?'

'You should never have picked it up. Something that's bad enough to scare the dogs is very powerful. If you are really feeling something bad, then I'll take you to visit a *sangoma*.' Jacob's accent is not very pronounced, but it nevertheless disguises his innate intelligence from anyone inclined to think lightly of him. Harry himself was genuinely surprised when he first found out that his new partner could speak six of the eleven official South African languages.

With a hollow laugh, Harry for the first time looks Jacob in the eye. The vacancy of his gaze makes Jacob shudder.

'You want me to go see a *sangoma*? This damn headache started even before I picked that thing up.'

'When *did* it start?'

'As soon as we got there.'

'That's my point – there was bad magic already there, and then you touched it. You saw the way the dogs were reacting, Harry. I'm not the only one who saw what happened last night. There were others there, too. And even if *you* don't think something strange is going on, the others may think so.'

'I'm just not feeling well, that's all. Since when did you become so superstitious?'

'It's not superstition. I just know what I know.'

'I've seen that crucifix you wear around your neck; you can't tell me you're Christian but still believe in magic.'

Jacob is taken aback and retorts, 'Don't change the subject.'

'OK, I had a fight with my wife last night and we ate breakfast in separate rooms this morning – which upset my daughter. I did have a headache – and a bad one at that. Point is, this morning isn't a good time for me.'

Jacob does not say anything.

'It's a coincidence, nothing more.' Harry sighs. 'I didn't have any bad dreams, and I can't explain what happened to those dogs yesterday, but I'm sure it wasn't magic. I don't need to go to a *sangoma*, and I'd never want to either.'

Jacob shakes his head. 'OK, forget it, man. I'm going to attend the muster.'

'Jakes, give me a break.'

'Harry – ' Jacob pokes a finger at Harry – 'there was a time . . .'

'Yes?'

'I won't want to work with you if you're going back to the way you were. Your wife, she maybe understood you then, but *I* didn't.'

Harry is stunned. 'What do you mean?'

'There was definitely something wrong with you. I don't want to work with a dead man again, a man who just sits in the car or in the office saying nothing all day.'

'What's with you?' Harry is suddenly angry.

'I am going now, OK?' says Jacob. He stares at Harry for a second longer, gives a nod and then leaves, closing the door behind him. Harry throws his eyes up to the ceiling, his hands gripping the armrests as he tries to bring his anger under control. His partner lecturing him is definitely the last thing he needs today.

18

Harry, himself late for the briefings, joins the knot of people gathered in the doorway. When Jacob spots him, he abandons his well-placed chair deep inside the room and comes over to stand beside his partner. Detective Superintendent Ryan Bornman barely notices Harry's arrival as he continues reading out summaries of the last week's crime statistics, his thick brown moustache quivering as if it has a life of its own. Only when Bornman cites Harry and Jacob as investigative officers in the little girl's murder does Harry look up.

The detective superintendent fixes Harry and his partner with a stare over his reading glasses. 'You two better get a grip on this case fast. Molethe's in a really bad mood this morning.'

'Shouldn't the Occult Unit be handling this case anyway?' asks Bobby Gous, a young detective recently seconded to the unit. 'I thought this is what their lot was created for.'

'This is a murder, detective, and it gets treated as such,' answers the overweight detective superintendent, in the tone of a teacher reprimanding a child. 'If you're suggesting another unit can do our job better, then you're obviously in the *wrong* unit. Got that?'

Harry hates the daily muster as much as he hates the cramped room itself – with its smells of dust, floor polish and body odours and its sickly yellow light. It is the same routine every morning, people squabbling over timetables, assignments and, most importantly, car allocations for the day – holding up daily progress for some and buying the slackers time before they need start work. Harry's thoughts drift as he stares at a familiar community-policing poster stuck carelessly to the wall. It is one he has read and reread a thousand times during these ritual meetings.

'Harry, are you coming?' murmurs Jacob.

Harry blinks in surprise. Everyone else is now filing out of the room.

Back in their office, Jacob gets on the phone to contact all the different registered organizations of traditional healers operating in the Witwatersrand area, while Harry sits down with some fresh coffee in the purple mug with DAD scrawled lovingly around it. He decides to call the pathologist's office for a date on the autopsy and is eventually put through to an old acquaintance, Dr Malcolm Wilkes, only to be advised that nothing will be happening before Thursday.

'Can't you do anything sooner?'

'What do you mean, can't I do anything sooner? You people normally have to wait two weeks for an autopsy. No, Harry, we're full up. You're going to have to wait your turn.'

Harry stays quiet.

'Hallo?'

'Malcolm, I know I can catch this killer, but I need the autopsy results sooner than that.'

'I'll be honest with you, we have to prioritize and, after reading the report from the coroner present at the crime scene yesterday, it looks like there isn't much left for us to analyse here. That cadaver is at least a week old. The weather has been hot, and it's been raining, too. I've got a dozen other bodies waiting here that will yield more useful evidence than yours could.'

'The removal of organs suggests this is a muti killing, which means there's a good chance it might happen again. Do you really want the next innocent child's murder on your hands? Do you want us dealing with riots like when the Station Strangler was still loose and the public decided we weren't doing enough? Come on, Malcolm, you've got kids of your own – I don't know how many other children might be lying out there in the fields. I need to move fast, and for that I need your help.'

There is a sigh from the other end of the phone, and Harry can hear the doctor paging through reports.

'These are *kids* that are getting knocked off here,' continues Harry.

'All right! All right!' snaps Wilkes. 'I'm counting this as a favour – a *moer* of a big one. I'll do it tomorrow, personally.'

They make arrangements for the afternoon of the following day.

Jacob is now speaking rapidly to someone in a native tongue, tapping a pencil against his chin. Harry pulls a copy of the case file towards him and surveys what they already have. It is not very much: a mutilated body, a fetish – that is all. Any tyre tracks or footprints were long gone. Jacob's interview with the old man yielded nothing substantial either. The witness had been dropped off that morning to visit a friend in Riverlea, had hung around there for a while, then headed back home, taking a short-cut over the ridge later in the afternoon. He had already crossed the ridge, heading towards the highway, and descended into the dry riverbed when he smelt something rank and found the little corpse.

As Jacob puts the phone down, Harry asks, 'What's an old-timer like that doing crossing open veld to reach a highway? Why didn't he just catch a taxi?'

Jacob shrugs. 'He didn't have the money.'

'Surely he couldn't have been the only witness, if other people regularly walk over that hill?'

'Maybe, but you can see for yourself those trails don't get used often. I guess most people prefer to cross the N1 at Commando Road or the Soweto Highway, but those roads are quite far away from the location he was visiting,' says Jacob.

'We'd better talk to that friend of his. How come you were arguing with the old man, anyway?'

'He was very scared.'

'Oh?'

'He is traditional in his ways, believed that place was polluted, full of bad luck – just like that object you picked up was full of bad luck. He didn't want to stay there any longer – just wanted to get away as quickly as possible.'

Harry sips from his mug of fresh coffee. 'We need to solve this, Jacob.'

Jacob is glad to notice the predatory glint slowly returning to Harry's eyes. Someone curses loudly further up the corridor and there follows the sound of something crashing into a wall. A door is flung open and heavy steps come towards them. Senior Superintendent Simon Molethe stomps into their office, looking sweaty and beleaguered.

'I don't believe it! I've just had three newspapers in succession on the phone. They're putting that murdered girl on tomorrow's front pages, with or without our say-so.'

'Shit,' grumbles Harry.

'I've barely read the report, so how do they know about this so fast? Who leaked the story?' asks the chief. Molethe used to be a keen boxer in his youth and his heavy frame still ripples with strength, reminding Harry of an old bear with plenty of fight left in it. His age could be anywhere between forty and sixty, his white beard, pitch black hair and the naturally serious lines of his expression making it a difficult guess. There is a star-shaped scar in one corner of his mouth: a memento from his days as a Bantu constable in the old republic, when some miner not carrying his pass attacked him with a screwdriver.

Harry and Jacob glance at each other. 'Neither of us did,' says Harry firmly.

'The *Beeld* wants to do a split cover featuring the whole Ngubane Maduna mess *and* this dead child, too. *Eish!* I'm going to suffer a heart attack the way things are going. The area commissioner has been shouting at me all morning because we haven't yet solved that double execution at the Berea Shell station *or* the murder of that damn Nigerian family. What have you got so far that I can feed these idiots?'

'We've got nothing yet, boss. Autopsy is done tomorrow, but the scene was about as clean as they come.' Harry realizes the ashtray is still on his desk and barely manages to sneak it off before Chief Molethe looks his way again.

'Nothing, hey, so why are you still here? Go *do* something!'

'We're just about to,' says Jacob, then he switches to Sotho. 'We're just waiting for some faxes that will give us the names and addresses of any traditional healers operating in that area.'

Harry, catching some of what was said, adds, 'I want to go visit some of the houses beyond that ridge and speak to the people that work there.'

'Sort it out, then. Tomorrow's a big day,' growls Molethe. 'I've given them some basic facts already, but tomorrow *you're* the ones speaking to the media.' The phone in his office, far down the gloomy corridor, begins to ring shrilly and he charges out. He yells over his shoulder, 'Harry, I don't want you smoking in that office!' The chief's office door slams shut a moment later, and the shrill ringing is abruptly choked off.

'Nice mood *he's* in,' says Harry, emptying his ashtray into his wastebasket.

Jacob is laughing. 'What, any worse than yours?'

'Watch it,' warns Harry, cocking an eyebrow, but with a grin on his face.

Two hours later the expected faxes have all finally come through and the two detectives begin sorting all the contact details into manageable groups before heading out to Riverlea.

Driving south on the De Villiers Graaf motorway, through heavy commercial development, they cut west on Main Reef Road towards Riverlea itself. Harry gazes out over the bare brick houses that rise above them on the hills that will eventually terminate with the old mine heaps further south, and he ponders these gated communities now springing up all along the major highways. These popular residential communities, virtually unheard of a decade ago, with their high walls, their electric fences and their armed security patrols send out a clear message: the police service is fast losing the war against crime. Families do not feel safe any more, and the fact that the houses dotted along this ridge do not look particularly affluent intensifies the general message. Even poorer people would rather hole themselves up in a security village than face head-on the New South Africa.

'You think we're going to get any help at all on this?' asks Jacob, following a railway line on his right.

'I should bloody hope so,' replies Harry. 'That list is a mile long.'

When the interviews with local homeowners and their domestics fail to yield anything constructive, it is Harry's idea to call in officers from the Langlaagte police station to help comb the whole ridge all the way down into the riverbed just five hundred yards from the security wall surrounding the last clutch of the new-built houses, before the open fields start to the west of them. Even then, no leads are found.

It is as they are driving back to the station that Harry begins insisting that he does not want the media involved.

'Why not?' asks Jacob. 'We need to identify the child somehow.'

'We'll probably find a match with the help of the Child Protection Unit.'

'Harry, you're not making any sense. What if they don't have her on file at all?'

'Look, that poor little girl deserves to be left in peace. She doesn't need the media torturing her family, raking through her past history. We can do this discreetly.'

'I know you don't like the press, but we've always released selected statements whenever we need additional help. So why not now?'

'This is different,' grumbles Harry, and clams up.

Jacob's mind drifts as he is left to wonder just how it is different.

Stopping at a red traffic light on his way home that evening, Harry watches a flower vendor entertain tired car-bound commuters by whistling an enthusiastic tune while dancing to its rhythm. As the vendor approaches Harry's car with a wide toothless grin he suddenly decides to buy Amy a bunch of red roses. At home, Amy seems happy to receive them, and it briefly looks like they might be reconciled. But once she realizes her husband is still not entrusting her with his inmost feelings, she starts to withdraw again. Meanwhile, picking up the general mood, Jeanie stubbornly refuses to eat her supper or to go to bed.

Hours later, Harry lies on his back still awake, his stomach churning with nausea. He is keenly aware of Amy not even saying goodnight to him.

19

Harry wakes up early and lies staring at the ceiling, listening to Amy's soft breathing beside him. Then he slips out of bed quietly to wake up his daughter, having decided that there is only one way to deal with the silent misery that has been steadily creeping through their house. They need to talk, just as Amy already suggested.

The pleasant smell of a warm child greets Harry's nose as he opens the door and peers into his daughter's darkened bedroom. With dawn's light glowing through the yellow curtains, he discerns that Jeanie is not lying in her bed under the window but is sleeping stretched out on the floor instead. Having clearly rolled off the bed sometime during the night, she is still fast asleep with one thumb tucked in under her chin. Harry pulls the curtains apart before gently shaking her awake.

'You wanna help Daddy cook breakfast for Mommy?'

'Yes!' Jeanie stretches and nods with enthusiasm. She grins up at her father.

Before long she has helped him make a mess of the kitchen, while Harry has managed a tomato and pepper omelette for his wife. Along with a cup of black coffee, he takes it to her on a tray sprinkled with petals gathered from the garden. He wakes Amy with several soft kisses on her forehead. As her eyes flutter open, her expression becomes confused.

He says, 'I'm sorry, love.'

'Mhm?' She sits up and notices the tray. 'Thank you,' she murmurs sleepily.

'Amy, we can talk about it tonight, if you still want to.'

A deep frown creases her forehead as she recalls they did not go to bed last night on the best of terms.

'Harry, it's OK, we really don't have to,' she says. But he has seen something light up in her eyes.

'No, I want to. We can't go on like this. Better nip this in the bud before it starts getting serious again.'

'Come here,' beckons Amy, a glad smile spreading over her face. She hugs him to her tightly and nuzzles him on the cheek. 'Thank you, baby, and I love you, too.'

Harry leaves her to her breakfast and finds Jeanie now perched on the sofa in front of the television, her face smeared with jam. She complains loudly as he helps her change for preschool. Barely making it into work on time, he encounters a small group of journalists already congregated outside the police station, waiting to be briefed on the developments in Harry's case.

Superintendent Bornman is standing at the front of the common room addressing the detectives of the Murder and Robbery Unit. 'Ladies and gentlemen, your chief would now like to have a few words with you,' he announces, 'and so would his special guest, senior state advocate David Gildenhuys.'

'Good morning people.' Chief Molethe moves to the front of the room, which feels even more crowded than usual. Harry notices a few familiar faces that are not in their unit but with SANAB, the South African Narcotics Bureau. 'By now I'm sure you know what Inspectors Mason and Tshabalala found on Monday night. Judging by the number of journalists phoning this station, I'm sure by now the whole country knows, too. I want to insist you all take extra care of who you talk to about this case, since I don't want this situation developing into something worse than it already is. And I certainly don't want it turning into a circus, the way the narcotics investigation already has.

'As you know, Ngubane Maduna is currently being sought for skipping bail on the Randburg heroin bust. Detective Superintendents Ryan Bornman and Kobus Niehaus are working with Narcotics to try to establish links between their case and certain homicides occurring over the last week. Only last night another three victims were gunned down in Braamfontein. With that Nigerian family of four, the two youths executed at the petrol station and two pushers killed in a stairwell over the weekend, that now totals eleven fatal shootings. The fifth and youngest member of the Nigerian family is still missing, so keep an eye out for a seven-year-old boy on the loose – his picture is available from Superintendent Kobus Niehaus.

'Man, I don't know exactly what to say to you. We don't know if there are links between our drug bust and this shooting spree, but when ten million rands' worth of heroin ends up with us, there are bound to be repercussions. I suppose all I can say is: be careful and assist each other as best you can.' Chief Molethe gestures for Kobus to step up. 'Superintendent Niehaus.'

Kobus looks uncomfortable in front of such a large crowd, a lanky forty-six-year-old dressed in grey slacks and a white-and-blue checked shirt. He nervously scratches his thin, jet-black moustache while consulting some notes he has made for the occasion. When he finally speaks, his English is clear but hesitant.

'Narcotics are still interviewing the five men arrested with the cache of heroin. The two women with Maduna at the time of his arrest have been released. So far the suspects have told us bugger all. They're either feeling bloody sure they'll walk free, or they'll happily go to jail rather than talk.

'There haven't been any further tip-offs from the anonymous caller who started this ball rolling. A trace couldn't be made, but we're hoping he'll re-establish contact. All we know at this stage is that he was an Afrikaans-speaking male. We've invited some of the narcs over to discuss the case with us. Just try to find out a bit more from them, so long as you don't ask them out on a date, OK?'

99

There is the obligatory laughter at Niehaus's tepid joke, before Molethe steps forward again.

'Right, people, all we can tell so far is that no one is talking. As said, the suspects certainly aren't talking, and one of the reasons we think these cases may indeed be linked is that the recent executions in our city seem closely linked to the heroin trade in Hillbrow. Potential witnesses to those executions aren't talking either. People are running scared of something, and that makes me very uneasy. Here with us now is senior state prosecutor Gildenhuys.' Molethe holds out his hand to a man in his fifties, who is standing in the doorway. He has drooping eyes and a large downturned moustache, his face looking frozen in a permanent expression of sarcasm. Though his habitual unkempt appearance makes him appear dull and slow, Jacob has occasionally been witness to the man's ferocity in court. He chews up the defendants in his cross-examinations, and what he spits out is not usually worth locking up afterwards. It is for this reason, perhaps, that a few hand claps and hoots of appreciation break out as he steps forward to address the assembled police officers.

'Gentlemen, the justice and police departments seem to be screwing up, and screwing up *bad*. I'll be the first to admit it and I hope you can, too. We're just not getting any results.' His tone is sharp enough to cut glass. 'Last week Ngubane Maduna himself walked out of the High Court after winning his appeal for bail. First mistake! Then the people who were detailed to tail him somehow *lost* him, although he was driven away in a convoy. Second mistake! So there he goes, *poof* – ' Gildenhuys gestures like a magician – 'like magic.

'Now, I'm glad the public doesn't know yet that those

same three vehicles were implicated in the execution of those two young dealers at the Berea petrol station – on the very same day. Right now the public hates us enough as it is, the newspapers have made sure of that. We have eleven dead so far, blown to pieces in roughly similar ways, which gives us good reason to believe this might be mushrooming into some kind of all-out turf war. Like Simon here said, suddenly there's a ten-million-rand gap in the drug market.

'What I don't understand is that we have only one eyewitness at that petrol station and none for any of the other killings. That's *bullshit*! You hear me? That's fucking *bullshit*! How can a petrol station full of people suddenly all look away at once or disappear while Desert Storm is suddenly breaking out in the forecourt? Answer me that.'

The room stays quiet.

'I'll answer it for you. It's got to do with *credibility*. We hardly had any left after that incident with our police dogs chewing on defenceless immigrants for the BBC. But now, with this Maduna bastard vanishing into thin air while on bail, we have none. In fact, we have *fuck all*! The papers are having a laugh at us and the politicians are shitting themselves. That just pisses me off!'

Gildenhuys deftly controls his pause, angry eyes trawling the dead-quiet room, searching for somebody who might challenge his opinion. Very few eyes meet his directly.

'I'm pissed off, too, because I've been pulled off some really important cases for this. A bunch of dealers killing each other – I personally couldn't care less. This is a lot of my own time down the toilet. Now, I *want* that asshole Maduna, I *want* to find the killers of these eleven people and I *want* the killer of that little girl, because *maybe* then we'll get some respect back, *maybe* the papers will back off us and actually help and *maybe* ordinary people might once again be willing to help us with vital information.'

'Why such special interest in the little girl?' Harry interjects.

Gildenhuys licks dry lips and peers over at Harry. 'Because the politicians like something that gets people going, and nothing gets people going like harm done to children. So if the brass can get the case of a dead child dramatically solved, and thus keep people looking the other way while all hell breaks loose in Johannesburg over our heroin epidemic, then that's all to the better.'

'What?' Harry places his hands on his hips in disbelief.

'*Jissus*, Harry, I'm telling you, we need some suspects *fast*.'

'This Maduna thing is at its height right now,' retaliates Harry, 'but I haven't even got an autopsy on the child yet.'

'You're an experienced cop – so deal with it.' The two men glower at each other until Gildenhuys turns to the rest of the unit and addresses them as a group again. 'Remember, it's not my job to pick a fight with you boys and girls. It's my job to get convictions.'

'You really think that potential witnesses keeping this quiet is all about police credibility?' asks Bobby.

Gildenhuys throws his hands in the air. 'I don't know. I just don't know.'

'I don't want any press releases issued about my case while it's still under way,' interjects Harry.

'Why not?' inquire Jacob and Gildenhuys at almost the same time.

'Because it's likely going to become even more of a mess.'

'Is that right?' says Gildenhuys, frowning.

'Yes,' says Harry, 'that's right.'

There is a nervous cough beside Harry, and someone whispers to him in Afrikaans, 'Relax, *moena*. What's wrong with you? He's on our side.'

Chief Molethe is loudly tapping a pen on his notepad, staring directly at Harry.

'We'll talk about that in Molethe's office,' says Gildenhuys. 'Right now we're not about to bite the hands that feed us. We play this the way the area commissioner himself and the others want it.'

While Gildenhuys is still speaking, a man enters the room and takes up position near the doorway. Turning to the new arrival, Molethe says, 'Mitchell, I want you, Mason and Tshabalala in my office in fifteen minutes. God bless the rest of you. Adjourned.'

20

'Come in,' comes the muffled command from behind Senior Superintendent Inspector Molethe's door when Jacob knocks. Inside, Gildenhuys is talking at a furious pace on his mobile, while staring out over the ugly concrete parking lot outside one floor down. Molethe stands near him with his arms crossed.

'What's your problem, Harry?' asks Molethe the moment he catches sight of him behind Jacob.

'Nothing, chief.'

'Then why were you giving Dave so much trouble?

He's locked up some very important cases, and he's a friend of this department.'

'Chief,' says Harry, glancing over at the prosecutor, 'I don't like people interfering with my work, and I especially don't like having to answer to the media every morning I come in. As far as I can tell, that little girl's murderer could already be on his way to Cape Town after the press coverage so far. On the one hand, I'm being instructed to arrest the killer as soon as possible, and on the other it sounds like I should spend my time window-dressing, to distract people from what's really going on in this city. The trail is already going cold, and I don't care to waste my time liaising with the media when I should be out catching an innocent child's killer.'

'It's tough, *boet*, I understand, but you'd better play the game. And play it our way, you understand?' Molethe retires behind his desk and flops down in his green leather chair. The office is plain and unattractive, the sign of a man who clearly has no interest in adorning his workspace with personal items. Only a single framed poster of his favourite football team, the Orlando Pirates, adorns the wall directly opposite his desk. 'You're a good detective, Harry, and you've been in worse situations.'

David Gildenhuys puts his phone down and turns to them, clapping his hands together loudly, then rubbing them as if anticipating food. 'Right, sit down, people. I'm not here to shit on you – that's your chief's job,' says Gildenhuys, unperturbed by Harry's obvious hostility. 'We've skimmed through your reports, but I want to hear it from you directly. What exactly are we dealing with?'

'Yesterday, we spoke to any local people living and working in the vicinity who might have had cause to go down into that field. We also thoroughly searched the whole ridge above it. We found nothing,' says Jacob.

Gildenhuys acknowledges Jacob's report with a nod, although his eyes have been holding Mason's stare. 'Harry, I'm not here to fuck you over. In fact, I might just do the opposite. There's a chance your case might tie into something I was working on before I got yanked from it and put in charge of sorting out this Maduna *kak*.'

'What are we talking about?' asks Harry, puzzled.

'You first,' says Gildenhuys.

'I don't want to rule out the possibility of a serial killer with his own bizarre rituals, but on the face of it this looks like a muti murder. In either case, this might not be the first or last such incident.'

Molethe sighs, leaning back in his chair as if trying to distance himself from this observation. Gildenhuys begins rolling up his sleeves, as if getting ready for a long session. Harry does not like the look of this gesture.

'It's either one or the other in this case. So which, detective?'

Jacob answers for him. 'This is a muti killing – and it will happen again.'

Molethe stares at Jacob, surprised. 'You sound very sure about that. Why?'

'It's a gut feeling we have, chief,' answers Harry quickly, afraid Jacob might mention the furious reaction of the dogs.

'No, it's more than that.' Jacob's face clouds. 'The body parts removed are those typically used in muti rituals.'

'Yes?' beckons Gildenhuys.

'I think the child's blood was drained from her. People have been known to bathe in it, in order to gain courage and strength. The missing hand could also have been taken for strength-enhancing rituals, but hands are also known to get buried in the concrete doorsteps of businesses, so as to beckon hesitant customers in and bring the owner great wealth. The heart is always a potent item, particularly because she was so young and innocent. Her eyes would have been taken to allow the ability to predict the future, or else to gain insight in some difficult situation.'

There is a stunned silence in the room, which continues until behind them the door suddenly opens.

'Morning, chief, Advocate Gildenhuys.' Mitchell walks in, offering Harry and Jacob barely a nod. His grey eyes, blond mullet and a bulbous nose flecked with dirty pores give the overall impression of unkempt violence. The tension in the room is jacked up several notches.

'Detectives, I'm sure you know Captain Francis Mitchell, on secondment from the Occult Unit,' says Gildenhuys, as Mitchell takes up a position to the left of Molethe's desk. 'His experience in dealing with witch doctors or traditional healers, whatever you prefer to call them, will be appreciated by you two, I'm sure. But, then again, Tshabalala, you've just been sounding like a walking encyclopaedia of witchcraft. Have you worked on a case like this before?' asks Gildenhuys.

Jacob casts his eyes at Mitchell. 'No, sir.'

'So how do you know all this stuff?'

'It's my job,' says Jacob, suddenly hesitant to talk. Harry notices the cloud on his partner's face has now become a thunderstorm. He knows why.

'Well, I grant it's a strong enough case for labelling it a ritual murder,' says Gildenhuys.

'There are going to be more killings,' warns Mitchell. 'This business should be handled urgently.'

'I agree it should be dealt with as soon as possible,' says Harry, although the idea of siding with Mitchell disturbs him. He has always felt Mitchell, who significantly helped in creating the Occult Unit after he went through a flurry of rebirth as a Christian, to be a morbid sensationalist, constantly banging on about the danger of the country's traditional black practices and the steady Satanist invasions of schools, hospitals and graveyards. Sure, there had been serious incidents in the past, but none warranting Mitchell's wild claims of a society facing imminent collapse.

'I want us all to slow down,' says Gildenhuys, pushing his sleeves up even higher. 'This child may have been killed for a *specific* reason. There is as yet no basis on which to found your theory that it is going to happen again, is there?'

'Somebody tried to make damn sure the victim wouldn't be traced,' says Harry. 'Her body seems to have been deliberately washed clean. From what I know, one-off muti killers very rarely bother covering their tracks to such an extent.'

Gildenhuys nods. 'I don't know if the two cases are linked, but this is where I begin my own story. Two months ago airport security picked up a suitcase left at Johannesburg International. Inside, packed in bubble wrap, they found a human skull and an embalmed human hand. Mitchell's been handling that case since, but there's not much to go on, so the trail's running cold.'

'My apologies, advocate, chief,' interposes Mitchell, 'but I still think things would go quicker if I was appointed the investigating officer for this girl's murder.'

'We discussed that already, captain,' says Chief Molethe firmly. 'Tshabalala and Mason stay on the case.'

Mitchell's face goes red. 'I can't agree with that approach. My own team was formed especially for such cases.'

A thought occurs to Harry. 'Chief, are we two being kept on this case simply because we're a nice black-and-white double act for photos in the papers?'

'I'm saying you two look good together, *and* you're both good cops. Like the advocate here said, we've had a great deal of negative publicity with that immigrant incident. This is a chance for us to rectify any opinion that the police service is still fundamentally racist. Don't worry, you'll solve the case. You'd *better* solve the case.'

Gildenhuys bursts out laughing. 'They make a cute couple, all right.' No one but Molethe shares in his humour. 'Oh, fuck it,' continues Gildenhuys. 'You people need to lighten up. Hell, if I didn't love the bad jokes in my business, I would have died from my ulcers already.'

'But this stuff is what our unit has been especially trained to handle,' reiterates Mitchell, dissatisfied with the turn of conversation.

'These two were on the crime scene first. They already put in all the work, the reports, the hours.' Molethe sits forward in his chair. 'They're just as qualified as you are to handle this case, because a *murder* has been committed. The newspapers that keep harassing me will be hovering over everything we do. I prefer to have *them* in the papers.' He indicates Tshabalala and Mason.

Mitchell nods reluctantly.

Molethe grabs a pen from his desk and, clicking it agitatedly against the table, he continues. '*Jissus*, when are you people going to learn this is a *team* effort? Brief them, Mitchell.'

Mitchell sighs and leans heavily against Chief Molethe's

table. While he speaks, he looks either at his superiors or straight ahead, with never a glance at Mason or Tshabalala. 'We don't yet know whose bag it was, or where that person was heading. There wasn't a name on any of the personal items inside. We suspect some smuggler got cold feet and just left the bag at the airport.

'We've narrowed down to about an hour the time the suitcase spent abandoned in a toilet cubicle. Judging from the timetable and the proximity of the toilets to certain departure gates, the smuggler could only have boarded three planes in good time: two destined for London and one for Dakar, Senegal.'

'Tell them about the grave robberies,' urges Gildenhuys.

'In the past two months we've listed seven cases of defiled graves, where the corpses were mutilated and body parts were stolen. We've also had four reported cases of cadaver mutilation actually in morgues. So far we've only apprehended two ambulance drivers, of all people, after it was discovered they themselves had removed the genitals of a deceased man during transit.'

Molethe whistles in disbelief and Harry shakes his head in disgust.

'It seems one of the drivers wanted the items to cure his impotence, after he learned the deceased had fathered nine children. In this case the ambulance man was going to perform the ritual by himself, without any help from a witch doctor. At the moment we have no idea whether the remaining cases are related. All we know is that statistics have gone through the roof; we've never before had to deal with this many grave robberies and mutilations within such a short time frame.'

Harry interrupts. 'A relationship between Mitchell's

case and ours isn't necessarily substantiated by these incidents. We can't assume that these various crimes involving witchcraft all link up; that's like claiming that every murder is related.'

It is Gildenhuys who answers Harry. 'The skull and the hand were identified as belonging to a female child between four and eight years of age. The morphology of the skull indicates that the victim was probably black. You're right, Harry, these things are perhaps not related, but are you willing to take the chance that they're not?'

'*Your* murder victim, I think, is part of something bigger,' nods Mitchell, for the first time looking directly at Harry.

Gildenhuys turns to Mitchell. 'Do we have enough information to pursue the issue with Scotland Yard and with whoever's in charge up in Senegal?'

'What do you want me to report to them? That we have found a suitcase with human bones and we think maybe there's someone in their country who's missing a suitcase?'

'God, I hope I'm just being paranoid, but the increase in such statistics unnerves me,' says Gildenhuys.

Shortly the detectives are all dismissed. Mitchell disappears without a word, clearly still angry that the case has not been handed over to him. Back in his office, before leaving for a meeting with the prosecution in the panga murder case, Harry puts a call through to the forensic lab to check on their analysis of the blood-soaked fetish. It turns out that the wings belonged to a common pigeon, while the grass could have been plucked almost anywhere in the province. It is what was inside the horrible object that is most interesting to Harry. The rat had been an albino, its head severed with an extremely sharp instrument. Also, both the ashen substance and the dried blood caking the rodent's head had been of human origin.

'Human?' Harry repeats, and Jacob looks up from his desk.

'Yeah,' says the technician. 'I've got a blood group for you already, but you'll have to wait a bit longer for a DNA analysis.'

Harry writes down the blood group he is given and hangs up.

'Human?' asks Jacob.

'Your curse thing was filled with human blood and bone ash. The rat was an albino – that suggest anything to you?'

Jacob nods thoughtfully. 'Such a rat itself is uncommon, abnormal, which could be significant for some people. Albinism has always been associated with the occult in Bantu lore. The human blood and ash will have rendered the fetish more powerful. I guess, from what we saw, those ingredients were used to make a deadly curse, a charm that would remain powerful for a long time even after it served its purpose.'

'You're not altogether sure?' asks Harry.

'There is no standard for African magic, no set recipe. It all depends on the demands of the spirits at any specific time and the needs of the person who is asking for the magic. When people seek black magic from a *baloyi*, they often want misfortune to come upon a person they're jealous of. But sometimes they want someone to be killed by the spirits, and then they invoke the most deadly magic of all. It's very expensive and very dangerous.'

'Are you saying we're looking for a *rich* believer in African magic, then?'

'Yes, but it still doesn't mean anything for sure. A lot

111

of black businessmen these days feel insecure about their new-found position, so they turn to African healers to support their own good fortune or bring bad luck to their competitors. We'd have to interview literally thousands of people.'

Harry grabs his keys off his table and pauses in the doorway. 'You know, we're going to have to talk about this. I still want to know how you know all this stuff. You never told me about this little sideline of yours.'

'It's nothing much, Harry. It's only what you pick up when you grow up in our culture. Any other black person could tell you this.'

When Jacob closes the door to the office they share, he is relieved that Harry has had to go off to attend the autopsy. There are some things better left untold.

21

Harry is nearly late for the scheduled autopsy. Arriving at the state morgue in Hillbrow, he is struck by how familiar it all still seems. Instead of spending two conscription years fighting in the Border War, he went to the police academy straight from school and subsequently became a uniformed officer, then a forensic photographer showing a keen interest in autopsies and forensic pathology in his spare time. He expended much youthful enthusiasm learning procedures and came in regular contact with a wide range of forensic specialists.

Harry continues along the main corridor with its olive-coloured walls, the familiar stench of formaldehyde and disinfectant mixing with the smell of floor polish currently being applied to the black lino tiles by an old janitor, who recognizes Harry and greets him warmly.

The doctor he is seeking appears round a corner. He is already dressed in his surgical garb, with a tough white apron, and long black rubber gloves pulled up to his elbows.

'Ah, Detective Mason, I'm glad you are so punctual,' he greets Harry in mock surprise. The forty-two-year-old practitioner's blond hair is immaculately permed and styled, while aquamarine contact lenses lend his eyes a striking blue. With his skin also a deep, artificial tan, Harry feels he looks more like a volleyball coach.

'It was either coming here or talking to a bunch of reporters.'

Wilkes grunts. 'I'm glad to know an autopsy is not the worst thing a cop ever has to face.'

They enter the examination room, where two assistants have just carried the black body bag from its allotted fridge and are laying it out on a solid slab. Harry eyes the cruel runnels which drain any blood down through a hole in the centre of the operating table's white porcelain.

The stark white light, sharp angles and sharper instruments always make Harry think that morgues resemble interrogation rooms for the dead, torture chambers rather than places of science. And now they are going to tear the truth out of this little body, too. The reek of her week-old corpse is already seeping through the plastic.

'Smells like the deceased enjoyed her lie out in the sun,' comments Wilkes.

Harry barely nods as the examiner chuckles at his own ghoulish humour. 'We found the body lying out in the open, just off the western bypass of the N1. By the looks of her, she'd been badly affected by the weather, so I'll appreciate even the smallest bit of information you can get off her.'

Wilkes looks sharply at Harry as he shifts his cold steel instruments around in readiness.

'It's a corpse, detective – it's not a "her" any more. You start thinking like that, you'll find yourself heading for trouble. Here, stick this in your nose. It smells like orange peel, but that's better than what this cadaver is going to smell like.'

Harry takes the two wads of cotton he is offered and sticks one of them in each nostril. The sudden sharp smell brings tears to his eyes. When Wilkes pulls the zip open, the stink that escapes is overwhelming. Despite his long experience, even the expert looks like he has taken a punch to the chin. Harry, too, feels his stomach hitch.

'Jesus!' says Wilkes. 'I haven't smelt anything quite that bad in a while. Isaac, come and help me lift this thing out of the bag. Uh, last time I worked on one as far gone as this, my little fox terrier wouldn't come near me for a week, no matter how many showers I took.'

As they lift the girl's body free, Harry steps back and looks away. He hears loose soil fall off her back and patter onto the bag that had enclosed her. For the first time he grasps just how long she has been dead. Up to now he had somehow managed to envisage to the finest detail the little girl she had once been, something he has never experienced before. For some reason he can imagine her running around playfully, flapping her arms as if she is a bird. In his mind's eye, the child has a cute toothless grin; she has glittering black eyes; her hair is braided into long strands that sprout wirily from her head. She is dressed for church in a white dress with blue trimmings and wears her favourite yellow shoes, shoes like . . . well, like . . .

Maybe the doctor is right: somehow he must begin thinking of her as just another victim.

Isaac slips away the body bag and carefully tips its remaining contents onto the table: more sand and some dead insects.

'When did you last see one of these, hey, Isaac?' Wilkes asks his assistant.

'Not for a long time, boss,' says the man, his broad nose twitching as if to dodge the stench.

The victim's mutilated body is bloated and distended with gas, its skin bruised and blistered. As frozen maggots roll off her body, Harry cups his mouth with one hand and takes a few steps backwards.

'*Jenne!* What a mess,' mutters Wilkes.

Harry stares across the table at this clean-cut man who looks as if he might never even have taken out the garbage in his life and wonders what anyone so immaculate is doing practising forensic medicine at the University of the Witwatersrand.

'We're pretty sure it's a muti killing,' Harry volunteers.

'*Ja*, I can see why you'd think so,' mumbles Wilkes, as he fidgets again among his knives and saws, 'but this sort of thing would happen more in the Limpopo province, don't you reckon?'

'Yes,' replies Harry, 'but it does still crop up in the townships.'

'Let's get started, shall we? I've made arrangements for later at Woodmere Country Club, and I have a lot of work to finish first. You owe me big time for this one.'

'I'll buy you a drink at the Arms and Boar then, like old times,' suggests Harry.

'Hey, no, there's a *lekker* place in Rivonia – a good Scottish single malt is more what I had in mind. Were there any clothes on this corpse?'

'None that we could find.'

'Hmm,' murmurs the examiner, and switching on his Dictaphone begins to document the autopsy: 'Presented 29 October 2001, is the cadaver of a black African female. Normally muscle tone would be indicative of age, however heavy putrefaction forces us to hazard a guess at between five and eight years old. Radiographic and bone examination will be able to determine the age more accurately.

'The head is intact, with no fractures present. Both eyes have been removed, the lids cut away, leaving evidence of long and penetrating wounds. The instrument used may well have been sharp, but extensive post-mortem damage by insects has enlarged the lesions. Mason, hand me a few of those vials there.'

The detective does not budge.

'Harry?'

Harry snaps out of his contemplation, slides over to the cabinet the doctor is indicating and hands him the containers requested. With forceps the doctor plucks some of the larger dead maggots out of the wounds at the eyes and neck.

'These should also help us establish the approximate time of death, or at least clarify when the body was dumped.'

There is an audible sound of gas escaping as Wilkes probes the head further to examine the mouth.

'On examination of the oral cavity, no damage is present to the teeth and surrounding tissues, except for the tongue which has been severed. No foreign matter is evident. It is not possible to distinguish any bruising on the neck because of the advanced state of decomposition and discolouration, but a deep incision – let's see – cut from the left ear to the right ear, has punctured the trachea, oesophagus and all major veins and arteries. Again, post-mortem damage by animal life has obscured the exact nature of the wound.

'Moving onto the thorax, a large penetrative wound just below the ribcage on the left-hand side is an entry point to the chest cavity . . . Isaac, bring some light closer. I need to see better.'

Wilkes bends down close to the body and, with a scalpel, prises the wound open further. More putrid gas escapes.

'Christ!' Wilkes shrinks back, coughing.

Isaac manoeuvres some additional light towards the doctor's head, so it shines directly onto the wound.

'Yes, the heart's definitely been removed, but nothing else. The other organs have hardly suffered damage from contact with a foreign instrument. Not much blood left in the cavity either. Whoever did this is an expert.'

Harry's stomach hitches again. Hornets seem to be buzzing around in his head and black dots blur his vision.

'Sorry,' gasps Harry, before hurtling from the room.

He bursts through the swing doors, accidentally tearing off the top two buttons of his shirt in his desperate attempt to breathe more easily. He opens his eyes to find two students gawking at him, then barges into the nearest toilet and stumbles over to a basin in search of cool water. He makes fists of his trembling hands in an effort to control their shaking, before going over to the door and collapsing against it to prevent anyone entering and seeing him in this state.

*

An hour later Harry is still sitting outside the examination room, on a wooden bench in the stark corridor, when Wilkes finally bursts out through the black double doors. His clinical gown and rubber gloves are gone, but Harry immediately detects the odour of death still clinging to him. A batch of forms is tucked underneath one arm.

'Now *that* you don't see every day,' the surgeon says, coming to a halt in front of Harry. 'You feeling all right?'

'It must've been something I ate,' lies Harry.

'Stupid thing to do – eating before attending an autopsy.'

'I felt obliged to be here,' answers Harry, defensively.

'Right,' says Wilkes, 'let's go talk in my office.'

Entering the examiner's office, Harry sees a sturdy oak desk holding a computer and heaps of neatly piled files; the large bookcase behind it, lined with specialist texts, displays a single photo of the doctor himself, looking every bit the golfing playboy.

'Harry, you're one of the few cops that still does come to attend autopsies. I don't mind that – it shows you're committed – but you seem to be treating this one different, and I want to know why.'

'I'm not treating it different.'

'Cut the crap. You normally can't stop asking me questions, man. Hell, you know how that's irritated me in the past. Today you just stood there goggling, like some rubberneck at an accident. So what's the matter?'

'I'm just really tired, that's all.'

'We all get *gatvol* sometimes.'

'So what have you got for me, doctor?'

'The body is badly decomposed, as you well know, so things were a lot more difficult to distinguish. I discovered linear abrasions, lacerations and rope burns around the deceased's ankles and arms, meaning the victim was tied up real tight, which may also explain why there aren't any defensive wounds. Pushing the legs together, the pattern of discolouration suggests the feet were tied together and then £the deceased was strung up by them. Must be how they bled the victim, because inside there isn't a drop of blood left worth mentioning.

'The stomach was filled with a lot of unfamiliar matter, although her intestines didn't contain any partly digested food, suggesting she might've been starved until just shortly before she was killed. I'll have tests done on the later contents of the stomach as soon as possible, but in this case I suspect we may need a horticulturist and a geologist.'

Harry shakes a cigarette loose from his packet, then holds it up.

'May I?'

'Not normally, but on this occasion, yes.'

'I didn't quite catch that. A geologist and a horticulturist?'

'I'll tell you now, what's in her stomach isn't stuff that she would have normally eaten.'

'How long will all this take?'

'I can't say,' says Wilkes. 'I also can't tell for sure if the victim suffered any form of sexual penetration, even though it's highly unlikely.'

'Why do you say that?' asks Harry.

'The younger and purer she is, the more potent her body parts are considered, or so I've heard from my colleagues.' The doctor shifts uncomfortably in his chair. 'Small consolation to the victim, though. This kind of stuff makes me want to take early retirement – leave the country. Maybe I'll move to Florida. The golfing there is great.'

'Yeah, really?' Harry comments without interest.

'You yourself are British by origin, as I recall. Do you ever think of going back there?'

'I might still have some of the accent, but I've never felt like returning. This country's been good to me, you know, my wife and daughter and all.'

'But how many cops have got killed in the line of duty since the free elections? I read a statistic somewhere that you people suffer more problems than soldiers returning from Vietnam.'

'As I said, I like it here.'

Wilkes laughs. 'Yeah, the place has its moments.'

'When you said it would take an expert to do all that to the victim, what did you mean? What or who are we looking for here?'

The examiner's expression clouds. 'The damage to the arm itself is crude, the hand was hacked off roughly with a long instrument like a butcher's knife. The wound to the abdomen is curious, though. That incision was most likely done with the same instrument used on the throat, eyes and tongue. The person who did that clearly knows a lot about the human body; the cuts were all very precise, single strokes. Normally, you'd have someone constantly correcting the position of the blade, thus leaving traces of ancillary cuts. I'd say it was either a surgeon or someone else who has had a great deal of experience. Maybe a witch doctor who specializes in this kind of thing? Possibly, but I don't know. Like you said, the total damage suggests classic muti work, so I doubt we have an old-fashioned ripper on our hands. My only surprise is that no further organs were taken. It's as if this victim was killed for some special purpose, and not just . . . harvested.'

'With the contrast between the crude removal of the arm and the more precise removal of the other organs, are you saying there might have been two different instruments used – or even two different people that did this?'

'No, I'm not, although those are possibilities. The difference in the types of wound could be simply explained by the relative difficulty of removing an arm. It's a fair struggle to cut through bone when compared to the soft tissue of the neck.' Wilkes looks at his watch. 'I've got to run now. Are you taking the box with you?' Harry nods. 'Then just sign these for me.' The examiner slides over to Harry's side of the desk the release papers for custody of the girl's stomach, kidneys and liver. 'I've retained the necessary samples; your lab will want the rest.'

'Malcolm, I really appreciate you coming through for me like this. I know it involved quite an effort.'

Wilkes holds his hands up. 'No problem. One last thing though: I tried to check whether the victim was conscious when all this happened. Normally one can tell by burst capillaries in the eyes, caused by pressure when someone is screaming in intense pain. Since the eyes had been removed, I opened the larynx. Harry, – ' and here the doctor turns a sickly colour – 'she ruptured her vocal cords with screaming. It was all done to her before her death.'

It is the first time Harry has heard the doctor refer to a victim like a person. He nods, visibly shaken, and leaves to collect the child's organs.

Harry's arms feel numb as he carries the box outside to the parked Toyota pickup. As he sets it down on the tarmac to retrieve his keys, he stares down at the box lid, with its large printed biohazard sign. *Samples in transit*, it states, in large aggressive letters.

Hot rage suddenly wells up inside him. He smacks both fists into the hard steel canopy of the pickup. '*Fuck this!*' he yells, and kicks the rear bumper hard enough to rock the vehicle.

As the pain erupts in his foot, he snaps out of it. A handful of people stand watching him, shocked. He turns back to his truck, and leans against it. Finally he opens up the back and slides the box in gently. By the time he gets into the driver's seat, his hands are swelling up and bruising a dark purple. Driving away, he keeps thinking of what he would do to anyone who killed his own daughter.

22

Amy looks at herself in the mirror and adjusts the pink freshwater-pearl necklace. She has always liked the provocative satin dress she has put on specially for tonight. So does Harry, she suspects, from the way his eyes admire the way it flows over her legs and reveals her prominent collarbones. She runs her hands over her body, easing out small creases, amazed by how well she weathered the pregnancy.

He'll talk it through tonight, and then we'll make amends properly.

She felt such a fool after Harry left the house this morning, because he had been desperately trying to make it up with her – bringing her flowers, repeatedly telling her that he loves her, pleading silently with those genuine sad eyes of his – but all she herself had been able to think about was her own insecurities. After all, can she be sure he is trying to exclude her? Does he really not trust her? Is he about to slump back into the state he was in shortly after they got married? She is not at all sure if she is being too sensitive, but there is only one way to find out. If he really means that he is willing to talk, then she should try to be more supportive. The last thing she wants is for him to withdraw again, not after they have come this far.

Right now the champagne is cooling in the fridge, the food she ordered in is piping hot, their living area glimmers with candlelight, casting everything in rich mysterious shadows. Amy puts a Robert Palmer CD on as soon as she hears the garage door rattle open and Harry's car pulling in.

He sits inspecting his burning hands by the car's interior light. Ashamedly, he wonders how he is going to explain to his wife the broken skin and plum-coloured swellings. Any way he puts it, she is going to be alarmed. He gets out of the car and makes his way to the kitchen, already feeling uneasy about the promise he made her this morning. He wishes he could enjoy just one last cigarette – and maybe forget about the whole damn business.

In the living room, Amy lounges invitingly against the back of their green sofa. As he opens the door she laughs at Harry's astonished expression.

'And?' she asks, getting up.

Dumbstruck, he looks her over and asks, 'What happened here?'

Amy slides her arms around his waist. '*I'm* saying sorry, too.'

'What for?'

'I haven't been the most patient person in your life lately, have I?'

'You don't have to apologize for that,' says Harry quickly.

'Isn't he great for foreplay,' says Amy – meaning the music – and leans forward to kiss him. Harry pulls her closer and kisses her in return, relishing how the tension inside him seems to drain away in an instant. Suddenly this moment is all about her: her feel, her scent, just her *presence*. He has missed that so much.

When she draws away from him, grabbing both his hands, Harry barely manages not to wince with pain. 'You hungry, detective?'

'Who cares about food with a wife as gorgeous as you?' blurts Harry. 'But where's Jeanie?'

'She's with Mum,' answers Amy, 'so we've got the whole night to ourselves. Boy, I'm *starving*. I've had a really long day. And you?'

'It's been hectic, I can't deny, but I don't want to talk about it before dinner, if you don't mind.'

Amy narrows her eyes and she growls jokingly, 'All right, but I'll want to hear about it later. Promise?'

'Promise.'

As they sit down to eat, their conversation turns to Amy's working day. But suddenly she clasps her mouth with a horrified look. 'Jesus! What happened to your hands?'

Harry had forgotten about concealing them, and his heart sinks. 'I hurt them lifting a box into the back of a van this morning.'

'Let me see.' Amy gets up and switches on the main

light. The sudden flood of brightness dispels the moment's softness as Amy grabs one of his hands and examines it.

'I said, don't worry.' Harry laughs nervously. 'I'm not going to die.'

'What did you *do*? It looks more like someone dropped a steel safe on it.'

'I just got them jammed under a heavy load.'

'Does it hurt very badly?'

'It did.'

Amy cannot tell whether it is Harry's apprehensive expression or the severe nature of the wounds themselves, but suddenly she feels deeply suspicious. Later she will wonder whether it was her personal insecurities acting up again. 'Are you really telling me the truth, Harry?' she demands.

'Yes, why wouldn't I?'

'Did you hit someone?'

'No, I told you . . .' he falters. 'Why do you have to question absolutely *everything* I say these days?'

Hurt spreads like fire over her beautiful face. 'You know what, Harry, for*get* it.' Amy stabs the air between them with an index finger. 'I'm sick of you *lying* to me. I'm just sorry you can't bring yourself to trust me.' Tears well up and she bolts from the room.

Shamed, Harry follows her to the bedroom, but she slams the door in his face. 'Wait, Amanda . . . Amy, come on. Look, I'm sorry. We *can* talk. I know we *have* to talk.'

'*Fuck* talking! And fuck *you*!'

'How do you expect me to feel when I get home after a bad day only to face twenty questions? I don't come home to see a therapist – only to have some peace with my family. But every time I get home I feel like I'm defending my sanity. You knew what the deal was! You knew about that before you married me.'

Through the wooden door Harry can hear his wife crying. 'Things have changed, Harry. I . . . we have a child now. You can't expect me to look after both her *and* you.'

'See, there you go. I don't need looking after! There's nothing wrong with me – except my wife watches me like I'm a lunatic.'

'Stop it!' she cries.

'No! *You* stop it!'

'Jesus, when are you going to finish being so concerned with dead people and start living with the rest of us again?' The en-suite bathroom door slams shut. Harry is left staring at his feet.

With his back pressed against their bedroom door, Harry slowly slides down till he is sitting on the carpet. He picks at its thick pile, wondering what he should do next. When Amy does not emerge from the bathroom, he decides to go and clean up the living area. But looking over the ruins of their promising evening, the food and the burning candles, Harry is suddenly overwhelmed by despair.

He pours himself a bourbon up to the rim of the tumbler and flops down in front of the television, keeping its sound turned down.

He must have fallen asleep, because he is startled awake when something lands next to him on the sofa. It is a blanket and pillow. He turns around to see his wife leaning miserably against the wall. Her pretty dress is badly creased and her make-up is smeared.

'Harry,' she says quietly, 'I do trust you, but I'm warning you: I'll protect our daughter from anything harmful, even if it's you.' She begins sobbing loudly and

126

hugs herself for comfort. 'Christ, I know you too well. When will you realize you can't save the whole world?' Before he can manage a reply, she storms back into the bedroom, slamming the door behind her again.

Flinging herself onto the bed, Amy feels thankful that he has never hit her, has never been abusive. But in the years she has known him, she has witnessed how morbid he can be. Harry becomes a stranger to her in those moments when he withdraws, seemingly deaf and confused. He also appears capable of unpredictable behaviour.

That is what scares her the most.

23

In his hideout the boy sniffs and wipes his nose on his arm again. He badly needs a pee, his stomach has started rumbling and the afternoon air is getting colder. He does not need to peep outside to know the clouds are gathering into the tight darkness that comes before heavy rain. The air smells of it already, and the light filtering into his hideout is fading.

Harry has still not heard Rodge call out. This worries and scares him. Rodge is *always* loud when he comes crashing about looking for him. He wonders again who it was who passed nearby earlier.

The boy feels confused and small and not brave enough to be sitting here in a bush when it's getting cold and dark and rainy. The wood has suddenly become a threatening place and, though he does not know how long he has been waiting here, he knows it is more than long enough. If Rodge has not found him by now, he is never going to find him.

The boy is not enjoying this game any more. He felt

something tickling its way down his neck earlier, gave a yelp and smacked it. It squished under his fingers with a small crunching sound. Harry hopes it was not a spider. Rodge claims people have died from smacking spiders with their bare hands, because their poison can soak into your skin. The boy wipes his hand on his pants again, just to make sure he does not die.

Abruptly there is a long scream outside. It could be animal, maybe even human, but it suggests *pain*. Further silence follows.

'Roger?' he whimpers.

A car swishes by in the distance and even the birds have quit their songs.

The only way out to get home is the way he came in.

'Roger, where are you?' he moans.

He remembers their parents' constant warnings: stay together and keep away from those houses. Why, oh why, did he come this close to the Morwarghs?

He crawls forward, hoping to poke his head out far enough to check his surroundings. Sharp leaves scratch his face and twigs snag his clothes. As something drops off a leaf onto his nose he swallows a scream and wipes frantically at his face. Something else rustles the undergrowth nearby, followed by quick steps and the snap of a branch. He quickly reverses back into his hidey-hole.

Safely concealed again, he hears twigs snapping under the swishing of legs through the long grass. He looks up just in time to see the daylight blotted out completely.

That is when he screams. He scrambles further backwards into the darkness as something starts forcing its way inside. The boy starts sobbing loudly and kicks out defensively. Someone grabs his leg. 'Leave me alone!' he shrieks.

'Shshshsht, Harry. It's me.'

'Rodge?'

'Yeah, so shut up. I'm comin' in, so make some space. Something weird is going on out there.'

'What?'

'Fuck, I don't know!' says Rodge, and it is the first time Harry has heard him swear. The word hangs like a forbidden fruit in the air between them. He grabs at it.

'Fuck,' says Harry slowly. It describes perfectly what he feels.

'Did you hear it?' asks Rodge.

'What, the scream?'

'Yeah.'

'What was it?' Harry whispers. He cannot see Rodge's face, but he can sense he is scared, too.

'It was a girl or a woman, I think.'

'I thought it was you,' confesses Harry.

Rodge does not reply to that. The hideout is getting warmer from their combined body heat. The air is heavy, like a constricting blanket.

'So what do we do now?' asks Harry.

Again Rodge says nothing.

'Rodge, we need to get home. It's going to rain.'

'I know, I know, but I'm not going out there yet.'

'What did you see?'

'I didn't see nothing.' Roger pauses, then admits, 'I'm glad I found you.'

Harry feels a sudden burst of pride. 'Hey, it's a good place, isn't it?'

'Yeah, it's OK.' Rodge's dejected response is not what Harry was hoping for.

'At least we're safe here, right?'

'You're stupid,' Rodge hisses suddenly. 'You're so bloody stupid. You know we shouldn't have come this close to the houses.'

Harry feels shame brighten his cheeks. His parents will have a serious go at him over this.

'You're just scared of the Morwarghs,' he taunts.

'Just stop it, Harry! We're not playing any more.'

They fall silent again. Rain starts pattering on the leaves around them.

'I think it was definitely a girl,' whispers Rodge at last, as if talking to himself.

They are quiet for a few more minutes, both lost in thought, both thinking about the blonde girl they saw not so long ago getting slapped around viciously by a Morwargh in one of those backyards.

'We've to get out of here,' says Harry after a time. 'We can't just stay here, Rodge. I'm hungry and we're going to get wet.'

'Quit your whinging.'

'But Rodge—'

'Shu' up already. I say we wait here till my dad comes looking for us.'

Harry wonders how Rodge's father is supposed to find them here.

'Maybe I should go do some reconsorcering?'

Roger sniggers despite himself. 'You mean reconnaissance?'

'Yeah, that.'

'OK, OK. Jeez! I get the message.'

But Rodge himself shuffles around in the darkness, then crawls towards the opening. He begins to push through it, then stops again.

'What is it?' whispers Harry anxiously. He hears Roger mumble something inaudible. 'What is it?' he whispers louder.

'I can't,' whispers Roger, suddenly reversing his bum into Harry's face.

'I said I'd do it,' says Harry, suddenly annoyed.

130

'OK,' says Roger, 'but don't go straight home. Come and fetch me if everything's clear.'

Harry squeezes past him to reach the entrance. The water collecting on the leaves has begun to dribble down into their hollow. He pushes further into the open air and breathes in deeply.

'This really stinks,' he mutters.

24

Thursday is the day scheduled for Harry to appear in court as investigative officer in the case of the panga murder outside the *shabeen*. He will probably be tied up the whole day, overseeing any requests from the prosecution and giving evidence. After spending much of the morning updating Chief Molethe and the press about their progress, Jacob spends the rest of Thursday interviewing the herbalists and diviners on his list, but concentrating on those operating in the central Johannesburg area. Molethe has promised the pair of them more men and resources from Monday. By lunchtime, Jacob is not only frustrated by his lack of progress, but also angry. Only two traditional healers could answer his enquiries plainly and directly, although they had nothing significant to offer him. The others spoke of omens, embellished their answers with vague premonitions and regularly touted the services they could offer his investigation, at a price of course.

As the afternoon wears on, Jacob begins to question their own approach to this case. Surely people capable of slaughtering a young child would not be associating with highly visible registered healers who constantly lobby for the legitimacy of their profession? Climbing back into his car for the seventh time, Jacob is certain of one thing: he and Harry are going to need a lot more manpower to interview the sixty or so names on their list – a list which does not even include all the unregistered practitioners and muti dealers.

Having left his most intimate visit for last, Jacob now makes his way down a rough dirt road in Soweto, past comfortable houses built of bare brick with modest gardens, near Freedom Square. The townships – legacies of apartheid – have not disappeared in post-election South Africa; instead they have grown. Few people seemed willing to leave their communities, where they have family, friends, a history around them, in favour of white suburbia, and even fewer in truth could afford to do so. To Jacob it seems that the inner city is the only area where diverse racial groups are living next to each other in any *real* sense: the poor amongst the poor, and students side-by-side with them.

A group of children runs alongside the police vehicle, waving at Jacob and screaming with laughter. He pulls up before a small home whose exterior is freshly plastered and painted white with just a tinge of green. A chicken-wire fence surrounds its small yard, which is packed with tall sunflowers and maize, with green vegetables in neat rows, as well as flowers planted in old rubber tyres serving as containers.

Sitting together on a bench under the kitchen window is a line of women dressed in bright colours. They are chatting and smoking, drinking tea from tin cups. As they gossip loudly, two teenage girls are busy tending to the washing and another is gardening on her knees in the yard. The girls are *thwasas* – pupils of a traditional healer – and so are dressed distinctively in beads and wraps.

'*Sawubona.*' Jacob greets them at the rusty garden gate. The eldest, a grey-haired woman, jumps and screeches, 'Is that our child? Our Jacob?'

'Yes, Mama Poleng, it's me.'

The other women hoot out enthusiastic greetings.

'Well, come in. I'll call her right now.'

She rushes inside to announce Jacob's arrival. He can hear her belting out the news of his arrival in every room while looking for the frail *inyanga* Jacob has come to visit. Suddenly there is a wail of recognition from around one side of the house and Hettie Solilo comes waddling towards him as fast as her short plump legs will permit. Wrinkles have inscribed her skin with the passage of countless years.

'My child! My boy!' she calls out, as her dutiful *thwasas* drop obediently to their knees one by one the moment they see her. Hettie, however, omits all the formalities as she reaches Jacob, and she hugs him warmly. He towers over the diminutive herbalist and has to stoop to embrace her with the same joy.

'*Magogo*, it is good to see you again.' Jacob greets her as 'old mother' as much out of a feeling of kinship as out of respect for her wisdom and age. The diminutive family friend has watched over him like a son ever since he first moved to Soweto, shortly after his initiation into manhood.

Jacob is obliged to sit outside in the sun, drinking honeybush tea and chatting with the other women, before Hettie finally ushers him inside the house and into her private sitting room. There she seats him in one of the two armchairs, both of them draped in bright yellow sheets. Otherwise the room features a worn green carpet, a small television and a rectangular coffee table. Above the television hangs a smiling photograph of Nelson Mandela at his inauguration. Other photographs of family and friends are arranged on the shelves fixed along the walls, with mattresses and blankets piled up neatly in the space underneath them.

'You had a celebration this weekend?' Jacob nods at her supply of blankets, knowing how *sangomas* and *inyangas* from all over the huge city would travel to Hettie Solilo's home at weekends to celebrate the old traditions and commune with the ancestors together.

'Oh no . . . just a few friends that slept over.' Hettie comes to a rest in the other armchair with a loud, satisfied sigh. 'We've missed you dearly, Jacob,' she says.

'I'm very glad to visit you. What a wonderful welcome I always get.'

'You don't come to see us enough, boy. But now you can talk, because I sense you have not come here for a friendly visit. Your mind is elsewhere.'

Setting his cup down on the coffee table, Jacob nods gravely.

'*Magogo*, I need to ask you about an unfortunate incident that has occurred not far from here.'

She nods, holding up a hand before Jacob can continue, then calls to summon one of her *thwasas* from outside. The girl approaches the sitting-room door on her knees, with her head bowed, as tradition demands.

'Landi, close the door now, please.'

After the door is shut, Hettie rises up and walks over to the small altar to the ancestors, positioned in a corner of the room. With a hasty prayer she lights some incense.

'Yes, child, speak. Is it about that girl found there by the mine heaps?'

'Yes.' Jacob nods.

Hettie sighs deeply, shaking her tired old head as she limps back to her armchair.

'My son, this is an evil thing. My heart bleeds for that child. I am so sorry. Creation never meant for us to hurt each other like that.'

'Do you know anything about it?'

'There is nothing I can tell you about that girl, except what Anna has read me from the newspapers and, of course, the signs we have all witnessed.'

'What signs do you mean?'

'Three stillborn children – occurring just here.' With her hand she widely indicates the immediate neighbourhood. 'During the last month a small dark figure has been seen out at night, trying to open house doors, but so far he's been scared off. People claim they still hear him screaming at night-time. Doepie, who works at the Spar shop, he says he saw hyena tracks out in the veld last week.'

Jacob sits back in his chair and runs his hands over his face. 'I know about all those sorts of omens, but I need something more concrete. Can you tell me something I can *use*.'

'You think such omens are not important? Don't be a fool, boy. I'm telling you the story the way I know it. You must not be impatient. You must see it as a whole.'

'When did all this start?'

'Oh, these things are so difficult to tell, and I'm just an old woman who understands my plants. I really wouldn't be able to say *exactly* when these things began to show. But, yes . . . maybe it was around the time those graves were found desecrated.'

'The graves?'

Hettie sinks deeper into her chair, curling bony fingers around each armrest.

'It was reported to the police at the time, but no one's been caught yet. It started, I think, when a young girl committed suicide a few months ago. She hanged herself from a tree after she was raped. The father found her and they took her down, but they either forgot, or didn't have the money, to purify and protect her body before she was buried. That same night people came and dug her up. They cut off her head and took her heart, her hands. You know how potent the evil ones consider a suicide's body to be.'

'This is not the only time this has happened?'

'No, five other graves have been desecrated since. And, thinking now of your child, so many other children have gone missing over the years. But I cannot tell what is just rumour and what really happened, or why all these children go missing. Some of them just run away from their terrible homes to go live on the city streets, thinking that will be better for them.'

'How many children do you reckon?'

'I don't know. I myself maybe know of eight children by name. But people continually bring me news from many other parts, so I don't always know if they are talking about the same child.'

Jacob presses her for further details about the grave robberies, then the names of the children she mentioned, making a rapid record in his notebook.

'Have any of them ever come home again, do you know?'

'Yes, some, but not nearly as many as have disappeared.'

Jacob leans forward, rubbing his hands anxiously.

'*Magogo*, do you know of anyone who may be dealing with a *baloyi* in Soweto?'

The old lady begins to pick at a loose thread on the armrest. 'You can never be sure of that.'

'Is there anyone that might be buying or providing human muti?'

She flattens the thread by spreading her hand over it. 'No,' she says, eyes concentrating on the armrest.

Her sudden abstraction makes Jacob suspicious. 'I don't think this will be the last time this happens to an innocent child.'

She takes a while before answering. 'No, I don't think so either.'

'Oh, please tell me *something* I can use.' Jacob's voice rises with frustration. 'I have spent the entire day talking to so many people, but it's like . . . it's like people don't care about this evil hovering around them. Everyone seems so obsessed with their own concerns. Why is everyone so unresponsive?'

'How is your father, Jacob?' Hettie changes the subject abruptly.

Surprised by her question, Jacob stammers, 'I . . . I still haven't spoken to him.'

'You promised me last time to contact your family soon.'

'*Magogo*, I don't see how that has anything to do with my visit here today.'

'It has *everything* to do with this visit. If you were on better terms with your father, if you hadn't decided to abandon him, like so many young people do nowadays, you wouldn't need to ask *me* all these questions.'

Wondering why she has suddenly become so angry with him, Jacob says placatingly, 'I speak to Mama now and again – I hear from Landi, too. But my father . . . I'm sorry, I've just been very busy.'

Hettie Solilo snorts sarcastically and Jacob can see her frail arm trembling on the armrest. 'You've been *busy*? What does that mean? We are *all* always busy. But what's more important than your family? No, you all go to the big city, find work, find money, and forget who raised you.'

Jacob bows his head, staring at the floor in silence. Then he gets up to leave.

'Where are you going?'

'I don't know why you are saying these things to me,' says Jacob softly. 'You know very well that is not how things were with me.'

Hettie's gaze softens, but her voice is still firm. 'I want you to contact your father.'

'Yes, *magogo*, I will. Now I must leave. Thank you for your time,' he says with deliberate formality.

'These days there are many prepared to have dealings with the people you are looking for,' says Hettie suddenly, causing Jacob to stop dead in his tracks. 'There are many, too, who will offer such services. Times are tough, and our new government is not doing as much to help us as they promised. People are very scared about the future; they want something firm, something *powerful*, to believe in. They seek someone who can manufacture good fortune for them – luck *and* prosperity.' Mama Hettie rouses a shaking hand to her face, suddenly overcome by emotion.

Jacob goes over quickly and kneels beside her. 'What's wrong? What's happened?'

'Oh, Jacob! I've wanted to contact you, but . . . but I've been so scared. This old woman here and her friends,

we talk a lot, and it seems we've made someone very
angry. It's someone very powerful.'

'Yes?'

Hettie inhales deeply, shakes her head, and suddenly
Jacob knows she is about to change the subject again. 'I'm
just a silly old woman, scared of her own shadow.'

'*Magogo*, you had better tell me what's going on. I'm
sure I can help somehow.'

Hettie stares at him for a while. Then she gets up and
shuffles over to her little altar, where she begins toying
with the ornaments. 'Yes,' she sighs, 'maybe you can. I
don't know much except that people started hanging
around my house, snooping around outside at night. I have
some men now, good men, who help me, and they sleep
here in my sitting room, guarding me. Can you believe it –
needing people to guard me? The snooping has now
stopped, but I know I'm still being watched. Yet I don't
know who it is, or why.'

'There must be something you *know*? Something that
set them off?' says Jacob.

'I don't know, Jacob. My greatest mistake is perhaps
to be seen just sitting here enjoying gossiping with other
people from all over the place. Sure, I learn things about
this community, but people change the stories I tell myself
and pass them on as gossip. This watching – it could be
due to anything or anyone, because of people I don't even
know. Perhaps you are looking in the wrong place, Jacob.
Maybe you should speak to someone in Newtown. Speak
to a man called Hlopheka Sepang, near the taxi rank.'

'Newtown? In Johannesburg?'

'Yes, my boy.' Hettie shuffles back towards Jacob and
pats his shoulder.

'But why him?'

'He has hinted to me that someone very foul is ruining the traditional businesses down there, someone who makes use of the *evil* ways.' She grasps Jacob's fingers in her tiny palm.

'Thank you very much for that, *magogo*.'

She smiles somewhat shyly, then gives him a warning glance. 'But before I see you the next time, you will have spoken with your father, you hear me? I know he misses you.'

The door suddenly bursts open, startling both of them. Mama Poleng rushes in, her eyes wide with alarm.

'What's wrong?' asks Jacob, bracing himself.

Poleng barely notices him. 'Hettie, it's them. I'm sure it's them.'

'Jacob, go now, please,' says Hettie.

'Who is it?' insists Jacob.

'Jacob, you are alone here! You cannot deal with this by yourself. Go! Just act like you don't know anything, please.'

Jacob slips the net curtain aside and peers out. A sporty red BMW is parked two houses down and in it he spots a young man of about twenty, wearing a black skullcap, apparently observing Hettie's house before turning to his companion to strike up a conversation.

'*Magogo*, you're not making any sense.' Jacob pulls his phone out of his pocket, ready to call for back-up. 'If these people are harassing you, something has to be done about it.'

'No, please, leave them be. If you can't deal with it yourself now, just leave it. They will be back outside either here or someone else's house. They know who we are. So if you cannot arrest them immediately, don't antagonize them.'

'I can't arrest them for just sitting in their car,' Jacob is forced to agree, wondering what he can do. He looks out again and notices the vehicle is missing its registration plate. Deciding to act, he is out the door and at the gate, the two women remonstrating loudly behind him, before the skullcapped man notices him.

Jacob reaches his right hand round to the holster tucked in the small of his back and unclips his service pistol. As he draws near to the car, he notices a third man in the back seat, who is scrabbling for something in the footwell while the driver starts the engine. Jacob is suddenly aware of blood pounding in his ears as he moves right up to the front passenger's window.

'Police,' he says. 'Can I help you?'

The skullcapped twenty-something leans through the window, measuring Jacob up. 'No, man, we're cool.' His muscular chest is the size of a bank safe, with arms like sledgehammers. Jacob stoops to peer in at the man sitting on the back seat. He is a big character, too, but considerably older, with a thick curling beard and large Ray-Bans perched on his nose. The driver himself is a thin, nervous type, breathing audibly through his wide-open mouth. From his neck hangs a beaded pouch on a leather string, clearly some sort of charm. All three of them stare at Jacob with obvious aggression, but it is the character in the back seat, now stooping forward as if to hide something below eye level, who makes Jacob most nervous.

Jacob nods towards him. 'What you got down there?'

The guy smiles like a shark, flashing two gold teeth, and shrugs.

Jacob turns to the driver. 'Your plates are missing.'

'I know. They fell off. You know what these roads are like.' He titters nervously.

'What's your registration?'

'We forget,' says the youth, who looks like he was born in a boxing ring.

'You men scaring the ladies over there?' asks Jacob, nodding over his shoulder. Behind him all the women have congregated at Hettie's fence and are staring at the scene apprehensively.

'No, we're just lost,' answers the boxer type.

'Where you going?'

'We forget.'

The driver is tapping the gear shift nervously, ready to make a quick getaway. Jacob's hand twitches on his pistol. If the guy in the back seat is holding a gun, he will be dead before . . . well, before he does anything other than retreat.

'You better think of where you're going then, and do it fast,' says Jacob.

When the skullcapped man replies, 'We might just be going to your funeral, pig,' the man in the back breaks out in an ugly grin.

The driver laughs nervously and puts the car in gear. He then takes off at a slow leisurely pace. Once they vanish around a corner, Jacob gulps for air like a stranded fish and rubs at his face with shaky hands. No rear registration, either.

Hettie comes racing out through her garden gate, wagging a finger at him furiously, but Jacob jogs over to his own car and radios through.

'Jacob Tshabalala! I've *never* seen a man do anything as stupid as that.' She stands and scolds him from the middle of the road.

'Wait a minute, *magogo*, I need to find out who they are.'

'Don't you ever listen to a word I say?' Her lecture goes on for another four minutes, while he tries to convey the remembered details to the few patrolling officers surviving in this township.

Driving back to the station, Jacob tries to contact his partner, but finds that Harry's mobile is switched off once again.

25

Nina is staring at herself in the mirror when she dimly realizes the bedside phone is ringing. She has been wondering whether she is at all properly prepared to go as far as she has planned. She studies her Toni & Guy haircut, fixed especially for this trip, and broods on how inexperienced she still feels. Is she just being irresponsible, selfish? Or is she seizing the initiative as a good journalist should?

When she finally answers the phone, her mother's voice catches her completely by surprise. Soon Nina finds herself again defending her presence here in South Africa, although her mother does not even know the full reason she is there.

Nina's eye is caught by the snapshots she has stuck to part of the mirror, pictures of different women of her own age, which she has taken over the last week in the streets of downtown Johannesburg while getting a feel for the city and its diverse cultures. Besides that, she has been raiding the public and university libraries to find information on the subjects of ritual murder and trafficking in human beings.

'I want you to come home. I don't want you staying there any longer,' wails her mother. 'I watch the news. It's not safe there. Things have gone from bad to worse ever since I left.'

'Mother, let me do my job. I *wanted* to come here.'

'Baby, I know you're an adult now, but look at all the murders, look at the horrible rapes committed there. You must find people there treat you badly for being a coloured? Why not just come home, my dear?'

'Mother, don't get things out of proportion. Don't make it sound like I still have to use a segregated restroom – that was all back in *your* time. Besides, it's not safe anywhere in the world these days. I'm a journalist and—'

'Why couldn't you just find a nice safe TV show to work for over here in London?'

'Mother, it's not that easy. Besides *investigative* journalism is what I always wanted to do, remember?'

Unconsciously, Nina has struck a defiant pose, jutting out her hip and resting her free hand on it. When her mother finally finishes, Nina replies, as calmly as she can manage, 'I appreciate all you're saying, but I *chose* this as my profession. I'm *happy* with what I do, so surely you can respect that?'

The phone line goes so silent Nina wonders whether she has lost the connection. Then she hears a small sob, like a mouse's squeak.

'Don't you *dare* do that to me. Don't you dare start crying! I've worked fucking hard to get where I am now. This is my chance to do something useful and you're not going to rob me of it!'

As the sobs grow louder, Nina reacts in frustration. She grabs the useless Zulu phrasebook she brought with her and hurls it across the room.

Why does it always have to end this way?

'Oh, Nina, my dear, can't a mother be worried? Your uncle writes regularly and tells me what it's like over there.'

'Mother, you *know* I would never do anything rash or irresponsible.'

There is an abrupt silence from the other side, and the sobs miraculously cease. 'Nina,' her mother continues sternly, 'that's *exactly* what I'm afraid of.' She sighs. 'But I suppose there's not much I can do. But, *please*, if anything goes wrong, just phone your uncle. But don't try driving to Alexandra by yourself. Just phone him – promise me that.'

'I promise,' answers Nina, her fingers crossed. 'Mother, I have to go now. The call's getting too expensive for you.'

'I love you, and your father loves you, too.'

'Bye, Mother.'

As the line goes dead, Nina breathes a sigh of relief.

Back at the mirror, weighing the newly purchased hair clipper in her hand, Nina finds herself experiencing renewed doubt. This is her first major story, so she does not want to screw it up. She glances at the Zulu phrasebook lying abandoned on the floor, then at the second-hand clothing laid out ready on the bed, still pondering whether she is truly competent enough, or *confident* enough, to pull this thing off. Before her concerns can grow any worse, she heads into the bathroom.

Seconds later the whine of the little electrical clipper mingles with the sound of running water. Half an hour later Nina stands in front of the full-length mirror in the main room again, gazing intently at her self-wrought transformation.

26

'Tell me what to do,' slurs Ngubane, his breath heavily tainted with rum, while he spins the 9 mm Beretta around one index finger.

Although the diviner is about the same age – in his early fifties – he has clearly weathered more of life's hardships than Ngubane. His tired, drooping eyes are set in a gaunt face spotted with patches of white beard. A busby made from water-buffalo hide covers his head, which would make him look rather ridiculous were it not for the pervasive atmosphere of his muti shop. From an old paint can standing next to him is wafting sweet perfumed smoke that irritates Ngubane's nose.

'Tell me,' his visitor repeats quietly.

The tin roof above them cracks and pops occasionally in the day's heat. The gloom within the shack is in stark contrast to the searing midday sunlight in the street outside. Entire baboon skeletons hang from nails on the walls, while crocodile skins dangle from wires strung beneath the roof. Behind the *sangoma*, rows of powders and potions stored in recycled tot bottles line the rear wall of the establishment.

'What's the matter? Will you tell me what I must do, or am I going to have to shoot you?' Ngubane growls, as he raises more rum to his lips. His pistol is now pointed threateningly at the *sangoma*.

With shaking hands the diviner opens up a pouch lying between his knees and pulls out a small collection of bones, cowrie shells and polished gemstones. Still holding Ngubane's angry eyes, he spits into his cupped palms and gives the bones a vigorous shake. He throws them onto the mat lying between them.

Ngubane closes his eyes. 'Read me what it says.'

'You have lost respect.'

'Ha! What else?'

'You want it back. You feel you have been betrayed.'

Ngubane bursts into wild laughter. '*Eiee*, tell me what it says there that it doesn't already say in the newspapers.'

The *sangoma* glares at him. 'You came to me because you have been betrayed by *him*.'

Ngubane makes himself more comfortable by resting on one elbow and stretching out his legs. He takes another leisurely swig from his bottle. 'That's better. What else?'

The *sangoma* shifts position. 'You want to know how to recover the respect you've lost. Also your money and your power.'

An exaggerated grin spreads over Ngubane's face, and he nods vigorously. 'Oh, you are so right. But tell me, are you just a smart operator or do the spirits really speak to you?'

'They speak to me when I pray to them, or when they have something to say.'

Ngubane sits up, raising the gun to his own head. 'How do they speak to you? In here?' He pats his temple with the barrel. 'Or here?' He rams the tip of it into his chest. 'Or in the air around you?' Ngubane brandishes the gun at the empty space above him. 'Where are they, these spirits?'

'Mr Maduna, I don't want any trouble.' The elder's hands are now shaking uncontrollably in his lap.

'There's no trouble here. Why do you think there's trouble? I've come to you because I need to hear what the ancestors have to say – to get some clear advice on what I must do. Now – ' he cocks the hammer of the Beretta – '*how* do they communicate with you?'

'Here.' The *sangoma* points. 'They speak to me in my head because they are with me. They are a part of us, part of everything.'

'Can *I* hear them?'

'Yes, if they want to speak to you.'

'I hear them.'

A short silence passes before the *sangoma* replies. 'Then you must know what they say, what they want you to do. What do you need me for?'

'Because I want *you* to explain to me what to do. The voices – ' Ngubane shakes his head bitterly – 'they . . . they're confusing.' He drops his gaze to the gun. 'I don't know what to do any more. For so long I felt so strong, I knew what was needed from me. I had guidance, I had purpose – I was doing their bidding through him. Now I don't know any more.'

'You know he is looking for you? He has put out word.'

'Yes, I know, but he can wait. *He* can wait for once, damn it!'

The diviner exhales heavily, then adjusts his buffalo-hide hat. 'You need to confront him yourself.'

'Is there nothing you can do for me? Can't you put a curse on him?'

The other man looks shocked. 'No, I cannot do that.'

'Why not?' Ngubane leans forward.

'He is too strong for me.'

'He's a bastard foreigner.'

'That doesn't matter.'

'He is not what he claims he is.'

'He is very, very dangerous,' argues the *sangoma*.

'I am strong, too!' shouts Ngubane, thumping his chest with the rum bottle. He struggles to his feet, the flailing pistol making the other man wince. 'I have worked so *hard* to achieve what I've become. *I* made the money. *I* directed all the people he recruited. Now I'm *nothing* to him – why? Just because I made one single mistake, he now wants to kill me?' Ngubane stumbles slightly, peering around the gloom of the muti shop.

'I don't believe he wants to kill you,' mumbles the *sangoma*.

'Let me tell you something.' Ngubane belches loudly. 'For a time together we became invincible, except now I'm invincible no more. That must mean he is weakening too, or else he's after me. So, I'm asking you . . . *do* something about him.'

The *sangoma* shakes his head as he watches Ngubane tottering around his shop. A few customers had come in earlier, but hurried away discreetly when they saw the drunk man with a gun.

'You know, I paid a lot for where I am,' Ngubane stops to take another swig from his bottle. He suddenly begins to sob as he wipes his mouth. 'I paid for it in blood, so not even *he* is going to take it all away from me. You know why? I made a pact with the ancestors. *They* listen to me! *They* speak to me! Even he can't interfere with that, can he?'

'Why are you so afraid?' asks the *sangoma*, keeping a watchful eye on the drunk as he circles closer.

'Shut up, you!' cries Ngubane, his flabby face suddenly bulging with rage. He shoves his gun hard up against the back of the *sangoma*'s head. 'Who said I'm *afraid*?'

'If you really have the ancestors on your side, you

should be able to confront him,' protests the *sangoma* quickly.

'I can't do that. Just do something!' wails Ngubane, collapsing on the mat.

'I can't help you. You and him, with your men and, your guns and drugs, you have invaded our lives here and run everything to suit yourselves. So why do you now come to me and ask me for help? I can't do anything against him. He will have me killed. He will have my family killed. This is *your* problem to deal with.'

'Don't talk like that,' snarls the drunk.

'I will talk to you any way I wish.' The *sangoma*'s eyes suddenly glow with hate-fuelled anger. 'If he's going to kill you, then let him do it. Right now you don't look like you could defend yourself against even a child. It is clear you are a coward and a man who is easily led.'

Stunned by such sudden venomous honesty, Ngubane raises his Beretta, then begins to chuckle. 'Did *they* tell you to say that? I did all of it for him, you know, but now he barely acknowledges my existence and everyone laughs at me.'

A car comes to a stop outside the muti shop. Ngubane scrambles to his feet and runs over to peer through a slit in the tin wall. The *sangoma* stays calmly on the mat. Ngubane spots a police van outside, its driver and another officer talking to each other inside.

'What is this now? Cops? Fucking *cops*?' Ngubane feels a sobering rush of adrenalin surge through him.

The *sangoma* looks up and also makes a decision. If there is one chance for the community, one person who might destroy the albino, it is this unstable man.

'Hide over there, quick!' The diviner points to a corner where a great heap of mats is stacked halfway to the ceiling. 'Hide!' he repeats when they hear the car doors open. Still Ngubane hesitates.

Finally, Ngubane Maduna's survival instincts kick in. He shoves his rum bottle at the *sangoma* and scurries over to the corner, where he buries himself flat between the pile of mats and the wall.

27

'So this contact of yours said we should go interview this guy?' says Harry, slamming the car door shut behind him and clipping the holstered gun onto his belt.

'Yes, but it doesn't mean he's in any way involved. He might have some information for us, though.' Jacob stretches his lower back as he climbs out. He looks over at the heavy traffic booming along the Selby overpass some distance away.

Harry nods towards it. 'I couldn't handle that noise all day.'

'Some people don't have a choice,' mutters Jacob. 'Are you coming?'

Harry looks over at the hubcap dealer next door. The man is eyeing them suspiciously.

'What else did she tell you?'

'Nothing much.'

'She know anything about the little girl?'

'No, only vague rumours about missing children and grave robberies.'

'Missing children? Did she give you any names?'

'Yes, I wrote them down. We can check out all of them, although she says some of them might have returned home by now.'

'She just tells you these things out of the blue?' asks Harry.

'Yes.' Jacob wonders what Harry is on about. 'Why do you ask that?'

'I don't know,' says Harry, eyeing a group of children at play further down the street. Their game seems to consist of chasing a tyre downhill, accelerating it with a stick to see how fast they can make it go. For Harry, like most white officers, it's difficult to even get to meet with *sangomas* or *inyangas*, let alone have intimate conversations with them. Yet Jacob somehow commands enough respect to encourage even the most reticent black man to offer him information. 'How do you do it, anyway? If you're a cop in these parts, people don't just invite you in for milk and cookies, then jabber on about all the crimes occurring in the neighbourhood.'

Jacob laughs. 'I smile a lot more than you do, that's my secret; I smile more than all of you white boys. That's why they invite me in for tea – and also because I don't like cookies.'

The two men approach the shaded entrance to the *sangoma*'s stall and Harry raps his knuckles loudly against its tin-sheeting wall. There's no immediate answer.

'What's his name, anyway?'

'Hlopheka Sepang.'

Suddenly someone calls out from inside, '*Ee!*'

Jacob and Harry enter. In the gloom their eyes need a few moments to adjust, although the structure barely offers any protection from the sun's heat pounding down on its metal walls. There is a dusty smell, the musk of different animals mixing with the scents of aromatic plants. They eventually discern the diviner himself sitting on his red mat in the middle of the room with smoke slowly trailing upwards next to him.

'*Tokhosa*,' cries Jacob, clapping his hands in the traditional greeting reserved for healers.

Harry's first impression is that the man looks anxious. When the *sangoma* nods in reply, Jacob approaches and bends over to speak to the man in Sotho. Harry meanwhile turns his gaze to examine the bizarre items on display in this muti shop.

Jars containing what looks like sand, a wide variety of rocks stacked here and there, ground powders in old ice-cream containers and unidentifiable fatty objects rolled up in newspaper – Harry becomes utterly engrossed with this paraphernalia, never before having had the chance to pry so closely into one of these places. As the discussion behind him is being conducted in a native language, he is not able to contribute anyway.

Jacob takes his shoes off and sits down facing the diviner on his mat. He glances at the sheepskin unfolded before him, at the *sangoma*'s hands still clutching his sacred bones.

'Were you busy with a customer when we arrived?' asks Jacob.

'Mhm?' grunts the man, peering reflexively over Jacob's shoulder. 'No.'

Jacob eyes the bottle of rum standing next to the makeshift brazier. He barely manages to suppress a frown. 'We were hoping you could spare us some of your time, wise one.'

The man's eyes finally meet Jacob's and, with sudden animation, he says 'OK, speak.'

'A muti killing has recently been reported,' says Jacob.

'Yes, I heard.' The *sangoma* is busily packing the bones away in their leather pouch.

'Have you had any customers ever coming in here asking for human muti?'

'I have not.'

'Have you ever had anyone offering you human muti?'

'No, never.' Just then Harry sniffs at an open bottle and coughs in disgust. The *sangoma* looks up sharply. 'Leave that alone, please.'

'Excuse me?' challenges Harry.

The diviner turns to Jacob and says in Sotho, 'Tell him to keep away from my stuff. If he cannot show respect, he must wait outside.'

'Harry, take it easy,' says Jacob.

'Will you look at that thing?' Harry points to the corpse of a small animal. 'Isn't that a vervet monkey? That thing can't have been cured properly.'

'Harry, leave us to talk, please.'

'Sure.' Harry shrugs.

The *sangoma*'s eyes again flick involuntarily over Jacob's shoulder, which causes the black detective to glance behind him this time. All he can see is a table covered with dried tubers and a pile of mats stacked messily in a corner. Jacob turns back to the diviner.

'Do you know of any traders specializing in such items or diviners who might be performing rituals requiring human body parts?'

'I told you, I will have nothing to do with such people. I run a respectable business. Even if I did practise such abominations, does it look like I could afford to acquire human muti? I am situated way out here not because I am a criminal, but because rent is too high elsewhere. I have nothing at all to hide from you.'

There is a loud crash from where Harry is now standing and the diviner turns on him, furious. '*Wena!* Leave my things alone, man. You can't come in here and treat my shop like this!'

'Sorry,' grunts Harry, bending down to retrieve the item he has knocked from its place on a deep shelf. 'I just wanted to see . . .' His face disappears into the murk of the shelf as he reaches for something tucked behind several other objects. 'Ah, now, what's this? This looks like a cheetah's pelt. It's an endangered species, Mr Sepang. Have you got papers to show you acquired it legitimately?'

Sepang jumps up. 'That's not a cheetah. Put it back!'

'Look, I don't hunt myself, but I do watch a lot of television.' Harry's casual tone suggests he is deliberately implying that the *sangoma*'s anger runs off him like rainwater. 'It looks to me like this definitely comes from a cheetah.'

The *sangoma* balls his fists in silent anger.

'Mr Sepang – ' Harry advances, holding out the pelt for Jacob to inspect – 'if you're prepared to sell the skins of endangered animals, would you not be willing to traffic in human parts, too?'

'I told you, I never deal with things like that.'

His expression now steely cold, Harry leans closer to the *sangoma*, in the process stepping onto the man's holy mat. 'I have reason to believe you have information for us on the murder of a child for the sale of her body parts. If there already is one highly illegal item here, then there might be others equally incriminating. So if you don't want me tearing the whole place apart, I suggest you'd better start talking.'

'That pelt was given to me in reward for a service I once rendered to a tribal leader. He made a gift of a fur

155

that had been in his family for generations. Now take your shoes off this mat. It is an insult to tread on it.'

Harry looks down at his feet, then at Jacob, who nods. Harry steps off it. 'OK, there, see, I can be reasonable.'

Suddenly there is a commotion from a corner of the shack. The three men look round to see Ngubane emerging from his hideout. The man's pistol is raised.

'Down!' yells Harry, already drawing his service pistol. The *sangoma* falls backwards, knocking over his incense burner, while Jacob throws himself to one side.

But Harry has not drawn fast enough this time. With a series of ear-splitting cracks, cordite blossoms from Ngubane's Beretta. The rum bottle sitting on the floor explodes. As a round whizzes past his head, Harry back-pedals desperately to duck for cover. He returns fire, but misses, as the gunman is already on the move, heading sideways along the wall. Ngubane sprays another burst of bullets into the close confines of the tin shack.

Jacob's frantic roll sideways has brought him close to the panicking shooter, who kicks him viciously in the face. The detective crumples over against a table.

As Harry raises his head to shove his gun over the surface of another table, the first thing he sees is the gunman disappearing through the doorway. The second thing he sees is his partner collapsed with blood running from his nose. The *sangoma* lies dead on his sacred mat, a deeper red stain spreading from underneath his left collar-bone. The smells of rum and gunpowder mingle in the warm air.

Harry scrambles past the table towards his friend on the floor. 'Jakes!'

Jacob moans loudly, touching the deep cut just above his eye. 'Go after him,' he urges, barely above a mumble.

Harry bolts for the entrance, swings his gun around the doorway, sees all is clear and moves out into the street. No sign of the mysterious killer.

But one of the children who had been playing earlier in the roadway points shyly towards an alleyway. Harry hurtles down the street and ducks around the corner, into a narrow passage about three feet wide. Keeping low, he hurries forward, his pistol clasped in both hands. Garbage litters the muddy passageway, which smells like a drain. Harry rounds another corner to find the alley divides.

A frightened man is standing in the left fork. He drops the pair of shoes he is carrying and raises his hands. Harry turns away and plunges down the right-hand fork.

A shot erupts, followed by a loud crunch close to Harry's head. He throws himself flat against the shack opposite; there is nowhere else to go in this passageway. As he returns fire, his bullets ricochet off metal. A woman starts yelling frantically nearby.

When nothing else happens, Harry unglues himself from the wall, takes a deep breath and sprints forward. He rounds another corner and finds himself trapped.

Before him is another passage, maybe twenty-five yards long, its end blocked by the last remaining wall of a partially demolished building. Within that stretch, four separate alleys run off sideways, down among yet more shanties. Harry holds his breath, but cannot hear anything except the commotion of people hurrying away behind him.

Ngubane manages to calm his breathing, inhaling and exhaling in long measured breaths. He is able then to remain completely silent, concealed in a narrow space that is perhaps six feet deep. It looks like another side passage

157

to Harry, but is in actual fact also a dead end confined by the ruinous wall. Squatting on his haunches, Ngubane can make out the cop moving forward cautiously, concentrating in turn on the first two openings off the alleyway. Ngubane wants him to get just a little closer.

This time he will not miss.

But his target suddenly retreats to the previous corner, sliding cautiously around it so he is partially protected again. Ngubane is aware of him checking his clip, leaving the gunman uncertain whether he can yet risk a shot.

Harry is now nearly down to his spare clip. He pauses, trying to recover his breath, hoping the gunman will panic. He is reluctant to proceed further for fear of ambush. If only Jacob was with him.

Harry listens hard for a few more moments, then swears in frustration. What does he do now? Sit tight or call for back-up? He does not have a radio on him and, for all he knows, the bastard might be sprinting for dear life down some faraway street by now, making his way towards the taxi ranks by Westgate station.

Harry decides to back off completely.

Heading back to the car, the violent scene in the muti shop replaying in his mind, he suddenly realizes who shot at him. The same man's face has been posted in every station, in every newspaper and news bulletin for nearly two weeks. His name occurs every day in the muster rolls. Ngubane Maduna.

So the *sangoma* did know something of significance, but what would Maduna have to do with Harry's current case?

He rounds the corner back onto the main thoroughfare, in time to see Jacob radioing for back-up.

'You OK, mate?'

'I'll be all right.'

'What the hell was that all about?' asks Harry, a sudden fit of the shakes overwhelming him. 'Bastard shot at me – fucking *nearly* got me.'

The two detectives are still pacing around, burning off their fright, when just about every available police officer in Johannesburg descends on their position.

28

Ngubane eventually rises from the nook he is squeezed into and ponders which direction to take. He can hear people whispering inside one of the shacks beside him.

He sets off briskly through the constricted maze of paths, false turnings and entrances. He passes a young man skinning a chicken in his doorway and, at the man's shocked expression, realizes that he is still holding the Beretta openly. He shoves it down the front of his pants, easily concealing it under his heavy stomach.

Fifteen minutes later he is crawling through a rusty hole cut in a razor-wire fence, now very near to the taxi ranks, and heads north over the train tracks towards Braamfontein. Soon the stitch in his side feels like it is feeding on his innards and his breath heaves in hot rasps. Ngubane cuts into a dead-end tarmac alley, where he discovers a fast food diner's mountain of discarded boxes, flops down behind them and wipes his sweating face on his sodden shirtsleeve. He then begins to laugh, adrenalin and alcohol pumping through his veins, his recent escape making him feel invulnerable once more.

The stink of urine hangs heavily around him, and the

rats scratching in the heaped boxes nearby distract him as he tries to consider his next move. If those cops recognized him, the area will soon be teeming with police. Skipping bail on heroin charges, then killing a man and assaulting a police officer virtually guarantee that.

Ngubane needs to get off the street fast, and there is one safe place he can easily reach by foot. He just hopes he finds the woman at home. That hag gives him the creeps, but he knows she will take him in.

By mid-afternoon Ngubane Maduna is standing at the door of a ground-floor apartment in Braamfontein. The entrance, covered in tattered strips of old posters, suggests that the place is abandoned.

He raps loudly on the green-painted wood and hisses, 'Sibongile? Open the door. Sibongile?'

Moments later, multiple locks spring open, revealing a cramped and gloomy hallway at the foot of a narrow flight of stairs. It smells just like any other confined space with too many people living in it. The carpet is greasy with a wide streak of dirty footprints running down the middle, completely obscuring the original pattern.

'What are you doing here?' rumbles a woman, confronting him.

Her bulk, her deep voice, top-deck haircut and patchy facial hair give the impression that she is actually a man. But it is the protruding eyes that always make Ngubane avoid looking at her directly. She is not only the most repulsive woman he has ever seen, but also perhaps the most vindictive. What disturbs him most is that this creature is married, and with four children.

'Let me in,' he gasps. In the background there is the cacophony of a television cranked up high and female voices jabbering loudly. Somewhere close by, a baby is screaming. 'Who else is here?' he demands.

'Some of the girls,' she says calmly, 'and my kids.'

'I need to stay with you for a few days.'

'He's looking for you. I'll have to phone him.' There is not the slightest touch of surprise or fear in her voice. It is this quality that attracted the albino and Ngubane to her in the first place: a woman so capable of controlling her emotions must have her uses.

'Tell him I will come to him next week. Now is not a good time: they are looking for me everywhere.'

'In that case you can stay here until then.' She cocks an ear, as if listening either to the progress of the soap playing loudly on the television or the cries of the infant, before she lumbers back up the stairs, finally giving him space to step in off the street. At the top of the stairs she turns to stare back down at him. 'You have money?'

'Yes.'

'You'll give me two hundred rand for food and for use of the mattress every night. There is no empty bedroom, so you sleep in the living room with everyone else. You'll give me the money now before you make yourself comfortable.'

Though irritated that she should order him around, Ngubane has no choice but to pay her. He realizes this is the prudent thing to do. It is rumoured that before she began working for the albino, she murdered some of her clients as they slept, taking everything they had on them.

He follows her into her own apartment. Three women, all of them prostitutes familiar to Ngubane, are huddled around a tiny television standing on the kitchen counter, commenting loudly on the action. To the right is the living room, strewn with blankets, mattresses, clothes and toys.

Six children either lie sleeping or sit staring at him passively, their play interrupted by his arrival.

Ngubane greets the women curtly, then pulls the gun from his pants and unclips it to check how many bullets he has left. He now wonders whether coming here was the best idea.

'You can sleep there.' Sibongile points to a dirty mattress underneath the window, positioned right among all the children.

He does his best to swallow his indignation, his life now depending entirely on what might pass as this woman's hospitality.

29

In their pursuit of Ngubane Maduna, police officers turning up at the scene were immediately dispatched to check all the apartments, businesses and shacks in the vicinity. Some of the major roads leading out of Newtown, Fordsburg and Ferreirasdorp were blocked off and cars were searched, causing traffic jams that backed up large parts of downtown Johannesburg. Police officers from precincts as far away as Midrand were called in to help with the exercise and news crews hovered eagerly for information. In the end nothing came of it.

'In an environment like this it's too easy for someone to disappear on foot,' says Swanepoel, a commander from the Narcotics Bureau, to a group of disgruntled officers congregated near Harry and Jacob's pickup three hours later. 'Don't sweat it. We'll keep up the search for another hour or so, but he's probably long gone. I don't think he'd be stupid enough to hang around here.'

Somebody comments that he has obviously been stupid enough to remain in the city so far.

After the scene of the actual shooting has been thoroughly surveyed, and the alleys nearby trawled for bullet casings and other evidence, Harry and Jacob are on their way back to the station, asking themselves for a valid reason why Ngubane Maduna would be visiting the same *sangoma* as Hettie Solilo had directed them to.

'Maybe Sepang killed the girl for Maduna, and he gave him that valuable cheetah skin as payment for exceptional services rendered,' says Harry. 'After all, being out on the streets again, maybe he believes it was the *sangoma*'s powers that got him bail. The old man seemed very fussed about that cat hide.'

'It's not unusual for a highly ranking and respected *sangoma* to own such a hide. It is a token symbol of his occult powers and often handed down from father to son,' says Jacob. 'I think he may have been so tense because he knew a gun was being trained on all of us and that Maduna would open fire if you had started searching the place further. Something doesn't fit. Ms Solilo would have told me if Sepang was dirty. So I just don't know where Maduna fits in.

'On hearing about the dead girl, your contact pointed out Sepang, who is now dead, killed by Maduna, a drug baron who has been missing since his release on bail. I wonder what the link could be. Didn't you say the old woman was under surveillance herself? What happened about that red BMW, anyhow? Didn't a patrol car pick them up afterwards?'

'No. You know how few patrol cars there are operating in the townships. There weren't any available in the

163

area. I knew I should have tracked them myself, but those three would've been already looking out for me.'

'I say those guys were out there either looking for Maduna or working for him. In any case, your old woman may be in trouble, so I suggest we dispatch a guard for her. If it's them behind the murder of the little girl, then we'd better focus on that red BMW. But if it's Maduna then . . . well, then I don't get it. Surely he'd have moved on by now and be trying to recover his losses from the heroin bust? Why's he wasting his time with Sepang anyway? If the *sangoma* killed the little girl for Maduna, he would certainly never report it, so there's no real reason for Maduna to keep looking over the man's shoulder.'

'I think we should keep looking for both, Maduna *and* the car,' says Jacob. 'There's something we won't fully understand until we have *both* of them.'

After arriving back at the police station, Jacob sets off home early. His head feels like it has been crushed by a steamroller. A note lying on Harry's desk requests that he give Kobus Niehaus a call as soon as possible. Kobus had been significantly absent from the dragnet downtown, but when Harry finally reaches him on his mobile, the superintendent surprises Harry with what he has to say.

'We just found another victim. It looks like this one might be ritual-related murder, too, although I don't know how much it has to do with your present case.'

Harry sits up in his chair. 'What do you mean?'

'Early this morning a call was made to the flying squad by some hysterical woman living in one of those condemned apartment blocks in Hillbrow. Two Nigerians apparently broke down her door and threatened her life and the life of her child. They were looking for a guy called Oba, she says. Eventually they tracked him down to the apartment next door to her, smashed the place open and chopped off his head with a panga. She says she could hear them singing and clapping, even stamping their feet, before they did it.'

Harry whistles. 'Any details of the victim?'

'No, nothing, except that he spoke to his attackers in their own language – Nigerian, or whatever they speak. A building like this, people shack up on a short-term basis, mostly transients trying to keep a low profile. The bloody landlord doesn't keep any records, just collects the cash. The victim had no identification on him, nor any belongings to speak of. The woman who called said the men that killed the guy didn't stay long, which means they probably didn't take any of his things away.

'You should have seen this place, *boet*. *Yirre*, to call it a shithole is understating the fact. It *stank*! I don't know how these blacks can inhabit buildings like that. People shouldn't be made to live like that – black or white, *vokken* pink, I don't care. I'm passing the info onto the city council, in any case.'

'What else?' interrupts Harry.

'The woman from next door says she never even set eyes on this Oba character, nor did any of the other people there, except for the dirty little landlord, who says the victim just came in one night – he thinks the twenty-second of October – looking scared as hell and rented himself a room.'

'You said two Nigerians, not maybe *three*?'

'The woman says she recognized the language, but doesn't understand a word of it. Yes, only two.'

'Did you get descriptions?'

'Down to the teeth,' says Kobus. 'We've come up with some identikits.'

'What makes you think there's a connection to *my* case? It could've been just another crazy Nigerian way of killing people. You know how they are.'

'Maybe, but . . . this might sound strange, but I was hoping *you* could tell me. Something's been hovering on the tip of my tongue ever since I walked into that damn room. Do you want to come down here and check it out before we wrap things up? I might as well tell you now, I'm giving this case to Mitchell. With the Maduna thing, and that Nigerian family's murder last week, I can't handle this as well. He's been bitching to have a murder case – don't know why – so this has his name on it.'

'I nearly got killed by that bastard today,' says Harry.

'Yeah? Mitchell or Maduna?'

Harry snorts, then tells Kobus the whole story.

'That's fucking incredible, *boet*. Seems like that asshole is as slippery as hell. Look, if you want, I can hang around here a bit longer, so you can check things out before Mitchell takes over.'

Harry sighs and looks at his watch. Six o'clock. He still has to file a report on the incident in Newtown and then collect Jeanie from the neighbour. He really should go and check out the crime scene, but on the other hand he knows that Niehaus is a competent detective.

'I appreciate the offer, but I can't. I have to finish up here then head straight home. You know – family.'

Kobus laughs. 'You must be the only bloody cop who doesn't dread going home to face the wife on a Friday. I'll give you a call if I figure out what's still bugging me about this case.'

As Harry puts the phone down, he thinks about how relieved he is that Amy will not be home tonight. Maybe he is not so different after all from those guys who habitually go drink *Klippies 'n' Coke* after work, before facing up to the weekend.

Harry thanks Mrs Strydom for watching Jeanie after school and later makes his daughter promise she will not tell Mommy about their pizza run when she gets back from her office gala. By the time father and daughter have picked out some Disney videos, Harry barely thinks about the bullets that nearly ended his life some hours earlier. When he is with Jeanie, it does not seem to matter so much, but the moment he is with his wife it becomes a glaring issue, like staring into the sun. Amy is adamant that he does not need to do such dangerous work, that she makes enough money. But her constantly pointing it out to him only means that she still does not understand his reasons for becoming a police officer in the first place.

While Harry is slicing up their pizza on the counter, Jeanie sits next to him, swinging her feet in eager anticipation. Suddenly she pops the surprise question. 'Duddy, why is Mommy angry with you?'

Flustered, Harry puts the pizza cutter down. He takes a hold of his daughter by the shoulders and gazes straight into her green eyes. 'Baby, Mommy doesn't like the work Daddy does. Mommy wants Daddy to do something else.'

'So why don't you?'

It takes a few moments before Harry finds an answer. 'It's because Daddy needs to sort something out first. It's . . . it's like when Mommy tells you to clean up your room before you can go and play. Daddy first needs to clean up his room, before he can do something else. Understand?'

Jeanie nods silently, looking at the floor, self-conscious now under her father's serious gaze. He is not sure whether she really understands, or whether Amy herself would understand if he put it that way. Harry distributes the pizza slices and sits down with his daughter to watch the videos. Before too long, both of them have fallen asleep on the couch.

Harry is startled awake when the door connecting to the garage opens and Amy's high heels clack into the kitchen behind them. He turns around to peek at her over the top of the green couch and finds her glaring at him meaningfully. She must have noticed the empty pizza boxes. Without a word she heads for the bedroom and shuts the door firmly behind her.

30

Harry spends most of his Saturday staying out of his wife's way by concentrating on completing some carpentry work in the garage. The scents of pine and lacquer, of fresh-cut wood, help him forget about the past week, even if his resulting handiwork does not have any particular merit. Completely self-absorbed, Harry barely notices Amy periodically checking on him through the open kitchen door, biting her nails as if wondering how best to approach him.

Jacob had promised to help his neighbour, that same day, to construct an extension of his living room. As a result, he spends much of the day working in the man's garden with other men come to help, occasionally chatting to neighbours as they pass. He listens to their joys and grievances, easily losing himself in the people around him. When, prompted by his swollen face, they allude to his name appearing in the newspapers and on television, it is as if they are talking to their very own celebrity.

That evening, as Jacob and his partner, Nomsa, stroll past rows of identical matchbox RDP houses down to the small cinema located at the bottom of the hill, Nomsa voices her distress at his near fatal confrontation. Jacob manages to reassure her, finally, but in his own heart and mind the clouds begin to gather. All the time he is still trying to assemble the disparate pieces of an unlikely jigsaw. He can barely watch the film, his thoughts working at possible connections between the fury of the dogs, the various omens Hettie reported, the death of that *sangoma* and Harry's current volatility. Jacob wonders how much deeper he will get dragged into the evil side of both a religion and a way of life he has been trying so hard to leave behind.

The next day, after attending Communion, Jacob returns home feeling nervous, conscious of the sweating of his palm in Nomsa's tender grasp. On Hettie's behest, he has decided that he will phone his family. It's something he has not done in years. His mother answers, sounding older and frailer than he remembers. When he starts to speak, it feels like something heavy is stuck in his throat.

'*Sawubona*, Mama, it's Jacob.'

His mother is silent for a moment, then she answers, 'Jacob?'

'Yes, Mama.'

Their conversation is punctuated with long, uneasy silences. Jacob's voice is barely a whisper, his expression intensely serious. At one point he glances up to see Nomsa has sat down opposite him. He reaches out and grabs her hand tightly.

'They tell me you a detective now,' says his mother, proudly.

'Yes, I've come a long way. I've a good partner to work with, though he's a confused white guy, and it's going well.'

Jacob touches the wound on his forehead. Two days ago at least six shots were fired at him from very close range. Someone at that time not three feet away from him died. Jacob had nearly been killed while still estranged from his family. After being separated from his own kin so long, at times he has felt like an unripe fruit torn from the tree.

Suddenly he feels an enormous sense of relief well up in him. He should have done this a long time ago.

'I am so happy for you,' continues his mother.

Jacob can hear there are other people crowding around the phone with her, all trying to listen in. Abruptly she asks the question he has been dreading. 'Will you speak with your father now?'

Jacob pauses for a long moment before he answers. 'No, Mama, I can't. Not yet.'

The phone goes silent as at her end Martha Tshabalala clamps a hand over the receiver. Jacob closes his eyes and feels Nomsa squeeze his hand.

'Jacob,' says his mother shakily after a moment, 'your father, he would very much like to speak with you. You know, he's not well, and . . . Please, Jacob, will you not speak to him?'

Jacob swallows hard. 'No, Mama, not tonight. I will phone again soon, I promise.'

'You do that soon, son. We miss you. Will you come visit us, sometime?'

'Maybe, Mama, we'll see.'

After he puts the phone down, Jacob walks into the bedroom he shares with Nomsa, and closes the door quietly behind him.

For the Mason family this Sunday means a previously planned visit to two long-standing friends, and surprisingly it is then that the chill between Harry and Amy begins to thaw. Compelled to hide their personal difficulties, they begin to forget their grudges at each other and are soon touching each other occasionally as they talk and finding themselves finishing each other's sentences again. And, as they gaze at each other over the barbecue, apologies are written all over their faces.

By the time they get home and put Jeanie to bed, their conversation is once again smooth and easy. Exhausted, Amy flings herself onto the couch, talking happily about the day. Harry grins as he brews them fresh coffee. He never gets a chance to pour it.

Sleek fingers suddenly run over his shoulders and descend to explore his chest. Amy bites at his ear and whispers, 'Harry, I'm sorry. I never meant to lose my temper.'

Deeply inhaling Amy's fresh jasmine fragrances, Harry turns around and grasps her around the waist. 'I don't want us to go on fighting either.' He kisses her gently. 'To tell you the truth, I've been thinking of giving it all up as well. But . . . but this girl's murder – I have to get to the bottom of it. Then I'll think properly about what to do next.'

Amy cups his head in both her hands and nods vigorously. 'You just better come out of this OK.'

Harry pulls her closer and Amy runs her hands further down his chest, then across his stomach, and brings them up under his shirt. His skin is hot to her touch. Harry's fingers bury themselves in her hair, and they kiss deeply.

He whispers, 'Come here,' and leads her to the couch, stopping on the way to switch the light off. Only a streetlamp illuminates the room with a ghostly orange glow. There he unbuttons her blouse slowly, running his lips down her neck and collarbone before proceeding to undress her completely. He admires her naked silhouette briefly before he pulls her down on top of him.

He wakes up with a screaming headache from a dream he cannot remember. He is drenched with sweat. At first he does not know where he is, then senses Amy's breast pressing against his side and her arm resting on his chest. Her breath is cool against his neck and he realizes they have fallen asleep, entwined, on the sitting-room sofa.

It feels like a screwdriver has been jammed into each temple. He extracts himself carefully from Amy's arms.

'Mhm?' she protests in her sleep.

'Just stay there. I'll be back.'

Finding his pills on the dresser, Harry swallows one feverishly. The world swims before his eyes, and the curtains dancing in the breeze seem to glow with an unearthly light. He breaks out in gooseflesh as his body temperature suddenly plummets.

Something heavy crashes to the ground outside. Then a shadow creeps across the open window and is as suddenly gone. Alarmed, Harry holds his breath and listens. He rushes to the window and peers outside.

Nothing.

Pulling his pants on, he hurries through the house and opens the front door quietly. He creeps around the side of the building, depending only on the streetlamp to see where he is going.

Again nothing.

The breeze is chilling and the air smells like rain. A dog begins to howl in the distance, raising the hairs on the nape of his neck for some reason. Desperate to know what has fallen, Harry searches the area where he heard the noise.

Still nothing.

Unnerved, and realizing he cannot think clearly while the headache continues driving nails through his skull, Harry finally abandons his search, and back inside the house he makes his way into Jeanie's room. He finds her window wide open.

Sneaking across the room he closes it and stops for a moment to appreciate his daughter, her contorted sleeping body, her soft breathing, before touching her lightly on the head and closing the door behind him. Curling up next to his wife on the couch again, Harry ponders what he might have heard outside, but pain and exhaustion soon force him to abandon the effort. Somehow he manages to fall into a deep sleep – the last peaceful sleep he will enjoy for a long time.

31

As night falls and Ntuli brings in the goats, young Jacob's father and grandfather still have not returned.

Feeling cold since the night before, Jacob is wrapped in a

warm blue fleece blanket. Sitting close to his mother and aunt, who are already busy with the cooking fires, he ponders where the two men can be. He earlier overheard the women say something about their having gone to hunt down the witch who tried to abduct him. Yet Jacob does not quite understand how they might achieve that, since the witch seemed able to turn into a hyena and disappear off into the night.

'Mama, where is grandfather?' They are the first words he has uttered all day.

His mother exchanges a worried look with her sister-in-law before putting aside the ladle and sitting down next to him. She pulls the blanket more tightly up around his shoulders. 'They will be back soon, little Jacob. Don't worry, our troubles are over now.'

Her son fixes her with a piercing stare, as if he is seeing through a lie being told to him. 'But *when*, Mama?'

Unnerved by her young son's desperate expression, she mutters uncertainly, 'Soon, my boy, soon.'

His aunt comes over, wiping her hands on her white apron. She grasps Jacob's chin and turns his face up towards her own. Holding the boy's eyes with a firm gaze, she runs a hand over the crown of his head. 'Jacob, tell me, are you feeling OK?' She asks it with a voice that demands an honest reply.

The boy shakes his head and whispers, 'No.'

He could not sleep at all during the remainder of the previous night, staring at the dark ceiling and reliving constantly that horrible sense of paralysis that overcame him. By first light the whole compound seemed to know about the incident, and people kept coming to visit his absent father's hut, where Jacob was resting safely under his mother's vigilance. Where before he had felt totally part of an extended family, suddenly now he was feeling like an oddity. They peered in at him and commented in whispers, as if apprehensive to speak to him directly.

Jacob's own memories of the dark events the night before are growing more and more confused. He already barely recalls anything beyond his own frozen body and the intense eyes of the man who had picked him up from his bed. Had there really been a hyena? Had that man really appeared out of nowhere?

'What do you mean "No", child?' his aunt asks gently, settling down on her knees in front of him. 'Do you feel sick in the stomach? Is your head sore? What?'

'No, not sick like that, just that . . . something is wrong,' the boy answers.

'In what way, wrong?'

Jacob glances over at his mother, wringing her hands in her lap. 'Things are different now,' he announces, fixing each woman in turn with wide, solemn eyes.

Martha wonders at how distant-sounding his voice has grown. *My son's little laughing spirit has been stolen from him,* she thinks.

'What do you see that is different?' presses his aunt.

'Leave him alone, Grace. You're scaring him,' interrupts Martha, grabbing her sister-in-law by the arm. 'Just let him rest.'

'No, this is very important, Martha.'

'Where are my fathers?' insists Jacob, casting the blanket off his shoulders.

A sudden loud hissing behind them startles the two women. The blackened wrought-iron pot is spilling water onto the coal stove. Jacob's mother leaps up to tend to the damage, but his aunt still does not budge. The alarm just exhibited by the two of them would normally have little Jacob cackling with laughter, but now he just sits staring vacantly into space. Grace continues to watch him intently, gradually convincing herself that a certain clarity has surfaced in the boy's eyes — a brightness she has watched dawning before, in her own brother, the boy's father.

She gets up and walks over to join Martha, who is stirring

the stew. First glancing over her shoulder to make sure he is not watching them, she leans in close to whisper to the boy's mother. 'Martha, his head is opening up to the ancestors. I think they are speaking to him.'

'*What?*' hisses his mother, glancing over at her son. 'That can't be true. He's still far too young.'

'He may be young, but remember his soul is that of this family's first-born. It is powerful and restless, and it is looking for answers.'

Even as they whisper, the sound of Jacob's breathing seems to intensify and quicken, causing both women to glance at him in consternation. Suddenly the door is flung open with a mighty crash. Martha yelps, starting back in fright. A young, barefooted man enters, his eyes gleaming wild under the paraffin light. Between ragged gasps for breath he announces that he has come all the way from a little village lying south of Goosen's farm. Then he begins to jabber incoherently about a clash between the *sangomas* and the *baloyi*.

'Stop!' cries Grace, holding up a hand. 'You're not talking like that in here. Outside, *now!*' She grabs the young man by the arm and propels him out the door. Tears welling, Martha holds her hands up to her mouth. She glances at her child, who even seems to nod in understanding, before she, too, rushes outside to hear the young man's story. But she carefully closes the door behind her.

Jacob sits watching the steam from the pot slowly lifting the lid again, expelling its hissing heat into the silent room. Meanwhile he cocks his head in an attempt to hear the frantic news being related outside.

As the two women's loud wailing suddenly rises in volume, piercing the silence of the room with their agony, it seems that Jacob's premonition has come to pass. The boy gets up slowly, shrugging off the blanket completely. Slowly he walks to the door and opens it wide.

His mother and aunt stand hugging each other and weeping, his mother's neat blue bandanna now pushed askew on her head. The young man stands close by them, staring solemnly at his feet.

How could this have happened?

Jacob thinks back to all the other children that have gone missing over the years. Could one *baloyi* truly have proved stronger than both his fathers, more powerful than two such highly respected *sangomas?*

32

It is Jacob's habit to arrive half an hour before work. Invariably a newspaper is tucked under his arm, which he begins to read through after making himself some tea. The phone surprises him just as he is sitting down.

'Sorry, Jacob,' says the desk sergeant, 'but I've got a woman on the line who wants to speak only with you.'

'Put her through, then.'

'Is that Detective Jacob Tshabalala?' a fierce voice asks in Sotho.

'Yes, it is. Can I help you?'

'I'm going to kill you, you hear me? I'm going to kill you for what you did to him!'

'Sorry?' Jacob shifts the phone on his shoulder.

'You told him you'd be careful, you told *him* to be careful, and see what it's brought him!'

'Who are you talking about?'

'My father, Walter Mbewu.'

The old man who found the child's body.

Jacob's heart skips. 'What's happened?'

'You gave his name to the media, you filthy bastard! Once people read about it, they thought he must be involved. They came to our house last night. They beat him. They beat him badly. They wanted to know where the other children are.'

'But I made particularly sure to keep his name out of the paper.'

'Don't lie to me!' screeches the nearly hysterical woman. 'My brothers will be paying you a visit!'

'Wait a minute. You don't ever *dare* threaten me like that, understand? I am *not* the one responsible for what's happened, so calm down.'

'My father is now in hospital! He only did you people a favour. He could've just walked on past that girl's body, but he called you up instead. Just see where that's got him.'

'At which hospital is he now?'

'Chris Hani Baragwanath.'

'Ward number?'

'Four.'

'Right, what's your name ... Lebo? I'm going to get to the bottom of this. Do you know which newspaper this article appeared in?'

'The damage is done. How's that going to help us?'

'I'll go visit him as soon as I can. In the meantime can you tell me the people he was assaulted by?' Jacob takes down the same few details she has already given to an investigative officer from the Orlando station – she does not know any of the members of the mob that attacked her father. By the time Jacob has written the name of the guilty newspaper, the old man's daughter sounds a lot calmer, more assured that something might be done.

Jacob phones the *Sowetan* journalist with whom he has been working and confronts him firmly. All he receives is an insistence that his contact did not write the article. It was another reporter who composed the filler, but the man in question will not get in until nine o'clock.

Then, digging through the previous week's newspapers in the tearoom, Jacob discovers the minor article in question. Titled 'Hesitant Witness Possible Suspect in Muti Case', it appeared in last Friday's late edition and refers briefly to Jacob interviewing an elderly suspect, who is then named. The rest of the article is devoted to conjecture of tabloid proportions.

Suspect? How did the idiot journalist conjure that up?

Flopping back into his chair, Jacob wonders where this misinformation might have come from. The *Sowetan* being a respectable newspaper, they would not just publish any rubbish without substantiation. Then he suddenly remembers those three men from the New Canada satellite police station who were supposed to be helping them out that day, but instead stood idling at the top of the embankment, discussing the developments while occasionally throwing glances towards Jacob and the old man. He should have sensed trouble at the time.

With a vision of that same frail old man now lying battered in a hospital bed, Jacob abruptly leaps up, grabs his keys and heads out the door – leaving his tea to cool and his newspaper unread.

When Harry arrives at the office later, he is faintly surprised by the untidy state in which Jacob has left his normally orderly desk. He phones his partner, suspecting something important has come up. Jacob answers promptly and describes what has happened.

'I hate to say it, Jakes, but I feared something like this. That's why I've been so against the media being provided with extended briefings.' Harry pauses to light a cigarette, after shutting the office door. He retrieves his ashtray from the bottom drawer.

'I'm on my way to sort things out now,' continues Jacob. 'It's down to the source of the information, not the newspaper itself, although I'll need to speak to the journalist, too.'

'You wouldn't happen to know whether your friends in the red car were Nigerians, would you?' asks Harry suddenly, thinking back to his conversation with Niehaus the previous Friday.

Jacob's answer is almost immediate. 'No, I don't think so. Why?'

Harry then fills his partner in on the gruesome decapitation in Hillbrow.

'Interesting, but I'm not sure it has anything to do with our case,' says Jacob. Harry agrees with him.

As Harry joins the muster, a number of fellow officers congratulate him, slapping him on the back and insisting on hearing his version of Friday's shoot-out with Ngubane Maduna.

As the meeting drags on, Harry's mind once again begins to wander. He remembers receiving a bad fright last night. Checking his garden again this morning yielded nothing out of the ordinary, which leads him to believe it was just some side-effect of his migraine that was causing him to imagine things.

Throughout the day the phone rings periodically, usually media grunts seeking more information. Harry turns them down roughly, insisting that Detective Tshabalala will handle all queries as soon as he returns to the office. Harry does not bother to write down any of their messages.

Ten minutes after the pathologist's preliminary faxed report comes through, Harry's phone rings again. This time it is Gildenhuys, the state prosecutor, congratulating him on locating and nearly capturing Ngubane Maduna. 'That was some good work; the area commissioner loved it. As far as I'm concerned, it's one helluva boost for morale,' he enthuses. 'How did you find the bastard?'

'I didn't – that's what's not making any sense. We were just chasing a lead on the little girl's murder.'

'Well, next time he pops up, arrest the prick, will you? Have you spoken to Mitchell yet?'

'No, why?'

'Our office received an interesting request from Scotland Yard this morning. It seems they might have something connected to our investigations, something about a kidnapped girl having her foetus forcibly removed during a ritual before she was brought to England. They're now trying to locate her parents. I don't have all the specifics yet, but it increasingly looks like we might be dealing with an international syndicate or such.' Harry whistles in disbelief before Gildenhuys continues. 'I want you to talk to Mitchell though. He's picked up a case you might be interested in.'

Harry lets the prosecutor know that he has already received some information on the Hillbrow decapitation, quickly ends the call and turns his attention back to the medical examiner's report.

His leg jigging impatiently under the table, Harry

ascertains that the little girl's blood group was the same as that found soaking the fetish. The child had also been older than they previously thought. Radiographic examination of her bone structure indicated that she was an underdeveloped seven-year-old. The state of her bones correlated with the condition of her empty intestines: she had been severely undernourished, a situation which does not bode well for Harry's investigation. That meant that either she did not receive much attention at home, or else that she was living out on the street. In both cases the possibility of finding someone able, or willing, to identify her could prove very difficult.

The good doctor had also managed to lift from the girl's hair some beige fibres which most likely came from a fleece blanket. Harry puts a call through to forensics, asking them to compare the DNA sample taken from the fetish with the girl's.

Just as he puts the phone down, a fist raps on the door. Scrambling to remove any evidence of his smoking, Harry finds himself too late. The door swings open and Francis Mitchell walks in.

'Morning, Mason. I need to speak with you.'

Harry instinctively pushes his chair back from the desk. Mitchell might look like a parish priest in his long-sleeved shirts, always buttoned to the collar, and his neat polished shoes, but to Harry he more resembles the snake in Eden's undergrowth. 'Go ahead,' he growls.

'It's been a week now, so how you doing with your muti girl case? You haven't been in touch with me.'

'We're doing fine,' retorts Harry. 'You haven't been in contact with us either.'

'It's water under the bridge, I know, but just how *did* you get saddled with what should be one of *our* cases?'

'As I said before, because it's homicide.' Harry's eyes narrow with distrust.

'It's devil worship, man. And that's my territory.'

Harry lets the comment hang in the air for a moment. 'You know what the score is, Mitchell. Why not quit whinging about it? Shouldn't you be out arresting kids for playing their vinyl records backwards or something?'

'Don't get smart with me.'

'You wanted to talk to me, or just stir up trouble?'

Mitchell sighs heavily. '*I'll* start the sharing first, then. There's a darkie lost his head in Hillbrow last week, Thursday night or early morning Friday.' Mitchell's eyes glint, as if he is bringing Harry really good news. Harry decides not to tell Mitchell that he already knows. 'Two of them in two weeks – that must be a record even for Jo'burg, hey?' Mitchell moves closer to the wall to peer at Harry's notes pinned there, then at photos of the young victim. The case map has been growing steadily. 'Will you look at that?' Mitchell's bulbous nose is hovering before one shot, depicting in close-up the damage done to the girl's head. 'You know what I think, Harry? I think these kaffirs are never, never going to change. We bring them civilization, we bring them Jesus Christ, but they still go practising this kind of barbarism.'

He cracks his knuckles and looks up at Harry. 'What?' Mitchell asks, as if genuinely confused by the resentment he notices on the other man's face.

Harry shakes his head. 'I don't know how you manage it, Mitchell.'

'What do you mean?'

'Things have changed so much for the better around here, but you'll never realize that, will you?'

'What's wrong with *you*?' Mitchell holds out his hands

in feigned innocence. 'Can't you see we're dealing with wild *animals* here?'

'What's *wrong* here is that you somehow assume I'm paddling in the same boat with you. You're mistaken. I have to cooperate with you just to keep Gildenhuys happy, but I don't have to listen to your bullshit opinions.'

To Harry, people like Mitchell have always seemed moral cowards of a kind, masking their insecurities with religion, race, sex – anything – and finding it easier to lash out at the world rather than understand it. They fear everything that seems different, conjuring up devils composed of one part paranoia and six parts speculation. It has always been difficult for Harry to make many friends in the police force, simply because that mentality very much persists there.

'I'm not the bad guy here, Mason. You just take a good look at these pictures and remember we're fighting a war.'

Harry sighs. 'Look, I have work to do. Is there anything special you wanted from me? Anything you wanted to share with me about that Hillbrow business?'

Mitchell glances at Jacob's desk. 'Doesn't look like this one has too much work to do.'

'He's just naturally tidy.'

'Maybe you should give your boy a bit more to do.'

'My partner can take care of himself.' Harry kneads his temples in exasperation.

Mitchell makes his way back to the door. '*Ja*, I can see that – and he's taking good care of you, too. I hear you've been cursed by something not even a stinking dog would go near. How does that sit in your stomach at night? Have you, by any chance, wondered how your partner knows so much about muti?' He pauses to look at Harry. 'Oh, I can see you haven't.'

Harry stares back at him, fighting to keep his composure.

'You're so out of your depth, Mason, and your stubbornness is going to get you killed. Come talk to me if you need anything. I can see from the way things are going here that I won't be needing much from *you*.'

'If you have something particular to say, just spit it out, ghostbuster,' mutters Harry. 'No use you talking to me in circles.'

Mitchell leans a fist on the door handle and grins smugly. 'Well, why not ask that boy of yours? And, if I were you, I'd advise him to stop stirring, because the shit will really hit the fan if he keeps on doing that. I've seen it happen before.'

Mitchell slams the door behind him before Harry can react.

33

The moment Jacob Tshabalala strides into New Canada police station, he recognizes again how glad he is to have been promoted to the Murder and Robbery Unit. A lone African female sergeant is the only person behind the wooden counter, attempting to deal with a long line of complainants. Her denim uniform is oversized, clearly intended for a man and washed out to the point where the seams are frayed, which suggests it is her only complete outfit. Occasionally she throws poisonous glances at the men lounging at their desks behind her, clearly enjoying a lazy conversation rather than attempting to help.

RICHARD KUNZMANN

Of the three officers who had been present at the crime
scene, only one is currently available. Jacob corners him in
the locker room. A few local officers look on aggressively,
wondering what this uptown hotshot is doing down here,
apparently ready to attack one of their own.

'Who did you speak to, Sephaka?' yells Jacob in Sotho,
slamming his fist against a nearby locker. 'Which one of
you talked to the press?'

Some of the other men jeer at this outburst, telling him
to calm down. Sephaka goes on changing into his uniform,
defiantly avoiding looking him in the eye.

'Do you realize I could have all three of you hauled in
for compromising a criminal investigation? A witness was
badly beaten – a *witness*, not a suspect! He had been
reluctant to talk precisely because he didn't trust us, and
now you lot have proved him right. Do you think any
other witnesses will be ready to come forward after this?
Talk to me, will you! Which one of you did it?'

'Look at this guy,' says Sephaka to the spectators. 'He
comes in here and starts throwing a fit like a little girl.'
He finally makes eye contact. 'You know what, you can't
prove it was us. Just because we were the only other black
officers there doesn't mean *anything*.'

Jacob grabs him by the front of his denim uniform
shirt and shoves him with a crash backwards into the row
of green lockers. Instantly hands drag him off Sephaka,
holding onto him firmly.

'You don't mess around with someone relying on me
to protect him. You're going down, Sephaka! Call yourself
a police officer?' Jacob snorts with contempt. 'And don't
think I'll take your side after this, just because you're on
the force.'

Embarrassed, Sephaka laughs. 'From what I saw, you

and those whites you were with are screwed anyway, whatever we did or didn't do. Why are you still messing with that case, after what happened with the dogs? If I were you, I'd stay far away from it. And you'd better stay away from me, too. I don't want to get polluted by you or that case of yours. I'm not at all surprised things are going so badly for you.'

Sephaka makes his way rapidly from the room as Jacob is violently shoved forward, falling to the damp concrete floor. A few moments later the station commissioner himself charges in, but the only person left to yell at is Jacob himself.

As Harry heads out to lunch, the sergeant on duty greets him from the front desk. '*Sawubona*, Harry!'

'*Yebo*, yes, Samuel,' says Harry, and their hands run through a complex pattern of handshakes.

'*Daars die donder! Howzit*, Harry!' hails another voice, sounding dry and parched from years of tobacco smoke.

'Hennie, I'm fine.' Harry smiles, shaking the older man's hand vigorously.

Hennie continues in Afrikaans, 'The boys tell me you picked up something nasty at a crime scene last week. So how you feeling now?'

Harry thinks briefly of the pills that he has begun swallowing again regularly, after such a long abstinence.

'Feverish, Hennie, but maybe I'm allergic to *you*.'

All three laugh, although Samuel is also shaking his head. 'Harry, you must take this seriously, man. You should not have touched that thing. You must go see a *sangoma*, and she'll make it right.'

'Sammy, I'm fine.'

'You know what I would do if I was you?' insists Hennie. 'I would sneak that thing out of the evidence room and hang it from my rear-view mirror.' He bursts out laughing. 'Then no *tsotsi* alive would ever dare steal that nice pickup of yours. You'd even be able to stop paying insurance on it. You'd save yourself a bloody fortune.'

Harry merely grins at him. Hennie, although close to retirement, is still responsible for the evidence room and for the storage of prisoners' belongings. The man looks like everyone's favourite grandfather, with bushy grey hair and eyebrows and a deeply wrinkled smoker's skin.

'You think I'm joking, son? I have a friend, he wrapped a chicken leg with some beads and feathers, and propped it up on his dashboard. His car's never been touched since. He can even go off and leave it without locking the doors.'

'It's probably just a pile of rust sitting in the corner of his garden, on flat tyres,' comments Harry. 'Maybe they just felt sorry for your friend when they looked at it. And maybe they'll even get him a new car when that chicken leg *really* begins to smell.'

Samuel roars with laughter and slaps the desk.

'Could be, could be – ' Hennie pats Harry's shoulder – 'but I reckon these *tsotsis* understand muti better than they do car alarms. Alarms are a white man's thing. Break into a car that's fixed with an alarm, it's all about timing and skill. It's about beating the rich at their own game. Now, dealing with ancestors and spirits, that's different. Get *them* guarding your car, and they're bad news.' Hennie moves off with a wave and a final cackle. 'You think about that: there's no one better to do it than a spook.'

'*Ja*, Hennie, something like that,' sighs Samuel, waving the older man on before turning to Harry. 'That one's maybe old and mad, but he's right. Muti is good for protecting your car, but it's expensive.'

Harry declines the offer of a recommended *sangoma*'s phone number – one who apparently specializes in securing cars – and walks out into the hot sun. The heat rises off the baking pavement in waves, and almost immediately Harry breaks out in a sweat. It is running down his back by the time he reaches the rooftop via a steel staircase on the outside wall of the police building. It is his favourite spot for a quiet lunch on the rare occasions he is still in the office at midday. He sits down in a scarce nook of shade, from where he can watch the cars hush past on the street below.

Keep Jacob on a tight leash? What did Mitchell mean?

The steel staircase rings with footsteps. Jacob himself appears with two chilled cans of ginger ale. His white shirt is soaking wet and his brown skin glitters with beads of sweat.

'*Yebo*, Harry,' grumbles Jacob.

'Jacob, you look tired, mate.' Harry moves over to give Jacob room in the limited shade. Together they pop their cans and drink deeply. 'So, what happened here this morning?'

Jacob tells him more about the woman's hysterical phone call, his subsequent inquiries at the newspaper and his suspicions about who might have been responsible for the leak. 'I've lodged formal complaints with the New Canada superintendent.' Jacob laughs. 'First he wanted to throw me out, but after a little talk he saw things my way and called in that idiot Sephaka to dress him down properly. I've also requested an indictment against the *Sowetan* and that bogus story of theirs. And, after all that, I contacted the Kliptown station to keep an eye on Mrs Solilo as best they can.'

'You did well. It's a pity you can't trust the media. Even if you try to control the information through press releases, one of them will find a way to screw things up. It's just not worth it, getting them involved.'

'But, Harry, we need them if we're going to get more information from the public. I spoke to some more traditionalists this morning, but none claims to know anything about the victim, or about recent human muti trading.'

'Are you driving around by yourself, dropping in on these people, after what happened on Friday?'

Jacob shrugs. 'We need to work fast. We still know very little about this case and other children may disappear. I just hope her own family is not involved in the murder, because then it might take months for information to surface.' Jacob finishes his can while staring down at the cars passing below.

Harry informs his partner of the girl's true age, her evident malnourishment and the fibres found in her hair. Jacob unclips his holster, stands up and pulls his sticky shirt off. He carefully brushes dust off a pitched section of roof nearby and lays his shirt out there to dry in the sun. His body ripples with muscle and sinew, the body of a man who has known hard work from an early age.

'If I find the parents actually sold their child, or just gave her over to a *sangoma* to have muti cut from her, I will kill them myself, I swear.'

Jacob grunts in disgust. 'So you would do that, make them suffer? You couldn't possibly make them suffer more than she did, unless you yourself could become as evil as the *baloyi* that tortured her to death. Then what? Then what would make you different from the witch who

190

utilized her as a sacrifice to the spirits? The only difference would be that you will have killed the parents out of revenge, while they let her be slaughtered in the belief that her death would make their own lives easier – or make someone else's worse. In that case, Harry, you might actually come out of it looking worse than they do. Although you'd probably have lots of hate-filled people cheering you on.'

'Are you trying to explain away the kind of parents that would do such a thing, simply because to them it's a sort of religious exchange?'

Jacob grabs at the small gold crucifix that dangles on his chest. 'No, I've just seen enough anger to make me stop and think.'

They grow silent, and after a while Jacob attempts to break the ice. 'It's getting hotter every year now, don't you reckon?'

Harry nods with a small smile.

Jacob dents his empty can in meaningless shapes, 'Harry, I'm getting very worried. This thing is looking bad. I don't know . . . but I'm thinking about Maduna a lot. How does he keep on evading us like this? How did he contrive to get out of jail despite all those serious charges? How did he manage to throw off a tail on the way from the High Court?' Jacob shakes his head. 'He could have shot me so easily, so . . . why did he just kick me? Now my old witness is lying in hospital, and you . . . you're struggling with your demons again.'

'I noticed you grab your little crucifix, Jakes. Why worry so much when you believe in God?'

'Harry, there is evil in this world that's stronger than either of us. The omens, all these things happening . . . it looks really bad.'

'Don't worry about all that. We'll catch him, or them, whoever they might be.'

'You don't understand. Someone very powerful is involved. It looks like . . . *he* looks like he might be for real.' Jacob finally crushes the can.

'What do you mean?'

'There are many *genuine* people who are spiritual leaders, people that have learnt how to give proper guidance. There are many cheats and liars, too. But I can't get last week out of my head. It makes me think back to the powerful ones, the *sangomas* that used to rule side by side with our tribal leaders, and also the witches that lived up in the mountains, plaguing entire communities. Both could accomplish powerful things.'

'Are you being *serious*?' Harry asks, his mouth dropping open.

'Yes, I am,' replies Jacob.

'Bloody hell, Jacob, the last thing we need on this case is you talking like some superstitious *sucker*.'

'You think I'm an idiot for believing in some of the old ways. You witnessed how those dogs behaved, you *must* understand.'

Harry knows how the *baloyi, inyangas* and *sangomas* still hold tremendous power over many people in this country, even those who have been urbanized, westernized, converted. Out in the townships and rural areas, where poverty and luxury are oddly combined, mobile phones, boom-box music and stereo car-radio are all mixed up with ancestor worship, tribal ceremony and ritual drums. The concoction is tangible: the modern and the tribal cultures bonded together haphazardly like so many of those rainbow-coloured corrugated shacks that many people are forced to inhabit. Harry understands that such traditions remain strong, but surely they have no place in a police investigation.

'Jacob, I can see how these things concern you, but remember you're a cop. I really don't appreciate you suggesting to other people that I'm screwed from here on in just because I touched something you consider tainted with bad magic.'

'Harry—'

'Are you telling me you would jeopardize a murder case involving a seven-year-old just to protect yourself from a ritualistic parcel of dead bird?'

Jacob looks away because the direction of this conversation is now giving him pause for thought.

Harry, his temper rising, misreads his colleague's reaction. 'You *would* do that? You would *really* do that? Did you see what that little girl looked like when they'd finished with her? That was somebody's *daughter*. You might not have children, but I do. My girl's almost the same age. That could've been *my* daughter; do you *understand* me? Can't you see that somewhere out there are parents who might've *lost* that child, not deliberately sold her? They might be keeping quiet right now for the same superstitious reasons you wanted me to abandon that vital item of evidence. Are you really so scared of some bastard who murders little kids? This psycho *lives* off people like you, Jacob – and likely so do her parents. You be afraid of these bastards, fine, but don't let it mess with my case.'

'Harry, don't get angry with me.'

'I *am* angry!'

'I didn't say we had to abandon that piece of evidence. I just meant that we needed to handle it right. You just picking it up there, you've invited *rubbish* into your life.'

'Don't worry about the rubbish in my life. I'm a regular

trash compactor. The only two things keeping me afloat right now are my wife and my daughter.'

'Yet your head is hurting again – doesn't that mean something to you?'

'What?' Harry is astounded.

'I'm telling you, this is really bad muti.'

Harry jabs a finger at him. '*Bullshit.*'

'It started that same day.'

'Don't go any further, Jacob. You're not making sense.'

Just then Harry's mobile phone rings. The two men glare at each other in exasperation, but the phone persists. Jacob pulls his shirt from the flat roof as Harry unclips his phone and turns away.

'Yeah?'

'Harry, where are you?' asks Samuel.

'Just outside, up on the roof, having lunch.'

'Come in, quick. There's a woman on the phone urgently wanting to speak with you. She wants to talk to you about that little girl.'

'Is that Detective Harry Mason?'

'Yes, Mason speaking. Can I help you?'

'I believe I might be able to help *you*.'

The British accent puzzles Harry. 'What do you mean?'

'My name is Nina Reading; I'm a freelance journalist over here on assignment from London. I—'

'I don't have time for you, sorry. I'm busy.'

'Detective—'

'Damn it, can't you people *ever* leave me alone?' Harry slams the phone down. He stares at it for a few seconds, his fingers drumming on the reception desk, before he crashes off through the side door.

Samuel looks inquiringly at Jacob, who has just followed Harry down. '*Aowa*, what is wrong now?'
Jacob shrugs.

34

Nina stares at the phone, not sure she can have heard him right. What kind of reaction is that from a police officer?

Screw that. She tosses her mobile onto her backpack, lying over in one corner. Her hair has been shorn off and her previous, cosmopolitan clothes replaced by a brown frayed skirt and discoloured white blouse, while a washed-out yellow bandanna hides her cropped head. On her feet she wears simple blue thongs.

This crude disguise seems to have worked so far, although her appearance has at times been to her both hilarious and depressing.

The interior of the building has been gutted by fire at some point. Crushed beer bottles now lie amidst mounds of caked ash; weeds and moulds flourish in some of the moister corners. The low drone of traffic on the overpass is occasionally punctuated by loud vocal exchanges in the streets below, by cars hurrying by through the desolate neighbourhood.

Nina has made herself reasonably comfortable on the second floor of the building in front of which she had parked little more than a week ago. Yesterday afternoon she noticed that she could just about squeeze in under the chain meant to secure the boarded-up doorway and discovered with some surprise that the building seemed free of squatters and drifters. She has been carefully exploring this rundown area of the city by foot over the last few days, leaving her car out of sight some blocks away.

Her investigative excitement has died down quite considerably in that time. What she has been witnessing here among the market stalls has much sobered her up. Amid the inevitable clothes, blankets, matches, fruits and sweets there are carcasses of blue monkeys strapped to wooden poles, the skins of unidentifiable animals stacked next to African tribal drums; there are containers filled with strange powders or hooves, or other things less discernible, stained newspaper parcels over which flies buzz in the heat; all of this is punctuated by the occasional stench of improperly cured meat. The sight of a dried grey head of an ostrich made Nina feel dizzy with revulsion. All the bound-up clumps of dried leaves, roots, bark, pods and seeds might have recalled another era if not for the razor blades and radio batteries, cheap perfumes and plastic toys on sale beside them. Strangely, most of the pedlars themselves appear to be of Indian or Pakistani origin, while the clientele is exclusively black.

It has so far been difficult for her to gauge the full extent of the shack whose open front is draped with a covering of blue plastic sheeting. The numerous shanties in this crumbling wasteland are packed together so densely that the neighbourhood resembles a tin insect hive stuck together with plastic and human will power. She has not yet got close to the shack itself, since a group of young men, bare-chested in this heat, seems always to be hovering by it. They look far too edgy and alert to be part of the aimless humanity that shuffles endlessly through the market.

All the time that she has been lurking in this neighbourhood, she has been wondering which of these men might be Tumi's abominable uncle. The few people she has successfully caught on film hardly correspond to the girl's description.

She watches intently as a silver Honda carefully jumps the kerb and coasts to a standstill in front of the shack. The group of young men reacts hastily, spilling their card game over the upturned wooden crate they have been sitting around. Nina grabs her camera again. The men move forward cautiously, two of them carrying their guns as discreetly as possible.

Out of the car steps a man dressed in olive trousers and a shirt printed gold and black. Four women also climb out, one of them notably obese. Two men, both smartly dressed in dark tailored suits, emerge from the shack to greet the newcomers. One of the two is a huge man with a neck as thick as a tree trunk, the other one is much shorter.

Nina's camera buzzes with a life of its own as the guards return to their card game but do not yet sit down.

Suddenly she hears the ominous rattle of the security chain downstairs. Something heavy falls. Then she hears a voice.

Nina lowers the camera and glances at her mobile, wondering who she could call for help if she is discovered here. *Nobody, probably, since that damn cop hung up on me!*

A wooden tread creaks somewhere on the stairs. A sudden loud burst of children's laughter dances up the stairwell, the chain rattles once again – then there is just the thrum of constant traffic again, as if nothing has happened.

Nina rises slowly to her feet, her heart pounding, and

wonders whether she has indeed been found out – and how she is going to make her way out of the building unnoticed.

35

His hair glittering with wax, his chest radiant with jewellery, Golden Boy – as he is known on the street by most of the Asians he trades with – is renowned for his love of bling-bling. Chewing a toothpick, he watches Sibongile rummaging for a soft drink, before turning his gaze to the three women chatting opposite him, all sitting on upturned plastic crates. The room is dark except for whatever blue-tinged light can seep through the groundsheet draped over the stall's entrance.

The women are talking in Portuguese, all being immigrants from Mozambique. They have acted as his couriers for a year now. This will be their last run – he was bound for that period by an oath of loyalty to himself and to the albino – although Golden Boy is now reluctant to let them go.

Boy is annoyed at having to come here to pick up the merchandise, after last Friday's police operation little more than a mile away. Not that he is worried that anyone would detect the true purpose of this building at a glance. The shack has been cunningly reconstructed, with false walls and frontages concealing all the original recesses and passages below ground, discovered by the albino's men and incorporated into the structure to suit their needs. No, Golden Boy's concern is that his foreign business partners will lose their cool in the neighbourhood. His constant fear is having to face one himself while transporting a car full of prostitutes or abducted children.

'Here.' Sibongile hands him a fresh Coke she has located in a cooler-box.

'Thank you, my lovely.' Boy smiles up at her, one of his canines flashing gold. 'Will you now take care of our ladies, please?'

Sibongile nods and invites the other women to accompany her on a short walk outside. They follow her towards the entrance obediently.

There ensues the sound of a trapdoor opening in the small room adjacent to the one Golden Boy is seated in. Two of the albino's enforcers climb up out of one of the old maintenance shafts running underneath, remnants of the old factory which once stood on this site. They are followed by the albino himself, once again wearing a white *boubou* with beige threading in parallel lines down the front. Adusa and Taiwo position themselves protectively just inside the blue sheeting that conceals them all from outsiders, while Boy clasps and kisses the albino's hands. After the boss sits himself down on the single threadbare couch, they turn to discussing current business in Yoruba.

'Where is Ngubane?' asks Boy, concerned. 'The two Englishmen aren't happy with the situation, as they trusted him.'

The albino sighs. 'Don't worry. Ngubane is safely out of the police's hands for now.'

'They want assurances that their operation is not in danger, since you seem to be losing a great deal of money, my friend, and perhaps influence with it. It looks like the Alexandra crews are moving in on your territory, and El

Hadji's men recently beat the hell out of your girls operating in Melville Road. There are even rumours that people don't fear you any more. With Ngubane's arrest, your shipment confiscated and some of your people facing jail, they're beginning to believe your luck has dried up. These Englishmen, they represent a lot of money to us both.'

The albino blinks rapidly, as if even the dim light filtering into the room is painful to his eyes. 'They don't know our ways, so how can they possibly understand? Yes, there are people who think there's an opportunity to encroach on my business, but they are quickly finding out how wrong they are. Do not get worried about that.' The albino leans forward and shakes his fist for emphasis. 'My power has *never* depended on money, and that's what these Brits don't understand. My fortunes lie with the afterlife, and my purpose is not affected by threats from imbeciles who cannot fathom my true nature. I'll cut anyone down who doesn't remember his place.'

Boy takes a long swig from his Coke can and nods in approval. 'The girls are expecting you to release them now from the pact we made with them. They want to know their souls will be safe when they get to England. But I'd like to keep them longer – they're good couriers.'

'Let them go. Sibongile has others waiting for you. I'm not in a position to break the pledge with them. The spirits oversaw that bond.'

'I'd still rather hang onto them for a bit longer. It's risky now taking on anyone new.'

'It's a far worse risk to strain our relationship with the shadow world. You let them go, you understand?'

Boy gestures his acquiescence.

Another car arrives outside, and Boy jumps up to greet the new arrivals. The albino remains sitting in the hot dark interior of the shack, while his own two men follow the smuggler outside.

One of the Brits has started arguing with Boy even before the dust stirred up by their vehicle settles. 'Let's have two things clear here, guv. We flew a fuckin' long way to meet this bloke Ngubane, and now you're telling me he's *un*available? We're the money in this story, a' right, and if I don't get to speak with Ngubane, you won't be seeing any of our money. And I don't fuckin' care for getting driven out here into a soddin' African slum either. I prefer clean, air-conditioned hotel rooms, guv. I'm too fuckin' important for a pisshole like this. In future *you* come to *me*, understand?' As he speaks, he repeatedly clutches at the crotch of his blue nylon tracksuit. His name, Duff, is tattooed across his knuckles, and a gold St Christopher medal hangs on a chain around his neck.

'OK, I'm sorry to bring you down here, but it's for all our safety.' Boy flashes his golden smile. 'Come in, have something to drink, and we'll talk with the real boss, OK?'

'I don't know, Rhaj,' says Duff, eyeing his partner over the roof of the shimmering green Peugeot that had fetched them. 'This stinks, I reckon. They're up to something.'

His Asian partner, a dyed red beard encircling his mouth, wears large sunglasses perched on a nose as prominent as a vulture's beak. 'It is a bit strange, innit?' he agrees mildly, seeming better able to hide his nervousness. Rhaj is dressed in a Manchester United soccer shirt. 'What you up to, Boy?'

Boy laughs disarmingly. 'Come, let's go inside and get out of the sun. We'll do some business.'

The new arrivals follow the west Africans indoors. When he sees the albino for the first time, Duff takes an instinctive step backwards. 'Jesus, what happened to you?'

Without getting up, the albino motions them to sit down. 'It is merely a gift from the gods,' he replies calmly. 'Welcome.'

'This is the man you've really been dealing with all along,' explains Boy.

'Fuck this, mate,' mutters Duff. 'I'm *not* dealing with the likes of that!'

'Careful.' Adusa's rumble from behind startles the white man. 'You're far from home here.'

'You threatenin' us, guv?' asks Rhaj, now looking incensed. 'Cause if you are, we're packin' up and leavin' right now.'

'Don't worry,' intervenes the albino, although nothing about his demeanour is reassuring. 'We're all friends here, and we're sorry for the change of plans, but recent circumstances have demanded drastic action.'

'Where's that guy Ngubane?' insists Duff.

'Our only concern here should be with the money,' continues the albino.

'Why should I trust you?' says Duff. 'I ain't never even heard about you. What's your name, anyway?'

'My name is not important.'

Rhaj is the first to sit down. 'Chill, mate, we're here to do business. Let's do it quickly, so we can get back to the hotel.'

With a groan Duff throws his hands in the air, then settles himself on one of the crates. 'I'm sitting here on a sodding *box*, Rhaj, is what I'm saying.'

Adusa pulls aside the blue sheeting to let the four women back in. Sibongile and the Mozambicans nod to the newcomers, whom they have encountered before. Sibongile then leads the three prostitutes on into the back room, from where they disappear deeper into the bowels of the complex structure.

'Look, we're prepared to do business as usual, but Boy said on the phone there might be somethin' extra you want transported?' asks Rhaj.

The albino nods towards Taiwo, who hands Duff a thick envelope.

'That is for you personally,' explains the albino, 'if you're prepared to carry some packages back to London for me.'

Duff opens it up and counts the sterling banknotes. Rhaj gives a low whistle.

'What do you want us to take? Guns? Drugs?'

'No, nothing that dangerous. These items are considerable rarities where you come from, and certain people will be willing to pay a high price for them.'

'What are they then?'

'You don't need to know.'

Rhaj insists. 'I'm not fuckin' this trip up by carrying stuff I don't know about. All I do is fly in, check that the couriers flying with me get to the other side and then I go home. If I'm going to carry something, I like to know what it is. That's only fair, innit?'

'Just some powders and oils.'

'What?'

'Made of rare African ingredients.'

'Mate, if it's just beauty products, then why the hell give it to us? No, mate – ' he shakes his head – 'what am I *really* meant to be carrying?'

'Adusa,' commands the albino. The man digs for a moment behind the makeshift counter, then presents Rhaj with a single neat box wrapped up like a birthday present and two coffee bags professionally sealed and labelled.

'Coffee?' Duff takes one of the bags from Adusa and tests its weight in one hand.

'No one will know that it's anything else,' says Boy. 'Security won't be looking out for what you're carrying, so just play it cool.'

'Where's it going?' asks Duff.

Rhaj is blowing nervously over his knuckles. 'Duff, I'm not taking any extra risks. I make enough money to suit me looking after them women and kids.'

'Shu' up,' says Duff. Still weighing the bag in his hand, he is eyeing the money. 'Another five hundred – ' he shoves a nervous cigarette in his mouth – 'each.'

'No,' growls the albino.

'What?' asks Rhaj. 'You hear me, Duff? I'm saying I'm not doing it. What's the matter? I thought *you* didn't trust him?'

'Fuck it, it's money. And if we're gonna do this, we might as well do it proper. You know, kill two birds with one stone, and all that.' To the albino he says, 'No, mate, I'm not carrying this stuff for anything less.'

The albino's nose flares and his neck swells up, making him look, if possible, more sinister. 'Five hundred between the two of you.'

Duff stares at him for a moment, taking a deep drag of his cigarette. 'Aye, mate, it's all right. We'll do it that way, then. Five hundred.'

'Good,' says the albino.

After the money is checked and the packages are handed to the two British couriers, Rhaj lifts his shirt and removes a bundle strapped to his body, which turns out to be a serious wad of US dollars. 'Here you go, guv. Pretty, innit? Now, can we fucking get out of this place? It's too hot in here; I don't know how you stand it.'

'You will please wait patiently. I have to prepare the women first, and the children will then be brought to them shortly.'

The albino disappears into the rear, in the direction he first came from, leaving his two enforcers with Boy and the English visitors.

Duff gets up and starts pacing again, managing to sneak a look into the back room the albino entered. He turns to Boy. 'Oi, where they all got to?'

Boy just smiles and shrugs; the enforcers say nothing.

Someone suddenly calls to Adusa from outside, one of the guards who was playing cards earlier on. After Adusa lets him in, they converse in hushed tones just inside the entrance, until the man gives a nod and disappears again. All the people in the room look at Adusa expectantly, but he whispers only to Taiwo.

It is nearly half an hour before the albino returns with Sibongile. Accompanying them are the three Mozambican women, their faces smeared with some white substance. Two have eyes shining with tears of gratitude. Three children, a boy and two girls, accompany them. Aged between eight and eleven, they are dressed in fresh clothing and look well fed and clean. The youngsters seem wide-eyed and grateful, already bonding with the three women who will pretend to be their mothers for a short while, before abandoning them to ruthless strangers in a strange land.

36

For a long time Nina remained frozen, uncertain whether she should attempt escape or stay where she was and wait it out. In the end she stayed on the upper floor, nervously scanning out the window to check for any sign of those kids bolting across the street to warn the guards about her presence in the building opposite.

Eventually her decision was rewarded. With ever more people arriving at the shack she was spying on, she managed a number of good shots of them without further interruption.

Much later, the day drawing to an end, and after everyone seems to have left the shack, she packs up, preparing to leave. Even inside her vantage point, the air is heavy with exhaust fumes. As she shoulders her bag and heads downstairs, her mind turns to the cop again. She was surprised as much by his English accent as his severe rebuttal of her approach.

At the boarded-up entrance Nina holds her breath and listens intently. After a minute she pushes the boarding open as far as it will go and peers outside in all directions. Reassured, she squeezes herself through the narrow gap. She hurries up the derelict street, heading towards her car, which is parked a few blocks east outside a vehicle parts shop. She tosses her equipment into the boot before unlocking the door and falling into the driver's seat with a sigh of relief.

It is only as she is turning the ignition that she notices a movement out of the corner of her eye. She looks up just as a gun butt smashes through the side window. Glass sprays over her, and she stalls the engine in shock.

Hands quickly tear open the door and drag her out of the vehicle. She struggles desperately, but the giant she saw earlier has her arms pinned to her sides with a vice-like grip.

'Let go of me, you *fuck*!' she screams.

She notices a few frightened-looking bystanders, but no one reacts.

Her attacker's smaller partner comes into view and unlocks the boot with her car keys. Nina is quickly stuffed inside it, suddenly plunged into a claustrophobic darkness. Soon after the boot is slammed shut, the car starts up and makes a rapid U-turn.

No! Dear God, don't let this happen!

After a short journey involving a series of turns which utterly confuses her, the car comes to a halt. She hears footsteps on gravel and the key sliding into the car boot. As the lock springs, she tries to fight her way out. But her captors move faster: one hand seizes her by the upper arm, another by the throat and Nina is lifted clear. The leaner of two suited men is standing nearby with a wicked grin. She lashes out with her foot and connects viciously with his shin.

The man cries out, grabbing at his leg. He yells something to his colleague that she cannot understand. The grip intensifies on both her throat and arm.

'You *bastards* . . . let me *go*!' Nina manages to thrust an elbow hard into the giant man holding her, but her blow is totally absorbed by solid muscle.

Looking around, she sees she is back in the shanty town. A radio is blasting Lucky Dube close by.

'Shut up, you bitch,' growls a voice close to her ear. A big arm hugs her tightly across the chest, squashing her breast painfully and minimizing her power of movement. 'Shut up or I'll *really* hurt you.'

They enter a shop lit by a paraffin lamp standing in one corner. The proprietor nods cheerfully at her captors, saying something in an African language. The big man holding her laughs, but his smaller friend, somewhere behind them, is still grumbling with pain.

Nina screams for help again. This time she is dropped to the floor and whirled around. A heavy hand slaps her across the face. The force of it stuns her, causing her eyes to water and her ears to ring.

'I told you to shut up!' the massive one snarls.

A wooden trapdoor is raised and she is pushed down makeshift stairs into complete darkness, the two men following closely. The corridor before her is narrow, running between bare brick walls. Its ceiling is barely higher than her head. Though the air is cool, it is thick with dust. Soon she begins to cough and sneeze.

Nina is eventually shoved into a small room opening to her left, where candles and a paraffin lamp have already been lit. The big man's hands press down on her shoulders, forcing Nina to kneel. The smaller one, who she notices has prominently slashed scars around the eyes, examines her closely in the candlelight, causing her to look away in fear.

It is in those eyes of his that she realizes how bad things are going to get.

When a woman lumbers into the room, Nina feels a glimmer of hope. Maybe, just *maybe*, this woman might stop the worst of what is to come. But when her protuberant eyes briefly meet Nina's, the young journalist sees there is no hope.

Out of the darkness behind the newcomer appears another face. Though smiling, barely illuminated, his face is more obscenely grotesque than any she has ever seen. Nina instantly recognizes the albino from Tumi's account. She begins to shiver violently.

All the newspaper articles she has read, all the violence she has researched over the last two months, invade her mind in a rush. She knows that now she is facing the real thing.

Her slighter-built captor steps forward to hand the *baloyi* her belongings. The albino switches his gaze from Nina to the film he begins to pull out of her camera. His glance moves back to her and then to her wallet. Each time they make eye contact, Nina flinches.

'So, Nina Reading,' begins the witch in a deep, almost hungry voice, 'are you going to explain why you were taking photographs of us with this camera?'

37

The red Toyota Corolla coasts off the road onto the hard shoulder, halting fifty yards before an unlit T-junction. There it turns its headlights off. While the occupants wait in the darkness, the clouds that have been gathering all day burst like a dam wall, the deluge wiping out all visibility. Large raindrops smack onto the windscreen like bullets.

Taiwo cocks his Kalashnikov to the sound of thunder echoing in the hills of Roodepoort. He exchanges a meaningful glance with his partner.

A number of cars some distance behind them pull off onto the shoulder as well, not daring to continue driving in this storm.

'Are they going to be a problem?' asks Adusa, though barely able to discern the other vehicles' headlights in his rear-view mirror.

'Not in this weather. Actually it's better this way. Just

us stopping here could make someone suspicious, but with a whole bunch of other cars waiting for this rain to stop, he'll never know. They can't see shit anyway. That suits me fine.' Taiwo positions his rifle more comfortably across his lap.

'What if it lets up suddenly?'

'Then we'll have to follow him if he goes past.' Taiwo laughs and strokes his AK-47 lovingly. 'Relax, you get in close enough to him with this big machine, nothing's left. I'll make it short and sweet.'

Lightning flickers across the sky, briefly illuminating the scene around them. This isolated off-ramp, cutting through the side of a hill, follows a long curve down to the traffic light at the junction.

'Didn't take us long to find out who he is,' says Adusa.

'Nobody likes a nosy cop,' answers Taiwo. 'Especially racist fucks like this one, as I've been told. Sipho comes through for us so often, I just wish we had someone like him in Murder and Robbery, too. That would help me sleep a lot better at night, knowing that I have another little helper.'

The two men fall quiet for a few moments, watching water crash onto the windscreen.

'You think that English bitch was telling the truth?' asks Taiwo.

'I don't care,' mutters Adusa.

Taiwo laughs. 'I haven't seen you get worked up like that in a long time.'

Adusa looks at his partner. 'No one kicks *me*, least of all a slut like her.' His angry eyes seem to glow in the darkness.

The storm eases up after half an hour. Soon a few of the parked cars start up and go trundling past them.

'Hmm, might have to follow him home after all,' says Taiwo.

Adusa's mobile trills and he answers it. After a short exchange he says, 'He's coming up the ramp now.'

Taiwo glances at his watch, then turns in his seat to look over his shoulder. 'Right on time,' he murmurs.

Adusa starts up the car. Though the rain is still gushing down, they notice a car that has been parked behind them get back onto the road. It passes them at a crawl, and a minute later a fresh column of vehicles rolls down the off-ramp and takes the gradual curve leading down towards the junction.

'You see him yet?'

'No,' says Taiwo, his voice sounding distant. 'Be patient.'

The traffic light turns green, and the unwanted vehicles soon disappear off to the left and right. Moments later, the headlights of a single car appear behind them. A grey Opel Kadette passes them, its driver clearly unconcerned about a car still sheltering at the roadside from the downpour. The traffic light then turns red however, and the driver stops.

'That's him,' says Taiwo. In one deft movement, he throws his door open, steps out of the car and, holding the assault rifle close to his side, hurries down the road and moves round the halted vehicle on the passenger's side. He stops dead centre in front of the Opel. The rifle finds his shoulder just as a white face, blurred behind the rain running down the windscreen, leans forward to squint out at him.

The weapon kicks viciously against Taiwo's shoulder as he fires a long burst at the driver's head and chest. The

211

high-velocity attack tears golf-ball-sized holes into the glass before it caves in completely.

The bright orange gun flashes finish, and Taiwo squints inside through the pouring rain. 'Shit,' he says in mild surprise.

Inside the car, Sergeant André Viljoen, from the Dog Unit, is miraculously still alive, though his fat chest looks like a bloody sieve. Taiwo comes up alongside the car, shoves his rifle through the collapsed glass and snarls, 'You arseholes just never learn, do you?'

'What?' the dying man gasps.

'You tried to lean on the *wrong* people, motherfucker.'

The rifle cracks again and Viljoen's body convulses one final time.

Adusa pulls the car up next to Taiwo just as fresh headlights appear in the distance behind them. The assassin throws open the passenger door and leaps in. Their Toyota has disappeared around another bend before anyone can realize that the driver of the Opel in front of them will never again care whether the light has turned green and he can proceed.

38

The next seven days see the Murder and Robbery Unit buzzing with activity, while its morale drops to an all-time low. The ferocious ambush of Inspector André Viljoen on his way home on Tuesday night has everyone now looking over their shoulder, even more so because there is no clear reason for the crime. All leave is cancelled until further notice. The two partners' coordination of interviews with the hundreds of traditional healers and muti shop proprietors moves forward only by inches. A couple of hurried search-and-seizures yield arrests of various gang members, confiscations of unregistered weapons, small amounts of drugs, as well as stolen cars and goods – everything, in fact, except Ngubane Maduna. In the opinion of detectives on the streets, these searches are poorly planned, more public-relations gimmicks than anything else. Also, they seem to be driving any potentially key figures in their investigations deeper underground.

The media coverage of Mason and Tshabalala's emotive case leads to a breakthrough when two motorists separately report seeing a Chevrolet parked on the highway's shoulder near where the child's body was eventually found. But newspaper reportage, including a release of statistics claiming up to six hundred children disappear annually in occult-related cases, does nothing to stem the influx of increasingly twisted and utterly useless phone calls the unit is forced to take, and then investigate, daily.

Among these phone calls is one from a hysterical white Sandton housewife who claims she has found a curse tucked neatly under her mattress. She is therefore convinced that her eighteen-year-old housekeeper is the killer and that the muti found in her house was made from the same murdered girl. Asked why she thinks so, she answers, '*Yissus*, man, what do you take me for? God knows, I recognize human ash when I see it. Anyway, the little bitch looks at my kids funny, too, so I've been watching her. I've also been getting these strange pains in my abdomen and my knees, which my doctor can't explain. Isn't that enough?'

Besides such colourful claims, more credible ones come in. Suddenly Ngubane Maduna is cropping up everywhere, and everyone's neighbour is either a witch or has paid a *baloyi* to curse this or that individual with muti concocted from human organs. On Wednesday a serious incident occurs when an innocent woman's house is surrounded by a lynch mob, clamouring for a necklacing. A group of women collecting money in the vicinity for the Love Life Aids charity manages to keep the crowd at bay until the police finally show up. When the threatened woman is taken to safety and inquiries are made, no one in the crowd can explain for sure why she is suspected of being a witch. All any of them could do was repeat the same rumours: she is a monstrous Zimbabwean who has already eaten four children, yet the police have refused to do anything about it.

Although Harry and Jacob managed to bury the hatchet, after their conflict on the police station roof, their truce is uneasy and they prefer to work alone. Every single possible lead is followed up. On the Wednesday, late afternoon, Harry is finally contacted by Tienie Fourie from the Child Protection Unit providing a list of all the children gone missing on the West Rand. Her results are shocking.

'*Thirty?*' blurts Harry. 'Thirty little girls aged between age four and eight?'

'No, detective. There is ten of the childrens that is girls. The rest is boys, but I thought I should tell you about them, too. It's not only the girls that get murdered for muti, first-born boys are favourites, too.'

The meticulous task of interviewing the parents of these missing children begins immediately, as regional police officers are organized to help with taking statements. Naturally the priority is to identify the murdered girl. It is heartbreaking work.

Reports and statements swell into mountains of documentation that make even Jacob's normally clean desk look like a paper mill. But the chaos in the bureau does not nearly reflect the chaos erupting in the station detectives' personal lives. With the knives of the area commissioner and his director of detectives constantly hanging over the heads of the various units, and with the memory of André being mown down on his way home, the officers are working overtime. Meanwhile three more men are killed in a bloodbath. This time they are the owners of a notorious rave club in Randburg, who turn out to be ex-narcotics detectives who had embarked on their own venture, officially as club promoters, but unofficially as ecstasy distributors, after having been summarily dismissed from the force on corruption charges back in the mid-nineties.

Jacob manages to find time to visit the old witness in hospital and even manages to make peace with his daughter and her brothers by securing an officer to guard their father while he recuperates. He, however, fails to make that phone call home which he promised his mother, and Nomsa barely sees him now as he buries himself in mountains of paperwork, mostly the statements taken by other detectives or desk sergeants. His mind frequently wanders back to that day in the riverbed when he forced André to take charge of the parcel with the fetish inside it. The detective shivers at the thought that he may have condemned the dog handler to death by passing the curse on to him.

Harry gets home late every night, but he cannot sleep. He too keeps thinking back to the last time he spoke with André Viljoen, at the same crime scene. He has nightmares in which all the other police officers present at the scene die, too, shrivelling up as if sucked dry by some unseen force. Twice he wakes up in the night with a start, thinking he might have heard something moving outside. Harry cannot shake the feeling that someone or something may be stalking him now. His constant checking on his daughter keeps Amy awake, too, wondering what her husband knows that she does not. What scares her most of all is the loaded gun he now insists on keeping openly on his bedside table.

39

On Monday night at 7.25 p.m. Harry is on his way home when his mobile rings.

'Mason, Kobus here. I have something for you.'

'What?'

'You know that Nigerian family massacred three weeks ago? A neighbour now remembers that he spotted the father using one of the lock-up garages there one evening. Guess what we found when we opened it up?'

'Tell me,' Harry demands eagerly.

'A car fitting exactly the description of the one your witnesses noticed standing by the side of the highway on the twenty-second of October. A grey Chevy.'

Harry slams on his brakes. 'I'm there in ten minutes. Just give me the address.'

He parks outside a Pick 'n' Pay which is busy closing up and looks up at a block of apartments facing onto Pretoria Street. It seems like every balcony is piled high with stuff that rightly belongs at a jumble sale. Many of the windows are cracked, and the walls are stained black where burst piping has been leaking for years over the baby-blue paint. Bobby Gous and Kobus Niehaus approach by the concrete path accessing the parking space located behind the apartment block.

'The technicians are busy inspecting the car right now,' explains Kobus, 'but we've found a few interesting things already. Let me show you.'

'What else do you know about that Nigerian family?' Harry follows his colleagues up the ramp.

'Bugger all,' says Bobby. 'All five of them were living crammed into a bachelor apartment the size of a sardine can, they paid rent in cash and they liked to keep to themselves. They were civil to the neighbours, but there were frequent rows with the seventeen-year-old son. The people that lived next door couldn't follow a word, though, as they didn't understand their language.

'Several descriptions and the family's travel documents confirm that a seven-year-old was living there as well. He's the one that's still missing though: the mother, father, sister and elder son are all dead and accounted for. They had a regular visitor, it seems, but the description of the man is vague. One neighbour assumed he must be a relative, but he certainly didn't live here with them.

'The other neighbour I mentioned on the phone says he noticed the father helping this same guy park his car in one of the empty garages. That happened the same week the family was killed. He claims the unknown guy looked very distressed. Since then, the landlord insists he didn't give them permission to use the garage. When we got to inspect it, we found the lock had been forced.'

Kobus interrupts his colleague just as they round the corner of the block, and Harry sees a glow of bright light from where the technicians are working on the car discovered. 'I think you found your victim in the week after

217

this car was left here. The Nigerian family was gunned down shortly after one in the morning, Thursday 24 October. That's close enough time-wise for me to believe this unknown character killed the girl and dumped her, went into a flat panic and then persuaded his acquaintances here to stash the car. He then maybe thought it was too risky for the family to know what he'd done and so he swung by again to pay them one last deadly visit.

'We checked the four of them out with Internal Affairs. There's no record of their being awarded refugee status, nor receiving permission to reside in this country. Illegal immigrants, therefore. I don't want to sound like I'm stereotyping here, but if they were here illegally, it probably means they were trafficking in coke or H, maybe even something else. These types of people are often smuggled in over the borders by the drug gangs, who then make them work for them to repay what they owe.'

'Damn it! What the hell's going on?' snarls Harry. 'The whole of this bloody month's been full of silences and people we can't seem to trace.'

Bobby shrugs. 'That's what happens when you get a large migrant population no one can really keep track of – and that's not counting all the refugees. There are thousands jumping our borders from every damn country between here and Timbuktu.'

They come to a stop at the garage entrance. 'We're going to impound the vehicle as soon as we've got from it as much as we can find. In the meantime, you'll like this.' Kobus walks over to the pile of evidence being tagged and bagged outside the garage door. 'This blanket here is a likely bet: we've found traces of blood on it. And then there's this.' Kobus scoops up the battered .22 Smith and Wesson. 'It hasn't been fired recently, so I'm not sure what it signifies. The family was killed with larger calibres, 9 mm's and .38s.'

'We'll have to try and get a better description of this man who visited them,' says Harry, squatting down to examine the blanket. 'I'll want to speak to everyone here that might've encountered him. Let's hope the vehicle registration number gives us a clue at least.'

'It must've been last registered when dinosaurs still walked the earth,' chirps one of the techies. 'There's also a Ford engine inside, and the whole thing is one big jury rig. Ten to one this bucket was assembled in a chop-shop or rebuilt in someone's backyard out in the townships. Naturally there aren't any papers in the glove box.'

'This definitely looks like the one,' murmurs Harry. 'Fibres the same colour as this blanket were lifted from the victim's hair. It doesn't matter too much how old that registration sticker is. We can trace the last official owner and take it from there.'

'Hey, you guys really think he killed the Nigerian family as well?' asks Bobby.

Harry looks down doubtfully at the gun, the blanket, and then over at the car the new suspect left behind. 'I don't think so. Someone went to great lengths to clean that little girl up before she was dumped. That's rare in these cases. And why would the guy clean her up so carefully, then just leave his car here, right beside where the massacre occurred? That doesn't make sense. Jeez, nothing about this case makes sense so far.'

Harry inspects the car for a few more minutes, chatting to the techies, yet does not come up with any more than he has already learnt.

'Tell me something, Kobus.' Harry offers round his packet of Lucky Strikes. 'You mentioned that something was still bugging you about the decapitation here in Hill-brow. Any further light on that subject?'

'Oh, sorry, *boet*, I clean forgot about that. I keep meaning to look up some old case files, but . . .' Kobus rubs his forehead and suddenly looks a hundred years old. 'I'm just so fucking tired of this *kak*. This month has been hell.'

'I know. You don't need to remind me.'

The two men smoke in silence, watching while Bobby Gous signals for the tow truck to haul the evidence away down the narrow access route. Kobus remarks, '*Weet jy*, Harry, the last time I felt like this was during the goddamn war. I was barely as old as him then, and I had a *kak* time on that border, let me tell you, *boet*.'

Mason exhales smoke. 'Yes . . . well, this whole bloody city is looking like a war zone at the moment, and I think we're all starting to feel like you do – some more than others.'

40

The wood is dripping with rainwater, the light has turned yellow and the trees look greener, the earth even muddier. A sharp smell of rotting roots hangs in the air. Harry shivers; the air's summer warmth has been sapped. His soaked underwear chafes uncomfortably as he scrambles to his feet.

Surely someone else must have heard the scream and reacted by now? It occurs to Harry that the world is frozen in time, holding its breath and waiting for *him* to do something.

'Roger, *please* come out,' he whispers.

'*No!*' whispers Roger. 'You go and check!'

Harry creeps away through a patch of long grass. He

reaches his father's ordained boundary – the muddy bridle path – and crosses back into safer ground. Conscious of being very exposed, he hurries across the clearing towards the footpath beyond, which is thankfully overhung by a thick growth of oak and holly. That path will eventually take him within a short distance of home.

As Harry reaches the footpath his feet splash to a stop. Underneath the silent canopy of the trees a repetitive sound echoes through the wet undergrowth. Over to his left somewhere, a shovel is crunching into earth.

Harry wavers, wanting to turn away from the sound. Before he can decide what is best to do, he is creeping through undergrowth. Moments pass while he moves forward, then he freezes as the shovelling suddenly stops. Strangely he feels calmer, his attention now focused on discovering what is going on.

Through the wet foliage Harry begins to distinguish the bulk of a man in a heavy black overcoat. The man grunts as his shovel again crunches deep into the soft ground. Without noticing the watching boy, he throws a load of mud directly in Harry's direction. The big man's efforts are hurried and frantic.

It is the same Morwargh man they watched beating his daughter.

A scuffed yellow shoe catches Harry's eye. It is lying next to the fat man's foot. The boy hesitates, then lies down in the mud and crawls to one side, anxious to see what lies behind the mound of excavated soil.

Suddenly he hears a furious roar. Harry looks up just in time to see the shovel aiming towards him. The man jumps over the pile of mud, ready to take a swing.

Harry scrambles backward, then leaps up and runs. The shovel narrowly misses his head and splinters a sapling.

Harry keeps running, belting through the foliage. Suddenly he is out in the open again.

'Roger!' he yells. 'Roger, watch out!'

Close behind him branches snap violently and spur the boy on. Without even thinking, Harry runs towards his recent hideaway.

That is when he slips on the wet grass.

His feet fly out in front of him and he lands hard on his coccyx. The breath is knocked out of him as agony tears through his back.

And still the fat Morwargh is thrashing his way through the bushes. Harry drags himself on, gasping, stars erupting in his vision. He makes it to the hideout just in time.

Roger is not there.

Harry turns around inside his refuge and pokes his head back out.

Where has Roger got to?

A small figure suddenly shoots past the entrance. 'Harry!' screams Roger. 'Harry, where are you?' He stops dead in the clearing, peering around him. Then, hearing the foliage snapping behind him, Roger whips round.

The Morwargh's bulk crashes out of the undergrowth. Roger looks up in confusion – just as the edge of the shovel is driven deep into his collarbone. The boy drops immediately, like a severed fruit.

Harry begins to screech hysterically.

41

Jacob's house phone begins ringing an hour before dawn, the sound of it shattering a peaceful dream. Yawning, he swings his legs out of the bed. He gives Nomsa's arm a quick, affectionate stroke before he makes his way into the living room.

'What?' he asks gruffly, picking up the receiver.

'Jacob?' A troubled old woman's voice replies.

At first he thinks it is his mother, then he recognizes Hettie Solilo. Suddenly Jacob is wide awake, his flesh crawling with premonition. '*Magogo*, why are you phoning this early? What's happened?'

'You better come quick.'

'Are you in trouble? Is it them again?'

'No . . . I don't know. You better just come. It's horrible.'

Speeding down the abandoned early-dawn road, Jacob nearly collides with a donkey cart transporting four youths. The encounter forces him to relax and slow down. He wonders whether his father might have died but his family did not feel at ease with phoning him directly. His mother had warned him that his father was ill.

At 6.00 a.m., with the sun already risen and the dew nothing more than a scent on the wind, Jacob finally turns into Hettie Solilo's familiar street. He immediately spots the small crowd gathered outside her house. Coming to a stop, Jacob jumps out and pushes his way through the group, noticing how their expressions are all drawn and grim. A slow, rhythmic wailing ebbs and flows from the house itself, causing Jacob's hair to stand up. At Hettie's front gate a tall, shaven-headed, middle-aged man attempts to keep him back with the rest of those assembled, but Mama Poleng, who is sitting stooped and alone on the wooden bench, waves Jacob in with a heavy hand.

'What happened, Mama?' he asks, approaching her up the short garden path.

'Go inside. She will show you.' Mama Poleng shakes her head bitterly.

Jacob enters the house and discovers the kitchen full of young men. A few of them hold traditional weapons such as knobkerries, sjamboks and assegais. They greet him solemnly, and Jacob hastens past them towards the mournful singing coming from the living room. There he finds just a handful of people, the women amongst them producing the slow, sad dirge. Wrapped in full traditional garb, Hettie Solilo is kneeling beside her altar, on which red candles and incense are burning. The ancient *inyanga* slowly sways from side to side, as if drunk, keeping her hands cupped over her face. Jacob notices the thick blanket-enveloped bundle on the floor in front of her.

'*Magogo?*' asks Jacob gently.

The keening does not cease as Hettie removes her hands and looks up at him with tearful eyes. 'How could they do this? What purpose does it serve?'

Jacob approaches slowly and squats down next to her. She gestures for him to investigate the bundle. One of Hettie's *thwasas* abruptly skitters from the room and they all stop singing altogether.

Jacob carefully pulls open first the left fold, then the right. He sighs loudly and drops his head in despair.

Harry has been awake since four o'clock, unable to sleep but also unable to concentrate on the various witness statements he brought home the previous evening to work through. His mind keeps skipping back to that woman with the English accent who phoned him last week. She had claimed she could help, but he had rudely hung up on her. He now cannot believe he just slammed the phone down on her. What the hell had been wrong with him?

BLOODY HARVESTS

His dreams have become increasingly bizarre and violent. Once or twice he has woken with the impression of hearing a shovel biting into the soft earth out in his yard, but he subsequently cannot be sure whether he heard this noise while dreaming or awake. During the past night he had a dream of which he can now only remember that it caused him to wake screaming and sweating, lashing out so violently that Amy leaped from their bed. It took him nearly a quarter of an hour to calm down, and only after his wife had switched on both the lights and the television.

Harry shakes his head in disbelief and lights a cigarette, staring at the statements laid out in front of him without actually registering them. Tendrils of smoke crawl through the yellow halo cast around Harry's face by the desk light. The small study is quiet except for a low electrical hum from Amy's laptop. Pretty soon the ash on Harry's cigarette grows into a long grey curl waiting to fall off at his slightest movement.

When the kitchen phone rings, Harry spills both ash and coffee over himself in his hurry to get to it before the shrill clamour can wake the rest of the household. He is surprised to hear Jacob's voice sounding shocked. When Harry hears his partner's news, what little colour is left in his face drains away completely.

The drive to Soweto takes about forty minutes in the heavy workday traffic, during which time Harry runs over in his mind the few firm facts so far. On Monday 27 October the naked body of a murdered seven-year-old girl is found in a dry riverbed off the N1 highway's western bypass. The organs specifically removed suggest a muti killing. Either the murderer had wanted to concoct his own medicines, or else he had intended to sell the essences derived from these body parts to others. The girl clearly had been malnourished, so might have come from a broken home or right off the street. She had been skilfully kept alive during the surgical removal of her organs, then bled to death.

A fetish found nearby the corpse is the only object that can be definitely linked to the unidentified child. So far they know only that the blood contained in the fetish and the girl's blood are of the same type. The reports due on the DNA samples and stomach contents are still outstanding.

Anxious parents from all over the Witwatersrand have been contacting the Murder and Robbery Unit, wondering whether the girl was theirs, but comparing the information provided by them with the few characteristics known for sure about the body offers nothing to suggest any positive identification. This leaves Harry more and more irritable, because the continued failure to establish an identity increasingly suggests that the girl's family themselves might have been involved in her murder. That could mean the corpse will remain unidentified, so her killers may go unpunished for ever.

The strands tying any suspects to the case are equally fragile. Different aspects of it point to different people. There is Ngubane Maduna, who shot that *sangoma*, then the gang Jacob accosted at Hettie Solilo's, and the unknown driver of the car Niehaus discovered the night before. Even the dead *sangoma* himself is a faint possibility. Try as he might, Harry cannot construct a working hypothesis he feels confident about from the evidence collected so far.

Harry takes the Klipspruit Valley thoroughfare into Soweto, passing Avalon Cemetery on his left. It is a vast expanse without a single tree, without even a single patch of green, just a great dry expanse of fine red dust surrounding thousands of crosses and gravestones. This is Harry's first visit here travelling by himself; it is unnerving him, and Amy would throw a fit if she knew where he was heading.

Even after all these years the townships remain bewildering and mysterious places for him, the Englishman's uneasiness stemming from his earlier years spent in the service of the former apartheid police state. The country has come a long way since then, but as a white man – never mind a white police officer – he still experiences a range of emotions whenever heading into one of these segregated communities. Chief among these feelings is remorse, but also awe, uncertainty and fear.

The tarmacked streets are easy enough to follow, but then the potholed tracks begin, as the newer, more affluent districts give way to crude state-built housing, and finally moving into the older districts crammed with shacks and rickety outhouses. Harry is becoming ever less sure of where he is going. Fifteen minutes driving, however, bring him into a newer neighbourhood, where directions can be followed by street signs rather than landmarks. Glancing from side to side, he drives along a narrow dirt road at a crawl. Now and again he meets gazes that seem hostile, although he has no sure reason for believing that. Finally, spotting two white-and-blue police pickups and a large crowd gathered outside, Harry feels sure he has found Hettie Solilo's house.

As the detective steps out of his pickup he immediately senses the crowd's edginess. Harry hurries over on shaking legs: in the past he has witnessed restless mobs such as this grow deadly. He presses his way through the crowd before coming up against a chicken-wire fence. Three burly types stand at the rusty white gate, casually brandishing weapons by their sides.

'I'm looking for Inspector Tshabalala,' grunts Harry.

'Yes,' intones one of the men slowly, 'you are Harry?'

The detective is about to head on through when a voice yells, 'When you police going to do your jobs *properly?*' Other voices mutter in agreement.

Harry turns around and stares at them incredulously. 'We're here now, aren't we?'

A middle-aged woman with large pink curlers in her hair pipes up. 'Yes, *now*, but we must always wait. And things always happen again in the meantime.'

'We're doing the best we can,' protests Harry.

Jeers greet this answer. A man in his early twenties wearing a bright yellow Pan African Congress T-shirt pushes his way to the front of the crowd. 'Go home, *Boer*, go back to Europe. What do you know about Soweto, anyway?'

'All right, just stay calm.' Harry holds up his hands. 'Police work takes time. With your cooperation, it'll go faster.'

More catcalling erupts.

'I tell you, *Boer*,' threatens the man in the T-shirt, 'just take that *dog* of yours and leave. It's all because of him that this happened to the Old One. He's a disgrace to his family and he's brought his bad luck into her house. So take him and his bad luck with you, and *go!*'

'What are you talking about?' demands Harry, puzzled.

But the young man merely hawks and spits on the sand by Harry's feet.

'Harry! In here,' shouts Jacob from behind him.

Harry turns around to see his partner standing in the doorway beckoning. Two local officers file out to join Hettie's protectors at the gate.

In the kitchen Harry finds a third officer who is interviewing a man sitting opposite him at the Formica-topped table. A cup of tea stands where Jacob must have been sitting. Harry's partner now directs him along a narrow hallway towards the living room. The dirge has long since stopped, and the room is now empty except for Hettie's three *thwasas* seated with bowed heads near the sad bundle, which has been covered up again. Her eyes firmly closed, Hettie performs a slow, laborious shuffle around the wrapped-up blanket, rasping a chant uncertainly from her throat. She is shaking her *ichoba* emphatically over the bundle, its buffalo hair whisking wildly this way and that.

'We must wait until her purification is finished,' whispers Jacob, pulling Harry back into the hallway.

'Isn't that the job of a *sangoma*?' Harry peers round the edge of the door again, spellbound by the ritual, never having seen anything like it before. The old woman is barefoot, wearing a red skirt with a *kaross* wrapped around her narrow shoulders. Beads encircle her head like a simple crown, from which one cowrie shell dangles over her forehead, one over the nape of her neck and one over each ear. Pouches of herbs are woven into bandoliers that criss-cross her chest. Similar woven satchets are attached around her waist and to the hemline of her skirt.

Harry is entranced by the sombreness of her appearance, her air of nobility and her venerable beauty.

'In a pinch, the lines between the healers blur. The child must be blessed as soon as possible if there is to be any hope for its soul,' says Jacob.

Turning his gaze to the bundle Harry sighs. 'So it's another one?'

Jacob merely nods.

The two men retreat further back into the passage, where Harry describes in a whisper his encounter with the PAC supporter outside. 'What was he talking about?' he demands.

In the dim light, Harry notices Jacob's face crawling with anger and shame. 'It's nothing. That idiot has *no* idea what he's talking about.'

Jacob abruptly turns away and returns to observe the ongoing interview in the kitchen. It is the first time Harry has ever experienced his partner acting so evasive – which leads him to wonder again about Mitchell's cryptic innuendos.

42

When Hettie Solilo finishes, she turns and gestures for the two cops to enter; then she herds her three pupils out of the room. The men are left alone with the body and each other. Harry steels himself. Approaching the blanket, he crouches down next to it and pulls it aside.

'Oh, *Jee-sus*!'

After a moment Jacob explains, 'At about four thirty this morning Hettie and some of the men staying here overnight were woken up by the sound of a car slamming on its brakes outside. Doors were opened and closed hurriedly, but by the time anyone here got to the front window there was just a cloud of dust as the car went spinning off. They say it was a red vehicle, although no one can confirm whether it was that same M3 BMW seen on previous occasions.

'They rushed outside but at first saw nothing. Then Zukile – the tall one with the shaven head – spotted the head lying in the flower bed, up against the wall of the house. The rest of the body was lying under the peach tree. They must've tossed it over the fence like a sack of corn, leaving it behind as some gruesome message.'

Harry stares at the severed head – the face barely recognizable as that of a young boy, silently screaming at him. The damage here is far worse than that inflicted on the little girl found in the riverbed.

'This corpse can't be more than a day old,' mutters Jacob, squatting next to Harry, 'and his skin colour is too dark for him to be a South African. He must be from far up north somewhere.'

'What does that matter? What can it bloody well matter when this is all that's left of him?' exclaims Harry, still in shock.

The mutilation is so extensive that it is hard to think of this corpse as human. It reminds Harry more of a side of meat lying in some abattoir. He fumbles for his cigarettes, but his fingers encounter the container of pills instead. When he shakes out two and pops them into his mouth, he draws a reproachful stare from his partner. Finally finding his cigarettes, Harry lights up, turning to look at Jacob with haunted eyes. 'I mean, what do they want with *all* of his innards? And did they *have* to sever the head after digging around in it?'

'There's a reason for that.' Jacob pulls out a pair of latex gloves and snaps them on. He grabs the head and rolls it slightly away from the body, so he can inspect the damage at its base more closely. As he sticks a finger into the hole, he grimaces.

'What the *hell* are you doing?' demands Harry.

Jacob nods to himself, realigning the head with the body. 'The atlas bone is missing, too.'

'The *what*?' asks Harry.

'The atlas bone is the topmost vertebra, linking the body to the head itself. Since it connects the brain, or mind, with the rest of the body it is believed to be the seat of the soul. Hence it is considered the most powerful and sacred element in the whole body.'

'Where's the rest of it, then?' asks Harry, letting his eyes roam over the corpse. 'Have you checked whether bits of it are still lying around outside?'

Jacob pulls an ugly face. 'Yes, of course we have, but we won't ever find the rest of this child. Everything has been taken. This boy wasn't killed just for a specific ritual. He was murdered for the harvesting of *all* his muti-significant organs.'

The two detectives stare at each other in the fresh morning light that filters through the windows. The red candles are still burning close by.

Harry speaks first. 'It's time we sat Hettie down and grilled her.'

'Harry, you can't just *grill* someone of her status. You must—'

'Look at this child! Take a good look at that before you tell me to back off. We've postponed talking to her for long enough.'

From behind them comes a voice that rustles like papyrus. 'There is no need for any of that in my house,' says Hettie. 'We will talk, but not in this room. That child has suffered enough in life. Let him sleep now in peace.'

43

The kitchen is hot, mainly due to a massive pot of oats popping and bubbling sloppily on the stove. The other three officers have also crowded into the kitchen, and they lean attentively against the walls and work counters. One of them is the detail selected from the Kliptown station to check up occasionally on the Solilo house. Outside, the crowd has all but dispersed, except for the two or three men who have appointed themselves protectors of the little *inyanga*.

Hettie alternates between Afrikaans and Zulu, grasping for the right words so that Harry can understand. 'Besides the omens of which I have already spoken, there is really not much more to tell you. I am so sorry to hear that Hlopheka was murdered by this man, Ngubane Maduna. I did not myself know Hlopheka well, but he would occasionally join our drumming circles at the weekends. He was a humble man, but also deeply troubled by some-thing, something which he carried in his heart for years without ever revealing.

'During one of those weekends, when we celebrated the initiation of a young *sangoma*, and after the goat and cow were slain, he walked right past me looking particu-larly troubled. I asked him to sit with me and speak his heart – while the drums thundered and the *thwasas* danced the *Umdawu* for us. He settled down next to me and, after a long pause, began to speak freely. "Hettie," he said, "there is a darkness stirring in the city. It has been growing for years now, but it's getting worse. It is an evil power which neither I nor the others know how to cope with. It is a nameless power come amongst us, and it is destroying the community. It's very smart, too, holding us like a beating heart is held in a fist. It has woven webs of threats around us. We fear for our families, for our businesses, even for our souls. We've thought of going to the police with this burden, but you know how they react when we speak of spiritual matters. Besides, this dark power seems able to smell out any move made against it, whether using the lure of money or with help from the spirits. It is ruthless, and we are helpless."

'I was shocked to hear this from a *sangoma* of his age and experience. I asked him who he spoke of, but he just shook his head and refused to say more. He was clearly afraid that this person's ears might begin itching and he would retaliate. Now, with all the protections laid at the gates and fences of any house where an initiation is in progress, this *baloyi* must be very powerful indeed to deter a senior *sangoma* from conferring with his fellows.'

Jacob gets up and begins to pace the room, a fist pressed tightly to his lips.

Hettie continues, 'I saw him only two or three times after that, but he never spoke to me of his concerns again. One day I even went to visit his shop to satisfy my curiosity. The moment my taxi crossed into that part of the city, I could *sense* it clearly in the air. There *is* something there that is very dangerous, I'm telling you.'

'So this person you speak of doesn't yet have a name?' interrupts Harry.

'A person who truly has no name possesses much power,' answers Hettie. 'One cannot grasp him, one cannot see him, one cannot place him. He is invisible and therefore invincible.'

Harry takes a moment to consider those nameless children whom he himself cannot identify without knowing their names and concedes that what Hettie says has some truth in it. He asks her about the cheetah skin and tells her how Sepang had explained his possession of it.

'I do not know for sure if some tribal nobleman gave it to him, but I do know he's owned it for many years. A cheetah skin is a proud possession indeed, a revered symbol of a diviner's status. He always carried it with him to any special occasions.'

The two detectives glance at each other, realizing that their theory of it being a recent reward for his services has crumbled to dust.

Harry persists. 'So why, Ms Solilo, is this nameless guy coming after *you* now?'

'I think he is trying to extend his presence wider, like an infection.' Hettie gets up to stir the oats. 'You saw all those people outside my house this morning. Imagine the fear he can now stir up in this community by attacking me directly in such a way. By doing this he has said clearly to them that I am nothing in his eyes, that he is not scared of me. He has told me to shut up, to *fear* him, or *I* will be next. We don't have to see this *baloyi* or know his name to be scared of him. All he needs to become is the ghost on everyone's tongue when we speak amongst ourselves.'

'Why hasn't he killed you, then?' asks Harry. 'Surely that would be a much more powerful statement?'

'*Harry*, what kind of questions are these?' interrupts Jacob, perceiving his partner's direct approach as rudeness.

'No, Jacob, don't worry. He is right, and I have thought about it, too.' Hettie walks to the window and peers through the net curtains at her protectors outside. They are standing conversing with her *thwasas* and Mama Poleng. 'My only answer is this . . .' She gestures widely, encompassing her house, the neighbourhood and her followers outside. 'We have a strong little community here, and he does not want to totally outrage it. He merely wants it to *submit* to his will.'

The two detectives thank Hettie for her information. Once outside, they agree that Harry will head back to the office to inform Chief Molethe of this morning's developments, while Jacob finishes up here in Soweto, with the rest of the officers at hand.

Harry decides to again broach the accusations levelled against Jacob earlier. 'What's going on, Jakes? Why did that guy earlier say that about you? And why am I hearing strange rumours back at the station? How do you know so much about this muti business?'

Jacob stares sadly at his colleague. 'Maybe we are both cursed, you and I.'

The silence that settles between them is distinctly uncomfortable and uncertain. Suddenly Harry appreciates how badly this case is affecting not only himself, but also his relationship with his partner. Ever since the little girl's body was discovered in that ditch, their confidence in each other has been steadily unravelling. Fumbling with that realization, he nervously looks away.

'I'm sorry, it isn't right for me to talk with you about such things. Just like you have your secrets, I have mine.'

'Fine,' Harry nods. 'I respect that, but if it has any bearing on this case, I have a right to know.'

'It has nothing to do with this case,' replies Jacob earnestly. 'And how about you? Is there anything else *I* should know?'

'No,' says Harry firmly and slams shut the door of his car. Lowering the window he says, 'Let's keep it that way, then.'

Jacob nods silently and watches Harry drive off before returning into the house.

The forensic lab calls on his mobile just as Harry eases onto the highway heading back to central Johannesburg. At the station they have a confirmation waiting for Harry: the DNA samples from the little girl and the blood-soaked fetish match. The revolting object *did* contain her blood.

'Do me a favour, Piet,' says Harry, thinking back to the crime scene yesterday. 'Compare those two samples with the blood traces Superintendent Niehaus discovered last night on the blanket found in that car. And compare the fibres from the blanket with those found in the little girl's hair – I want to know for sure.'

The technician agrees to get onto that right away and hangs up.

Harry has already convinced himself they will find a match there, too, but he has no idea where such information might take him. The evidence against *someone* is mounting, but without a firm suspect it means very little.

Harry is feeling heavily sedated as he drives, the pills he took earlier now having their full effect. When he first saw the boy's body he had reacted immediately, swallowing the tablets for fear of having another attack in front of complete strangers. But now that he has dealt with the situation without the familiar panic rising, he feels an odd sense of guilt surfacing. Why is he not taking this murder personally, too? Why can he not feel as much for the boy as he does for the girl child? Perhaps the medical examiner was right: the more he thinks about her as someone's *daughter*, the more he seems to unravel emotionally.

Fingers drumming the steering wheel incessantly, Harry

forces himself to consider the recent information he has received from the lab. Could Ngubane Maduna really be the 'nameless' entity spreading this fear everywhere? Say somebody rats on Maduna, leading to his capture and the confiscation of his heroin, but Maduna happens to be a firm believer in African occultism, so when he surprisingly wins his bail application, he decides to make a sacrifice. He kills the girl, makes an evil fetish from her blood, drives her out to a secluded spot in the Chevy that Niehaus found yesterday and dumps her along with the fetish he so painstakingly concocted from her. Then he takes the car back to be concealed by that Nigerian family.

The theory seems flawed, but Harry thinks it has possibilities for exploration. Key questions will still have to be answered. For example, why would Ngubane go to the trouble of manufacturing an elaborate curse, only to abandon it? Did he actually make the fetish himself, or was a witch doctor involved? How do the other men in the red BMW fit in? Or this dead boy?

The boy!

Harry calls Superintendent Niehaus to brief him on the morning's gruesome events. 'Do you have a picture of that missing Nigerian kid you mentioned last night? I have a feeling we've found what's left of him.'

'I'll fax it through to your office right away,' comes the reply.

Convinced he has found Niehaus's abducted child, Harry ponders any other weaknesses in his theory. He will need to confirm with the neighbour of the murdered Nigerian family whether Maduna might have been the mystery visitor to their apartment block. His thoughts turn to the muti discovered at the airport. He still has not received any more information about that from Mitchell, although he has heard plenty more from Niehaus and Gildenhuys about the decapitation in Hillbrow. The former's suspicion that the Hillbrow case may be connected to Harry's investigation still seems unlikely to him, since the MO is radically different from everything he has encountered so far. The deceased in that case was not a child, and none of the body parts were missing.

Harry, nevertheless, decides to pay Francis Mitchell a visit, after he has had a word with Chief Molethe.

44

It takes him more than a week to drum up the courage to leave Sibongile's apartment. In that time Ngubane sobers up in more ways than one. He finally finds himself walking down the street, disguised in an old tracksuit, a baseball cap and sunglasses, with his pistol resting reassuringly in his track top's pocket. He is thinking about how he should have taken care of Adusa and his sidekick before they gained such influence over the albino. Now he knows only one thing for sure: his life hangs in the balance. If he cannot revive his former relationship with the boss, he will die on the streets or in jail.

It has been a miserable time for him, being constantly bothered by noisy children, the women coming home from their work at all hours of the night and Sibongile's damn husband constantly eyeing him suspiciously – as if he would ever lay a finger on that monstrosity of a woman. It was a degrading and embarrassing sojourn, but strangely uplifting, too. He has come to realize that, whatever their past differences, his and the albino's fortunes are still closely tied, so he feels hopeful despite his sense of betrayal, that they can re-establish a close working relationship. He will do anything to get out of that godforsaken house.

The day is still overcast after last night's rain. Braamfontein, once a hub of money and culture, is now a swathe of struggling barbers' shops, haberdasheries, pawnbrokers and cheap furniture dealers, all of them catering to the masses of poor that flock into the city in search of a better life. Most whites do their best never to penetrate this deep into the city's heart nowadays, preferring the familiarity of their suburban enclaves. Only a few administrative and industrial offices have remained located here. Further down the road, the Carlton Tower, tallest of the city skyscrapers, stands nearly empty, a relic of a time when big business felt safe here in the city, when blacks needed passes to get into work, when the townships and homelands were still wage-slave borderlands. Now the streets heave with exactly the same people once denied access to eGoli, the City of Gold. There is a different kind of life here now, and its vibrancy is one that Ngubane understands.

The albino's web is clearly unravelling. His reputation was once as subtly binding as a spider's delicate thread. So many people, including his rivals and even the cops, kept quiet about his spreading organization for fear that the albino's pervasive influence would invade their own lives. His money, his violence, his uncanny ability to sniff out the slightest dissent, had made him seemingly invincible, even if one was sceptical of his rumoured powers as a witch. With such potential enemies cowed by gossip and rumour, Ngubane and the rest of them had been totally safe. But after the news of Ngubane's arrest and crimes appearing daily in the papers, people seemed to be realizing that the albino was not omnipotent. With such doubt blossoming, Ngubane wonders how long the criminals facing jail sentences will keep quiet, how long the politicians who have accepted bribes will stay loyal, how long it will take the pushers and prostitutes to see that the balance of power is shifting. How long will it take the albino's own people to overcome their fear of a spider whose gossamer ties are being blown away in the wind?

Perhaps if Ngubane returns to the boss's side, then all those rumours could be quickly dispelled; together they could consolidate their power and reassert themselves. The albino needs him because he is the man with the right contacts. He is the only one of the man's henchmen who can cut a decent business deal.

'*Daily Sun*,' says Ngubane, fishing out money for the barefoot newspaper boy who hovers at the intersection. The boy scrambles to oblige him, then holds out his hand expectantly after giving Ngubane his change. 'Boss, please, I'm hungry.'

'Get lost,' growls Ngubane.

He leafs quickly through the newspaper as he walks along.

Suddenly he stops dead, pedestrians brushing past him on the busy sidewalk. Ignoring their jostling, he reads the article carefully once again. In his mind the pin of a hand grenade has just hit the floor.

When Ngubane finally arrives at the blue-sheeted shack beneath the overpass, the albino's enforcers try to block his way in.

'He's busy,' growls Adusa.

Taiwo laughs. 'Ah, the dog finally found its way home.'

Ngubane's hand is already fidgeting with the pistol in

his track top's pocket. 'I need to speak with him,' he insists.

'You should know by now you can't disturb him when he is busy,' says Adusa.

'I'll do what I want.' Ngubane gestures them aside.

'You can *wait*.' Taiwo steps forward.

Ngubane cocks his pistol and brings it out fast. '*Wena*, I've had it with you two. I'm going to speak with him, and you're going to take me to him *now*.'

Taiwo exchanges a look of some surprise with Adusa, yet his tone is mocking. 'After all that's happened, it's not really smart of you to be waving a gun around out here in the open.'

'I need to speak with him.' Ngubane tries to conceal his nervousness.

'Just put the gun away, you idiot. He's been expecting you anyway – although you've taken your time,' says Adusa.

The two enforcers turn and enter the shack, opening the trapdoor that leads them briefly underground before they encounter a passage which heads back up into the hot dark interior of the rambling complex beyond.

Somewhere a loose sheet of corrugated iron vibrates under the shock waves from the dense traffic moving above them. The interior is only dimly lit by a few candles placed in brackets along the walls, or occasionally by daylight filtering through cracks and rivet holes in the rickety metal walls.

Ngubane has not been inside here in months, preferring to keep to his business locations. As his eyes adjust to the darkness, he becomes aware that extensions have been made. The convoluted structure looks much larger than when he was here last. It seems to him that a faint smell of death hangs in the air, permeated by an aroma of *impepho*, the fragrant herb often used by the albino in his rituals.

As he continues to follow the other two men, Ngubane hears a weak moaning sound from behind a flimsy pine door fitted in a crumbling metal partition. A moment later from behind another door can be heard the unmistakable sound of the albino's chanting.

'You can go now,' says Ngubane. 'I will speak with him in private.'

'You're mad,' says Taiwo, 'if you try to interrupt the boss now.'

'Yes, have fun.' Adusa laughs. 'I'm sure he'll be very happy to see you.'

Ngubane closes his eyes, takes a deep breath and strokes the Beretta in his pocket. He waits till the two Nigerians disappear before he steps forward to open the door and enters.

Braziers stand in each of the sanctuary's four corners, filling the room with smoke and making the darkness almost tangible. The albino kneels on a large reed mat with intricate patterns of white, black and red. He is dressed only in a wrap fastened around his waist, made of cloth depicting black spears on a red background. He is positioned in the very centre of the room, facing a large clay bowl containing some dark liquid on which various herbs float. His hands rest on his knees, and his spectacles lie folded in front of him, resting quaintly beside the short dagger he favours for such acts of worship. His face is turned up towards the ceiling, and in the depths of a trance his eyes are rolled up to show the whites, the lids fluttering feverishly. The man's body is drenched in sweat, hitching with rhythmic grunts expelled from deep inside him.

He shows no awareness of Ngubane's arrival, and for a brief moment his former right-hand man contemplates drawing the Beretta and ending his boss's life there and then. But simultaneously he realizes he cannot do that: his fortunes are too inextricably tied up with the albino's own.

Ngubane recalls his reason for coming here, and he turns to close the door behind him. The albino suddenly gasps heavily, before expelling a stream of incomprehensible words.

Laying the newspaper down and squatting in front of the albino, Ngubane begins. 'It looks like Oba didn't fulfil his task so well at all.'

The albino stops panting and screws his eyes tightly closed. 'What are you doing in here?' he rasps.

'Just read the newspaper.' Ngubane sounds more confident than he feels.

'You were not invited in here,' growls the albino, reopening his eyes.

'We need to talk.' Ngubane's hand creeps back into his pocket, needing the reassurance of cold steel. 'This whole bloody news story should interest you.'

'I will not read your newspaper. Just tell me what it says.' The albino senses a definite change in his former lieutenant. Has he misjudged Ngubane's innate cowardice?

Irritated, Ngubane grabs the newspaper and holds up the front page. 'Look at this.' He opens a second page. 'And that.' He flicks to a third page. 'And this as well.'

'None of this would've happened if you had followed my instructions.'

'So Oba is dead?'

'Of course, he's dead! Did I not already tell you he was responsible for the drug raid?'

244

'If he was really responsible for it, then why did he not run straight to the police for protection?'

'They could never shield him from the curse I put on him. And because Oba did not fulfil his duties his family have lost their lives as well.'

'But they were killed four days *before* the child's body was found. Now the police have a description of his car being parked next to the highway near where a dead girl was found. Why was the body not disposed of by your usual methods?'

'A strong message has been sent out,' snarls the albino. 'People are talking, and their fear is growing.'

'Their fear is *not* growing!' Ngubane stands up and begins pacing the room. 'Instead others are invading our space. This whole newspaper is full of stories that show people do not fear you as much as you think.'

The albino has not moved. Apart from opening his eyes, he has not yet responded to Ngubane's insolence at all.

Ngubane's indignation rises a few notches. 'This is a damn mess. What is now happening to all we had together? Even if we had the money now, we could not bribe anyone to help protect us. It is far too dangerous for anyone to come near us.' He waves a hand towards the newspaper he has dismissively dropped on the floor. 'Even our legitimate enterprises will now be under investigation. Meanwhile I am South Africa's most wanted criminal. So do you honestly think you yourself can go on hiding? We need a *plan*, I tell you.'

As the albino listens, his eyes follow Ngubane around the room, but still he shows no emotion.

'I . . . I'm confused about what to believe. You are

powerful and wise, but . . . I think the spirits have been telling me things contrary to your decisions. I . . . why was I arrested, anyway? I don't understand that. *How* could I be arrested after the honour we both paid to the spirits? I even sacrificed my fucking heir! I had a son once, you remember? I *committed* myself so totally to you that I sacrificed a *part* of me.'

The confined space of the sanctuary has steadily been growing darker and stuffier from the smoke pouring from the braziers.

'Speak to me!' yells Ngubane.

The albino remains silent.

'Tell me it was all worth it!' Ngubane thumps a steel wall with his fist. But he receives just a cold hard stare. He paces around in silence for another full minute, trying to judge what the albino is up to.

'You need me,' he eventually resumes, 'because I can make us the money we need to survive. You don't need those other two. Their violence is immature – it will only get us caught in the end. We must do this, like you taught me all those years ago, by working from the shadows. People will again learn to fear us, because we will have ears *and* money working everywhere to carry out our wishes.'

Ngubane stops pacing and hovers behind the albino. He notices rivulets of perspiration running down the albino's spine, over rolls of patchy-coloured flesh that remind Ngubane of a toad.

'Why don't you just say something? We built this up *together*. Now we must cut our losses and disappear into the night. We cannot afford to wage open war with the police – never mind the other gangs.'

Ngubane slowly moves around again to face the seated man directly. An icy shiver slides down his spine once he notices that the albino's fleshy sides are shaking. The *baloyi* is laughing at him.

'What?' Ngubane demands, disconcerted.

'I had not realized how much of a white man you've become.'

Ngubane is so taken aback he has no answer. Meanwhile the albino shifts his weight and reaches for something lying in front of him. Ngubane instantly drops a hand to his pocket, but the albino only retrieves his spectacles. He does not put them on, however; instead tucks them into his coloured wrap.

'I still possess much more authority than you realize. Or perhaps you have merely forgotten. Like I said, you've grown fat and slow, Ngubane.'

A truck on the overpass blasts its horn, and Ngubane cannot help but wipe hurriedly at his stinging eyes. The room is getting far too smoky for comfort.

'You and I, we are not equals, Ngubane, and you really don't know what you're talking about. It's a dangerous thing – the *most* dangerous – to lose your faith in me. Because that means I've lost your undying loyalty.'

'No!' Frustrated, Ngubane whirls around and again smacks a fist against the partition wall. 'You . . .'

There is a whisper of movement behind him. He turns. The albino is up, and has already stepped closer towards him. Unnerved, Ngubane's eyes flicker towards the bowl, where the ritual knife should be lying. He can no longer see it there.

'You . . . you have to understand, we need to work *together*.' Instead of drawing his gun, Ngubane backs away from the albino. The smoke burns his nostrils, his throat, most of all it burns his eyes, and yet the albino himself seems unaffected by it.

Ngubane slides to his left, along the wall, heading towards the door. The albino immediately outflanks him, stepping forward quickly to cut him off from the exit.

Ngubane licks his lips nervously and begins to shiver, even though he now spots the knife still lying by the bowl. His rising terror makes it difficult for him to control the hand desperately clutching the Beretta in his pocket.

'What's wrong with you, Ngubane? You said you wanted to talk to me, so now we're talking, right?' The albino almost croons the words, his tone of false sincerity insidious.

'Leave me alone!' cries Ngubane, before a fit of coughing overwhelms him.

'You're too dangerous for me to keep, but too dangerous to let go,' continues the albino. 'I don't need you for my business any more, and I certainly don't need any unbelievers.'

The smoke finally forces Ngubane to squeeze his eyes shut just for a moment. But that brief second is enough.

Hearing cloth rustle nearby, Ngubane fires the gun blindly from inside his pocket. Inevitably he misses, and the albino slams into him with surprising strength, crushing him up against the makeshift wall. There is a brief scream from the next room, then three quick punches land on Ngubane's stomach before a powerful uppercut connects to his chin. Ngubane's hand releases the gun still buried in his pocket. He drops to his knees, starbursts firing off in his head. The bullet hole in his track top has left a smouldering hole.

While Ngubane struggles to recover, the heavy candelabrum suddenly topples with a clang onto the floor. The room is plunged into darkness. Ngubane sits up and desperately tries to pull his Beretta free. There is the sound of metal scraping on concrete, then a hand suddenly grasps him by the throat and drags him upright. Ngubane lashes out frantically but cannot prevent the knife sinking deep into his belly.

He screams in pain as the blade is driven into him a second time.

The albino lets go of him. 'Come on, shoot me then!' he snarls. It is as if the gloom all around is speaking with the albino's voice.

Ngubane finally manages to free the gun from the torn material of his pocket. As he fires it, somebody screams again next door. Further away he hears a trapdoor swing open and Adusa yelling distantly.

'Boss? *Boss!*'

'Motherfucker,' croaks Ngubane, as he struggles to his feet and stumbles towards the door. His belly is slick with oozing blood. As he grasps the handle, the albino strikes like a snake. The sudden impact from behind drives Ngubane straight into the door, breaking his nose. The cold kiss of the blade plunges into his back. Ngubane manages only a groan; he lets off two more shots, but the gun is crushed ineffectively against the partition. The albino stands back and lets him slip to the floor.

The door is shoved open against Ngubane's body. 'Boss!' yells Adusa, staring first at the albino and then down at Ngubane. He begins to babble apologies.

'Shut up, fool!' The albino gathers up his ritual implements and the discarded newspaper and jostles his way

249

past him. 'Just come with me. Let the pig bleed to death. I want to know everything about these people who are talking to the cops.'

As the two men disappear out of earshot, Ngubane rolls over on his back and stares up at the roof. He feels his life slowly leaching from his body.

45

Nina listens to the man rolling around in pain above her. Occasionally he paws at the door and shouts incomprehensible things in a voice that has been growing steadily weaker. After hearing those two gunshots, she is amazed that he is still alive.

Huddled in the cold, in complete darkness that has surrounded her seemingly for days, her back pressed against the freezing concrete wall behind her and her knees drawn up tightly under her chin, she listens to the sound of another human being dying and finds it almost welcome company. She has heard little of anything else since she was thrown into this makeshift cell underground. It has disorientated her, the passing of time soon slipping from her mental grasp, so even the sound of someone else's pain is a reminder that she is still alive.

In the beginning she had explored the room by groping around it with her hands. The more desperate she grew, the less focus she could summon to resume her search. But now, with the sound of that man so near, her hope of escape revives like dying coals doused with kerosene.

Her cell measures only eight feet each way, and it is not even high enough for her to stand fully upright. A bolted scrap-iron door has been fitted to one of the concrete walls. Another wall has three circular holes drilled deep into it, and each is only a few inches in diameter, which convinces Nina they were once used to encase electrical cables.

A dusty chill wafts through her prison, bringing cold discomfort but some fresh air, too. The pungent stench inside the cell is almost overpowering. Try as she might, she cannot get used to it. Near one wall she has discovered some rough-cut grooves in the floor, inside which festers the smell's greasy source. Unwittingly in the darkness she had accidentally stuck her fingers into it, and immediately withdrew them with a horrified yelp. After that shock, her disorientated explorations in the darkness came quickly to an end. However, she now knows the basics of her confine-ment: it contains a bucket, a foul mattress that makes her itch and some tins containing food and water, both of which she has sampled as rarely as possible. Up till now she has luckily not shown any symptoms of being poisoned the way Tumi was.

Nina winces as she uncurls herself from her fetal slump and begins to move slowly towards the sound of the man's pain. The one called Adusa, the one with the deep scars tracking his face, had managed to sprain two of her fin-gers before his leader restrained him, leaving Nina to finish her story without the incentive of further torture. It was the big one called Taiwo who finally herded her into this cell, leaving her to wonder what was due to come next.

Lonely and despairing, she has oscillated between admonishing herself for her own stupidity and feeling sorry for herself. She should never have guarded her story so jealously. What was she thinking, attempting that stake-out alone?

Struggling to her feet and stooping carefully so as not

to crack her head against the ceiling, Nina approaches the side of the room where the sounds from above are clearest. Pressing up close to the wall, she notices a faint, dry odour of incense wafting in towards her. Feeling carefully with her undamaged hand, she detects that the concrete surface above her terminates before extending to the conjoining wall. Nina now realizes that the cool draught does not just come through the apertures she located earlier, but also derives from somewhere above her. Carefully exploring with her fingers, above her she feels a makeshift covering plugging the three-foot gap where the concrete is missing. Perhaps there was once a loading shaft.

Rising on her toes, Nina finds she can now stretch up to her full height. From what she can make out, sheets of tin and plywood complete the ceiling just there. Hearing the man's groans of pain much more loudly now, she presses gently against the separate sections of the added covering. None of it seems to be anchored very tightly, but if these cells are intended to confine young children, they would never be able to reach up so high anyway.

The excitement she feels quickly turns to desperation. Nina listens carefully for sounds of her captors before she proceeds to push harder at the tin sheeting with both her hands splayed. Pain shoots up her two injured fingers, and she barely manages to stifle a cry as she cradles them in her other hand. But before long she repositions herself, and tries again. This time she is rewarded with a cracking sound, which causes the wounded man above to quieten his groaning. But still the wood and tin will not budge enough to offer her hope. Nina's hamstrings suddenly seize up painfully, and she collapses to the floor in tears of frustration.

When her third attempt fails, Nina succumbs to an all-out panic. Her mind is clouded by visions of what they might have in store for her – of what might be kept in those cooler-boxes they haul out of the building from time to time. They could kill her right now or in a month. Would she be found like that girl on the highway verge?

She reaches up for the panelling again, this time jumping up to batter it with her fists. But instead she collides with the wall and ends up with a grazed forehead.

The groaning recommences above her. Then there is the sound of a heavy body dragging itself across the floor.

Nina reacts instinctively. 'Help me, I'm trapped,' she calls out, and is horrified by the high-pitched terror in her voice.

She receives no acknowledgement and the groans continue. She wonders if the man has even heard her. She searches her memory for the few Zulu words she can recall. '*Ungisize!*' she calls out, as loudly as she dares. 'I'm *begging* you – ' she turns to English – 'get me out of here.'

A drop of something warm falls onto her upturned cheek as she hears the wounded man's bulk rasping over the metal above her. She wipes it away heedlessly, then violently thumps at the sheeting immediately above her with her one good fist.

There is a sound like a door opening somewhere down on her own level. Nina freezes in panic, but the elusive sound is gone and the groans continue.

Suddenly there is a loud crunch overhead, like a tin can being crushed.

'*Yes!* Oh God, *yes!*' exclaims Nina as she sticks up her hand again and probes about with it. A narrow gap has appeared there and the air is smelling considerably fresher.

Above her the man mutters something under his breath.

'What?' she hisses, but there is no reply. 'You'll have to pull up another one. I can't get through,' she urges.

There is a heaving noise in the darkness above her and she flinches as splashes of some liquid fall onto her face.

There is now another sound, and it is coming closer. Soon Nina distinguishes voices.

'Hurry!' she entreats.

With another slow crunch, something above her gives way. Her hands immediately fumble through the extended opening, scrabbling desperately for a decent grip. Finding nothing better, she grabs hold of the rough edge of the tin. As she heaves, it bites sharply into her flesh in an explosion of pain, but she manages to pull herself up through the gap without screaming.

Nina quickly rolls to one side, colliding with a man who is gasping even more raggedly than she is. 'Thank you,' she whispers to the large shape barely discernible in the darkness.

She holds her breath, listening for the sound of someone coming to her cell door and discovering she is gone. Nothing follows, however, and the only other noise she can discern is a faint whimpering from another room nearby. With a shiver, she recognizes the fear of a lonely young child.

Faced with this new dilemma, Nina bites her lip hard. What should she do? How would she get a child out of here? She drags her attention away from distractions and focuses instead on their escape. She will be of no use to that child if she cannot get out herself.

From a distance she can make out the familiar hum of ordinary people chattering outside in the afternoon heat. The promise of a normal world outside infuses her with renewed energy. Once outside she can raise the alarm and thus rescue any kids still locked up in this abysmal building.

'How are you doing?' whispers Nina to the figure in the darkness.

'I'm bleeding, badly,' gasps the man. 'Stabbed in the stomach twice – and in my back. I need to get to a hospital, quickly.'

'Right.' Nina decides to explore further along the left-hand wall, where most of the daylight is filtering through. Her hands encounter a melange of hard plastic, metal sheets and plywood insulated with old plastic shopping bags. She attempts to find a firm grip between the various segments, but her damaged hands are not of much use to her. After a short while, she finally discovers two boards over in one corner which seem likely to yield to further probing.

'Hey,' she whispers, 'come over here.'

At first she thinks he has not heard her. Then he gradually shifts away from the other wall and drags himself towards her.

'Move over here.' She directs him by slapping on the floor. After she has managed to position the big man where she wants him, she listens again for the whimpering child. But all has grown quiet, and Nina wonders whether she just imagined it.

Propping herself between the heavy-set man and the weaker section of wall, Nina draws her knees all the way up to her chin, then kicks out viciously. The wall shivers with a sound of cracking and splintering, while the man groans in pain from the sudden pressure against him. The shock of pain up Nina's legs makes her momentarily dizzy.

As she quickly realigns for another kick, she mutters, 'If this ever works, we're going to have to fucking *run*.'

'I've been stabbed!' complains Ngubane. 'I *can't* run.'

Nina kicks out again, and this time one of her feet breeches the exterior wall. Gathering all her strength, Nina lashes out a third time. There is a satisfying crunch, like an axe demolishing a door.

'*Heeere's Johnny!*' cries Nina in triumph.

'What?' The man is confused.

'Just a line from a movie.' Nina scrambles forward, pulling away the debris. Bright afternoon dazzles her vision.

Suddenly there *is* a child just inches away from them, in the adjoining cell, clawing frantically at the wall between them, screaming out pleas that Nina cannot understand. She freezes in uncertainty about what to do about the little prisoner.

'It's still not big enough for me to get through,' hisses the man, ignoring the child's cries.

'We have to rescue her,' says Nina, assuming the young voice belongs to a girl.

'You have to get me to a hospital,' insists the man, anger suddenly growing in his voice. 'You've got to get me out of here! The kid will only slow us down.'

A shout goes up somewhere else in the warren-like building. In the distance there is the sound of a chain rattling loose.

'No, I'm getting the child out, too.' Nina stands up, takes a few steps back, then propels her shoulder full tilt into the makeshift partition that separates them. The force of the impact knocks her back onto the floor.

'You're being stupid,' gasps Ngubane. But then he struggles forward and starts desperately tearing at the ragged gap Nina has created. 'You're going to get us all caught.'

'Help me!' screeches the child, now scratching away on the other side.

Nina hurls herself at the wall a second time. Her shoulder and collarbone light up with magnificent pain just as she hears another section of the partition slide loose. Without a further thought she staggers upright and charges once more.

It does the job.

Nina slides to her knees, dazed and exhausted. Suddenly tiny fingers are fumbling around her face as they grope for freedom. Between them, Nina and the child manage to pull further sections free from the shabbily built partition. Nina recognizes Sibongile's voice as a confused alarm is raised close by.

A great deal more light suddenly floods into the cell behind her, causing Nina to look around as she lifts the child – a girl – free. The wounded man has already crawled out into the narrow alley beyond. In the light Nina sees that it is indeed a girl's face, casting fearful glances everywhere. The little girl clutches desperately at the journalist's neck, but Nina manages to prise her loose and urges her to crawl out through their escape hole.

Nina can see sandalled feet hurrying past the wounded man now lying prone in the dust outside. To her surprise, no one even stops to discover what is going on; they all seem to be scuttling away in panic.

She herself scrambles out through the opening, wincing painfully in the glare of full daylight. The man seems to be barely moving, and Nina is horrified to note how much blood he has already lost. The girl is about eight, naked except for a pair of green knickers and very thin. Nina lifts her up quickly and peers around for an escape route.

Suddenly shots ring out, bullets clanging loudly against

corrugated iron. Instinctively, Nina presses herself back against the wall. Further up the alley, she spots three men running towards them, herding two panicked pedestrians in front of them.

'Get up! Come on, run!' Nina tugs vainly at Ngubane's arm before herself turning to flee.

She barely notices the frightened faces peering out at her through the windows and from around the corners of this rag-tag shanty town. Most of them are women and children, but there are terrified male faces occasionally, too.

'For God's sake, *help* us!' screams Nina as she runs.

More bullets whine past her, forcing her to duck and weave. The girl is screaming loudly in her ear and her uncomfortable weight makes it difficult for Nina to keep her balance. She does, however, manage a series of quick twists and turns, diving through the densely packed back alleys of the market, hopping across garbage-filled ditches and discarded tyres. She exhaustedly rounds another corner and, desperate for breath, finally has to put the child down. Nina's weakened body aches and her vision is swimming. She momentarily closes her eyes and lets the darkness spin out of control. As she wonders where to turn next, she realizes the wounded man has not followed her.

She does not notice a door opening cautiously behind her, so when a rough hand falls on her shoulder, Nina squawks in surprise.

'In here, quickly!' urges a plump African woman with light brown skin. A maroon beret is perched on her head, and an African Zionist star pinned to her chest.

Nina grabs the little girl by the wrist and tugs her roughly into this unexpected refuge. The shack is hot and stuffy inside and seems crammed with junk salvaged from the streets. Their rescuer quickly throws two bolts, then gestures for them to duck out of sight beneath the crudely fashioned window sill. Nina tries desperately to bring her breathing under control.

'Where are you bleeding from?' the woman eventually whispers.

Nina glances down at herself and sees that her filthy clothes are stained with the big man's blood. She shakes her head and manages a wry smile.

Seconds later, two armed men sprint past outside. After another five minutes the woman suddenly gets up and unlocks the door. She indicates silently for Nina and the child to follow her.

Ngubane is still struggling to get up when two men hurdle over him in hot pursuit of the woman who helped him escape. His life is ebbing away fast, and his vision seems to narrow. He begins to feel cold despite the sun beating down on him. A shadow falls on him as a third figure hurries towards him.

'Boss, what happened? Who did this?'

Ngubane manages to choke out, 'It's all over . . . Go. Leave all this and get away.'

'I'll go after them,' promises the man, unaware of the power struggles of his leaders. He steps respectfully past Ngubane and hastens down the alley after his comrades.

What a way to die. Ngubane closes his eyes and groans at the pain burning in his innards. As he listens inside himself, he becomes sure he can hear the voices of his ancestors, urging him to join them.

As yet another figure looms over him, Ngubane opens his eyes again and recognizes the figure of Adusa sneering

259

down at him. The black mouth of his Glock is hovering close to Ngubane's face, demanding all his attention.

'I always knew you would prove the weakest link.' Adusa cocks the hammer of his pistol and spits directly in Ngubane's face.

A shot rings out, then a long pause before a second shot. Then after another, longer, pause, the entire magazine is emptied into the corpse of Ngubane Maduna.

46

As Harry approaches Mitchell's office on the other side of the police building, he hears a sudden loud whoop followed by a peel of victorious laughter. The door is flung open, and some officer Harry does not know walks out quickly, wearing a broad smile. Mitchell himself comes to the door, also grinning, and leans on the door handle. 'And make sure the prosecutor gives you warrants for *all* of them this time.'

The other officer brushes aggressively past Harry, not even looking up from the papers he is now studying.

'Anything exciting?' inquires Harry, already eyeing Mitchell with regret.

The man looks at him with that grin still in place, and it grows even wider as he senses that Harry has come to ask him for help. Harry's gut instinct is to punch him, but he forces himself to wait for Mitchell's reply.

'We've finally got someone to squeal on a gang of teenagers, operating in Soweto, that's been robbing graves for someone. I'm telling you, they've got it coming, I reckon they're responsible for all those other grave robberies, too. Come in and tell me exactly what can I do for you.'

As Harry enters Mitchell's office, the hand in his pocket is clenched around his yellow Bic lighter. It is not just the man's recurrent racism which gets to Harry, it is the way he always hangs back on the periphery like a hyena, snatching up titbits of information by listening in to others' conversations. His years serving as an officer at the notorious Vlakplaas Centre, where so many political opponents of apartheid were tortured and killed, still stick to him like a greasy film of old cooking. And no amount of his born-again Christianity will ever seem to wash him clean.

Curious on this, his first, visit here, Harry takes the time to peer around the man's office. A large but badly composed family photo-portrait hangs on one wall – Mitchell, his wife and three sons all looking suitably pious – while a wildlife calendar adorns the one opposite. Elsewhere pictures of Mitchell and his buddies out on hunting expeditions hang amid Bible verses inscribed on wooden plaques. Harry suspects Mitchell's wife manufactures the latter for church sales.

'Sit.' Mitchell indicates a chair, as he himself sits down. 'What can I do for you?'

Harry takes a seat and pulls out his lighter to fidget with it openly.

'I was wondering whether you've had a breakthrough yet with that airport muti case.'

'No, not yet, unless these *laaities* just caught robbing graves have something to do with it.' He pauses. 'How's your own case going?'

Harry shakes his head. 'This whole thing is still not

making any sense to me. There's no order to it. The connections seem to be completely arbitrary. Firstly, Ngubane Maduna, who never seemed to have anything to do with our case, turns up out of the blue and nearly kills us. Last night Kobus calls me over to an apartment complex where an entire family of Nigerians was gunned down and there hauls our primary suspect's car out of an abandoned garage. It's the right vehicle, OK, but who was the driver – and what was his connection with that family? I just don't know. Now, this very morning, we discover the mutilated body of another child – a boy this time.'

Mitchell's face grows serious. He scratches his head before pulling out horn-rimmed glasses and opening his notebook. 'Tell me more of the details,' he invites. His apparently genuine interest surprises Harry into relating more about the morning's events than he was intending to. All the while, the captain takes detailed notes.

'It's the devil's work, that's all I can say,' replies Mitchell finally, clasping his hands with resignation. 'But it's our job now to prevent him and his followers from wrecking any more innocent lives.'

Harry stifles his cynical response. This is not what he came here for. 'Yes, well, I was hoping by now you had some further information for me on the airport business. That might be the only case so far that connects with mine directly.'

Mitchell plucks off his glasses and leans back in his chair. 'I'm telling you, you need to get into the *minds* of these blacks. They're different from us, you know. They don't think rationally. This whole bloody race is dominated by witch doctors – traditional healers, herbalists, diviners, whatever you want to call these sinners.'

'Look – ' Harry holds up a hand – 'relax with the cant

about mumbo-jumbo. I want information, *leads*. In my book a killer is a killer, full stop. I don't care what *he* believes, or what *you* believe. I'm just trying to pursue the logical connections here.'

'Then you're bound to get it wrong. Occultism is about the *irrational*. What *you* haven't taken into account is that no witch doctor would risk exposing himself like this. They prefer working in the dark, manipulating people from the shadows. In the rural areas, especially up in the north, they still make their homes in caves, you know. They always operate alone, because that gives them power. They excel at melodrama and weaving a veil of mystery around themselves. You, on the other hand, seem to be looking for thugs similar to my grave robbers, people willing to grab children off the street, kill them and then sell their organs to witch doctors. These kinds of gangs love to have people living in fear of them – that's why they leave bodies strewn all over the place. They're "terrorists" in the truest sense of the word.

'But the serious ones, the *intelligent* witches, they disguise themselves carefully. You'll never guess who they are – they're like chameleons. I'm telling you, the only ones we ever catch are the quacks and the wannabes, because the blacks, they stick to their own. They'll protect their leaders, whether they're good or evil, because – like I said – they're so easily *controlled*. So unless they suddenly turn on one of these witch doctors – when they get angry because a *baloyi*'s magic doesn't work – you'll never get anywhere near the truth of their crimes.'

Harry's not sure whether he is being handed serious information or just more crap on a silver platter. He decides to change the subject: 'Anything new on the decapitation in Hillbrow?'

'So far, we've identified the two killers. Each man has been deported from South Africa at least once and has evidently returned subsequently. I don't know how long they've known each other, but as a team they've been implicated in a half-dozen killings over the last year. So far they haven't been caught on a murder charge. This is Adusa Okechukwu.' Mitchell hands Harry a picture of a man in his early thirties, with one of the coldest stares he has ever encountered in a mugshot. 'He's thirty-two years old, with a People's Republic of Benin passport. When he was arrested and deported in 1999, they found Guinea-Conakry papers on him, too, as well as two thousand US dollars. My guess is he's one of those backwater-state mercenaries who eventually found his way through Africa to us, where the real money is. He could be from any one of those abysmal West African countries.'

'This Michelin man is Taiwo Ejiofer. He's a thirty-five-year-old Nigerian. Now this guy's interesting, because we've just linked him with the CCTV footage from the Berea garage shoot-out.' Harry stares at him blankly, and Mitchell explains: 'Bornman's case where the two dealers were blown away?'

'Oh, yes,' mumbles Harry, studying the two men's faces.

'Not much came out of that CCTV film except this lunatic standing in the middle of the station as if he owned the place, spraying the joint with an AK-47. I wouldn't be surprised if he's also got some kind of military experience. He was deported only last year, but here he is again.'

Eyeing the girth of Taiwo's neck, the pronounced eyebrow ridges and the patterning of his tribal scarring, Harry whistles. 'Hell, Mitchell, you've really got your work cut out for you. Looks like you'll need a whole platoon to take these guys out.'

'That's the problem with Africa, every fucking kaffir can get himself military training and a machine gun nowadays. Why else do you think our country's going down the toilet?' He chucks the case file over the desk for Harry to look at. Harry studies the mugshots and reports on the two men, then the photographs of the slum apartment where Oba was killed. He is astonished by the filth evident in the bathroom and kitchen: what could possess a man, even the poorest of men, to inhabit surroundings like that? Harry notes the blacked-out windows and then the viciousness of the attack itself. What could scare a man enough to dig himself into a dump like that?

'Mitchell, this Oba guy was obviously scared as hell if he was voluntarily hiding in this filthy dump. He must have known someone was coming for him.'

'Why didn't he just run, then? There are hundreds of other cities and towns in this country where no one would find him.'

'What language were they using, again?' asks Harry.

'We've figured out it was Yoruba, apparently one of the main dialects in Nigeria and Benin.'

'And is this guy Oba on file with Internal Affairs?'

'No, which means he was also an illegal immigrant who had managed to escape attention.'

'So where's a Nigerian going to run to when he's in this country illegally and his own community is out looking for him? We know how tight the Nigerian underground is and how little our local tribal groups care for any foreigners.'

'So what are you saying?'

'I'm saying this guy probably believed he really had nowhere else to go, being therefore completely dependent on the Nigerian bosses who most likely smuggled him over the border in the first place. Or else, having got into this country by himself, and finding he couldn't get work, this character got in with organized crime and then managed to anger them in some way. Have we got any idea who these two men are working for?' Harry taps the photographs on the desk.

'No, no one knows. None of our informants knows about them, or at least no one is prepared to talk about them. It's as if these two guys are ghosts. We *suspect* they work for someone in the heroin trade, but then again they could be freelancing mercenaries.'

A light goes on in Harry's head. 'Like *ghosts*, you said?' Hettie Solilo used the same words this very morning.

'Yes?'

'What about the decapitations?'

'I'm looking through past cases involving decapitation right now.' Mitchell pats a small pile of files on one corner of his desk. 'They've become a lot more common in the last few years.'

'What about the singing and chanting?'

'Like I said, the worship of ancestors is the devil's work.'

'Whether it's the devil's work or not, I still need to know whether there's a link between this case and mine. Kobus has a reason to think there is, but what do you say?'

'Hhm – ' Mitchell runs a hand through his mullet haircut. 'I don't know where he gets *that* idea.'

Harry thanks Mitchell and is about to leave his office when he is summoned back. 'Listen, I have no worries with you, man – just understand that. We might have our differences, but you're a good guy. Just watch out for that partner of yours, though, because anyone that's personally involved in this *kak* is likely to be a liability.'

'My partner is a Christian like yourself, Mitchell. He just happens to know a little about *your* favourite subject, too.' Mitchell's face turns bright red, the reaction Harry hoped for. 'Thanks again for the information. I hope you catch your two killers soon.'

Stepping out of the man's office, Harry wonders what had been hovering on the edge of Niehaus's recall the night he called from Hillbrow. Harry needs a strong lead right now, and needs it badly. With the area commissioner and the public both watching his investigation closely, the pressure to resolve it is mounting.

Back in his own office, Harry notices that Jacob has turned up in the meantime. At the sight of the mound of statements sitting on both their desks Harry sighs heavily; they make him feel like Atlas, carrying the world on his shoulders. Surely no detective was ever originally meant to deal with all this paperwork? Instead of grappling with the reports, Harry flings himself into his chair and picks up his photograph of Jeanie. In the last week he has hardly found time for either his daughter or his wife. When he gets home at night, he feels broken and weary, often falling asleep unintentionally, only to awaken suddenly with an intense sensation of vertigo. On such occasions he will often find that Amy and Jeanie have already gone off to bed, leaving him alone to sleep on the couch. A considerate gesture, Harry supposes, but it leaves him feeling more alienated than rested.

Abruptly needing to hear his wife's voice, Harry decides to phone her office. Amy's assistant, however, informs him that she is attending an important meeting with a client and will not be available until the afternoon. Returning the receiver to its cradle, Harry experiences an exhausted depression creeping over him. Why is it that so often when a small necessity like an intimate call needs to be realized, it somehow cannot – or will not – happen? It all goes towards disrupting their relationship, and such small setbacks begin to matter when the larger picture is clouding and crumbling like a decaying painting.

Harry folds his arms on his desk, pillows his head on them and falls momentarily asleep.

In his dream he is walking down a suburban street in his dress uniform, smiling and waving at neighbourhood wives who are helping their housekeepers with the washing or watering their flowers. A red car shoots past him, then jerks to a halt in the middle of the street. Something sizeable is thrown from the back of the car to land on a beautifully manicured lawn. Too late, he races forward, yelling for the car to stop. Reaching the crumpled heap, he stares down to see a little black girl clothed in a white-and-blue floral dress. She is wearing yellow sandals and lies on her stomach, her face buried in the grass, which suddenly grows miraculously tall. When he stoops to see whether she has survived such rough treatment, one eye opens to reveal a bloodied socket.

He recoils in horror.

'*Baas*,' the child mumbles, as if her mouth is full of earth, 'can you tell me who I am?'

When a hand grabs him by the shoulder and shakes him Harry sits up with a gasp. He blinks up at Jacob.

'Someone wants you downstairs urgently.'

'Who is it?' demands Harry, and he shudders at the thought that it might be the little girl from his dream.

Jacob seems to sense something of Harry's dark disorientation because his face softens with concern. 'I don't know, Harry. I just got this call from Samuel at the charge desk.'

Still feeling queasy, Harry hurries downstairs. At the main reception he encounters a bemused-looking sergeant, who points to the door of a waiting room. Two Metropolitan police officers are standing outside it, looking equally anxious. Harry mouths a question at Samuel, who only shakes his head to indicate that he does not know.

Harry approaches the two officers. 'Can I help you?'

'Harry Mason?' asks one of them. 'Maybe you'd better ask the lady yourself.'

Just as he lays his hand on the door handle, Harry hears a sob from inside.

On opening the door, he is doubly surprised at the little black girl sitting on the interview table, wrapped in a blanket and weeping loudly. A coloured woman, her grime-caked face badly bruised and swollen, is seated next to her, wrapped in her own blue blanket.

The visitor's reaction takes him aback, as she stands up and moves furiously towards him.

'Yes, ma'am?' stammers Harry.

'You Detective Harry Mason?' she demands grimly.

'Er . . . yeah, I am.'

Without another word, Nina Reading takes a hefty swing at him. Her fist connects solidly with his mouth.

'Bugger you, *arsehole*!' she screams, while Harry barely gets his hands up in time to defend himself against further blows. He stumbles backwards, a new dread weakening his knees.

47

Although the little girl, called Yolisa, is immediately whisked away for a medical examination, the thought of others still being imprisoned there prompts Nina to forgo Chief Molethe's offer of a shower, fresh clothing and an early trip to the hospital. Instead she insists on telling her story first. So it is that Mason, Tshabalala, Molethe, Niehaus and Bornman now find themselves crammed into the two detectives' tiny office to listen. Nina begins with her surveillance of the shack and concludes with her dramatic escape with the help of a local woman resident. At that moment David Gildenhuys barges into the office, too.

'So what happened after you followed this woman out of there?' asks Superintendent Bornman, sounding almost awed by what he is hearing.

'She has an acquaintance who owns a car, and might have been persuaded to take us to the nearest police station. But just then this Met car pulled up at the traffic lights . . . But does all this matter?'

'You're right, madam,' says Molethe, jumping up. 'I can see you have much more to tell us, but for now we must get moving.'

Nina glances at Mason, who is staring into space. He is looking winded and ashamed, and a feeling of satisfaction surges through her exhausted and aching body.

Gildenhuys turns to Molethe. 'I want your entire unit ready to move immediately. I don't care where they are or what they're doing, I want them in a vest and ready to go within fifteen minutes.'

Turning back to the journalist, Gildenhuys smiles

warmly. 'Young lady, you did absolutely the right thing persuading Metropolitan to get you here to us straight away. Otherwise we'd be waiting till Christmas for your statement to reach us.'

With a frown, Jacob rummages through the papers stacked on his desk. He pulls out a photograph, squints at it and breaks out in a smile. 'Praise God.'

'What is it, detective?' inquires Bornman.

Jacob hurries over to Nina and shows her a photograph of Yolisa Sekhoto sitting happily with her mother. 'She's been missing from home for three weeks now,' he explains.

Nina takes the picture gingerly and studies it for a while. Biting her lip, she hands it back to him. 'There might be more children still imprisoned in that place. It doesn't look big from the front, but it's a labyrinth inside.' She gives them a hurried description of the building as best she can remember it.

As she finishes, Gildenhuys gives instructions. 'Harry, phone Sandra and ask her to take Ms Reading to the hospital. Make sure she'll be made as comfortable as possible. Then I want you to rejoin the rest of the team. Ms Reading, if I knew you any better I would kiss you.'

Another officer slides into the room, his face anxious with news. He makes his way quickly to Chief Molethe and whispers something in his ear, at the same time throwing Nina an incredulous glance.

'What's up?' she demands.

'Ms Reading, could you excuse us for a minute?'

'No. What are you whispering about?' she insists.

'I'd prefer to keep this police business for the moment. You've done enough to help as it is, and we're grateful, but please, for now, let us talk in private.'

'Are you chauvinists going to just shunt me aside after all I've been through?'

'Please, Ms Reading – ' Molethe holds up his hands disarmingly – 'we do need to get you to a hospital. Detective Mason will inform you of further developments as soon as possible. Until then, we have to treat all information sensitively.'

'You people really *are* a bunch of pigs!' Nina throws down the blanket and makes her way to the door. 'Screw the whole lot of you!' she yells in parting.

The door slams loudly shut behind her.

Gildenhuys gives Molethe a wink, but then turns an earnest gaze on Harry. 'What's all this about?'

Harry shrugs.

'Why did that woman attack you?' asks Molethe.

'I don't know.' Harry squirms.

It's Gildenhuys who delivers the final humiliation. '*Yissus*, Harry, there must be some reason she's pissed off with you. And I'll tell you this now: if I find out you screwed up somewhere, I'll not only have your badge, but your scalp and ears, too.'

Harry turns a bright red. 'Seriously, I don't know what this is all about.' He reaches for the phone and hurriedly dials, trying hard to ignore the eyes boring into him.

48

With Adusa Okechukwu, Taiwo Ejiofer, the woman Sibongile and their master the albino witch all now identified, Harry should be thinking positively of the ghosts he is about to expose to the light, but he feels a terrible sense of foreboding.

Could he have prevented the death of that boy by speaking to the journalist when she tried to phone him? Could he also have prevented the ordeal Nina Reading has gone through? The memory of her damaged fingers and bruised face causes Harry to grimace. She'd been covered in so much blood. The answers to those questions must be yes, he could have.

Harry sighs loudly enough to attract a quick glance from Jacob as they speed through the stifling city. Ahead of them race three police cars, behind them even more, all of them spraying blue emergency light over shops and over the traffic rearing out of their way. Pedestrians and shopkeepers watch silently as this column advances downhill, towards the Queen Elizabeth Bridge which feeds traffic into Newtown and Marshaltown. Neither man is keen to talk, intent only on what is about to happen. Their nerves are taut to breaking point.

Clutching the steering wheel till his knuckles show pink, Jacob has a terrible premonition that they will not catch any of the primary suspects but are taking themselves into some horrible danger. He is recalling that field of reeds where the dogs panicked; he is thinking of André Viljoen; of the dark omens Hettie Solilo described.

As a green sign for Newtown flashes by, Harry, too, is wondering about their chances of success. By the time they reach the target building, it will already have been over an hour since Nina's escape. How long would those murderers remain there? These days all it takes is one well-positioned man with a mobile phone to raise the alarm.

As they speed past, Harry eyes the crowds milling on the pavement: people going home, people arriving at work, hawkers with their wares spread over blankets and newspapers, gamblers shooting craps on the kerb, a group

273

smoking what looks like *dagga* under a blue haze curling slowly over their heads. Anyone out there could be working for this same albino witch.

Harry squirms in his seat to remove his wallet and keys from his back trouser pocket. He puts them safely in the glove box. For an operation like this, he prefers to be as unencumbered as possible. Finally he breaks the silence with his partner as Jacob steers them into Simmonds Street.

'You know, Jacob, I've never even seen where you live. What sort of place is it?'

Reacting as if this is not rather an odd question at a time like this, Jacob replies, 'It's fairly small. Just two bedrooms, a kitchen, a living room. Outside it has a small garden with a surrounding wall, where I've recently planted a few fruit trees – peaches and apricots. I just finished painting the place green and white, like I think I told you.'

Harry takes out his Vector service pistol and extra clips from the glove box, and lifts a box of ammunition from between his feet. 'You've never been to visit my house either.'

'No, I haven't.'

'You should come. We'll have a *braai*. You can bring . . . what's her name again, Nomsa?'

'Yes, Nomsa.' As Jacob briefly turns to Harry, their eyes meet and share the hopelessness they both feel. 'That sounds good.'

The two-way radio suddenly buzzes and officers already cordoning off the streets report shots being fired in two different locations. They want back-up, and they want it fast. Chief Molethe's distorted voice assures them that his men will be there in under five minutes.

Jacob is sucking in his cheeks, a sign that he feels he is facing extreme danger.

'You need any?' Harry shakes the box of bullets.

'Mm.' Jacob shifts in his seat and unhitches his weapon and spare clips for Harry to double-check. There are two shotguns resting between Harry and the door, and he knows some of the other men will be carrying R4 assault rifles. Some liberals still believe such firepower excessive; everyone else appreciates it has become a necessity these days. In Harry's opinion, once a large proportion of the criminals on the streets of South Africa is carrying Russian semi-automatics, the time for discussion on whether the police force should or should not be carrying guns at all is over.

Looking out the window, Harry spots a young black boy's face briefly illuminated by a flash of revolving blue light. It is a face filled with awe and wonder. 'You really enjoy driving, don't you?' observes Harry, conversing mindlessly, but he cannot dwell on his mistakes now, not before something as big as this raid.

'*Ja*,' replies Jacob, still hollowing his cheeks. His eyes rest on the rear-view mirror, where he spots two ambulances following them.

Harry presses on. 'So what will you do when you win the lottery?'

Jacob gives a strained smile. 'I'll first pay for Nomsa's *lobola*, then marry her and buy us a house in some better neighbourhood. After that, I'll be happy to have a few children.'

'What, no Ferrari?'

Jacob laughs. 'Maybe, if there's any money left.'

The streets which were lined with glittering multi-storey buildings fall behind as they crawl further south into Newtown's older district. Open spaces now appear, filled with the rubble of a changing inner city, and then the outer rim of the shanty town appears further down the hill. The police come to a stop about half a mile further along the road, just as the roadblock units report more gunfire.

'It seems they're being pinned down for some reason,' says Harry.

Jacob does not reply.

'Jacob?' His partner still does not react. 'Jakes, listen to me – you'll be OK.'

Jacob stares at Harry and forces a nod, his gaze now glistening with fear.

As they step from the car, Harry immediately notices the smell of diesel and rubber. He peers down the hill and spots a thick column of black smoke billowing up over the shanties. A section underneath the overpass has begun to burn.

'Call the fire departments. It's all gonna go!' yells Harry, as he sprints down the road on impulse, leaving Jacob to stare after him, dumbfounded.

It is only when Jacob leans back into the car to radio for help that he realizes his partner has left both his bullet-proof vest and his shotgun.

49

Harry hurtles towards the action, reacting in panic. He thinks of nothing other than reaching the burning building and forcing his way inside. He cannot allow the death of another child to happen. Not when the last one may have resulted from his own negligence.

The blood thundering in his ears, Harry ignores his commander's order to return to their amassing group. Reaching one of the roadblocks, which has now been pulled further back up the street, Harry veers towards the three Met officers who have plastered themselves against a street corner. To their immediate right another three officers are peering out at the emerging chaos two hundred yards away. A number of civilians are even darting about, investigating the flames that threaten their lives and livelihoods.

'What's going on?' rasps Harry.

'Gunmen,' says an officer in his late twenties with eyes like black pools of ink. 'Shots were exchanged, but nothing from our side since we pulled back. It's as if they're determined to stop us coming any closer. I think that crowd down there is trying to organize some means of extinguishing the fire. If that blaze spreads any further, the whole camp might burn down.'

Harry can see flames licking out of a structure located almost underneath the overpass. It stands close to a concrete support column, exactly where Nina Reading said it would be.

'In that market these shits can move around and take pot shots at us in the darkness for as long as it takes that whole place to burn down,' grumbles one of the Met officers. Harry watches a trickle of sweat creep down the side of the man's head.

But what about the children? his thoughts prompt him, urgently.

Unable to wait for the larger police force to organize itself, Harry leaps ahead, sticking to the left-hand pavement. He draws nearer to the blaze without incident. Just as he hopes the gunmen have already made their escape, gunfire erupts again like firecrackers. Harry hurls himself sideways as he runs, and tumbles downhill, slamming painfully into a doorway. Nozzle flashes erupt to his right, forcing him to scramble for safety behind a defective street light. Bullets spray the concrete everywhere. The anxious crowd further down the street dissipates in seconds, people screeching in fear as they flee in every direction.

Tearing out his pistol, Harry returns fire, aiming towards the four snipers he has now identified partly concealed in a narrow alley adjoining the nearside of the burning building. But the distance is close to forty yards, so Harry's return fire falls short.

There is a sudden loud crash from inside the blazing structure as automatic fire rakes his own position again, the bullets ricocheting loudly off steel.

Desperately glancing behind him for support, he spots men grouping behind the two patrol cars that seal off the street. Harry turns his gaze back to the gunmen. His lungs heaving, he wonders whether he can risk an all-out sprint for the building itself, past their line of fire.

Suddenly the roar of R4s echoes down the street and Harry sees the gunmen scramble backwards as their tin cover is shredded by military calibres. Niehaus, Bornman and a third officer kneel blatantly in the middle of the road, their suppressing fire bringing a quick smile of gratitude to Harry's face. Keeping close to the walls, police officers advance quickly down both sides of the street.

Hunched low, Jacob sprints towards Harry, but before he can reach him Harry scrambles up again and heads straight for the burning building.

'Harry, what the *fuck* are you doing!' yells Kobus, jumping up.

A sheet of blue plastic is slowly curling in on itself, like a drying leaf, fluttering in the gusts of hot air escaping from the building's entrance. Harry hurtles in underneath it, slams straight into a kiosk counter and waves his gun from side to side. There is no one in the cramped room, but he spots a back room and hurries through to it.

Nothing but a dead end. Smoke is, however, pouring out of a hole in the floor, reminding Harry of Nina's account: how the place is riddled with crudely constructed secret rooms and passages. With his nose and mouth jammed into the crook of his elbow, he manages to fan sufficient smoke away to inspect the floor and wall nearby.

'Harry!' shouts Kobus from the entrance. *'Kry you gat daar uit, man!'*

Chipboard in the walls is blackening, the plastic used to insulate the imperfections of the structure's walls is shrinking and all around him metal is creaking and whining.

Having noticed a bolt set in the floor Harry tugs it aside, meanwhile breathing in a lungful of black smoke. Retching and coughing, he manages to lift open a trapdoor to reveal makeshift stairs leading into darkness below. Throwing caution aside, he holsters his pistol and jumps down into the gap.

50

'We have to go in after him!' cries Jacob. 'He's not thinking clearly.'

'We can't go in there.' Kobus shoulders his rifle. 'It's bloody well about to explode.'

'We have to!'

'No way am I going in there . . .'

There's a loud crash from inside and Jacob winces.

'*Aykona*, I'm not going in there,' reiterates Kobus.

The two detectives hear others moving behind them and turn hurriedly to see a fireman and four police officers approaching. Kobus informs the young, clean-shaven fireman that one of his police colleagues has gone inside. The fireman stares at him incredulously. 'That's bloody *insane*. These shacks are so damn flimsy, it'll collapse completely in a few minutes.'

Kobus tugs at a fistful of hair in frustration. 'Oh fuck, Harry, you bloody idiot.'

The blue sheeting suddenly tears loose and flaps away on a current of hot air. There is another crash as something else gives way. Jacob glances up the street to see three fire engines now inching past the hastily erected police barrier. Officers are fanning outwards through the squatters' camp in all directions, hunting for the gunmen.

'We'll have to focus on containing this fire. It's too late to rescue the building,' says the fireman. 'These shacks are all linked up together, so they'll go up in a chain reaction. If we don't prevent that, this whole block will burn down within a matter of hours.'

'No, *you* don't understand.' Kobus wags a finger menacingly at the fireman. 'We need this building in the *best* fucking condition possible. There's evidence inside there we can't afford to lose. This is bloody important, understand me, *boet*?'

'I—'

'Is that *understood*?'

The man is silent for a moment, then gives a curt, apprehensive nod. 'Right, we're on it. Just get your man out of there; I can't afford to send a team in after him.' He turns and jogs towards the fire trucks, which are now coming to a stop in the middle of the road.

'I can't just stand here and wait,' groans Jacob, tugging at the Velcro of his bullet-proof vest.

'What are you doing, Tshabalala? You can't go in there, too. Didn't you hear a word that fireman just said?'

The vest drops to the ground, and Jacob throws himself inside the building just as the first flames come licking over the roofline towards the entrance.

'Jacob!' shouts Kobus. 'Come back here, you bull-headed Zulu. What is it with you two?' Niehaus steps back from the heat and shields his eyes, but the detective has already disappeared into the smoke now belching sporadically from the entrance.

51

The heat is extraordinary and Harry is finding it difficult to breathe. His lungs feel as if he is inhaling straight from the spout of a boiling kettle. His eyes are swimming and his shirt feels burning hot against his skin. Nevertheless, Harry is glad that the structure seems more solid underground: cooler here, and with less smoke. He can see a few feet ahead of him, thanks to the flames that lick along crudely patched areas in the ceiling. The light they provide is eerily golden.

Already feeling disorientated, Harry is hesitant to proceed, but when another crash sounds somewhere close by, showering sparks into the underground tunnels, he is spurred on at a stoop through the narrow confines. It is not long before he arrives at a T-junction, where he opts to turn left into a darker network of the tunnels, expecting, for no reason at all, to find there the cells he is looking for.

Suddenly he stops and peers over his shoulder, listening intently. From somewhere behind him, a high-pitched scream sends a familiar chill down his spine. After all these years the sound reminds him of the Morwargh child's last moments.

No, not again. Not ever again.

Harry Mason turns around and rushes back towards the epicentre of the inferno, paying no heed to the ash and embers dropping down from cracks in the roof above him, landing in his hair and on his shirt, where they smoulder and burn. He disregards the snapping of this dark warren's structural bonds as they disintegrate a floor above him, threatening to cave in on him through the makeshift ceiling. His eyes bleed tears in his effort to see, and his sinuses feel as if hot gravel is embedded in them.

Reaching a bolted metal door, Harry lunges towards it. He bellows in pain as the hot metal singes his bare palm.

'I'm coming!' he yells desperately. 'Hang in there a little longer.'

There is no verbal reply, but Harry does not need one. The screaming is still audible, although considerably diminished, and still brutally agitating him. Finally he pulls the belt from his trousers, wraps it around his burnt hand and grabs again for the bolt, which this time slides open.

The door blows open with enough force to knock Harry to the floor. Like steam released from a pressure cooker, the scorching air bursts from the room into the colder passageway, closely followed by flames.

He rolls over and shakes his head to focus with bleary eyes on the naked child lying motionless inside the small room. Harry scrambles over, sweeps it up in one arm and hurtles back into the passage.

52

Jacob hurries on through the abandoned kiosk, where a week before Golden Boy and his couriers negotiated the transport of three abducted children. His partner is nowhere to be seen, but Jacob soon finds the open trapdoor, with smoke spiralling up lazily over the dark void below.

Down the steps he plunges, already sweating profusely from the intense heat. Immediately below, he is confronted with the choice of two directions. Wondering which way his partner went, Jacob listens intently, but cannot hear anything other than metal popping and the faint din of water hitting the structure's tin exterior. Jacob scrambles first one way, then the other, unsuccessfully trying to discern in the gloom any sign of Harry's passing.

Where is he? God, where is he?

Jacob pauses, feeling for an answer, a premonition – anything that will suggest to him where his impulsive friend might have gone.

Jacob closes his eyes and looks inward. Abruptly his thoughts turn to his grandfather. It hardly comes as a surprise to him to be thinking of the old man in this dire situation, for he is, after all, one of the many in a long line of ancestors who have watched over Jacob all these years. The sense of having someone with him, to help him make decisions, has always calmed Jacob in moments of crisis. What does come as a surprise is a sudden feeling of his head opening up to the will of his ancestors in the way he remembers his father describing to him. Having for so long turned his back on such teachings, Jacob finds this unfamiliar prickling sensation at the crown of his head disturbing, yet welcome, too. He feels stirring inside him the spirit he first encountered during his initiation into Zulu manhood, and suddenly he is overwhelmed by a renewed surge of confidence. He calls to mind the image of his grandfather stooping over him as a child all those years ago. What was it he had said on that last occasion?

You're going to be the kind of man who will know what someone's going to say before he knows himself.

Like you, grandfather? the young boy had replied.

Maybe.

The sound of a small explosion suddenly snaps Jacob out of his trance. Without delay, he continues in the direction he is now facing, in the direction which Harry also took.

53

Jacob's back is beginning to ache with the effort of running hunched over to prevent knocking his head against the low ceiling. Sweat is streaming into his smoke-irritated eyes. He arrives at another T-junction just as a sudden blast erupts somewhere above him. It is followed by the sound of hissing steam. Debris and waterlogged ash rain down on top of him.

He races instinctively down the left-hand passageway, after scarcely even a glance in the other direction. Suddenly he is tripped up and sent flying. Barely managing to throw his hands out in time, he hits the floor hard, biting his tongue in the process. Rolling over, with a painful groan, to see what he has stumbled over, Jacob is shocked to discover Harry lying face down in the flickering darkness. His hunched silhouette suggests he is holding something in his arms.

'Harry!' cries Jacob, scrambling back towards his partner. 'Get up, Harry.' He grasps Mason's neck and feels for a pulse, finding it is there, but rapid and irregular. A bright flare of orange light briefly illuminates Harry's smoke-smeared face and a large bruise rapidly spreading on his forehead. The back of his shirt is pitted with holes where fragments of burning debris have charred through to the skin.

As Jacob tries to roll Harry over, his partner abruptly stirs, then springs to life. 'Leave her alone!' he roars. The man struggles to his feet, and for a brief moment Jacob distinguishes the form clutched to his chest.

'Harry, it's me,' announces Jacob solemnly.

Another hiss of steam behind him causes Harry to whirl around. It is more dirty water gushing through the ceiling. The little light in the tunnel fades significantly as the flames above them fizzle out.

Jacob speaks up softly. 'Harry, we need to get out of here. We need to *go*.'

'Roger?' says Harry in a confused voice.

'No, it's Jacob – it's me, we have to go. Just give me the child.'

'No!'

The edge on this rejection is sharp enough to cut. Sensing something is desperately wrong with his partner, Jacob hesitates. Another brief flare of plastic bursting into flames above them confirms his suspicions. Harry's unfocused eyes are glittering wildly in the dark.

'OK, *you* carry her,' says Jacob. 'Take her now and lead the way. We need to get out of here quick, though, Harry. Just make sure you get us out of here.'

By now the slimy rain filtering through the damaged ceiling has soaked them with grime. In the distance Jacob hears someone call out. 'Shall I take the lead?' he asks.

After succumbing to a coughing fit, Harry takes half a minute to answer. 'Yeah, go on then, you take the lead.'

His partner's peculiar tone of voice makes Jacob's hackles rise. Giving the man a wide berth, Jacob quickly slips in front of him.

With occasional anxious glances over his shoulder, he guides them towards the way out. When they round the last corner, Jacob is momentarily alarmed to find their exit blocked by a large and shadowy figure wielding a massive axe. But it is only a fireman in full protective gear, hacking away at a collapsed section of the roof to clear the entrance. Noticing the two men approaching, the firefighter directs a bright torch beam on them before giving the thumbs-up. He kicks away the worst of the smouldering debris and waves them through.

As they burst gasping from the building retching for breath, the two detectives stagger off in different directions. Jacob is still bent double when he hears Niehaus's horrified voice behind him. 'Harry, what the fuck are you doing? Can't you see she's *dead*?'

Jacob turns around just in time to see Harry pull away from the child he was trying to resuscitate. Now visible in her soot-stained forehead is an obtrusive bullet hole.

Jacob drags his eyes away from the murdered child to look at Harry. He sees the wild expression on his partner's face flicker and die out, as Harry slowly sits back on his haunches. Grasping his hair with bloodstained hands, Harry looks up at the fireman and police officers silently staring at him.

In anguish he suddenly sobs, 'Oh, *fuck.*'

Niehaus sighs and, crouching next to Harry, grabs his shoulder. 'It's OK, *boet*, you tried. God knows you tried when no one else would.'

Harry's shoulders begin to hitch uncontrollably. Abruptly he shoves Niehaus's hand away, jumps up and starts towards the other side of the street. He only manages a few steps before he succumbs to another violent coughing fit, then sways and drops to the tarmac.

54

Doctors, medical tests, more doctors writing reports or giving advice, nurses constantly flitting in and out. She has given further statements to Sandra Pienaar, the detective who accompanied her to Johannesburg General, then finally a trauma counsellor arrives to warn Nina that any emotional reactions she suffers over the next few days will be entirely natural and would she like some sedatives to help her sleep. They have since then given her slop to eat rather than anything solid to get her teeth into, advising Nina that her stomach will need to be reconditioned after several days without regular meals.

The barrage of attention mounts, eventually irritating her to the point where she shrieks abuse at the latest nurse who dares enter her room to check up on her. After that outburst they finally leave her alone.

Even with the medication, Nina finds it difficult to fall

asleep. When she was confined in that dark hole of a cell, all she could think about was her freedom. Yet now, with her freedom won, she cannot stop thinking obsessively about her abduction and the horrors of the past week. When she finally got a chance to clean up and examine herself in the mirror, she saw that the entire left side of her face looks like it has been caught under the wheels of a truck. Her cheeks are sharp and gaunt, her eyes wide and fearful. A week in that place has made her unrecognizable even to herself.

In that harrowing week she was forced to betray her own story as well as Tumi's to the people who least deserved to know it. That makes her feel untrustworthy and ashamed.

Nina tries to find comfort in the soft, clean sheets and the privacy of occupying a ward actually meant for four, but the bed feels as if it is made of nails and the room is just like another cell. Her splinted and bandaged fingers and multiple bruises cause her continual discomfort, till she sits up impatiently and clicks on the television bracketed to the wall.

After a while her thoughts meander towards the policeman, Harry Mason. She feels a lot calmer about him now. The memory of his surprise, as her fist crushed his mouth, brings a satisfied smile to her lips. The bastard deserved that and more. Yet she could not bring herself to report him for misconduct once she was given the chance. She omitted explaining her reasons for attacking him, both in the presence of his superiors and in a statement later made to Detective Pienaar. None of them has asked her any more about it, yet. Nina is coming to the realization that she would very much like the whole incident to be forgotten, probably because she knows she cannot entirely blame him for her recent predicament.

From Mason her mind wanders to the big wounded man who saved her and whom she tried to rescue in turn. Did he manage to escape, too? She certainly hopes so, although a gnawing instinct deep inside her argues otherwise. The room in which he had been imprisoned was already slick with his blood when she climbed up into it. Her brief glimpse of his face in daylight just before she fled has left her with the feeling that he was already close to death.

And also somehow that he looked familiar to her.

Try as she might, she cannot reach the itch of recognition this man is causing her. She rolls over again and sighs heavily. The only thing she feels remotely pleased about is Yolisa's escape. She had felt such a temptation just to save herself without the child. She hopes that by now the child is reunited with her family.

Nina looks at Harry Mason's mobile, which he has lent to her in case she needs to call someone. It was a nice enough gesture after his previous disagreeable behaviour. Nina decides that, to make amends, he deserves to pick up the charge for a phone call home. When her mother answers, she becomes completely hysterical at the sound of her missing daughter's voice. When finally she calms down, they conduct a conversation of sorts, with Nina evading any questions as to what she has been through.

'When's that going to be, my dear?' demands her mother.

'Soon, but I can't say for sure. I . . .' Nina suddenly feels a knot in her throat. 'I just want to come home *now*. I'm not so sure if I'm cut out for this.'

When she puts the phone down her veneer of toughness

finally collapses. Nina buries her face deep in the pillow and weeps uncontrollably.

Detective Mason's mobile rings on her bedside table, waking Nina up. Uncomfortable with answering a stranger's phone, Nina nevertheless answers the call, thinking it might be the detective himself checking up on her.

'Detective Mason's phone,' she announces.

'Hello?' asks a female voice hesitantly.

'Yes?' Nina yawns and looks at the time – still only eight o'clock in the evening.

'Is my *husband* there?' The woman suddenly sounds a lot more determined.

Oh shit. 'Mrs Mason? No, he's not here. This is Nina Reading speaking. I'm ... I was mugged and am in hospital at the moment. Your husband was kind enough to lend me his phone.'

'Oh, I'm sorry to hear that,' says Amy more amiably. 'I hope you're all right.'

'I'll be fine. Your husband said he'd be by to pick up his mobile first thing tomorrow. Perhaps you could try calling one of his colleagues to find out where he is.'

'I tried his office number and they said he'd gone out on some big operation.' She sounds distracted. 'But I guess that doesn't concern you. Thank you in any case.' Mrs Mason breaks the connection, leaving Nina to wonder what it must be like to be the wife of a cop in a country as dangerous as South Africa.

55

Lying down, with an oxygen mask clamped over his mouth and nose, Harry feels a sharp pain in his forehead and an intense burning sensation in his right palm and all across his shoulders. He realizes that his shirt has been removed. When he opens his eyes, he discovers a furious-looking Jacob sitting just across from him in the stationary ambulance.

'What happened?' wheezes Harry, propping himself up on one elbow. He pats gingerly at one shoulder and winces at the huge blisters he feels there.

'That's what I'd like to know,' counters Jacob.

Harry pulls off the uncomfortable mask and coughs raggedly. He spots his shirt on the floor of the vehicle, its white cotton material now ruined by the number of holes burnt into it. Outside, dusk is quickly spreading over the city's skyline.

'So who is Roger?' Jacob demands.

Harry looks up sharply and all the blood drains from his face. 'What do you mean?'

'What do I *mean*?' Jacob narrows his eyes. 'I *mean*, I had to go after you into a burning building. You seemed to have gone raving mad – kept calling me Roger for some reason. Who, I ask you, is Roger?'

'I don't know what you're talking about.' Harry swings his legs down from the stretcher and reaches for his discarded shirt.

'*Klau shapha wena*, Harry!' yells Jacob, grabbing his partner and ramming his head up against the storage units above the stretcher. 'I've just about *had* it with you! Don't shrug me off this time. You always do that, and I'm growing sick of it. I'm not an idiot! You were going to kill me back there – I could see it in your eyes. And now I *know* you're still not telling me everything, man. I don't want to risk my life every day with a partner who's crazy and hides things from me – things that could get me *killed*. So answer me!'

Harry's expression dulls as he goes limp, seemingly welcoming his partner's onslaught.

'In the name of God, *speak* to me!' yells Jacob. 'What *is* it with you?'

A fresh coughing fit, the sight of sweat beading under Harry's eyes, and his greying complexion force Jacob to release his grip. He throws himself back to sit on the other stretcher. 'I'm sorry,' he grumbles.

Harry pulls the oxygen mask back over his face, then massages his throat. Jacob stares at him with a mixture of rage and concern. As his breathing finally returns to normal, Harry mumbles indistinctly, 'I thought they might still be alive in there. I thought *she* was still alive.'

'She'd already been executed.'

Harry moves the mask aside. 'I was sure I heard her screaming.'

'Well, it was definitely not her you heard. So all you managed was nearly getting us *both* killed.'

Harry sits up. 'I didn't *ask* you to follow me in.'

'We've always worked together; why should tonight be any different?'

'Don't get so bloody holy with me. We've always worked together? What about your own little secret that Mitchell seems to know so much about, that some dick at Solilo's place was baiting me over? Don't lecture me about hiding things.'

Jacob stares at him in disbelief.

'Your shit's blown this all out of proportion,' continues Harry, with rising agitation. 'You and your damn beliefs – there's never a straight answer. Never making any sense, it makes me *sick*. You lot *allow* these killers to operate. That's what's really evil, not some fucking curse I picked up, not some shit frightening the dogs, but *your* culture. Don't tell me some *witch* is responsible for all this. It's people like *you*, who live in fear of those bastards that do this, who cause others to fear them with your bullshit stories. I honestly thought you had more to you than this voodoo crap.'

'I see,' Jacob replies quietly. 'And why is this about *black* culture and religion all of a sudden?'

Harry throws his hands in the air. 'This isn't about *race*.'

'No?' says Jacob coolly.

Harry pauses. 'Let's cut to the chase, then. What do you expect *me*, as a *white* man, to think about all this? Just put yourself in *my* shoes. Is human life really so cheap to you? If that woman reporter is right, this stuff could have been going on for years. How many other people must've lived or worked around that building? How many people must've *heard* something, *seen* something. But *nothing* happens! No one says a goddamn word. Traditions like those don't belong in the civilized world.'

Jacob chuckles sarcastically. 'Poor Harry, look at you. You always have to be able to understand something from where *you're* standing. And if you can't, you get mad at the world. That makes you very self-absorbed, my friend. Your concerns are not at the centre of the world, the world is not always against you, and neither did God make it just to be understood by you. God created it for you to *live* in.' Jacob draws a breath, holding up his finger. 'You have no right to judge my culture so harshly. No culture is ever perfect, and they are all responsible for their own atrocities. You're no better than I am. You might *think* you are, but that's only because you haven't made any effort to *understand* my heritage. Do you really know what it means to be a black man? Do you know what it is to be a Bantu? No, I know you don't, otherwise you wouldn't have been so resistant to everything I've tried to tell you about this case. You don't really understand people, do you? You know all about what people can do to each other – the science of understanding what people do wrong – but that isn't the same as relating to people, is it?'

Harry rubs his face sullenly and stares out over the driver's seat and through the front windshield. He can barely make out the overpass's droning traffic over the commotion outside. For a long time he thinks about what he is going to say. Eventually, 'I can't do this any more, Jacob,' Harry whispers. 'All this time I . . . I've been trying to relate to killers: getting inside their heads and anticipating their next moves. But I can't do it any more. It's not why I'm here, it's not why I joined the force. I joined the police service to get rid of them, not to have them take over my mind. All I can think about these days is what they do and why they do it. I think about their victims and the lives they must've led. There's now hardly any room left in here – ' Harry taps his temple – 'for other things.'

A medic arrives wearing a navy blue jumpsuit and promptly berates Harry for taking his oxygen mask off. The pencil light the man shines into his eyes causes Harry to gasp in pain. Concerned, the medic turns to Jacob. 'I'm taking him in now. His heart rate is still pretty erratic – and I'm not ruling out a concussion either.'

'One more thing, Harry,' says Jacob, stepping out of the back of the ambulance. 'We found that guy who helped the journalist escape, he was right where she left him – he didn't have a chance to run. He's been shot to pieces, so they clearly didn't like him much.'

'Who was he, then?' asks Harry.

'Ngubane Maduna.'

'*What?*'

Jacob shrugs. 'You just think about that until morning. Take care.'

As the medic slams the doors shut, Harry lies back and raises an exhausted hand in token farewell.

56

There is desperation in the pace at which the police and fire departments now work to salvage as much evidence as possible from the smoking building. They operate in the soft yellow glow of outdated street lamps and the stark white light from the fire department's generators, both illuminating the grim site. Red and blue lights flash across the hundreds of eyes now watching the investigation unfolding, which include those of the men, women and children who are spying for a man whom they believe to be special. He brought them hope just as much as he brought them fear, two strong emotions that can inspire people when he needs them most. For those in his thrall it does not matter whether he blesses them with a word from the afterlife or blesses them with money and a sweet kiss of heroin. What matters most to them is their association with him.

Three men in particular have stationed themselves in

an adjacent street, close enough to view the action. Lurking in a darkened doorway they wait, periodically collecting information as runners appear to report on new developments from the police operation. They are the three men Jacob encountered outside Hettie Solilo's house.

Cassius is leaning against a wall, lazily tracing a finger along the steroid stretch marks on his bulging forearms. His familiar skullcap is now discarded in the car parked around the back of a wholesale printer's building. 'You sure it's him?' he asks in Ndebele.

'Of course, I am,' rasps his bearded friend. Collin was sitting in the back of the BMW the day the cop came over to talk to them. He plucks at his frazzled beard. 'It's definitely him that ran into the building after the white cop. Pity it didn't cave in on their heads.'

The driver, Lucky, who is leaning against a lamp post, snorts with laughter.

'Besides, they were the two cops in the paper Adusa showed us,' continues Collin.

'So we'd better have a look at the car they arrived in,' says Cassius. 'Call Vusi – let one of his boys have a look.'

Cassius leaves the doorway and whistles up the street. At its far end a shadow separates itself from the corner and hastens towards them. Soon a boy of about fourteen wearing a tarnished yellow shirt has joined them, an eager glimmer in his eyes. Cassius issues a few quick commands, urging Vusi to hurry.

'I'll do it myself – ' the boy smiles wickedly – 'and if I get a chance to steal from these sons of bitches, I'll do it.'

An hour later, Lucky spots the same boy flitting back towards them. He arrives with a massive grin on his face, revealing teeth that are discolouring at their edges. In his hands he holds a key ring attached to a shark-shaped bottle-opener and also Harry Mason's wallet. Inside the wallet they find Harry's home address printed on an old receipt.

'How did you get it,' asks Cassius. 'Did you break the window?'

Vusi looks at him reproachfully, as if his professional pride has been deeply injured, and holds up a T-shaped iron tool that fits neatly into his hand and which has a thin fork at one end. 'These stupid police – no one is guarding their cars.' Vusi brandishes the keys. 'This little piggy won't even know I've been into his car until he gets back to his nice big house and tries to unlock the door.'

Cassius takes money from Harry's wallet and hands it to the boy. Then the three of them disappear into the parking lot behind them – to retrieve their own car and make a phone call.

57

It is ten o'clock at night. Her phone conversation with that English woman using her husband's mobile occurred two hours ago, and Amy has still not had any word from him. Earlier that afternoon she already knew that something was wrong after their neighbour called Amy during a company function to inform her that Harry had not dropped by to pick up Jeanie.

Amy had raced home, seething with anger and embarrassment, to grow ever more anxious as she gradually discovered Harry was embroiled in some kind of police emergency.

What kind of operation could be so crucial as to make him forget about Jeanie? Harry has never before failed to pick up their daughter.

Without much success, Amy has been trying to calm her spiralling apprehension. She clutches her hands in her lap and chews on her lip as she sits and waits by the phone in the hallway. The orange glow from a ricepaper lampshade contrived by Harry casts a warm light on the white tiles. Amy shifts her chair forward under its halo as if seeking comfort from her husband's creation as she worries about him being in danger.

Jeanie has already gone to bed: highly upset at first, but now sleeping soundly. From where Amy sits she can catch sight of the television, in case a special news bulletin is broadcast. Her mind skims over Harry's increasingly bizarre behaviour recently. He does not sleep properly any more, often pacing around the house until a few hours before dawn. In the past few days he seems to have made only the briefest human contact with either her or Jeanie before his eyes glaze over with that dumb, emotionless expression she cannot stand.

Then there is the gun.

Admittedly, she herself has not been sleeping properly either, waking up when she unconsciously senses the cold empty space where her husband should be lying, waking up alone in the room with that steel thing on his bedside table, the black eye of its barrel staring towards her.

And now seemingly Harry has disappeared – and a stranger has his mobile phone.

Is there something they're not telling me? How soon will they tell me the worst?

Amy is unsure. She has had only brief contact with Harry's partner, Jacob Tshabalala. Although she remembers taking a liking to him, she still considers him a stranger. All in all, she has never really enjoyed the rough crowd comprising the members of the Murder and Robbery Unit and their families, and usually declines to accompany her husband to their social events.

It is a terrible moment for Amy to realize how much of an outsider she really is, and how much of an outsider Harry must therefore seem, too. In a world where the servicemen and their families all function like kin, Harry and herself have always preferred the company of their own little world. So now, when she could use all the help she can get, she has no one to turn to for support.

When finally the phone rings, it startles her.

She seizes the receiver. 'Mason residence.'

Someone wheezes, 'Amy.'

'Harry, is that you?'

'I'm sorry I didn't phone to say I'd be late.'

'Where the *hell* are you? You forgot to pick up your own daughter from Mrs Strydom, do you realize?'

'I'm—' Harry begins to cough in loud whoops. 'I'm sorry, Amy. I . . . it's been a very difficult day.'

'Harry, where *are* you?'

'I'll be home soon. I've kicked up enough of a fuss for them to discharge me.'

'You're in *hospital*?'

'Just routine. They wanted to check I didn't have a concussion. And they also want to keep an eye on my lungs – chemical pneumonia or something.'

Amy stammers, then falls silent.

'I'm all right now, I promise. How's Jeanie?'

'She's in bed. What's going to happen? Do you . . . do you need me to fetch you? Of course, you need me. I'll fetch you, where are you? I'll wake up Jeanie right now and we'll come . . . we'll come see you. I . . .' Amy sobs, then bites her mouth shut.

'Amy, I'll ask them for a ride home.'

'You're in a goddamn *hospital*!' she cries. 'I was worried *sick*. I had no one to phone, I had no one phoning me. I'm worried *sick*.'

Over the phone, there comes the sound of Harry drinking something. When next he speaks his voice sounds better. 'I understand. Listen, can we talk about this when I get home? I'm exhausted.'

'Yes.' Amy regains her composure. 'Yes, all right. I'll come fetch you, though.'

Harry does not object, sensing that Amy needs to do this her way.

She disconnects and hurries into her daughter's room to wake her up. Jeanie immediately commences complaining. By the time her mother has her tucked into a warm blue blanket and securely fastened her into the passenger seat of the blue Mazda, the little girl is fast asleep again, leaving Amy to mull over her own conflicting emotions as she races towards Johannesburg General.

58

Harry smiles tiredly at the duty nurse as he hands back the receiver, and thanks her. It is the third time he has disrupted her duties in this way, first to receive concerned inquiries from Jacob and Chief Molethe, then to speak to Amy, for which he needed to ready himself.

To Jacob he apologized for his behaviour earlier. 'I had no right to say what I did.'

Jacob replied almost shyly, 'It's OK. You rest now and maybe we'll speak tomorrow.'

Sometimes Harry envies Jacob for his reserves of patience.

The fire had eventually been brought under control, but not before it had destroyed a great deal of the building itself and its contents. Three more bodies had been retrieved before Chief Molethe finally departed the scene, leaving behind a team of grumbling forensic specialists, from both police and fire departments. Although Molethe was frustrated about not capturing anyone significant, it seemed that a few arrests were made after people began to come forward with more constructive information.

'All sorts of scum were plying their trade quietly in that dump,' Molethe reported. 'It seems a massive extortion ring was operating there, as well. Now that people living and working locally know who we are onto, they'll be singing like sparrows perched on a fence.'

'Just don't make any further move without me, boss,' Harry pleaded. 'This means a lot to me.'

There was then a long pause before Molethe replied. 'Perhaps too much? Just get some rest, detective. I'll speak to you in the morning.'

Exhausted and dazed by painkillers, Harry makes his way down the ward towards the small open-air balcony the smokers use. Finding himself alone outside, Harry sinks into a plastic garden chair and contemplates the leafy suburb of Parktown, spread out six floors below him. The hospital, nestling on a hill, gives an excellent view west and north of the night-time city: cars inching along in the distance, halogen street lights shimmering in the heat from the suburbs, Harrow Road snaking its way up from the

M1 highway to disappear eventually into the bowels of Hillbrow. The powerful scents of frangipani and jasmine drift on a light breeze while bats squeak and gorge themselves on insects buzzing around nearby lights. Johannesburg looks and smells so tranquil and seems so unconcerned with its own savagery. Harry wonders whether he himself will ever be able to coexist so easily with his own internal demons.

He closes his eyes and turns his tired mind back to the day's events. The more he thinks about it, the more he feels responsible for that mutilated boy's death. The corpse, the traumas experienced by Nina Reading, and now the executed children all conjure vivid images to plague his senses. The more he thinks about his own part in this day's developments, the more he thinks that his usefulness as a police officer has come to an end.

Jacob was right – of course, he is being selfish. He is demanding that the world pay constant heed to his own misery and pain. Harry realized long ago how self-obsessed he becomes when his childhood memories surface. What good is understanding, though, if he cannot bring himself to change?

The balcony's glass door opens suddenly, startling him.

'Harry?' asks Amy in an intensely relieved tone.

He sits up in his plastic chair to see his wife turning to thank a nurse before stepping out into the fresh night air. Jeanie is sleepily draped over her mother's neck. Harry notices that his wife is still wearing her corporate attire of a beige skirt and white silk blouse.

As he jumps up, she comes towards him quickly and strokes his cheek. 'I was so bloody worried and . . . now you're just admiring the view out here?' Her expression seems to harden as she realizes that his condition is not as serious as she had thought. 'What's going on?' She feels he has a lot to explain.

Harry grasps Amy gently by the shoulders, but finds himself kissing an upturned cheek when normally she would offer him her lips.

Jeanie eyes her father cautiously, seeming unwilling now to relinquish the safety of her mother's neck for her father's arms.

'Hello, baby,' whispers Harry and touches her head.

'Are you going to answer me?' Amy asks bluntly. 'Are you OK?'

'Except for this terrible shirt, yes.' Harry pinches a fold of the shirt that the night staff found for him in some lost-property bin. It is an ugly, silver polyester affair.

Amy merely nods.

'Oh, I'm *sorry*. OK?' snaps Harry.

'Well, how do you ex*pect* me to react? You finally call me from hospital to say you're suffering "chemical pneumonia", when you should have phoned me hours ago. But instead of finding you writhing in agony in intensive care, I find you lounging out here on the balcony. The time for me worrying about you is *over* by the looks of it. Now I'm just feeling upset.'

'Mommy, don't . . . no.' Jeanie tries to clamp a small hand over her mother's mouth, distressed at the sharp tone of her voice.

The two adults stare at their daughter in dismay. Then both drop their gazes, feeling ashamed.

Amy shifts Jeanie to her other hip. 'Look, Harry, I'll cope – really, I will. I just had the fright of my life, that's all. Let's just get your things and go home. I don't want to stay here a second longer.'

As he is checking out, Harry realizes that he must have

left his wallet and keys in the glove compartment of the police vehicle. Sure that Jacob will have removed his property to safety, he doesn't give it another thought.

Harry sighs with relief when they finally turn into their familiar driveway at precisely twenty past eleven. During the journey, Harry has painted Amy a rudimentary picture of the evening's operation, referring only briefly to how he sustained his injuries. Amy takes notice of how bewildered her husband looks, despite sounding so much better than when he phoned her earlier. It does not take much to deduce that he is not telling her everything. For now though that does not matter – she is just glad to have him back.

While Amy puts their daughter to bed again and begins running herself a bath, Harry goes into the kitchen to fix himself a tumbler of whisky, filling it all the way to the brim. He flops down on the couch and switches on the television, hoping to fall asleep in front of CNN's repetitive images. But his mind refuses to wind down and keeps drifting towards the tasks facing him. For one thing, he will have to go back to Johannesburg General soon and hear the rest of that journalist's story. Then he intends to hunt that witch and his thugs – down to the last god-damned man.

So what happened back there, mate? Harry's mind limps back into the inferno. He replays the scene again and again, still convinced he did hear that little girl scream-ing. He had been so sure she was only wounded when he had found her.

Harry sighs and gets up to pour himself another bour-bon. The truth is that maybe he had not been so sure. Once he had pulled the door open and the backdraught knocked him over, the screaming had stopped immediately. Was the screaming just the sound of pressurized hot air singing through a chink in the metal? On entering the girl's cell, maybe he *could* register that she was already dead, but his mind had refused to accept the message.

He leans back against the kitchen counter and takes a deep breath, appreciating the quiet of the darkened room, the soft flickering of the television, the comforting smell of his home. All these familiar things secure him to his family and to reality. Above all, they give him hope.

'Harry?'

He starts at the sound of Amy's voice. She is wearing only one of his collared shirts, her arms crossed over her chest, and stands in the doorway looking very vulnerable. He admires the lean lines of her legs, her hair is still moist and curly after her bath. He savours the scent of soap in the air.

'Hey,' he says softly. 'Feeling better now?'

'Yes.'

As Amy steps towards him, he strokes the counter with one hand. 'I . . . I tried to save someone from that building tonight, except I couldn't. It was too late.' He bites his lip.

'Can you tell me everything that happened?' Amy asks cautiously. 'If you don't want to, I guess I'll understand.'

'But don't you want to go to bed?' asks Harry.

She shakes her head with a gentle smile.

Harry nods. 'Come here.' He hugs her tightly for a long minute, finding comfort in her warm body, completely losing himself in her presence. After a while he says, 'Sit down and I'll make you some tea.'

And so Harry shares his story with his wife: not only the previous day's events but also everything that has come to pass since the day they found the girl's body in the riverbed. He tells her everything except the bizarre details of his own behaviour in those dark passageways and his subsequent attempt to resuscitate a corpse. Harry is not convinced that he can trust her – or even himself – with the irrational causes behind these incidents. Nevertheless, as he speaks he finds himself relaxing, becoming increasingly entranced by Amy's attentiveness. Soon the horrible images he has witnessed over the last twenty-four hours also begin to recede.

When he finishes, she sidles up to him to hug him around the neck and kiss his forehead. 'Thank you.'

'For what?' asks Harry, genuinely confused.

'For telling me all this, and for trusting me again.' Amy gets up and holds her hand out to him.

When they are finally in bed, they do not notice a vehicle slowly coasting to a halt outside their high and seemingly impregnable garden wall. Car lights briefly flash across their white electrified gate before extinguishing and plunging the suburban street into silent darkness once more.

59

Still in her pyjamas, Jeanie jumps up onto her parents' bed and begins poking around in Harry's hair, investigating the scorched patches on his scalp, while he sits on the edge of the mattress trying unsuccessfully to put on his socks. His forehead has turned a nasty purplish green colour, and his lungs still feel as if he is breathing in needles.

'Ow – please don't lean on my shoulder, sweetie.'

Harry grabs her small hands and gives his daughter a peck on the nose. Amy coming out of the bathroom smiles at them. 'Come on, you two, or we'll be late.' She disappears into the hallway.

Harry hugs Jeanie close and speaks softly into her ear. 'You're the only one I've been able to keep safe. And you've saved me, too. I never want to lose you, just because I'm not there for you. I'm very sorry for not picking you up from Mrs Strydom's, OK?'

Jeanie nods and smiles shyly. 'Yeah, OK.'

Harry holds her at arm's length, taking a moment to appreciate how quickly she has grown up. It seems just a few days ago that Amy first handed him his newborn daughter all wrapped up in a white blanket.

As they leave the house, neither Amy, racing ahead in her MX-5, nor Harry, bringing up the rear with Jeanie, notices the bearded man leaning against a nearby tree, who has been watching their house intently.

60

The instant Harry arrives at the police station, Chief Molethe drags the detective into his office and proceeds to admonish him first for coming in to work so soon and then for his reckless behaviour the evening before. Just as Harry begins to think his commander has not learned of his macabre attempt to resuscitate a corpse, Molethe eyes him squarely.

'Was it just last night, or are you beginning to fray at the edges? You can tell me the truth – we all have our bad moments.'

'I'm fine.' Harry fiddles with his lighter and the unopened cigarette packet resting in his pocket. 'Just tired . . . and a bit beat up.'

'Hm.' Molethe gets up. 'I'm going to be blunt with you: I don't think you *are* fine. You charge into a highly dangerous situation without consideration for your family or colleagues, and you've been looking like shit ever since these investigations began. Tell me, what *did* you do to get our crucial witness so angry that she punched you?'

Harry coughs raggedly. 'Look, we've been hounded endlessly by journalists for weeks now. And, like I've warned, they can cause trouble; remember old Mr Mbewu who's still lying in hospital? They're just a bunch of sensationalists, I reckon, so when this Nina Reading phoned me up about a week ago, I let her know I didn't want to speak to her.'

'Come on, what else did you say? She wouldn't have hit you just for that.'

'That's all I said, honest.' Harry chooses not to mention how he slammed down the phone on her.

'Harry . . .?' warns Molethe.

'I'm telling you the *truth*. I think she somehow blames me for her abduction, because she reckons that if I'd listened to what she was going to say, maybe all that might not have happened and . . . and those children from yesterday might not be dead.' Unable to contain his dark emotions any longer, Harry jumps up and begins to pace around the room.

Molethe whistles irritably and shakes his head.

'I know I fucked up, chief. There's no one knows that better than I do. But I'm begging you not to take me off this case – not now, not this close to the end. We have so much dirt on these maniacs that with this breakthrough we just need to round them up and put them all away for life.'

The chief clears his throat. 'Harry, I checked your holidays and sick leave. You haven't taken time off in the last three years.'

'No!' interjects Harry, panic evident in his expression. 'Not *now*. This is too goddamned important! Chief, you've got kids of your own – just like I have my little girl.'

'That's exactly why—'

'Sorry, boss, I won't stand down.' Harry meets his commander's gaze with his own pale blue eyes. 'Suspend me if you want, and I'll understand. I even deserve it. But don't order me to take leave at a time like this.'

Molethe returns to his chair and nods his head. 'Fine,' he says severely. 'We finish this together. We need you now, but that doesn't mean I'm forgetting about this business. That journalist could cause a lot of trouble for this department with any claims of negligence she makes. If that time comes, I will judge your mistake in earnest, but for now I'll think instead about the hard work you've already put in, not just in this case but over the last three years. So I'll try to see your stupid actions last night as misplaced heroism.'

Harry nods humbly and thanks his commander.

'Gildenhuys has been pressuring me about what happened yesterday. I don't know whether he'll be satisfied with what I've said, but I'm warning you, detective, don't ever let anything like this happen again.'

As Harry closes the door behind him, he pauses in the corridor. Pulling out the small transparent container of pills, he shakes out a couple and starts to chew them. Back in his own office, he puts a call through to Johannesburg General, inquiring about Nina Reading. A severe-sounding matron tells him that the journalist is exhausted and still fast asleep. The hospital will contact him the moment she feels ready to talk.

Harry represses the urge to drive over there directly.

61

In Yeoville four cars file up a hill rising above the seedy residential district, barely a mile from Ponte City. The road winds all the way up to the top, where a large reservoir hulks behind walls like the fortifications of a colonial prison, not improved by its crown of razor wire. Opposite it lies a barren building lot, roughly the size of a football pitch, with a large eucalyptus tree towering above sweet thorn and sickle trees that grow amongst large blocks of rubble. Broken glass and empty bottles twinkle in the long grass.

The four cars leave the road and make their way onto this empty patch of land, startling the small group of African Pentecostals, clothed in their green-and-white robes, who are busy enveloping a black-clad woman with leafy jacaranda branches. At the sound of their interruption she bursts from her green capsule with frightened eyes, her face and arms freshly anointed with glistening oils.

From the two black Mercedes step Adusa and Taiwo. Instead of their usual smart suits, the pair now wear plain slacks and T-shirts, although they retain their expensive leather shoes. Both men wear dark sunglasses in the bright morning light that glitteringly reflects off thousands of windows in central Johannesburg in the basin below them.

'Get out of here!' shouts Adusa, advancing on the small congregation. His right thumb is wedged into the belt loop next to the holster plainly visible at his side. Behind him two young men, one wearing a bullet suspended from his necklace, the other missing one ear, are climbing out of the red Corolla. Lucky and Collin step out of a fourth car, the red BMW.

Taiwo opens the back door of the Mercedes he chauffeurs, opens an umbrella and waits for the albino to climb out. The *baloyi* emerges hesitantly from its dark interior, dressed in a gold-and-green embroidered *sapara* – a flowing tunic deriving from his homeland. A similarly embroidered cap is perched on his head, while sunglasses protect his fragile eyes and white gloves are drawn over his sensitive hands. He hisses, as if in pain, at the sun's bright blaze, and Taiwo swiftly shields his leader with the umbrella.

'Let's get this over with quickly,' mutters the albino. 'This wretched sun is going to kill me one day.'

'I said, pack your things and get going!' bellows Adusa, beginning to manhandle the hesitant priest. The man's followers are hastily collecting their shoes, their plastic bottles of blessed water and their oils. The reluctant worshipper glances angrily at Adusa, then picks up his wooden staff, shakes himself loose of the enforcer's grip and gestures for his little congregation to follow him. They do not disappear onto the nearby road, but instead start descending through the foliage covering the hillside that rises up from distant apartment blocks which face towards Harrow Road and Ponte City.

'Calm down, Adusa,' chuckles the albino. 'We don't want them running to the police, too.'

Adusa rips his sunglasses off his face. 'Wise One,' he says, 'are you sure this is the best place for it?'

'Where else would you have us go? We cannot risk

crossing half the city to get back to our own little nest. It's too dangerous.' The albino gestures towards the departed worshippers. 'Besides, don't you feel it – like that lot can feel it? We're close to Them up here, like we're standing on the tip of the Mother's breast that rises up out of this city. No, this place is *holy*, and here we shall make our sacrifice.'

Aided by Lucky and Collin, Taiwo is rummaging in the back of one of the black Mercs. They heave out four large containers of gasoline.

'Do we need to stay here in the city at all?' grumbles Adusa. 'Wouldn't it be better if we left the country for a while? We could go to Swaziland, Lesotho – even Mozambique.'

The albino strides over and grabs him tightly by the shoulder. 'Adusa, how many conflicts have you survived in your own country or wherever else your greed has taken you – Sierra Leone, Guinea, Senegal? After facing all those dangers, you fear a handful of cops? Do not worry, my proud warrior, you still walk with *me*. And though our fortune has ebbed of late, I foresee it will come again into full flood. I shall protect you, just as you now protect me.'

'It still seems a bit risky . . .'

'Everything is risky if you don't have faith, my friend.' The albino pats his follower on the back, then heads over to the edge of the steep slope while Taiwo trails close behind him, holding his protective umbrella. There the albino stands and contemplates his adoptive city.

You ugly thing, you beautiful destination, Johannesburg, eGoli, Place of Gold; you have so many names, as I have none.

He breathes in the scents that mingle on this hilltop: eucalyptus, with the sharp scent of flowering *khakibos* and the comforting fragrance of a camphor bush. All these natural aromas combine strangely with those of the city: the metallic taste of exhaust on the air and the pungent black smoke from a tyre burning somewhere in the streets below. How different, yet how similar, this place is to other African cities he has passed through over the years – ever since he was forced to leave the family compound on the banks of the Sokoto River in northern Nigeria.

His father used to claim that he was born into this world white because he had been bleached by the Great Spirit's holy light. In sunlight his condition was so painful that he could not emerge to help with the cacao crop like the other children, who clearly therefore had not been set aside by God to achieve great things. Instead, during daylight hours, he had remained hidden in the dark interior of his mother's hut within his father's compound, like a secret waiting for the right moment to emerge.

Beyond the compound existed a world he barely knew. By day he could almost smell the orchids and mosses growing among the fragrant pink-and-white blossoms of the chocolate plants, but he could not go to watch the pickers who worked carefully so as not to bruise either the trees or their ripe golden pods. He could stray out only at dusk or dawn, the times when the spirits moved freely amongst people. Sometimes his father would also take him out at night, when the sun's hateful stare could not hurt him any more, to show him what the family had achieved that day in the fertile groves. Very rarely was he taken along on family visits to neighbours and friends, because many people considered his pallid complexion a baleful omen.

In the end, night fell upon the rest of his family,

too, at a time only he, a creature of perpetual darkness, survived. After a coup d'état had overthrown the Igbo-dominated government, the other tribes grew restless and angry over this Igbo supremacy. One morning a gang of the local Hausa tribe approached their farm. They brought with them machetes and fire, and the albino remembers hearing the distant screaming that soon erupted. Scrambling over to the compound's entrance, he peered out into the blinding light of day but, try as he might, he could see nothing beyond, and he lacked the courage to venture further. He could, however, smell burning rubber and the destruction of his family's crops, while listening to their massacre as they fought to protect their livelihood.

The sight of his mother struggling towards the compound had seemed a blessing. But when she reached her child amid this chaos she could not lift him. In their bloodlust to seize possession of the Igbos' fertile acres, the Hausa had not only slaughtered most of the fieldworkers, but also severed his mother's arms just below the elbows.

As she lay dying on her own doorstep, herself now hovering on the fringe between darkness and light, she had pleaded with her youngest son to flee for safety into an uncertain future.

'Wise One,' Taiwo interrupts from behind him, 'they are ready.'

The albino sighs heavily before turning around. They walk back to where Adusa is waiting beside the cars. He is holding the small carved ivory box the albino was given by a hermit marabout so many years ago. The witch doctor takes the container offered by his disciple and removes from it what look like four scrolls of yellowing paper with enigmatic Arabic script stencilled in black ink. He places one sheet on the dashboard of each vehicle, which all now reek of petrol. With great ceremony, the albino produces a pouch of coarse, black powder and sprinkles this muti generously on each of the scrolls.

'Light them now,' he commands. 'Today the spirits will not hear our drums, our dancing, nor our songs. Instead they will witness our offering leap up into the sky.'

Adusa strikes the first match, and throws it into the black Mercedes he was driving only minutes before.

The albino backs away from the flames. 'Let them try to find us now,' he whispers to himself.

The youth, Godfrey, bearing the ugly scar of his severed ear, eyes the *baloyi* uncomfortably over his shoulder. Their leader seems so unconcerned by the rumours spreading within his own ranks that the boy suspects the albino is indeed privy to a knowledge of the future of which they, his servants, remain unaware.

As if his boss has caught him staring through his dark glasses, Godfrey hears the albino mumble, 'It's what you *choose* to make of your condition, not what you *allow* it to make of you, which will determine your future.'

The youth hurriedly turns his gaze back to the four burning vehicles, wondering what exactly the wizard means by that.

62

Descending the steep slope in the wake of the Pentecostals, the albino's entourage makes its way towards Ponte City, leaving four plumes of noxious black smoke billowing skywards behind them.

Moving among the shrubs and trees, the albino is

reminded of his wild flight out into a world he had never experienced as a young child. Gone was the cover of the compound where he had helped separate the aromatic cocoa seeds from their pods, where he had helped with the stamping of corn. He became lost in the forests, and all the while the hot sun, beaming through the canopy, ate away at his tender flesh. By the third day of aimless wandering and occasional hiding, his skin was marred with blisters that itched violently, his eyes were nearly swollen shut. After his initial panic subsided, he travelled only at dusk and dawn, or where the shadows lay thick and cool.

There was plenty of water to be had from streams running into the Sokoto, but the boy did not know how to find food for himself. Eventually he came upon a muddy road cutting through the forest and began to follow it. Thus he finally met other people uprooted by the turmoil devastating the country. But although they seemed willing to aid each other, they shunned the white-skinned boy. The albino soon realized that in their eyes he was not blessed by the Great Spirit, like his father had told him, but was an abomination that at birth should have been left in the forest to die of exposure or be eaten by predators. Some even pelted him with insults, calling him the son of a *tokoloshe*.

One group, heading towards the nearest town, nevertheless decided to leave something by the side of the road for him every time they themselves stopped to eat. They would not have this little creature travelling with them, for fear of inviting the wrath of their ancestors, but they were kind enough to leave him scraps to live on. But once more he was forced to travel by day, braving the agony of the sun's white glare in order to keep up with his benefactors.

The closer they came to the town, the more crowded the clammy red track became, and the more people there were, the wilder grew the rumours about the little outcast boy – the one who followed them so closely, lurking shyly under the protection of the forest. Various groups grew more and more nervous about him, the tension culminating when a number of men chased after him, hurling rocks and abuse and forcing him to flee. The albino ran headlong into the forest, deeper and deeper, until he was sure he had escaped them. In a place where the shade was deepest, he sat down on a large white stone, and for the first time wept for his family, and for himself. He cursed the Great Spirit for burning him. He cursed his ancestors and the spirits of his clan for not protecting his mother and father, and he cursed the entire world for reviling him because of the colour of his skin.

From then on, rather than expose himself, he followed only the narrow tracks in the forest. It was next to one such path that he found a tree with a large hollow amid its roots, into which he settled himself down to sleep – safely hidden away, or so he thought. It was the end of a staff striking him painfully in the chest that frightened him awake, and he tried to scramble away. But, like a snake twitching under a fork, he was firmly pinned.

The old man who held it finally released the pressure and beckoned the little boy to follow him. His mouth constantly on the move with Parkinson's disease, without a word of introduction, he led the child home to a thatch hut that stood even deeper in the forest. There he stripped the child naked, gave him rice to eat and proceeded to mend his tattered clothing. The albino's efforts to communicate with his rescuer were met with a stony silence.

And so the ancient marabout took him in and gradually warmed to this little creature who he believed had been born under that tree. The albino earned his keep by helping the hermit with the nimbler tasks the older man could not manage because of the constant shaking of his frame, while the mystic, in turn, taught him about the hateful world outside the forest, and the occult secrets of his art. He taught the boy how pathetic the human race really was, how much it depended on purveyors of spiritual indulgence; he taught him about his own special place in the world, constantly alluding to the boy's distinctive skin colour and his magical birth underneath the tree. Gradually the traumatized child absorbed the teachings of this wizard. He learnt about the jinn that stalked the forests, and how to befriend them; he learnt the ways of animals, of insects, of plants, of the winds and the clouds. The boy's contempt for those who had ostracized him – when clearly they should have revered him – grew as he embraced the marabout's way of life.

Occasionally people would arrive out of nowhere, seeking out the old marabout to concoct for them some powerful medicine. They were shocked to discover this little white demon aiding the ancient wizard, some of them even running away immediately in superstitious fear. Others would observe him cautiously while concluding their business with the old man before hastening away to spread rumours about the marabout's infernal allegiances.

It was of course these whispered reports about the albino that finally set the stage for his return to the outside world. After the old marabout died, the young man grabbed the substantial pile of money the old hermit had hoarded by selling his magic and headed off for the nearest town. The alienation in his heart having ripened into disdain and vengeance, he arrived there to rapidly instil a cloud of fear and awe. Soon the local administrators, police officers, soldiers and even criminals bowed to his pervasive charisma, and the albino set about undermining the precarious balance of the local community as it emerged from the Biafran civil war.

The only people he felt an affinity for were other outcasts – first refugees, then eventually criminals. But in time growing public reaction to his disruptive influence forced him to move on, and so he travelled the same paths as other social misfits. Together they lived in the shadow of Africa's moon and sun; they became the Mother's landless sons and daughters, who would never again possess a country of their own, nor somewhere they could bury their dead and pay respect to their ancestors in peace. They were eternal drifters crossing the Dark Continent, looking for food and work and not much else, as long as conflict continued to uproot them. Yes, they were similar, these fellow travellers, but he was very much different to them – these people to whom he gave hope and whom he cynically used as well. Because not only did he not have a home, a family, a tribe, unlike many of them, he alone was neither black nor white, in his own mind neither of this world nor the spirit world, neither completely revered nor utterly abhorred.

The albino knew he belonged nowhere and to no one.

From country to country he moved, along the routes of the Nigerian underworld, absorbing like a chameleon the local traditions of each country, while disguising his true origins. Wherever he went, he met the displaced, the desperate, other fugitives. He soon learnt that it was these needy and desperate people who were most likely to call on his occult abilities, and they were also the ones he could most easily bind to his service with oaths taken in blood before the spirits. Soon his cartel was based on the loyalty of worshippers.

To South Africa he came eventually. The gangs of the Cape fought constantly among themselves and also with vigilante groups like PAGAD, leaving a separate arena open for one as cunning as the albino. While the Hard Livings took control of drug trafficking in Cape Town, he chose to settle in Johannesburg, where he soon discovered he could command as much respect from local tribesmen as from the ever increasing swell of refugees who had made it this far south. It was in this city, where the former police control was fast crumbling, where there were count- less destitute black believers and many rich white narcotics abusers, that he could finally make his home and start bleeding a gullible community dry. This, after all, was much the same way his mentor the old marabout had operated, but on a much bigger scale.

The albino makes his way through the broken open gate leading into the basement parking lot of Ponte City. The air is humid, musty and tainted with the stench of burnt rubber he had smelt up on the hill earlier. A month before there would have been quite a number of familiar faces to greet him upon his return to his sanctuary. Now there are only two guards to hail him. He dismisses his entourage and ascends to the foyer alone.

Although he is confident that he still has control, he nevertheless feels somewhat taxed and fatigued. He had hoped that Ngubane's excessive spirit would have been broken by the shock of his arrest and the albino's subsequent threats, and thus his unruly lieutenant would have returned to him sufficiently chastened, to play a dutiful role as his skilled business adviser, but that had not happened. The man's death was unfortunate but necessary, since there can be no greater threat to the albino's leadership than an *induna* beginning to think for himself.

The albino closes the door to his sanctum and takes off his gloves. Walking around his desk, he strikes a match and lights the candle underneath the large bowl standing on top of his cabinet. He closes his eyes and murmurs something under his breath, before opening the top drawer of the cabinet. From a small turquoise vessel he takes a few cacao beans and drops them into the bowl. He pulls a strip of dried meat out of a plastic satchel and places it into the clay receptacle. The odour of chocolate mingles with the smell of sweet flesh and spreads quickly throughout the room while the albino continues to mutter litanies of reverence.

'Eat my mother, taste the fruits of your son's success, and be at peace in the eternally dark valley.'

When he is finished, the albino turns around, picks up the phone and dials a number. As he waits, his hand begins to fiddle with the lion's skull that rests on his desktop.

A secretary answers rather severely in educated English tones.

'I want to speak to Moloto,' says the witch doctor.

'I'm sorry, sir, the director is not in today.'

'When *will* he be in?' demands the albino brusquely.

'Not for the remainder of the week, I'm afraid.'

He has had enough experience of dealing with such people to know that she is concealing something. 'Woman, I know you are lying to me. Tell Moloto *now* that this matter concerns him directly. You know who I am, so tell him it's *me* who is calling and not some wayside toad he can lightly toss aside.'

There is a moment's hesitance from the woman sensing a veiled threat in the man's deep voice. 'Yes, sir,' she says.

There is a click, and a strained voice answers in Zulu, '*Yebo?*'

'You remember that gift your daughter received from me at her coming of age?' begins the albino.

'Yes.'

'I seem to recall you accepted it happily rather than reluctantly.'

'Yes,' agrees the director weakly.

'We have dealt with each other on quite a number of occasions, both on personal as well as business matters. How dare you now try to lie to me?'

'I wasn't lying to you specifically – I'm just very busy. My secretary was under orders to field every—'

'You are in a very delicate position. If the newspapers were to find out about your recent dealings with a businessman called Ngubane Maduna, there might be cause for an extensive investigation.'

'Look, it isn't very wise for you to be speaking to me just now,' interjects the director of detectives.

'*I'll* be the judge of that!' snarls the albino.

'OK, OK.' The director sighs. 'What do you want from me this time?'

'You will make sure your police service does not search Ponte. You managed that last time, and you will do so again.'

'I can't do that! They've already arrested far too many people. They have just too much evidence pointing towards you. They even have a witness! If they have found good reason to search the building, it would be career suicide for me to intervene. It's out of my hands now – this case has gained too much momentum. I can't just—'

'You *will*!' bellows the albino.

'But . . . they know who you are. No, I'm afraid I can't help you.'

'Gifts can be double-edged swords,' purrs the albino, suddenly adopting a notably different tone. 'Though seemingly innocuous gestures, they oblige the recipient to the giver of the gift. You were grateful at the time to receive an object of blessing from me for that whelp of yours, but know this: if you fail to help me now, that charmed figurine I gave to your daughter will instead curse her until the moment she dies young in your arms. You understand me?'

Moloto pauses to take a deep breath. He continues hesitantly, 'I truly appreciated your gift, but I don't believe it can contain such a curse.'

'Would you like to try me?' snaps the *baloyi*. 'I have here at hand the office numbers for Johan Breed from the *Beeld*, Jeffrey Nxumalo at the SABC and Tito Mayekiso at the *Citizen*. But on top of that, would you risk your daughter's life?'

'Please, I'm begging you, don't ask me to do this. Think about the repercussions. It could mean you losing your only ally in the police department.'

'I will be the judge of that. For now, Moloto, you will do as I tell you.'

'But the prosecution on this case has the ear of the commissioner himself!'

'That's *your* problem, and I suggest you deal with it effectively. Goodbye.' The albino replaces the receiver and for a few minutes contemplates the sacred mat laid out in

front of his desk. He decides he should not feel overly
worried. After all, the recent sacrifice of Oba's nephew
should be powerful enough magic to tilt fortune in his
favour.

63

Jacob is unusually quiet that morning, barely offering
support to Harry in the various meetings, interviews and
interrogations they conduct together, his silence leaving
Mason to ponder whether his partner is still upset with
him. However, just after one, Jacob appears at their office
door and announces that he will be paying for lunch today.
During the short walk to Guido's, their favourite pizzeria
a few blocks away, Harry remembers to ask whether his
partner recovered Harry's wallet and keys before returning
the vehicle they used yesterday to the police motor pool.

'No. I too seem to remember you put them into the
glove box, but I found only some spare ammunition, which
I put back in your desk drawer.'

Harry is surprised by this news, but leaves it at that. It
is possible that he still had the items on him when he
stormed into the blazing building. Did he drop them
somewhere inside? Did someone take charge of them –
even steal them – after he passed out, perhaps another cop
or a medic? There is nothing for it now but to hope that
some investigator finds these items at the crime scene and
returns them.

It is only when they sit down in a corner of the
restaurant, well away from a pack of noisy labourers, that
Jacob begins to talk – of his own volition.

'He was a great man. He was born with the helmet, as the Afrikaners call it.'

'Sorry?' asks Harry, totally confused.

'My grandfather, he was born with the gift of foresight – prophecy some might call it.'

'You mean he was born with the caul covering his head?' Harry had expected almost anything but Jacob's grandfather to be the topic of discussion.

Jacob nods. 'It's said that children thus blessed have the ability to see clearly into the spiritual world, that they are in union with the afterlife, and can develop great wisdom. My grandfather himself was a very wise man.'

'Your grandfather was a *sangoma*?'

'Yes, he was very well respected in his day. He devoted his life to routing out witches who were terrorizing any communities. Community elders from all over the region would request my grandfather's help if witchcraft was suspected. They were scared of him, but they also needed him, which is why, in the end, a witch came looking for his family and tried to take me.'

'You were also born with a caul?'

Jacob pulls something out from underneath his shirt, which looks like a little scroll attached to a long thong necklace. 'Custom demands that children born with this gift wear some of the dried membrane as a charm which should never be taken off.'

'So, can *you* see into the spiritual world?'

'No.'

'Why not?'

'*I* am doing the talking for now, please.'

And so Jacob tells Harry the story of his terrifying childhood experience, when his grandfather frightened off a witch in the early hours of the morning and saved Jacob from abduction. He pauses only when a young black waitress with her hair braided almost like a pineapple arrives at their table to take their order.

'This really happened?' blurts out Harry, stupefied by his partner's tale.

'Of course. Why would I lie to you?' Jacob sounds somewhat annoyed.

'For starters, people don't just seize up, all paralysed, so they can be kidnapped by invisible shape-changers,' says Harry. 'It's a bit hard to believe, mate.' Normally Harry might have laughed at Jacob's story, but his serious expression warns him not to.

Jacob sighs heavily, shaking his head. 'Like I said, Harry, you always ask too many questions about the world. Do you really *hear* what I am telling you or is your head just filled with all your questions?'

The waitress arrives with their food and places it on the table. Harry's confused expression causes Jacob suddenly to laugh out loud and clap his hands. 'OK, Harry, I'll tell you this: I *have* thought about what happened – and many times. Part of me *does* find it difficult to believe, but another part of me knows it is the truth. I was so scared that night that afterwards I tried to blot out the horrible thing that happened to me. But then my father insisted on reminding me of what had occurred, over and over again. Especially after . . .' Jacob shakes his head, and begins stuffing food in his mouth. Harry eats but waits patiently, studying the emotions playing over his colleague's face. At last Jacob wipes his mouth with a paper serviette and continues.

'The main point is that it was a *spiritual* experience, something only our ancestors and the spirits fully understand – either them or people like my grandfather. I was too young to pick up all the stories my grandfather had to tell before he died, but my father told me as many as he could. My people have witnessed things that you whites don't understand – or don't *want* to understand. You still think our culture is primitive, that our beliefs are stupid, but you know . . . maybe Africa is just different.'

'OK, so it happened that way,' concedes Harry, not wanting to antagonize him any more. 'What happened to your witch?'

Jacob shrugs. 'My grandfather recognized him. He knew who it was and he went after him.'

'What happened then?'

Jacob again attacks his food viciously, the subject clearly becoming more sensitive now. Harry has never seen Jacob balk like this before, but then this is a side of his partner he has never even suspected. Suddenly Mitchell's conspiratorial words begin to make sense. But how can he have known this side of Jacob before Harry himself did?

'My father and grandfather journeyed on foot to the largest of the villages that were dotted around the white farmers' lands. There they consulted with the elders, and soon messengers were sent to the other, smaller settlements. Men started gathering with their weapons, with petrol and tyres, all set to hunt down a witch. They knew where this *baloyi* lived, by himself on the side of a hill not far from the village, on the opposite side of a farm owned by a man called Oupa Goosen. Everyone was eager to catch this witch who had been terrorizing the whole district. For years children had been disappearing regularly, and recently the milk had been perpetually turning sour. Chickens were found dead, yet uneaten, with their throats torn out. Someone had to be responsible for all this, but up until the attack on me, no one had known for certain who it was because the *baloyi* was so clever and powerful.

'A mob followed my grandfather straight up the hill, though some went around by way of the valleys on either side instead, in case the witch tried to make his escape. By the afternoon he was caught, sneaking off across Goosen's land. They started to beat him right there and then. My father told me the men struck him first with their knobkerries, also kicking and punching him, then the few women following them joined in. After that, they necklaced him with a tyre, doused it with petrol and watched him burn to death in a cornfield. My grandfather himself performed the appropriate rituals to ensure that his spirit did not escape to possess any animal or person nearby.' Jacob finishes his tale with his face averted, pain and something else glittering in his eyes.

Harry wipes his hands vigorously with his own serviette. 'You see, that's *exactly* what I'm talking about. How is what your family did that day any different from the crimes we uncovered yesterday? How is it different from the killing of that boy or that little girl's shooting? There cannot be any justification for this stuff. It is just savagery.'

'Perhaps what you yourself believe in underestimates the power of these traditional practices. I agree with you, Harry, that it is barbaric. That is why . . . why I'm sitting here with you now and why I go to church regularly. The consequences of such practices have taught me a cruel lesson. But before you judge my family too harshly, I would like you to hear me out.'

Harry pushes his chair back a bit from the table, and nods for him to continue.

'When those people finally arrived at the *baloyi*'s hut,

they found there the half-cooked remains of several children. The sight was horrible enough to send grown men fleeing from the hut. They also found a lot of other things there that had been stolen from people in the neighbourhood. So my grandfather felt justified in what he did, and the others had acted appropriately according to ancient tribal laws, because they were led by a genuine wise man and not a charlatan.'

Harry shakes his head. 'Still doesn't justify what they did to the witch. You said they murdered him even *before* they saw what was inside his hut. For all they knew, the man could've been innocent.'

'Harry, there were fathers and mothers in the crowd whose children had gone missing years before. Didn't I recently hear you saying to me: "Have you got any idea what I would do to the bastard who kills my daughter?" Now I'm asking you – even if you don't believe that the man was a *baloyi* – what would *you* have done to him if you'd found your own daughter's body in the hut?'

'But how would I have known she was in that house?'

'That man came after *me*!' Jacob pokes his chest angrily.

Harry accepts that his partner has a point, in a roundabout way. It is so easy condemning people for necklacing someone, so easy to judge them after you see the news footage, or when you break up a lynch mob. Western jurisprudence has seemingly established ethical boundaries on such practices. But what *is* fair when your own child is butchered, when your child's *soul* is used as a commodity for evil ends? How do you react in the face of a Western judiciary which sees and understands only the physical harm done, not the *spiritual*?

Harry frowns and shifts uncomfortably in his chair.

'I don't know . . . I don't know if I could actually burn a person like that to death. But your case is a fluke, I say: you were lucky to be justified, and that your grandfather happened to identify the right man, but I can't believe that was because of any clairvoyant abilities.'

Jacob shakes his head. 'My grandfather had a definite gift, and he knew exactly what he was doing. That's just the way it was. You can't treat these killings we're now dealing with like any other sort of murder. The victims will see things differently to you – and so will the murderers.'

Harry raises an eyebrow. 'What happened next?'

Jacob leans forward, clasping his hands on the table top. 'When the police found out, there was an investigation. My grandfather and my father were arrested, along with a number of others. Back then it was not a good time for any black man in South Africa to get involved in a brutal killing, especially when he was as headstrong and defiant as my grandfather.' Here Jacob pauses to draw in a long breath. 'Without any consideration for the atrocities he'd uncovered, my grandfather was sentenced to death for his part in the killing.'

'But there were mitigating circumstances. Surely those would've been taken into account?'

'Harry, you sometimes think just like a child – you know that? This was during *apartheid*. A strong-willed *sangoma* standing up to the police – that was a sure-fire way to get yourself hanged.'

Harry's chin sinks onto his chest and he stares at the table, allowing this information to sink in. The mystic rationale behind much of what his partner has just said still makes no sense to Harry, but at least it brings Jacob into better focus.

Harry wonders whether this faith depends on an inherent blurring of the line between truth and fiction, whose fusion of the rational and the irrational strengthens the convictions of its followers. He remembers how some of the black police officers reacted to his picking up that fetish, as he reviews the story Jacob has just told him and how it all seems to depend on suggestions and symbolism significant only to a believer in such a faith. After a few moments Harry concludes one thing for certain: he cannot manage to fit himself into Jacob's shoes in this matter.

'You still haven't answered my earlier question. Why can't you see into the spirit world, if you were born with the same endowment as your grandfather? Why didn't *you* become a *sangoma*?'

'As the first-born son of my grandfather's lineage I was meant to,' says Jacob. 'I still *am* meant to.'

'But?'

'I was meant to begin my training once I was initiated into manhood. But I chose not to – I had seen enough. I had lost a grandfather who was very dear to me, and although I know he would've wanted me to continue in the footsteps of my forefathers, I could not bear to become part of that cycle.' Jacob raises his eyes to meet Harry's gaze. 'The time for the role my family once performed has passed. I deserted my father, who intended to train me like all first-born sons were trained before me. Instead I came to Soweto and . . . and tried to change my ways.'

'So that's what the guy was talking about yesterday morning, over at Solilo's place?' asks Harry.

'People don't understand that, you can still follow God as well as the old ways, that you sometimes *must* break with tradition to save yourself. *Magogo* Solilo understood that, even when no one else would.'

Jacob abruptly excuses himself and disappears towards the restrooms, leaving Harry to ponder exactly what his partner meant about deserting his father. If he renounced his own family, it must have been a serious thing indeed. For traditionally minded black families there is hardly anything worse you can do.

Harry becomes aware of how uncomfortable it must be for Jacob to exist by two sets of principles, one adopted by choice and one thrust upon him by birth – torn between two communities, two ideologies, belonging to both, yet to neither completely. He wonders how Jacob manages to walk so tall, burdened by this duality.

Harry is set to probe Jacob further when he returns from the restroom, but the dark cloud now settled over his partner's face makes it clear that their conversation is over.

Perhaps, thinks Harry, Jacob does not manage it so well after all.

64

From her hospital bed, Nina watches as the grim news report unfolds on the screen. When it briefly shows the corpses of another three children being wheeled out to the waiting mortuary vans, bringing the death toll to six, she begins to sob miserably. It seems they had all been executed with a bullet before the fire took hold – executed because her own escape from there forced the murderers to flee in a hurry. She points the control and switches off the television, and so misses the following report of Ngubane Maduna's death.

Tossing and turning, as if trying to escape the guilt

crawling through her mind, a desperate bitterness overwhelms her. Nina eventually falls into a fitful doze.

A gentle hand falls on her shoulder, startling her awake.
She looks up, trying to focus, then with difficulty registers
Detective Harry Mason's face.

'Sorry to wake you, Ms Reading. I just couldn't wait
any longer.'

Nina sits up in the bed, dabbing at her nose and eyes.
The wooden bench next to her bed creaks as Harry seats
himself. 'I suppose you found out?' he probes gently.

She nods, her gaze now fixed on her hands, which lie
in her lap.

For a moment they both sit in an uncomfortable
silence, before Harry continues, 'Ms Reading, I'd like you
to know this isn't your fault. If anyone is guilty of the way
things ended up, it's me.'

Previously she might have seized this opportunity to
berate him, but now Nina experiences only a large, black
void inside her – one from which she can draw no voice
and no emotions. 'No – ' she shakes her head – 'no, it's
my fault. I came out here thinking I'd do this all on my
own. But instead I fucked things up so badly that people
died – *kids* died.'

'Ms Reading?'

Nina takes a long, shuddering breath. 'I should've
stayed and done *more* – just anything.' She sniffs. 'So they
got away? All of them?'

'We made some arrests, but the persons you described
weren't among them. They must've organized their escape
shortly after you got free.' Seeing her wince, Harry adds
quickly, 'But they're on the run now. We already know

who two of them are, and we should have the rest of their names shortly. Once we have their identities, it's normally over quickly.'

Nina nods limply, still unable to look at him directly. 'So what now?'

'It's very important you tell me the *whole* story. We need to move as fast as possible, and any further light you can shed on this business may be of much greater help than what the suspects themselves could provide, I guarantee you.'

'What do you need from me?'

The woman Harry finds himself speaking to now seems completely different from the fiery, indignant journalist who confronted him the day before. She seems confused, disorientated.

Harry clears his throat. 'What you did yesterday was one of the most resourceful and courageous deeds I've ever witnessed, Ms Reading. And after such an ordeal, you showed the tenacity to sit in a crowded office with us and tell your story for the sake of getting those victims out of there. I know that everything looks and feels bad to you at the moment, but what you achieved is incredible. It proved the breakthrough in this case I'm working on. Without your contribution, there's no telling how long this string of atrocities might have continued.'

'Thanks – ' Nina finally raises her eyes – 'but they're still dead.' Studying his face more closely, she asks, 'What happened to you?'

'I got myself a little too close to the blaze,' says Harry, running a hand self-consciously through his ruined hair. 'A search for further clues has been under way since last night, and the fire department reckons they were using the abandoned passageways and ducts of an old factory that was razed about eight years ago. It'll be a while before we know exactly what has been going on down there since.'

Nina shifts uncomfortably in her bed. 'So why did you hang up on me that time? When someone phones you with vital information, do you normally just hang up on them?'

Harry tugs at his lower lip with one hand. 'I haven't ever cared much for dealing with journalists – especially from the British tabloids.'

'And whoever said I work for a tabloid?'

'It was a stupid guess, I suppose.' Harry stands up and paces around the room. 'Look, will you help me? If you don't want to deal with me personally, I'll understand, but will you at least speak to someone else? I realize you're in bad shape, but we need to move fast.'

'Why do you hate the British tabloids so much?' interrupts Nina.

'I just do, but look—'

'Don't dodge the subject.' Nina holds up a threatening finger. 'You owe me at least one straight answer.'

Harry sighs and his foot scuffs the floor awkwardly. 'Because they screwed me over once, totally.'

Nina looks at him for a moment, then nods. 'Fine, we can talk now – but you're buying me some cigarettes and coffee first.'

65

Twenty minutes later they are sitting in the hospital's ground-floor cafeteria, a packet of cigarettes lying between them while they are still weighing each other up cautiously over styrofoam cups of steaming coffee. The smoking-area tables are covered in shiny yellow plastic and each carries a cheap foil ashtray. A loud extractor fan is gasping in the corner, almost above Harry's head. A group of nursing students are gossiping a few tables away from them. Harry has just finished hearing Nina recount Tumi's shocking story, and the ramifications of it are settling in.

'Let me get this straight. Her uncle had her foetus removed for some ritual carried out by this albino witch doctor, then she was carted off to England and enslaved in a backroom sweatshop? How old was she then?'

'Only thirteen,' says Nina. 'She's nineteen now.'

'What's her full name?'

'Tumelo Maduna.' Nina then asks impatiently, 'Just how many bloody albino witch doctors can there be in Newtown operating a human abattoir under the overpass?'

'Well, does he at least have a name?'

'To me those scumbags only spoke English, but not to each other, so I don't know what his name was.'

Harry sits back, thoughtfully. 'I guess it shouldn't be too hard to track him down. Ms Reading, did you recognize that man you helped escape?'

Nina searches Harry's expression for a clue. She remembers thinking that the wounded man's face looked familiar. Then suddenly two disparate facts collide in her mind. For days, she had casually followed the newspaper articles concerning the escaped heroin smuggler, and now, having just mentioned Tumi's surname, it all finally connects. 'Oh shit! I *don't* believe it!' she cries, slapping her forehead.

Harry shrugs, and sticks his first cigarette of the day into his mouth. But he doesn't light it, his lungs still feeling far too fragile.

'But if it was him, then why did they stab him? They were obviously partners of some kind.'

'Probably for a dozen different reasons. It now looks like this albino character is the man on top, and Maduna nothing more than a sidekick. Obviously a disappointing sidekick, too. It all makes sense now. Trafficking in heroin, in people, in human remains – a syndicate smart enough, and with all the right connections, can arrange distribution for just about anything. We must've inadvertently torn the guts out of their enterprise by seizing that heroin shipment, which made their whole set-up come crashing down around their ears. I can't believe none of us knew more about this.'

But suddenly he *can* believe it. Jacob's lunchtime story had made him think at the time about fundamentalists; he just never thought of them occurring in tribal religious groups as well. Zealots are certainly a tight-knit group, difficult to crack at the best of times.

Albino? Harry's mind keeps skittering back and forth over that one word. There *is* something there, at the back of his consciousness, but what? The dead creature used in the fetish was an albino rat. And what was Niehaus always going on about? The superintendent had felt sure there was some connection between the Hillbrow decapitation case and the girl's body dumped near the mine tailings. Harry reconsiders the number of references to an albino man they have received over the past few weeks, each one sounding crazier than the last. He then thinks about Jacob's story of the witch's attempt to abduct him, and of the familiars these people seem able to use.

Another large fragment of the puzzle shifts. Niehaus was right: there *was* a connection between the three cases.

Oh, God, why couldn't I see it before?

'What?' asks Nina, noticing Harry's shocked expression.

'The albino – we came across him before, a few years ago,' replies Harry. 'An unreliable-seeming witness spoke about an all-powerful albino witch doctor who rode on a baboon, but that was naturally never followed through.'

'Why not?'

'How would *you* react if someone told you how he had discovered the decapitated corpse of a drug dealer just after seeing an albino riding away on the back of a large white primate?'

'I'd follow it up, maybe,' suggests Nina.

Harry smiles wryly. 'Ms Reading, in a country where so much credence is given to superstition, a journalist might have fun pursuing weird leads but a cop cannot necessarily do likewise. In court we need admissible evidence, not crazy stories. Take Atteridgeville, for example. It's a township west of Pretoria and has the highest incidence of serial killings in South Africa. Do you know how most of its residents explain that fact?'

'Tell me.'

'Some powerful spirit turned malevolent when it felt the locals were ignoring it, neglecting their traditions of respect. To this day it seemingly haunts the local streets, taking possession of men and turning them into psychopathic killers, the murders they commit quenching its thirst for revenge. Every time someone gets killed in a fit of rage, like a stabbing over a pint of beer, this same damn spirit gets blamed. Do you know what reaffirms that story?'

Nina shrugs.

'Most of the serial killers who have operated in that area for some reason choose the nearby Skurweberg hills to dump the bodies of their victims. That of course fuels the belief that those hills are sacred to this same demon.

My point, I suppose, is that we cops don't have the time to pursue every urban myth.'

'Fuck.' Nina scratches her head in sudden frustration. 'I can't *believe* I actually tried to save that arsehole's life. I should've bloody well offed him myself.'

Harry bursts out laughing. 'You're a hard woman, Nina Reading.'

Nina's smile is tight. 'Yeah, and not too shy to take a swing at a cop, either.'

'Don't worry about it,' says Harry, rubbing the wound on his lip. 'Now, we'll need to verify a link between your Tumi and Ngubane Maduna, then track down her parents as soon as possible.'

'Scotland Yard should be able to provide some info for you,' says Nina. 'If the hotel hasn't already thrown my things out, I should have details on file somewhere of the investigating officer for Tumi's case. William Ackroyd was his name.'

Harry jots down this additional information below his already extensive notes. 'I still find it hard to believe that any man could conceal himself so effectively in this city. We don't yet know where they've disappeared to, but we'll find them; we've got plenty of leads to chase up. They're on the run now and that gives us an edge in talking to any suspects we've arrested. If they know he's on the run, maybe they'll have less fear and talk more.' Harry's eyes begin to glint. 'We can implicate these bastards in a dozen high-profile criminal investigations. We should be able to get all the help we want to nail them.'

'As long as I get to report the action for my newspaper,' demands Nina.

Harry looks at his unlit cigarette, sighs and slips it

back into the packet. 'Sitting here with you over coffee and cigarettes – call it sharing the mundane things in life – suddenly life feels a lot less dangerous, Ms Reading. Sure, you can have the story, as far as I'm concerned, but you'll have to speak to the boss – and Chief Molethe can be tough.'

'He'll let me do this, just you wait and see,' says Nina, narrowing her eyes mischievously. 'So what's with your phobia about journalists?'

Harry meets her eyes with a penetrative glance. At first he seems about to clam up, then settles more comfortably into his chair. 'Like I said, you're probably no way as bad as they were.' Harry takes a deep breath, and gives Nina a summary of what happened all those years ago in Epping Forest. 'The man – Perkins was his surname – received two life sentences for what he did that day.'

Shocked by what she has heard, Nina can only nod.

'It didn't take the police too long to find him,' continues Harry. 'And it didn't take the British press long to find me, either. When I came out of . . . when I got home, my whole life had changed – not just because of what had happened but because there wasn't any privacy any longer. Anywhere and everywhere my parents took me, there could be reporters, or even just ordinary people, wanting to talk to me about it. My parents did their best to ward them off, to protect me from it all – to give me space to heal, whatever. But clearly, plenty of others didn't want that – they wanted a young hero.

'Eventually my parents decided they'd had enough. We packed our things and came out here to South Africa, where no one would know about us.'

Harry suddenly gets up to leave after a promise to

check on her belongings at the hotel. 'Once again, I appreciate what you've done, Ms Reading.'

Nina sits a while longer, tracing patterns on the ugly Formica surface. She grew up in Leyton, a poorish neighbourhood in the north-east of London, not far from Woodford itself. She tries to connect her mental image of that courageous child of twenty-five years ago with the detective, who now looks so haunted. They seem to have little in common. It is as if his spirit has been eaten away, all his inner strength used up.

66

As a kid, Harry Mason used to like experimenting with dams, building little mud walls round a central pool, testing the strength of his creations by filling the pool up with water until the walls eventually burst. It was that very moment which fascinated him the most: that first trickle breaking through and quickly dragging the rest of the wall away with it, tearing the gap wider open and destroying the entire structure. It seemed to accurately reflect the emotions toiling inside him. Even as a young child he understood the metaphor of his dam-building, but what he could not fully grasp was the point of critical mass – a point of pressure which would so often rise up in him, too. Try as he might, Harry could not master the engineering skills to strengthen the walls of his own heart. Eventually he gave up and just settled down within himself every time the flood waters of his emotions began to rise, watching hopelessly as they broke loose again.

The latest break in his inner wall began to reappear a

month ago, but it is only now, while driving away from the hospital, that he succumbs to the full impact of his early memories, roaring out of careful containment.

The crunch of blunt steel penetrating flesh and bone still rings in his head like it did that day of his lost childhood. In his mind's eye he still sees Roger's arm lying contorted and spattered with blood in the long, green grass. He remembers himself screaming like he had never screamed before. And the shrill noise that young Harry generates starts faces popping up over garden fences nearby. The Morwargh – later identified as Eric Perkins – had dropped his shovel and run off in blind panic. Harry's mother eventually found him still crouching in his bushy hideout, his throat raw from cries of terror. As she raised him to her shoulder, he caught a glimpse of what his father was staring at. 'Oh my God!' he had cried. 'Janet, get the boy out of here!'

His recollections of the following weeks are less clear, just moments occasionally separating themselves from a uniformly dark background: his mother coaxing him with a bag of sweets in a stark white room somewhere; his father clasping his hand protectively; staring at a red-brick wall immediately outside his window as a trail of ants moves up and down it endlessly. Then he was back home again in his own little room, yet in a life that seemed no longer his own. Slowly he begins to talk again, become human again. It was while he became reacquainted with his former life that the guilt over Roger began to gnaw at his insides. Tears came frequently, suddenly and unbidden.

Gradually something hard became lodged in his heart, towards which he desperately drew his mind and anchored himself. It at least helped stop him drifting towards those painful memories. His parents assumed he was finally getting over it, but that hard kernel of self-reproach continued to overshadow his emotions.

The ringing of the mobile Nina has just returned to him interrupts his train of thought. Bobby Gous sounds excited. 'Niehaus wants you to get over and meet us in Hillbrow, at the site of that decapitation. He's got something for us.'

'Let me guess, it's got to do with some *dagga* dealer from a few years back, right?'

'How did you know?'

'I finally remembered what Niehaus was going on about the other day.'

'He's digging out the file right now. He wants us all to meet at that victim's apartment.'

'I'll be there in five minutes.'

67

Just before five o'clock Harry pulls up in front of a large rectangular building whose exterior already gives an impression of what he will find inside it. The buildings that once clustered around it have been torn down, so the apartment block now looms like the last tree of a diseased forest. The plaster rendering has long since crumbled off the walls, leaving the red brick and insulation underneath it exposed to the city's gaze. Its ground-floor level is smeared everywhere with silver and white graffiti. In places, the drainpipes have rusted through completely, and now dangle pathetically from their moorings on the walls. All windows facing the rickety fire escape are smashed, boarded up, or sprayed with multicoloured designs. On each level, washing lines are strung from the fire-escape railings to adjacent windows. On the side facing Tudhope Avenue, the burnt-out remnants of a neon sign have left two sooty black words on the brickwork: Bates Court.

Harry spots Niehaus's car parked underneath a real-estate board proudly proclaiming the property's selling price. Inside, Harry discovers that there is no lift, so he has to take the stairs to the fifth floor where the fire doors have been vandalized. A figure far down the darkened corridor whistles to attract his attention. Harry finds Mitchell and Gous standing in the splintered doorway of an apartment.

'We only caught about half of the *laaities* we were onto.' Mitchell scratches his large nose. 'The rest of them got away.'

'You mean the grave robbers?' asks Harry.

'Yes,' Mitchell chuckles. 'You know how we got onto them in the first place? The mother of one of them discovered lime and mud all over her son's trousers. The sick little shit gave his mother his clothes to wash after he'd been out to dig up fresh corpses. Not one of those bastards was older than seventeen.'

'You reckon any connection to this albino affair?'

'Too early to tell, but I'll have it out of them sooner or later. Luckily they can't afford the same class of lawyer that Superintendent Bornman and the narcs have had to deal with.'

Niehaus's head pokes out of the doorway, a cigarette dangling from his smiling mouth. 'You know, that's funny. A month ago, just about every character we brought in on suspicion of heroin trafficking or gang violence surprised us by producing some beefed-up attorney. Now it's as if the legal crowd have all gone off to the Lost City to gamble away their spoils.'

344

'Or maybe they've realized the money's dried up at its source,' offers Harry.

Niehaus winks, holding up a file. 'Let's hope so. In the meantime, we've found another connection.'

'Tell me.' Harry is fingering the damage done to the door. He wonders exactly how strong a man must be to inflict such harm on wood. 'I think I may have already pieced this particular puzzle together, but let's hear it.'

'The decapitation itself was an obvious clue, but for a while I couldn't remember what else it was regarding this case that got me thinking about you. It was Mitchell here who helped me out a bit. There was another guy called Victor Lekota who also lost his head. He spent most of his youth in and out of juvenile courts, before hitting eighteen at a sprint, with the law already hot on his heels. He was convicted on numerous small-time charges – breaking and entering, various thefts, muggings, growing and dealing *dagga* . . . you name it. He ran with all sorts, so he became the kind of guy we pulled in just to gather information on what was happening on the streets. He was ideal for us – not too smart, and scared of going down one last time for the long haul. Vic was never really an informant, as such, but he did squeal easily under threat of arrest.

'His troubles began for real when one of the most sophisticated narcotics rings ever seen in South Africa suddenly appeared. In the years following the free elections of 1994, when the Apartheid Police Force became the Police Service, criminal organizations seemed to spring up everywhere. As you know, they often use the secret networks forged during the resistance movement to distribute their weapons and drugs. More criminals arrived, most notably from Nigeria and eastern Europe, and the Chinese triads also began popping up in numbers. The syndicate

I'm referring to seemed to be making use of all these different channels to supply top-quality hash locally, or to export grade-A compressed *dagga*. They also ran prostitution and extortion rackets, and they traded in guns. Their distribution was tight, and by South African standards the quantities they managed to move were astounding. Johannesburg International Airport, Durban, Richards Bay and Cape Town harbours – SANAB traced their shit everywhere, but the significance of the few arrests they could ever make always seemed to fizzle out.

'The syndicate functioned so efficiently that SANAB deduced it to be some kind of paramilitary group at work. A lot of freedom fighters and ex-police state specialists were suddenly out of work, and some felt cheated by the politicians they had been loyal to. The Soviet Union had also recently collapsed. The task seemed daunting, because SANAB had a lovely pack of suspects to choose from. Ex-Koevoet soldiers? Umkhonto we Sizwe fighters? Ex-KGB? Mercenaries from Angola or Mozambique? They couldn't be sure, but those are the types they started concentrating on.

'For SANAB operatives, infiltrating the ring itself proved impossible. The group seemed to be sealed airtight, and the few ever arrested had serious backing. They never talked, and if they did go to jail, it was almost always with a smile on their faces.

'It wasn't really by chance that the Narcotics Bureau finally caught their old friend Vic with a kilo of the same hash this group regularly imported. SANAB pulled him in and they leaned on him. They leaned on him *hard*, but this time Vic, surprisingly, didn't squeal. In fact he was in no mood to play at all. Instead of gibbering with fear of going to jail forever, he seemed cocky now, as if he knew he had

God himself on his side. He clamped right up and didn't give an inch.

'The fool would've gone down for six years at least, except our friends in the bureau were so happy over nailing their old friend with the actual goods on him, they fucking forgot to read him his rights – and the rest of it. So he laughed at them in triumph, muttering something about how his "high oath" had paid off, then walked out the door.'

While Niehaus talks, Harry inspects the rest of the apartment. The gloom of the place blends with the stench from the kitchen and bathroom to make the misery of this murder scene palpable in a way Harry has never felt before.

' "High oath"?' echoes Harry, retreating into the corridor for a cigarette.

'There exist different grades of witch doctors throughout Africa,' answers Mitchell. 'Only the very highest-ranking practitioners can bind someone with a high oath. It means that you essentially give your soul to the witch doctor as insurance for not breaking that oath. Of course, if you *do* break it, your own death and that of your close relatives will be of the worst kind imaginable. I think Lekota vouchsafed his loyalty for that level of protection.'

Harry retches violently as his fragile lungs reject the tobacco smoke, forcing him to toss the remains of his cigarette away. 'So SANAB wasn't hunting paramilitaries at all; they were hunting religious fanatics,' muses Harry.

'If you can call occultists that, then yes,' answers Mitchell.

'So what went wrong?'

'SANAB were onto them now,' continues Niehaus. 'It was just a matter of time before they found someone who wanted out, or until an honest customs official picked up on something. As it turned out, it was the latter, and it happened a few days after the narcs let Victor go. The problem for Vic, though, was that his bosses obviously thought he had broken his oath, so they came after him.'

Mitchell clears his throat. '*Something* came after him.'

Niehaus sighs. 'Mitchell, do you *always* have to—'

'Look around you, Niehaus! I know these people aren't the cleanest folk about, but you can't tell me these *boytjies* would hide themselves in places like this out of fear for ordinary men. Do you think even a man as big as Ejiofer could do *this* to a door? No, *boet*, these people are *possessed*, I'm telling you.'

Harry nudges a large splinter with the tip of his shoe. Standing in the doorway to an apartment as foul as this, Mitchell's outlandish occult explanation suddenly seems a lot more credible.

'*Ja*, OK, man,' mutters Niehaus irritably, 'whatever. The point is that Victor Lekota was sleeping at his mother's house on 14 December 1998 when a killer entered the house and butchered the Lekotas in their beds, decapitating the grandson and gutting the mother. The only clue found at the crime scene was a fetish clutched in Victor's hand. It had the same qualities as yours, Harry: an albino rat's head wrapped in broken birds' wings, with a generous helping of human blood and ash. Only Victor's blood didn't match the sample found in it.'

Harry nods. 'I suddenly remembered the story this afternoon while I was talking to that British reporter.'

'How's she doing?' asks Niehaus. 'I'll tell you one thing: that girl was impressive – *blerrie* impressive.'

'I think she's maybe doing better than us,' Harry

replies. 'Was this syndicate ever cracked, Lekota's murderer ever found?'

'No, the same thing happened every time. They'd follow the trail towards a core group, then, *bam*, they'd hit this impenetrable wall – or else their targets just disappeared.'

'Like magic? Hmm, are we talking about Maduna's operation here? The albino?'

'It seems plausible. The syndicate may well have mutated since those early days, diversified, with heroin smuggling becoming their chief source of income. Could be that even the muti trade has become a lucrative enough activity for them.'

Harry whistles.

'You're wrong, Kobus,' interjects Mitchell. 'It's not because it was a lucrative market that they started it; they began trading in human muti because it's in this group's *nature*. It's occult worship and the power it commands that lie at this organization's core, not just the pursuit of money. Smuggling human organs strengthens the group's spiritual contacts with other occultists.'

Niehaus holds Mitchell's gaze for a few moments, before admitting that he might be right.

Harry speaks. 'OK, I'll buy there's a weak link connecting this Oba, Victor and my dead girl, but that leaves me with more questions. First of all, why wasn't it Victor Lekota's blood in the fetish he was holding, like the little girl's was found in that fetish in the riverbed? Secondly, who the hell is this Oba?'

Mitchell answers, 'The human elements in those amulets suggest they were death jujus.'

'Death *jujus*?' inquires Niehaus.

'Practitioners of Haitian voodoo and West African juju sometimes use a fetish enhanced with blood to invoke a death curse. It doesn't, however, have to be the blood of the targeted victim. Once the incantation is completed, it's believed that an evil spirit will attack the victim, and even his family, so long as the spell made is powerful enough.'

'But we know it wasn't a spirit that killed this Oba character.'

Mitchell shrugs. 'We know that, but this witch doctor's followers, the ones not part of his inner circle, don't necessarily know it. The types who practise this form of occultism are indoctrinated in such a way that they don't ask too many questions, just accept in blind faith. The point I'm making is that the blood they use isn't necessarily the intended victim's blood.'

The last few pieces in Harry's jigsaw puzzle slot together, but his reaction is muted, not the euphoria he usually feels on piecing together a case. 'Niehaus, you said before that one of the slaughtered Nigerian's neighbours assumed the man who often visited them could be a relative. The Chevy found in the garage contained a blood-stained fleece blanket the same colour as the fibres found in the little girl's hair. And one of these death jujus was found in the riverbed, so here's the deal. This Oba is branded to die, along with his family. For some reason he has access to and then dumps the body of the girl, who was used in part to create his own death juju. He goes on the run, thinking that way he can escape death, but not before stashing his car with his own family. After a week or so, Taiwo Ejiofer and his friend eventually track him down. Then, having previously killed the man's family, they decapitate him in exactly the same fashion they killed Victor Lekota.'

'But why would Oba dispose of the body *after* his boss has obviously declared him a dead man to his face?' asks Niehaus.

'I have no idea, but I'm sure that's it,' says Harry, tugging at his lip in concentration. 'The question should be rather: why was he sentenced to death?'

Mitchell scratches his head. 'Wasn't there some kind of tip-off that led us to uncover that heroin cache?'

Harry snaps his fingers and points at Mitchell with an excited smile. 'I think you're right.'

'It would be great, *boet*, if that *was* it,' says Niehaus. 'But it wasn't Oba who tipped of the narcs, it was one of our own – a cop.'

'What do you mean?' asks Harry, astonished.

'When I spoke to Bornman late last week, he mentioned in passing that they'd managed to trace the call logged with SANAB. Surprisingly it came from Diepkloof, where the reaction units are based.'

'So a cop knows exactly where to find the biggest haul of heroin this city has ever seen, and then gives a tip-off to the Narcotics Bureau *anonymously*? That doesn't sound right.'

'*Ja, boet*,' answers Niehaus, 'it does sound far-fetched – unless that person had something to hide.'

Harry and Mitchell wait for Niehaus to replace the police tape and warning notice at the doorway before all three officers make their way down to the ground floor. Occasionally they are met by cautious eyes peering out at them from doorways, like so many church mice waiting for the aisle to clear.

'We could do with talking to whoever made the tip-off,' muses Harry. 'I reckon the chances are pretty good that *he* would know where we can find the albino.'

'That's true, but I don't think we necessarily need him.' Niehaus stops in the stairwell. 'I didn't bring this along for nothing.' He chuckles, holding up Victor Lekota's file. 'I'm sure, if you remember his case, you'll remember our star witness.'

Harry's answering smile is dry. 'Themba somebody-or-other – he was the only person to come forward. He claimed to have seen an albino witch riding away from the crime scene on the back of a massive white baboon – or some such garbage.'

'Did we laugh about that one for weeks?' Niehaus shakes his head. '*Jenne*, the things you hear as a cop in this country. But I suppose that after what we now know, I should fucking kick myself for not pursuing that claim further.'

'What else did he say?'

'Themba Msimang,' reads out Niehaus as they reach the foyer. 'According to his statement, this witch doctor of ours lives in a cave deep underneath Hillbrow, surfacing to do his evil deeds at night, along with his familiars – baboons, hyenas, chameleons and other such nonsense.' Niehaus snorts. 'He apparently controls the hearts and minds of everyone living in that neighbourhood. *Yissus*, what the hell was I supposed to do when the *chappie* told me all this stuff?' Niehaus slaps the document in disbelief.

'I suppose it could've been an allegorical kind of statement,' mutters Harry. The more he thinks about the tale in light of what Jacob told him earlier, the more it seems to him that that is the only explanation for these weird testimonies. 'Do we have a last known address for this kid?'

'*Ja*, everything – his last place of employment as well as his residence, which happens to be his grandmother's place, not far from where Lekota's body was found. Whether he's still living there is another matter.'

'Right, we need to track him down fast. I have a feeling we'll get more answers out of this kid than from any of our dear suspects already sitting in their cells. If it's OK, superintendent, I'll head out to his grandmother's, if you could go deal with his workplace.'

'I'll pursue the albino angle while I'm questioning my grave robbers,' chirrups Mitchell helpfully from several paces behind them.

Harry hurries to his car, his brain racing with the new information. The links definitely seem to make sense. Looking at his watch, he is surprised to discover it is nearing six o'clock – and he still wants to head out to Newtown. Realizing he will be working late tonight, Harry decides to give his wife a call. The house phone rings until the answering machine clicks in.

'Amy, just to let you know I'll be working late tonight. You'll be glad to know this is almost over. Don't wait up – and give Jeanie a kiss from me. I love you both.'

68

Jacob throws himself into a chair, still exhausted from last night's ordeal and further drained by the emotional effort of explaining himself to Harry at lunchtime. It proved a lot more taxing talking about his past than he had thought it might be, and he felt worse because Harry had not attempted to reciprocate. Yet he knows that man has his personal demons, too.

Jacob gets up and paces the room. He had not found the time to drive down to Newtown and help with the forensic investigations there, instead concentrating on allaying the fear that is still paralysing potential witnesses. Understandably the albino's rivals have been the most informative so far, detailing many intricacies of his tight grip on the drug trade in Johannesburg. That was something for the South African Narcotics Bureau though, not for the Murder and Robbery Unit.

The detective spots a new report from Dr Wilkes on Harry's desk and flicks through it. It includes the entomological and autolytic dating of the little girl's death, confirming that she had been dead for a week when discovered, but most likely dumped on the same day she was killed. The analysis of her stomach contents lists trace elements of plants and minerals that Jacob knows to be common ingredients used in purification rituals. He throws the report back onto the desk. The chief suspects are now on the run, with who knows what resources at their disposal. As far as he is concerned, the whole web of this case is still fluttering in the wind, waiting for them to tie its various loose ends together.

Beside Wilkes's file he finds another note. The night before, detectives in Heidelberg, south of Johannesburg, caught three men trying to steal a car. Upon further investigation, it turns out they were the hijackers identified in Jacob's own ongoing case of the couple found massacred in their Pajero. Jacob picks up the note and strokes the sheet of paper with a sense of disbelief. It now all seems somehow alien in the light of the occurrences of the last twenty-four hours.

When the phone on Harry's desk starts ringing, Jacob picks up the receiver.

A man with an unusually high-pitched voice introduces himself as one of the forensic technicians working at the site of the Newtown fire. 'We've got one helluva report to file. It's going to take us the greater part of a week, I'm sure. Been stuck out here all day in this heat, and it's not the best neighbourhood to buy yourself a drink in, if you know what I mean.' He guffaws loudly, as if he has made a joke. 'Anyway, we had a thorough search for Detective Mason's wallet and keys, but so far found nothing.'

'Did you find anything else that will help us trace these killers?'

'No, I'm afraid not. Just another body and a room containing charred remains: some bones and a skull, along with hatchets and some suspicious-looking packages. I have no idea what ten packets of filter coffee were doing in a place like that, but we'll be testing everything tonight at the lab. You boys obviously have a lot of high-powered backing on this one, hey? We're told we need to work through the night if we have to – orders, straight from the area commissioner's office.'

'If that's what it takes.' Jacob makes a hasty excuse and hangs up on the man before he complains further. The receiver is barely back in its cradle before the phone rings again. Jacob is surprised to be hearing from an officer at the nearby Brixton police station. He sits down to listen, disbelief spreading slowly over his face. When she has finished talking, Jacob hangs up and scratches his head in disappointment.

A quiet voice startles him. 'Problem?' asks Chief Molethe.

Jacob sees Molethe standing at the door and gets up. 'Early this morning,' he explains in Sotho, 'a patrol car from Brixton was called out to investigate a blaze, up near the Observatory water tower. They only managed to get out there this afternoon, and found four burnt-out cars, identified as a red BMW, two black Mercedes and a red Toyota Corolla. It's taken them a whole day to pass this information on to me, even though we'd put a priority on three of the vehicles.'

Molethe responds with a heavy sigh. '*Aowa*, these people are as slippery as catfish. We know about the three German cars, but why did they destroy the Toyota?'

Jacob shakes his head. 'As far as I know, nothing involving a red Toyota has yet been reported to us.'

'Hmm, better look into that. In the meantime, don't look so down. We've had a deal more luck lately – let's hope it's here to stay.' Molethe slaps him on the shoulder and leaves.

Jacob returns to his chair and thinks about what his superior has just said. It suddenly becomes clear to him that Molethe might be right – and one of the loose threads of the web has been tied up for them. The men who picked up Ngubane Maduna after his bail hearing at the law court, and who also were involved in the petrol station massacre, have just torched the BMW along with the two Mercedes, thus very likely connecting themselves with whichever gang dumped the corpse in Hettie Solilo's garden.

69

Harry parks his pickup outside a beige-coloured building dating from the early half of the twentieth century. It features sandstone balustrades beneath all its upper windows, creating the false impression of balconies, but whose cramped space only benefit the hundreds of pigeons nesting there. Harry climbs out of his car and is checking the address jotted down on a scrap of paper when his mobile rings.

'Harry,' begins Superintendent Niehaus, 'I'm at the Nando's fast-food joint in Cresta, where Msimang used to work as a griller. It seems he was fired about eight months ago, for coming in to work high on *zoll*. The manager suspects the *boytjie* was acting as courier for someone. He says his *chommies* were always hanging about out in the parking lot, playing craps or peddling stuff – might've been *dagga*, might've been something else. The friends are also gone, moved on to safer pastures, maybe.'

'Just reached the apartment building now, so let's hope I'll have more luck,' replies Harry, crossing the street. He enters a quiet foyer and locates a lift to take him up to the fourth level.

He steps out of the lift and heads along a concrete walkway with the front doors to apartments ranged to his left and an open view of the street to his right. Approaching apartment 402, he notices the brass figure two hanging upside down from one remaining screw. He knocks and steps back. There is no immediate answer, so he knocks a second time. Noting the kitchen window is open slightly, he leans towards it and calls out, 'Mr Msimang? Police. I need to ask you a few questions.'

Harry hears a soft rustling sound, but no one answers. He puts his eye to the peephole of the door and cups both his hands around it, in time to make out a shadow briefly flitting across the hallway beyond.

'Msimang, open up. You're not in trouble, mate. I just need to talk to you.'

When he still receives no acknowledgement, Harry curses, braces himself against the outer railing and kicks viciously at the door. After the fifth brutal impact, the lock buckles and the door springs open. Harry hurries inside, first checking the kitchen to his right, then heading into the living room, where he discovers the television switched on at low volume and a plate of half-eaten chicken and rice spilled over a battered maroon couch. A quick exploration of the two bedrooms and a small bathroom, ankle-deep in discarded clothes, reveals no one present. But the curtains are billowing into the living room from wide-open French windows with access to a black-painted fire escape running down the rear of the building.

Its steel treads are still ringing with someone's hurried descent, so Harry dashes through and hurtles down the metal staircase, covering each short flight in great leaps. When he glimpses an anxious upturned face two levels below him, he curses himself for not having brought Jacob along. Just as he reaches the first floor, he hears his quarry's feet hitting the tarmac of the fenced-off parking lot. Pausing to lean over the railing, Harry spots a youngster sprinting diagonally across the open space towards a security gate on the far side.

Without a second's thought, Harry leaps over the guardrail, dropping eight feet to the tarmac below. He rolls with the fall, ignoring the injuries already covering his back. Simultaneously pulling out his pistol, he comes over and up to see Msimang scaling the gate fifty yards away.

'Themba, get the hell down from that gate or I'll shoot!'

Msimang hesitates, looking up rather than back.

'I said, get your arse down from there.'

Msimang scurries up the rest of the gate and reaches its tiara of razor wire just before the two shots ring out.

'*Stop* there, you bugger!' yells Harry.

Msimang freezes, then turns and stares at the advancing cop with frightened eyes. He finally drops down from the gate in defeat.

'Right, get your hands up!'

The youth raises his arms, keeping wide and bitter eyes fixed on the cop.

'Up against the wall and spread your legs.'

Just outside the gate, gawking pedestrians hurry past the fence. Harry reaches his prey and pats him down. He does not find a weapon, but from Msimang's back pocket he pulls a large plastic sachet filled with marijuana. Harry holsters his weapon, grabs the youngster by the shoulder and swings him around roughly.

'Bloody idiot! You'd risk getting yourself shot for a banky of *dagga*?'

'What you want from me, boss? I haven' done nothing wrong.'

'What's this then?' asks Harry, holding up his gear.

Msimang looks away.

'You now dealing this from your *magogo*'s flat, eh?'

'Look, I'm sorry, boss. Jus' . . . please don' arrest me. I'm only sellin' to keep my ma and me alive, you know. I can' find the work, and my ma – she's too sick to work. You can no do dis, please, I'm asking you.'

Themba Msimang cannot be older than twenty-two, and despite an otherwise attractive face his cheeks are gaunt and his eyes bloodshot. His Harley Davidson shirt has seen too many washes and his North Star sneakers are ruptured in various places.

Harry sighs and gets to the point. 'I want you to tell me about that *baloyi* you saw after Lekota got killed two years ago.'

'Tell you *what*?' asks Msimang, terror instantly sparking in his eyes.

'You heard me, mate.'

'No.' He shakes his head vigorously. 'I can no do dat.'

'What do you mean, *no*?' snarls Harry.

'*No*, I can no do dis ting you ask of me.'

Harry grabs the hesitant boy firmly by his collar and gives him a violent shake. 'You better have something to tell me, something *good* – otherwise I'll have you up in front of a judge, and then we'll see how you like Sun City. You know what they do to pretty boys like you in jail?' Msimang's eyes grow considerably wider at the thought. 'I can see you do, mate, so you'd better invite me back up to your flat and we'll start talking there about what I want to hear.'

By the time Harry has secured the window and deposited Msimang on the maroon couch, the youth has gone deathly quiet, just staring at the carpeted floor in front of him. Harry quickly checks out the rest of the apartment – and finds a large brick of compressed marijuana under the young man's mattress.

He returns to the living room, brandishing the brick ominously. 'OK, if you don't want to spend the next ten years in jail, I suggest you start telling me about the albino you witnessed killing Victor Lekota.'

Tears suddenly well up in Msimang's eyes. Abruptly he bangs his head a couple of times against the backrest of the couch, before shaking his head. 'No, I can't.'

Harry nods and walks through into the adjoining kitchen. Tossing both the brick and the sachet into the sink, he rummages in the cupboards below it till he finds a bottle of paraffin. Dowsing his prisoner's stash with the

fuel, Harry turns around and stares at Msimang meaningfully, his cigarette lighter raised in his hand.

'What are you doing?' yells Msimang. 'I need that
stuff. Please, man!'

'Talk, then,' repeats Harry. 'I don't have all day.'

'You don' understand—'

'*Talk!*' Harry clicks on the flame.

'Las' time I talk, I couldna shit for a week, boss! Bad
dreams, dey come to me *every* fucking night for too long,
too long, until I go see this powerful *sangoma* – dere in
Limpopo – to get rid of his magic. I *still* owe dat one lots
of money for the muti he made me. I'm telling you, please
don' make me talk about him. She will hear me and come
for me – like she did with Vic, you know.'

Msimang begins to cry openly, his face reminding Harry
of a terrified child's. The way Msimang mixes genders is
not strange to Harry – many Bantus who lack a proper
education tend to struggle with their translations. Harry
decides to put the lighter away. Re-entering the living room,
he pulls a three-legged stool close to Msimang and sits
down. Softly he says, 'Look, Themba, you listen to me.
Whoever this man is, his hold on you is dying. We've taken
his heroin, his . . . his muti factory is destroyed and he has
killed Ngubane Maduna, his own right-hand man. The
other gangs are waging open war with him, and people
have started talking about the crimes he's committed. He's
on the run now, and he has no money. With your help, he
won't be able to touch anyone again.'

'You think prison will hold him? You think she will
let you take him into a court? You mad, you *stupid*! She's
not like you or me. You can' hold him. She will just disappear like a cloud. I've seen him do it.'

'Do you *want* this to be over?' Harry peers hard at the young man.

Msimang stares at him with wet eyes and sniffs, 'Yes.'

'Do you want this guy out of your neighbourhood?'

'Yes.'

'Then you talk to me, brother.'

Msimang grinds his teeth and clenches his eyes shut. Harry lets him wrestle for a while with his dilemma, but sure enough, when Msimang opens his eyes again, he nods hesitantly.

70

'Dey say she never see the light – that the light and he are enemies.' Msimang is nervous, glancing frequently around the living room. 'Dey say she half man, half demon. You can see she be of the spirit world, because she has red eyes, like the animal, that glow in the dark, and the skin of a white man although she is black.'

Where previously Harry might have begun to interrupt him here, the fresh memory of Jacob's life story forces him to bite back an urge to insist that Msimang talk more sense.

'No one knows what tribe she's from, or how she came here, except that she's from somewhere west. I hear she live deep underground, under Hillbrow, at the bottom of a very big tree dat grows underground. Its roots, branches, leaves, dey spread everywhere under the city. Only his people know how to fin' him. Dey also say she keep the world's most powerful muti buried under this tree's roots – secret, terrible things she learn in many faraway countries. Dey say the things she keep down there, if dey ever reach de sunlight, great fires will burn all the city. She keep things down there that will melt the skin on men's faces, and burn the eyes of women.'

Harry clears his throat, scepticism evident in his eyes.

Msimang's voice sounds even more delirious. 'No! You wan' hear, so now you must *listen*. He doesn' need guards down there, because who will go down there to anger the spirit tree.

'He has a secret army of *tokoloshe* – dey evil spirits that destroy anything living just for the fun. No one will ever find him, not even if the whole world tell you where he is, because he will already know and be gone again. What can the police do after he has already rub his skin with *bashimane* and disappear? This witch is so powerful because he has learn from many tribes. She know all different people of Africa; dey are his friends. He has earn the fear of everyone. How else can a foreigner get so many people to do his work in this city? The Xhosa and the Zulu, they hate each other, and everyone thinks the Venda are stupid, but this one gets all of them to serve him. No one refuse what she ask, once they start work for him.'

Msimang begins to whimper again, wiping his wet nose with a sleeve. 'He take all my friends, I don' know where dey are now. She kill Victor first, riding away on that evil white baboon of his. Then he kill Jim, and Daniel, and . . . and Godfrey has been taken to feed the tree or something. They all *dead* now.'

Msimang turns a terrified gaze back on Harry. 'Tell me, how you goin' get rid of this one, who curse me from many miles away after hearing me speak to the police about Victor? You think she is on the run, but I say he is juz moving. She putting himself in a place where you will not find him. From there she will strike again.'

Harry sits back, his hands firmly grasping his thighs. His first instinct is incredulity, but he takes a deep breath. 'You said he lives under Hillbrow. Where exactly?'

'You hear nothing I say to you?'

'I heard what you told me, but I want to know exactly *where* he lives.'

'You can' go there. It's a magical place.'

'*Look*,' says Harry, 'believe what you want to believe, but you better tell me what you know of this place where he's shacked up.'

'I've told you.'

'*Bullshit!*' roars Harry, jumping up to drag Msimang clear off the couch by his shirt. 'Tell me where he is or I'll *beat* it out of you.'

All the remaining colour drains from Msimang's face at this outburst. 'Ponte,' he whispers. 'The entrance is under Ponte City.'

Harry drops the youngster back onto the couch and stares at him thoughtfully for a long minute. Little pearls of sweat are forming on the boy's brows while Harry wonders what to make of his story. In the end he shakes his head and says, 'You lot do live in a brutal world.'

As soon as Harry has left, Msimang hurries over to the sink to check his weed. Finding it contaminated with paraffin, he first tries to rinse it off, before realizing it should dry out naturally. If he cannot then bring himself to smoke it, he is sure he will be able to sell it to someone else.

71

Harry fumbles with his mobile as he bursts out of the lift and rushes towards his car. Ponte City – it is unbelievable how obvious that seems now. For so many years the police have been raiding the huge building in an attempt to exterminate the criminal element periodically haunting the structure. Ponte City – again? And criminal West Africans holed up in there – again? The city council should have razed the place to the ground the day those four cops disappeared in its bowels never to be seen again. Something like that does not happen, *should* not happen, but it did.

It occurred back in 1998, after a sharp increase in the deaths of prostitutes hooked on crack finally drove the police service into action. The market for crack had suddenly burgeoned at the time, and some joker had been giving the girls helpful advice on how best to absorb the drug. Crushing the crystals and sprinkling it directly into the eyes was the best way to get high, he claimed. The problem was that it left the girls, some as young as eight, completely blind, their eyes almost melted away by the time they dropped dead.

SANAB eventually traced the drugs to a Zimbabwean group that had consolidated its power base inside Ponte. A green light had been given for a hastily organized raid.

The tower is massive, with many exits, by lift or staircase, on different sides of its cylindrical structure, as well as parking lots on various levels – basements and sub-basements – and numerous service corridors, which might as well lead down into the bowels of the earth, so complex a network do they form. More than one hundred officers arrived that day, only to find the key entrances locked and barred. By the time these doors were finally battered down with jackhammers, the drugs themselves were floating down the city's sewer network. All they achieved that day was the rescue of some near-naked twelve-year-old girls herded into two tiny apartments, while another unit recovered hundreds of stolen electrical appliances from the basements.

News reporters interviewed a beaming area commissioner standing in front of the towering monolithic building, along with the various investigative officers who had coordinated the dragnet. A profound pledge was made that, from that day on, the police service would keep the place free from criminals arrogant enough to barricade the building. The raid was deemed a great success, although no actual dealers had been busted nor any trace found of the crack that should have been stored there in large quantities.

As these things often go, calamity had struck while the area commissioner was already on his way back to the suburbs, probably happily dreaming his big political dreams. A headcount taken just an hour after the press interview revealed that four officers had gone missing during the search-and-seizure. Although each squad had a radio, and was meant at all times to stay within sight of another squad, somehow no one had noticed these men disappear. Another frantic search was organized, and this time the agitated and frightened cops became violent. Members of the public, as well as the media, were forced to vacate the area while more cops, firemen, medics and even a truckload of army reserves were brought in to help with the search.

Nothing was ever found.

The area commissioner subsequently made an abrupt announcement that there had been a miscommunication and that the four officers had in fact reported safe and sound to their precinct several hours later – hours after the whole city had been turned upside down looking for them. Neither the officers who knew them personally, nor their own families, of course, believed this hogwash.

Gradually an eerie picture emerged of their final moments. The unit that last noticed them reported that, upon descending into a second sub-basement, they found outdated transformers humming so loudly that in places it was difficult to communicate. The officers there could feel the hair on the backs of their necks rise. The third basement down contained a number of corridors feeding into a large central chamber, these passageways festooned with old-fashioned wiring and piping. The chamber itself being vulnerable to ambush, the search units proceeded carefully, but it was the four strange shafts sunk into the floor that unsettled them the most. Like wells, the shafts all looked extremely deep, and each was filled with black water covered by a film of undisturbed dust on its surface. It apparently smelt awful down there, too.

The team that mysteriously disappeared had been last seen heading down one of the radial corridors, following a set of dusty shoeprints.

A full month after the raid, a local scavenger hunting waste food climbed into one of the three massive garbage dumpsters placed permanently at Ponte City. But what he found was something else entirely. Four police uniforms were recovered from the dumpsters that day, soaked with human blood and other less identifiable gore, the tough denim itself shredded to ribbons. Nothing else could be found, however – not even the missing men's boots.

That was the last small-scale raid on Ponte City. After that, the only raids to be authorized demanded military and tactical police-squad backing, with a state-of-the-art communications system for every individual officer. And, even then, no politician would risk losing his office by sending cops down into the basements of the building, whose myriad nooks and crannies no architect could ever fully explain.

Is there a grain of truth in Msimang's story, after all? Harry shudders at the thought.

Back at the station, Jacob answers his mobile.

'Look, Jacob, I've got us a lead. And now that it's been raised, it's so bloody obvious. We bloody well should've thought of it sooner.'

'What are you talking about?' asks Jacob.

'Ponte,' answers Harry.

There is a split second's silence, then, 'How do you know?'

'I'll tell you later, but in the meantime we need some search-and-arrest warrants. We need to somehow convince Molethe to get authorization for another raid. Maybe Gildenhuys could help.'

'OK. Where are you now, though?'

'Right around the corner from the tower, down in Hillbrow.'

'You're not thinking of going in there by yourself?' asks Jacob, alarmed. After last night, he would not put any madness past his partner. 'Because I'm certainly not running in there after you.'

'Of course, I'm not, but we need both the boss and Gildenhuys on this as quickly as possible.'

'It'll take far too long to authorize that. Maybe we

should consider staking out the place or grab them when they try to leave.'

'No, there are too many things that could go wrong that way, plus they could either already be gone, or hide in there indefinitely. No, this damned albino has clearly been running his operation for years now without us knowing about him. He's far too slippery for us to just sit about and wait for him to make a mistake. It's time we go after him.'

'I don't know. You know how Director Moloto has blocked all suggested raids on that place ever since that area commissioner was forced to resign. Are you absolutely sure about this?'

Harry thinks for only a second before answering, 'Yes, it's obvious – for no other reasons than my own gut feeling and the word of a pothead scared out of his mind. This guy's been getting away with things for years precisely because we've been too scared to search that place properly. Who knows, maybe he's running something even worse down there than he was in Newtown. We need to get inside, Jacob. You speak to Molethe and I'll phone Gildenhuys.'

Harry hangs up and then dials the number of the state prosecutor. On the very first ring the man answers gruffly, 'Gildenhuys.'

'I have them,' says Harry, feeling calmer than in weeks. 'They're hiding out in Ponte City – exactly where we should be looking for them, but exactly where we don't *want* to go. They're hiding right under our bloody noses, and we need to get in there tonight, if it's not too late already.'

'Mason? Harry Mason?' Gildenhuys claps a hand over the phone. Harry can faintly hear the prosecutor excuse himself from a meeting, before the sound of a door closing and Gildenhuys coming back to him. 'Are you sure of that – Ponte City?'

'Yes, I'm totally sure.'

'Shit.'

'We need some warrants, and we need a search team large enough to cover every damned exit that place has, as well as search the building decently once and for all.'

'That's a tall order, Mason, and you know it.'

'Damn it, Gildenhuys! You promised us serious resources, and now it's time to deliver. This isn't just about *my* case; it concerns enough crimes committed throughout this city to keep an army of prosecutors busy for years – and you know it.'

Gildenhuys mutters, 'I can twist our superiors' arms on many things, but both the director and area commissioner can get very stubborn over Ponte City.'

'Just do what you can,' Harry pleads, and hangs up before steering his vehicle out into the traffic. What will he do if Gildenhuys comes back to him with a negative response?

Harry turns right at the traffic light, then hangs a left. He suddenly realizes he is in Saratoga Avenue, heading straight towards the grey cylindrical hulk of Ponte itself, rearing into the sky on the left-hand side of the street. Harry decides to park the pickup and study the building. The westerly windows facing him glitter in the late afternoon sun. Those windows that are not broken are closed, even in the summer's heat, giving him the impression that the building has been vacated. No one seems to be arriving or leaving the great multi-levelled parking lot built up behind the small petrol station surviving in Ponte's shadow.

Harry re-starts his car after twenty minutes' contemplation, having decided to head home after all. There he can think over his strategy in peace, while waiting for Gildenhuys's call. He will have to return to the office later tonight, but at least he can spend a few moments with his family before the storm breaks.

72

'So what did you learn at school today, sweetie?' Amy is steering her car down Republic Road on their way home. Her own day has been quite uneventful, but she is still exhausted from staying up all the previous night with her husband.

'We learnt about China, and its funny-eyed people – the Chi-*nese*.' Jeanie enunciates the last word slowly, as if she is teaching a new word to her mother, who is beginning to feel uncomfortable. 'Look!' she cries, when Amy stops at a traffic light. 'Chi-nese, Japa-nese, Portu-guese.' Her mother does look, and cannot help bursting out laughing as her daughter grins at her and pulls her eyes aslant with two fingers. 'That's what they look like, Mommy.'

'Funny-eyed people?' asks Amy, in disbelief. 'Who called them that?'

'Mrs Mostert.'

'Really? That's not a very nice name. I like Chinese much better, don't you?' suggests Amy.

'Yes, Chi-*nese*!' intones Jeanie again, before relating the rest of her day's history lesson.

They are now turning into their own street, with its green lawns, whirring sprinklers and ivy creeping up the walls. As she passes an old silver Cortina, filled with four dodgy-looking Africans, parked in the neighbour's drive-way, Amy immediately grows tense. Pulling out both her mobile and remote from the handbag tucked safely by her feet, she keeps a steady eye on the Cortina while wait-ing at the gate of her home. The men, however, seem to pay her no attention, but carry on chatting loudly enough for her to hear their jovial voices through the open win-dows of their car.

When the gate is fully retracted, Amy drives in, stops her car the moment it is safely inside, and, with an eye on the rear-view mirror, anxiously presses the remote to close the gate.

The gate comes to a stop, pauses a few seconds, then reverses its direction to a close.

She watches breathlessly as it inches shut, expecting at any moment for one of the men outside to come racing through the half-open entrance or jam a brick on the gate's slide-track.

Come on! She pleads silently.

The gate finally closes.

'Mommy?' asks Jeanie.

'What, my sweetheart?' asks Amy, her eyes still fixed on the rear-view mirror.

'Who's that man?'

Amy glances in the direction Jeanie is pointing. A young African is standing over to the left of her car, his hands concealed ominously behind his back. His bare upper arms are steroid-pumped, and a black leather skull-cap hugs his head tightly. His presence sends a ripple of ice down Amy's neck.

As she reacts quickly to lock the doors, the man casually strolls towards them. Jeanie looks hastily at her mother for guidance, while Amy desperately thumbs Harry's number but drops the mobile phone in her panic.

'*Shit!*' she cries and gropes for it under her seat.

'Mommy?' asks Jeanie apprehensively.

There is a hard tap at Amy's window. She looks up to discover the barrel of a snub-nose revolver staring straight at her.

'Open the door,' growls Cassius, his intentions deadly serious.

Amy shakes her head in mute shock, the phone now gripped in her left hand.

'Open the door or I shoot the girl.' He switches aim towards Jeanie.

As Amy's shoulders slump, Cassius smiles and fidgets for something in his pocket. To Amy's great surprise he brings out Harry's key ring, with its unmistakable pink shark, and points the remote at the gate. It begins to open. Puzzled, she glances over the young man's right shoulder and sees that the front door of their house is open wide. Her brief consideration of surrender turns into a glimmer of hope. If she can just make it into the house with her daughter, she may be able to save Jeanie and herself from these carjackers, or whoever they are.

'Jeanie, listen to me,' whispers Amy, the man's attention still fixed on the opening gate. 'When I tell you to run, you open your door and run for the house. I want you to lock yourself in the first room you can, OK?'

'Y . . . yes,' stammers Jeanie, pale with terror.

At that moment guffawing voices approach the gate, and the young man greets them with a laugh. Amy decides to act: with one sudden movement, she unlocks her own door, ramming it open with all her strength. '*Run!*'

The gun barrel clacks loudly on the glass as it is deflected. When Cassius is thrown off balance and stumbles backwards, Amy leaps out of the car, one foot catching the handbag underneath her seat and spilling its contents over the driveway. Yet she is still on the move before any of them can react. Behind her, she hears Jeanie's door opening too.

'*Run!*' screams Amy, as she lashes out with her foot at the teetering man and knocks him sprawling towards the lawn. Jeanie hurdles over his legs and races past her mother and through the front door, followed by Amy with three men in close pursuit.

Amy slams the front door shut and fumbles for the locks. But she is a little too slow, and a solid shoulder slams the door, throwing her back into the hallway. She screams for help as she stumbles against the small table holding a vase and the telephone. She recovers quickly enough to throw herself into the living room, but a rough hand catches her left wrist before she can get any further.

With teeth firmly clenched, Amy turns and throws a desperate punch with her free fist. The blow connects firmly with the man's temple, the impact sending a numbing shock up her arm. Although momentarily dazed, the bearded assailant does not let go.

'*Help!*' screams Amy futilely.

In their struggle, she manages to get the couch between them, and with a tremendous wrench she pulls her arm free from his grip when the man stumbles into the three-seater. She ducks into the kitchen, reaches the door leading to the small laundry room, yanks its key out and manages to slam it and lock it behind her. She immediately braces herself against the door and pinches her eyes closed in a silent prayer.

Hands grope at the door handle without any success. Abruptly, a man's voice swears loudly in an alien language, before the same man calls out to his friends.

Only then does Amy have time to think of Jeanie again. She has no idea where in the house her daughter is hiding, and, worse, Amy has left her mobile in the car.

Collin is still rubbing at his bruised temple as Cassius storms into the house cursing as he tries to dislodge soil from the barrel of his revolver. 'That bitch is going to pay for this,' he snarls.

Collin laughs. 'Mighty Cassius, thrown to the ground by a frightened white woman.'

Godfrey comes back from investigating the kitchen, his demeanour a lot less agitated than the other two's. 'She's locked herself into some room; I can't get through the door.'

'Let me try,' says Cassius, flexing his biceps so that the muscles ripple.

Collin laughs again. 'The lion's ego is bruised, so now it wants to show off.'

'Shut up,' snarls Cassius and heads through the kitchen to the locked door. He knocks on it loudly. 'Hey, bitch, open this fucking door or I'll shoot right through it.'

Amy says nothing, trying to get her racing breath under control.

Cassius pulls back his fist and throws a punch with all his strength. His right hand dents the light plywood. On the other side, Amy yelps in surprise.

'Open up, I said.'

'Go, just go *away!*' screams Amy from behind the damaged door. 'Take what you want – take *everything*! Just leave my daughter and me *alone*.'

Cassius laughs deeply. 'What makes you think we want any of your stuff anyway? No, my darling, we want *you*; we want *both* of you.'

Collin comes marching into the kitchen and announces in Ndebele, 'The child has locked herself in her bedroom.'

Cassius smiles maliciously, then knocks almost cordially on the door, 'Ah, *miesies* Mason, I think we have your baby. Are you coming out now?'

'Leave my daughter the fuck *alone*,' cries Amy desperately. *How do they know my name?* 'What do you want with us?'

'Oh, we just want to take you on a little trip.'

'Why?' she whimpers. 'What for?'

'Because your husband is a nosy cop.'

Amy feels herself go numb. She now realizes who they must be.

She hears the click of a gun hammer pulling back. 'Are you going to open up now?' whispers Cassius, with his ear pressed to the door.

'No,' whispers Amy, as if to herself.

Two deafening shots ring out in the confined space of the kitchen. Godfrey winces at each of them.

Jeanie lies hidden under her bed, the door to her room securely locked, just like her mother told her to. In the silence of her room, her breathing seems thunderous. She registers a few confused yells coming from the direction of the kitchen. When two shots ring out, the little girl gasps and flinches at each one.

After that she hears no more. Terrified, she crawls out from under the bed and moves over to the door to listen intently. Further indefinite sounds from the kitchen reach her up the corridor, followed by a sudden angry chatter of voices. What has happened to her mother?

Jeanie bites back from calling out to her and instead looks up to the window for a means of escape. It is heavily barred, however, offering her no hope there.

Suddenly her door handle rattles violently. 'Open up, *piccanin*,' growls a voice outside.

Jeanie whimpers and retreats to the bed. 'Where's Mommy?' she cannot help uttering.

'Open the door,' commands the same voice again.

Jeanie crawls back under the bed, as the first blow crashes against the door. Jeanie shrieks, '*Mommy!*'

Another crash, and this time wood groans and splinters, but does not give.

The third blow buckles the lock and the door sags inward. Under her single bed, Jeanie tries to make herself as small as possible against the cool of the wall behind her. Suddenly she sees silver-toned trainers heading towards her, before a massive hand suddenly seizes the edge of the bed and heaves it upwards. The face of a youth appears, with one ear missing. He grabs her arm and drags her out from underneath. As he lifts her up in one arm, Jeanie starts bawling openly. She manages to scratch him across one cheek. The youth barely winces, just throws her over his shoulder. Minutes later the house is seemingly abandoned as a silver Ford Cortina races away.

73

Even though the sun is setting on a horizon resembling an artist's palette smeared with lavender and deep shades of pink, its dying light through the windshield is blinding. Harry is stuck in the coil of congested traffic on Empire Road and trying to call home yet again. Surprised that no one has picked up, he tries Amy's mobile. Again it rings for a while before switching to voicemail.

Eight minutes later his own mobile rings. Assuming it is his wife, Harry answers more tenderly than usual.

'Where are you, Mason?' asks Gildenhuys, impatiently.

'On my way home,' replies Harry, taken aback by the controlled anger evident in the prosecutor's tone. 'Why?'

'You want the bad news first, or the good news?'

Harry groans. 'Give me the bad news.'

'Director Moloto has decided your information doesn't warrant the mobilization of another raid – especially one of the size we'd need to search Ponte effectively. He insists we can't do this every night – drain the entire city of its patrolling police officers. I take it he's referring to last night's operation.'

Harry is stunned. 'Are you *serious*?'

'He thinks we're now going over the top on this one just because Commissioner de Villiers granted us a favour.'

'What about de Villiers – what did he say?'

'I think he was with Moloto when I contacted him. In short, he's siding with Moloto on draining the city resources.'

'So what good news could you possibly have for me after that?'

'De Villiers isn't being entirely inflexible. He says the Murder and Robbery Unit is free to mount a dawn raid with whatever support we can muster from SANAB.'

'But that's only about . . . what . . . forty officers? That place is massive; it's called Ponte *City* for a good reason. It'll be like looking for a flea on an elephant's back.

They're bound to get away even if they're only half as smart as they've already proved to be.'

Gildenhuys sighs. 'I'm with you on this, Mason, and I'm as pissed off as you are. Listen, there's a stack of people in different units that still owe me some favours. Maybe they could help us without upsetting the main system too much. But you can forget right away about any army back-up.'

Harry stops his car in the breakdown lane and rubs his forehead. 'To be honest, I don't want to risk going in there with just a handful of people, even if you do come up with a few others from Tactical.'

'Are you thinking about what happened last time?'

'I'm thinking of a witch doctor and his cultists. If they can slaughter innocent children the way they've been doing, I don't think they'd hesitate to mow us down in those dark corridors. I know where he is, but I can't say for sure how many people he's still got on his side or to what lengths they'll go to protect their leader.'

'Harry, I believe you when you say he has been living in Ponte, but how can you be sure he's still there?'

'His little empire is crumbling, but he's still pretty safe there in Ponte, or at least I reckon he thinks so. If he's been operating from there for as long as we now think, he will have already survived a few raids without us catching even the faintest whiff of him.'

'Hmm,' rumbles Gildenhuys, 'you might be right there. Damn it, I don't know what to do – except go back to those arseholes at city hall. I'm sorry, Mason, I wish I had something better to tell you.'

Gildenhuys hangs up, leaving Harry with a sick feeling in his stomach. Though firmly clenched around the steering wheel, his hands are shaking.

74

In the wake of the portentous news that the unit will not, after all, be receiving support from the area commissioner, Jacob is sitting in his office, thinking of his father. He wishes he had him there to advise him now. Reaching with considerable hesitation for the phone, Jacob slowly begins to dial the number of his parental home. For a long time it rings with a sad drawn-out bleat, till Jacob is nearly convinced holding on is futile. His mother finally answers just as he is about to hang up.

'*Sawubona*, Mama. It's Jacob.'

'My son, you have called again!' The delight in her voice is almost palpable.

'Like I promised I would,' replies Jacob. 'And this time I *will* speak to my father, unless he has changed his mind.'

'Of course, you will speak to him. He has not changed his mind. But you must wait a bit, he is now very frail. I will have to find someone to help me bring him to the telephone.'

His mother leaves the connection open, and Jacob can hear her yelling for someone to come into the house and help carry the old man to the phone. The last time Jacob saw his father he was healthy and strong and filled with a spiritual power. That was the day he felt the sting of his father's sable-antelope switch viciously lashing his face and the *sangoma*'s heavy fists pummelling his unprotected head. That same day he was run out of the house for daring to question his family's profoundest beliefs, suggesting that they had led directly to his grandfather's death. At the time, Jacob would have ended up on the street like so many other kids, had his mother not secretly intervened and persuaded Hettie Solilo to take the boy in.

Unfortunately, news of his mother's complicity in this soon reached his father, and she was beaten severely for her betrayal in helping the outcast find a place in the world. Her husband sincerely believed that, by aiding the blasphemous child, she would incur the wrath of the gods and tribal ancestors, drawing down a curse on his family and descendants.

There is a rasping sound at the other end of the line, which puzzles Jacob until he realizes it is someone trying to talk.

'Sir?' asks Jacob, still hesitant to address the old man as father.

'Is it that boy, that stupid boy?' The aged *sangoma* sounds very asthmatic.

Does he intend only to berate me one more time before his death? wonders Jacob, as his discomfort rises.

'I hear you are a policeman now. You uphold the white man's justice?'

Jacob is about to excuse himself – this was all a mistake – when he hears his mother's voice chastising the sickly old man.

'All right, all right, woman, *enough*. Jacob, you know why I wanted to talk to you?'

'No,' replies Jacob. 'What is it you want to speak to me about?'

'I am dying,' says the old man in a sudden self-conscious whisper.

Jacob already sensed this was likely, but to hear his father admit it with such defeat hurts deeply.

He is bracing himself to inquire further when the old man mutters, 'Consumption.'

'Have you seen a doctor?' blurts Jacob, before realizing his mistake.

'A hospital is no place for a self-respecting *sangoma*.'

'How long do you have still to live?' is all Jacob can say.

'Not long.' The coughing fit that follows is so gratingly wet that Jacob winces. 'I should've been happy to join our ancestors, but I cannot do so honourably because . . . because I have no son now who will revere our lineage, sacrificing to those who came before him and feeding their hungry spirits.' The reproach rips through Jacob's heart like a barb. 'The spirits of our family have been refusing to speak to me. What use is an old man like me when his forebears refuse to proffer him their wisdom and protection? I have ceased to exist since you shamed us so.'

'If you wish me home just so you can die safe in the knowledge that I will pay homage to you for the rest of my life, you are sorely mistaken.' Jacob is now angry. 'You know exactly why I left you. You know I preferred to welcome into my life a greater God's mercy rather than endure the eternal vengeful schemings and threats of *your* ancestral deities.'

The old man clears his throat and abruptly calls out for a glass of water. The detective takes a few deep breaths to calm his rising irritation. An uncomfortable silence ensues between father and son, the tension between them fizzing like static on the telephone line, each waiting to hear what the other will say next.

After a while, the elderly *sangoma* continues a little more calmly. 'A telephone conversation is not the right way to discuss these things. The anger between us tells me that you would hold back from seeing this old man again before he dies, so I will now tell you why you should come. It is not for the reason you think, and I do not ask this for myself. Instead I implore you for the sake of those who have come before and those who will come after my passing.' The old man draws a long, uneven breath. 'I do this, because I have one more task to complete for all our sakes – the fulfilment of a recent vision.'

'What kind of vision?' asks Jacob.

The older man is quiet for a few moments, and when next he speaks, his tone is softer, more humble. 'It concerned a proud lion who learns . . . well, learns a hard lesson . . . in the face of death.' Jacob allows a long silence to pass, sensing that his father has more to say. 'Just come home, Jacob, that is all I can say . . . that is all I ask. *Please.*'

It is the wish of a dying man, one with whom Jacob has always wanted to make amends. In the end, whatever bitterness passes between family members, it is just bitterness, and the bonds of family blood are stronger than that.

'I will come, Father,' replies Jacob.

'Then we shall meet soon.' There is gratitude in the elderly *sangoma*'s voice as he finally hangs up the phone.

Jacob sits in the office for several minutes, his emotions in turmoil, before deciding to join the commotion up in the common room where preparations are escalating for the early-morning raid.

75

Harry stands outside the closed gate to his house, its white-painted steel bars shining brightly in the pickup's head-lights. His mind is numbed with scenarios of rising horror as he stares through at Amy's Mazda MX-5 parked in front of their garage. Normally nothing would be wrong with this picture, except that the car's engine is still idling, the driver's door gaping wide open. And Amy's house keys, wallet and handbag are strewn across the driveway.

Harry lifts his eyes again to the front door, which is standing partly ajar. There are no lights visible inside.

'Amy?' he calls out with dread. 'Amy? Jeanie?' He calls louder this time.

There is no answer other than a puff of smoke from the Mazda's exhaust.

Harry suddenly springs into action, yanking his spare keys from the pickup's ignition, pressing the remote to open the gate. His service pistol is quickly in his hand.

Moving at a crouch, he ducks behind his wife's car and briefly peeks inside it, before carefully advancing on the open front door. Reaching it without incident, he takes a few deep breaths to steel himself for what he may find inside, before gently pushing the door open wide and groping for the light switch.

The little table on which the telephone normally rests now lies on its side in a corner of the hallway, while the upturned receiver beeps forlornly on the floor. The vase that stood beside it is a glittering mosaic of pink-and-white ceramic exploded over the tiles. Harry proceeds gingerly across its fragments.

By the hall light, he can see that a considerable struggle occurred in the living room. A standing lamp has been knocked on its side, the couch stands askew and the ruffled carpet has been marked by muddy sports shoes. Here he discovers his missing keys, carelessly tossed on the floor beside the television.

Following the trail of footprints into the kitchen, he

notices a large hole smashed in the laundry room's door. It stands slightly ajar, and two bullet holes reproach him like little eyes drilled through the wood.

Harry feels his legs begin to shake uncontrollably. Did the struggle end here, with those bullet holes? What will he find inside the room beyond?

Abruptly, he turns away from the door. Taking a deep breath, he heads for the bedrooms at the rear of the house, suddenly confident that his wife and child will have found the safety of a bathroom or bedroom. As he switches on the light in the corridor, revealing cream-painted walls and a beige carpet, tears well up in his eyes. For lying abandoned on the floor is Jeanie's purple Barney toy – the one treasure she can never be parted from.

The master bedroom still looks the way he left it this morning: the bed made up, and the coverlet slightly creased where he perched to put his socks on; Amy's nightgown still lies on the chair where she deposited it after her shower. Whatever has happened here did not reach this part of the house.

Harry heads on to the very end of the passage, where Jeanie's room is situated. He instantly notes that the door is in ruins and sees Jeanie's bed has been shifted over to one side. Harry can guess what happened here.

Still no sign of his wife and child.

What about the laundry room? urges the voice at the back of his mind. But Harry knows he cannot face what might lie behind that brutalized door. He has witnessed too much already. He has an instant flashback to the woman lying riddled with bullets in the passenger seat of her husband's Pajero, her eyes drooping half open, her mouth frozen in a scream.

Harry drops the gun to the soiled carpet of the living room as his fingers lose all sensation. 'Amy?' he calls out, his voice cracking. 'Oh, God, Amy, answer me.'

There is no response – and he does not know why he expected one. They would surely not be in there if they were still alive. Harry's fingertips reach ever so lightly for the door's splintered wood. He listens closely before pressing against it gently.

76

Like a silver bullet, the car speeds through the evening, passing street lights glittering over its bonnet and windshield, and four pairs of eyes. For the moment all three men seem steeped in their thoughts of what transpired at the detective's house.

The interior smells rankly of tobacco and sweat, while the dull roaring of the engine is punctuated by occasional whimpers from the front.

Sitting in the back, young Godfrey shifts forward to peer into the front passenger footwell. There, trussed up under Cassius's feet, lies Jeanie Mason, her hair sticking to her tear-dampened cheeks, her terrified eyes flicking around wildly. In the panic in those glistening eyes, Godfrey recollects his brother's murder. Over and over again he sees Daniel get hit in the stomach by a bullet; in his mind he watches Collin – now sitting next to him – run up to Godfrey's wounded brother and execute him at point-blank range.

He could not even cry for his dead brother – like this little girl is now crying for herself. Ever since he was dragged into the albino's car they have been torturing him verbally and physically at any sign of weakness. But they are unaware that his grief has only grown over the last four weeks.

As he drives, Lucky toys with a beaded pouch strung around his neck. 'What do you think he'll do now?' he asks suddenly of no one in particular.

Cassius shrugs. 'Don't know.'

'Surely there's other ways of disappearing than burning our cars?'

'That BM was never yours to begin with.'

'But I liked driving it.'

'You liked it because the ladies liked it,' says Collin, leaning forward. 'Without that car you're pretty much nothing.'

Godfrey interrupts hesitantly. 'What will happen to this little girl?'

Cassius turns around and stares at him. 'Who are *you* to ask that? You obviously haven't learnt much in the last month, have you?'

'I was just wondering.' Godfrey hangs his head.

'If the police come looking for us, he'll just pull out his bag of tricks.' Collin continues their conversation as if Godfrey has not even spoken. 'Like he did before, like he did with Oba – like he does with *everything* that threatens him.'

'What exactly do you think it was that killed Oba?' asks Cassius, turning to face him with uncertainty in his eyes.

'I don't even want to talk about such things.' Collin shakes his head. 'It's only inviting bad luck.'

Biting his lip, Godfrey stares out the window, recognizing the deflections and insinuations so common amongst the albino's inmost henchmen. Poor Jim and Daniel had always thought Godfrey was too superstitious, but after dealing with the albino's men, he knows his own paranoia pales in comparison. He has even seen some of the albino's followers putting on women's underwear, so that any bullets fired at them would be confused and miss their targets.

Still gazing out the window, Godfrey mentally runs through the many escape plans he has been hatching over the last few weeks. Try as he might, whatever easy way out he can devise for himself, each would leave his innocent family prey to acts of vengeance greater than mere violence. For all that he is surrounded by idiots, the albino himself still stands out as a terrible force to be reckoned with.

77

'Right.' Molethe addresses the thirty-three officers assembled, some from his unit, some from the South African Narcotics Bureau and a few from various local precincts. They all crowd around Chief Molethe himself and two tables pushed together to hold the floor plans piled messily on them. 'This is Mr Uys, from Centaur Investment Properties, the company currently taxed with making something of Ponte.'

'I must point out straight away,' says Uys, a pale, bald-headed, lanky individual in a beige suit, 'that we have only just taken over management of the building, so its current state of degradation is not our doing, although it is of great concern to us. We have so far received very little funding to administer it and nothing at all to renovate it.'

'Jacob, where's Mason?' demands Molethe, annoyed.

'I don't know, chief. His mobile just keeps ringing, and his home number seems permanently engaged.'

'That idiot's chosen a fine time to make himself scarce.'

'He'll get here, chief.'

'Men, we'll all have a lot of ground to cover. As most of you know, that building is a giant hollow cylinder, with a circular light shaft running all the way down inside it. Mr Uys here tells me the building isn't in such a rotten state as it used to be, although I hear its central core is still piled up with stinking garbage as high as the fourth storey. A few armed guards patrol the most public areas, although there aren't enough of them to police the entire building effectively. Of course, knowing some of the types probably holed up in there, these eight-rand-an-hour guards might be tempted to cooperate more closely with the criminal elements than with their actual employers.'

'We've tried to deal with that issue,' Uys insists, 'but there may still be cases of it happening.'

'So be wary of the guards, but I think they'll soon start to play our game once we arrive in force.

'The building itself is four hundred and eighty feet high, rising fifty-one floors. It accommodates four hundred and seventy flats, with seven parking levels – of which only two are currently in use – and eight lifts, only three of them functional. That means, come four o'clock this morning, you men will have a chance to sweat off some of that blubber you've piled on.'

'So are you joining us, then, chief?' someone chirrups.

Chief Molethe glances down at his own sizeable paunch and smiles. 'I'm afraid not; I'd just end up blocking a stairwell. Now these lower levels here – ' he points to a floor plan – 'were dedicated to about eighty shops, most of them now abandoned and up for lease. There's also a church, a gym, a few laundromats and such things, so it's important for you to check the abandoned premises, too. I'm told it's a bit like a flea market down on these levels, so you'll find lots of nooks and crannies to keep you busy.'

Uys takes over, as if not wanting to be upstaged. 'Any floor higher than the shopping levels comprises residential accommodation. A typical floor contains an outer ring of apartments, facing out over the city, separated by a wide corridor with four foyers each featuring two lifts and a staircase from an inner ring of flats facing the building's central shaft. Conforming to government regulations, all the residences thus have access to natural light.

'After a spate of robberies, the reception area was secured with bullet-proof glass. These here are the lifts that we can still afford to maintain safely, and here are the parking levels currently in use. The upper eight levels, including the penthouses right at the top, are virtually abandoned, partly because so few of the elevators are functioning. You'll see that the very lowest five parking levels have been closed up and secured until such time as more car-owners move into the building.'

'Secured?' interrupts Bobby Gous sarcastically. 'That's shit, man. Back when I was on local patrol, we used to climb over the walls to surprise the whores and their customers. Those lower levels are just junkie hotels, with cardboard mattresses and needles all over.'

'Well, we continue to run them off the property if we catch such individuals,' replies Uys, lifting his chin.

'What about the sub-basements?' Niehaus directs a hard gaze at the property man.

'What about them?' asks Uys.

'The goddamned basements where four of ours disappeared a few years back,' Bornman joins in angrily.

'Ah, yes . . . Remember, we only took over the management *after* that most distressing incident. Since then, at a great cost to the new owners, all the plumbing and wiring have been rerouted to one basement only.'

'Is that possible?' Jacob looks incredulous.

'Oh, yes, very much so.'

'So there can't be anyone down there, then?'

'Not as far as we know,' says the man. 'We couldn't seal off the whole lot *completely*, so we placed a reinforced steel door over the only staircase leading down to the uppermost sub-basement, which is a utility section. The only key for that door is now kept safe by head office.'

'How many sub-basements are there?' asks Niehaus.

'There's just the main basement itself, which functions as a storage and delivery area for the whole building and the businesses housed there, and two more levels below it. But really, there's no need for you to go down there, as it's the only area I can guarantee is completely abandoned.'

'Like the parking levels that are used by the whores?' growls Bobby.

'That's enough, men,' interrupts Molethe. 'If Mr Uys says it's properly locked up, we have no reason to doubt him. We have a big enough area to cover as it is. I want you to be clear on one thing, though. Most of the residents are ordinary decent citizens with jobs and families. The place is big enough for them to remain ignorant of any criminal activity going on around them and of anyone dubious living nearby. Respect that fact. I know we have a bad history with that particular building, but it doesn't mean anyone you come upon is associating with criminals. Don't draw your weapons unless you really have to, and don't alarm the inhabitants unless you have good reason. I expect you all to be discreet in—'

'Yes, please,' urges Uys.

Molethe glares at him. 'Be discreet, but see you *find* these suspects. We'll go over our strategy in more detail later, but in the meantime you'd better familiarize yourselves with these building plans. Now, someone better go and fetch you some chicken and burgers. This is going to be a long night.'

Molethe turns and leaves the room. After a few seconds' hesitation, Uys hurries after him. As the rest of the men begin to mutter over the various maps, Jacob seizes the phone and redials both of Harry's numbers. When there is still no answer, he gathers up his keys.

'Tshabalala, where you going?' Superintendent Bornman calls after him.

'Something's very wrong. I'm going over to Harry's house.'

78

The house itself is dark. The street lights filtering through the open curtains cast deep shadows across Harry's haggard face. He is sitting on the floor in the living room, his back resting against the three-seater sofa, the chaos of his family's abduction all around him. Normally they would be finishing their evening meal about now, Amy and himself curling up on the sofa afterwards, and Jeanie messing about with her toys on the floor until bedtime.

He checked the laundry room, but the bodies he had been sure he would find were not there. Relief had washed over him briefly, but soon turned to dread of what might be happening to them.

Harry stares at the pistol in his clammy hand. A tiny

voice in the back of his mind is urging him to get up, to *do* something, but it is as if a poisonous cloud has blanketed his mind, immobilizing him. He cocks the weapon. What now? If the people who have taken his family are working for the albino witch doctor, does it mean Ponte City is still a viable target? He has no idea, just like he has no idea how he has ended up here in his living room, knowing both his wife and his daughter are kidnapped. The whole nature of this case has been much like the momentum of a flash flood dragging him and the rest of the police unit along, the normal procedures of detective work making little sense any more. Instead it feels like the dark forces that Jacob hints at have predetermined all of their fates.

Headlights flash over his gateway, filling the house with a brief fire of orange light before an engine is switched off. A car door opens, and moments later the intercom buzzes.

'Bugger off,' mutters Harry, wiping at his reddened eyes.

The visitor, however, does not relent and pushes the button repeatedly. When Harry still does not respond, he hears someone scale the gate. Moments later the foyer light is flicked back on.

'Harry?' It is Jacob's voice.

Harry does not answer, but when he hears Jacob draw his pistol and advance through the broken china, he decides to speak up. 'You'd better put your piece away before you shoot me.'

'What's happened here?' asks Jacob, locating the living-room light switch.

'I'm cursed, that's what's happened.'

'Your family – where are they?'

'They've been abducted,' answers Harry so matter-of-factly that Jacob is taken aback. One look at Harry's face confirms that the dishevelled wild man from last night has possessed his colleague once more.

'When?' asks Jacob, glancing around and noticing the bullet holes in the kitchen. 'Was it them?'

'Who else?'

'*Yiyo le!* You can't just sit here!' cries Jacob furiously. 'This is your family we're talking about, man!'

'I can't move,' mutters Harry, staring blankly at the television. 'I feel like some great weight is crushing me into the floor. I—'

'Get up!' shouts Jacob. 'Get up, you bastard!' He grabs Harry's left arm and tries to jerk his partner to his feet. But his partner remains limp. 'What's wrong with you?'

'I should be dead,' whimpers Harry.

'I'll kill you myself if you don't get up.' Jacob backhands Harry violently across the face. 'You call yourself a cop, but you won't even rouse yourself to save your wife and child!'

Harry gazes up at Jacob imploringly. 'You don't understand.'

'There is *nothing* to understand, except what I'm seeing here. Stop acting like they're already dead. We *still* have a chance to save them!'

'You don't understand, Jacob. If I go near them they'll just get killed.'

'What are you talking about?'

'You were right all along. I *am* cursed. I've been cursed for a very long time.'

'The only thing you're cursed with is self-pity. Now get up, we're leaving.'

Harry gets up lethargically and puts a hand in a pocket to pull out his little container of pills. Jacob lashes out lightning-fast, striking Harry's hand and sending the container flying. 'Enough of that rubbish, too. For God's sake, man, pull yourself together!'

'You don't know what these headaches are like. And the panic, it's—'

Jacob ignores Harry's moans. 'Come on, *move.*' He shoves Harry roughly towards the door.

At this point Harry decides he has had enough and takes a clumsy swing. Jacob evades it effortlessly. 'What the *hell* do you think you're doing, Tshabalala?' he yells, planting his feet stubbornly and balling his fists.

'If your family dies because of you wasting our time here, it will be entirely on *your* head for the rest of your life.'

Harry backs off and pulls his shirt straight. He looks at the floor, before nodding sheepishly. 'You're right.'

'Let's go,' growls Jacob.

Minutes later the two cops are strapped into Harry's pickup and tearing down the street, the massive engine howling like a wounded buffalo.

'What about the rest of the guys?' asks Harry.

'They're getting ready at the station.' Jacob starts to tell him about the strategy planned, then about what the building looks like inside, but eventually realizes that his partner is no longer really listening. 'They'll be OK,' reassures Jacob gently. 'We just need to find them fast.'

'Why did they take them?' asks Harry. 'What are they planning?'

'I don't know,' answers Jacob honestly. 'Perhaps they only want them as hostages.'

Harry thinks back on the atrocities these people have already committed. How long has he got? 'We don't need them,' he says suddenly and steers a hard left. 'It's too risky with all of them.'

The car jerks violently as they mount a kerb. Jacob grabs hold of the dashboard and stamps down with his feet, as if looking for the brakes. 'Who do you mean? The team?'

'No one goes but us. We need the surprise.'

'But it's Ponte, for God's sake! How are we going to surprise them?' replies Jacob in disbelief. 'Didn't you hear what I just told you about that place? They could be anywhere in there. And they'll probably know we're coming even before we park the car.'

'In that case, they'll have to believe they can either take us both or escape from us. Damn it, Jacob, don't you see? If the entire force corners these men while holding my wife and child, it'll be the end for Amy and Jeanie.'

'Not necessarily,' answers Jacob, inwardly conceding his partner has a point. If these men really are guilty of all the crimes they are being pursued for, they are hardly the sort to give up without a desperate fight.

'I'm not taking any chances,' says Harry, in a strange, distant voice. The tone makes Jacob shudder, since he has heard it before, a long time ago, when his grandfather fatalistically accepted the death penalty delivered against him.

Harry takes his eyes off the road and stares coolly at his colleague. 'The question is, are you coming with me or am I stopping now to let you out?'

'Don't be an idiot,' replies Jacob, wincing as they narrowly miss another vehicle changing lanes. 'Of course,

I'm coming with you. This kind of stuff has been my family's business for generations, remember?'

'I remember,' says Harry, in that hollow voice, the echo of a man readying himself to embrace death.

79

Amy is finally freed from the car boot, and then both mother and child are untied in the dark, damp depths of some unused car park. Outside, Amy can hear heavy traffic passing, so she assumes they are somewhere in central Johannesburg. When Amy does not move fast enough, Cassius gives her a shove hard enough to send her flying to the ground. Jeanie courageously stops her crying and tries to help her mother up. After that, Harry's wife is careful to avoid doing anything that might further annoy her captors.

As they enter a concrete stairwell stinking of ammonia, Amy picks Jeanie up wordlessly and steps carefully over the garbage accumulated inside. At an upper level they spill out into another car park, this time utilized, where Collin abruptly moves some distance ahead of them. The one they called Cassius slides a restraining arm around Amy's throat and sticks his gun painfully into her kidneys from behind. The reason becomes apparent when she notices Collin start to engage a security guard with jokes and laughter, distracting his attention from the silent group now advancing towards the lifts. All the time, the kid, Godfrey, keeps well to the rear.

The orange indicator light above the lift door eventually announces that they have reached the fifty-first floor. The door slides open with a tired scraping sound to reveal three anxious-looking men beyond, all of them armed. Tense greetings circulate as mother and child are forced quickly past them.

Heading along the dark curving corridor, with brown fabric-covered walls, Amy clears her throat and finally asks anxiously, 'What do you want with us?' The corridor, she notices, is ominously abandoned.

'You'll soon see,' answers Collin cheerfully.

'Stay quiet,' snarls Cassius, nudging her in the back with his weapon.

With wide eyes, Jeanie looks silently up at him, her left hand tightening its grasp on her mother's grey business pants. The child's right arm carries an imaginary Barney doll close to her chest.

Amy remains quiet from then on and they eventually arrive at a large white-painted door guarded by two edgy-looking youths, one of whom is propping a submachine gun on his knee. Amy picks her daughter up again, giving her a protective hug. The shorter of the youths, with a sharply elongated face and very flat nose, turns to open the door behind him.

Amy is not sure what she expected inside, but the evident luxury of the penthouse they enter stands in stark contrast to the rest of the shabby building. The entrance hall alone is larger than any room in the Masons' home. The pastel orange walls smell of fresh paint, the few pieces of African art displayed on them look priceless and other items are arranged on tasteful pedestals in little alcoves. In the living room large windows afford a breathtaking view of Johannesburg's nocturnal cityscape, and from the red neon light periodically flashing through the glass, she guesses easily which tower building they are in.

The whole apartment seems a hive of frenetic activity,

as men and boys pack items away in boxes stacked along one wall. A giant of a man is reclining on an oversized green sofa, casually chewing an apple. He looks up from the football game screened on a massive television set and says something to Amy's captors which she cannot understand. Mother and child are hustled past him towards a closed door on one side of the room, its heavily ornamental wood panelling stained as dark as cacao.

'Mommy, I'm scared,' Jeanie whispers into the nape of her mother's neck.

'Ssh, honey, I know,' murmurs Amy, stroking her daughter's hair as she advances. 'Don't you worry. Daddy will come for us.'

'What do they want?' asks Jeanie, peering at their abductors over her mother's shoulder.

'I don't know, sweetheart.' Amy swallows hard, forcing back her panic. If that big man sitting on the sofa is who she thinks he is, their chances of survival are looking pretty slim indeed. She sends up a silent prayer: *Please help him find us. Please let him find us soon.*

Cassius steps in front of her to knock on the door. Again he speaks in a language she cannot understand. There is no audible reply, but Cassius retreats.

Feeling Jeanie's breath quicken against her, Amy strokes her daughter's back soothingly. The heavy copper handle set in the dark wood begins to turn, and the door swings inwards. Behind it Adusa's face appears, a cruel smile splitting his face in approval.

'Hello,' he greets them. 'Come in and take your shoes off.'

Amy lifts her chin and steps into the room beyond, determined to retain as much dignity as she can muster. After glancing down to kick off her shoes, she finally notices the strange-looking man seated behind a large desk adorned with animal skulls.

'Mrs Mason.' He acknowledges her, but says nothing further.

There is an audible gasp from underneath Amy's chin as her daughter also notices the albino. Amy reassuringly presses her daughter's head against her shoulder. 'And who do I have the pleasure of meeting?' she demands, surveying the room. The air is slightly pungent with the hint of sweet incense, while bowls standing in each corner hold tender pink blossoms and some unfamiliar types of fruit.

'My name is not important to you.' The albino stands up suddenly, dusting his hands of some imaginary encumbrance. 'All that is important is that now you are my prisoner – or hostage, if you want to call it that – and will remain so until such time as I can evade your husband and his police colleagues.'

'And then you'll let us go?' asks Amy, feeling a glimmer of hope.

'We will see what happens when that time comes.'

'So you are the man my husband has been searching for.'

The albino moves part way around his desk, then pauses to tap thick pink-tipped fingers on a mummified baboon skull. She now sees clearly that he is a rotund man in his mid-fifties, who moves again to plant himself squarely in the middle of the room, his arms folded. He chuckles and shakes his head. 'You Westerners – I can see your eyes brimming with questions that are best left unanswered. You none of you know your place, woman. It's from people like you that one of my men learnt a terrible habit of questioning. Eventually it forced me to have him removed.'

'*Are* you guilty of all the things they say about you?' demands Amy rashly.

The albino raises his eyebrows at Adusa. 'I am guilty of *nothing*, because I exist way outside the boundaries of your society and the laws of ordinary men. I serve no one but the masters I have chosen for myself.'

'And that gives you the right to butcher children?'

'White woman, our religion is older than Christianity. What do *you* know about it? What do you really know about the history of the black man? I am a vessel for the will of spirits far mightier than you or I.'

'Don't try to bullshit me,' spits Amy, her slender frame shaking. 'You do what you do for your own *gain*, that is all. Don't make yourself out to be this . . . some blameless kind of shaman.'

'I uphold the truth, that is truly African, that has remained uncorrupted by your God or your Western culture.'

Amy looks around the rest of the room with growing disgust. 'You enjoy a very nice Western-style lifestyle here, I notice.'

'I have accumulated the wealth that is owed to me, but I have never adopted your decadent ways, if that's what you are thinking.'

She is suddenly livid. 'You're a fucking abomination who abuses the fragility of people's beliefs and their desperation. How can you murder children to sell their bodies as trinkets? You cannot tell me you're so different from us that you can prey on us all, like a different species.'

The albino crosses the sacred mat that covers the floor

and stops close enough for Amy to feel his warm breath on her face. 'I tell you *exactly* that, Mrs Mason.'

He reaches out suddenly and touches Jeanie's red hair. Amy starts back violently. 'Don't touch my daughter!' 'I will do as I please. Now give me the child, woman.'

'I'll kill you first!' snarls Amy, backing away from the witch doctor.

Understanding the threat, Jeanie begins to bawl loudly. 'Mommy, don't let him take me!'

'He won't get you, I promise,' whispers Amy in her ear. She backs into something warm and pliant behind her and looks up to discover Adusa's horribly scarred face grinning down at her. He grabs Amy by her upper arms, crushing her biceps. The pain is extraordinary, but she keeps her hold on Jeanie. The child keeps screeching, desperately clinging to her mother.

Amy tries to pull herself loose, but she cannot manage it without the risk of letting go of her daughter. Then suddenly the albino reaches out and seizes both her hands, and at last the two men together manage to wrestle Jeanie from her grasp.

'No! I'm begging you, give her back to me.'

The albino issues Adusa a rapid order in their unfamiliar language. The albino is now clasping the child around the waist, while the little girl holds her hands out imploringly to her mother. Adusa seizes Amy by one arm and the back of her blouse and abruptly he bundles the frantic mother from the room.

Taiwo then enters and approaches his leader. 'They've come after all,' he announces in Yoruba. 'Mason and Tshabalala are here.'

'Just the two?' asks the albino in disbelief, over the din

from the screaming child now lying discarded on his sacred mat.

'Yes, that's what our men say. They're keeping a close eye on them right now. What do you want us to do?'

The albino erupts in joyous laughter. 'Send some men down to capture them, but quietly. That fool Moloto must've been lying to me. If a larger force was really on its way, those two fools wouldn't have blundered in here on their own.'

Taiwo nods and leaves the room. He quickly sets about gathering five armed men, having decided to lead the party himself. On their way out, the giant Nigerian pauses to collect the Kalashnikov with which he killed André Viljoen – the cop responsible for this whole mess.

80

The compact bullet-proof office located in the main entrance is now deserted, although a cigarette still burns in a large white ashtray.

'What now?' Jacob peers at the dead surveillance camera dangling from its cords over the entrance to the lift.

'Msimang said the albino lives in a cave deep under Hillbrow – a cave at the base of a large tree, or something like that.'

'You want us to check the underground areas first?' asks Jacob.

'Yes.' Harry tests the management office's door and finds it locked. 'It doesn't look like we're going to get any help from the locals.'

A lift abruptly announces its arrival with a lethargic

ting. The two police officers look up expectantly. Three students, jabbering loudly and hanging onto each other like tired soldiers, drift out of it without acknowledging the presence of the two intruders.

Harry locates a staircase and they quickly make their way down into the bowels of the vast building, past several fire doors leading into the unused parking levels. Minutes later they arrive at a door marked Authorized Personnel Only. The bottom of the stairwell is littered with cigarette butts, joint roaches and used condoms, while the red wires that once connected the door to a security alarm look like a blood lily protruding from the wall. The detectives glance at each other, both their faces looking pale and strained. Harry gives a silent nod to Jacob and they draw their pistols in unison.

Harry gently leans against the door with his right shoulder and slowly pushes it open. Dim fluorescent light illuminates a large empty chamber, with a floor of raw concrete and thick black pipes running along its ceiling. The walls are adorned by silver ribbed ventilation tubes. It is a storage facility and large wire cages line the walls. All of them locked, they contain assorted materials: black insulation tubing, rolls of carpeting, various sizes of dusty boxes, and catering, gardening or cleaning equipment. Harry listens carefully, but all he can detect is the constant hum of machinery close by. Deciding it is safe, he pushes the door open all the way.

Wordlessly, the two men enter the square space, which must measure about thirty yards in each direction. Harry breaking left, Jacob right, they quickly search the area and find it surprisingly clean and tidy, with none of the squalor that was apparent beyond the doorway.

'Over here,' calls Jacob suddenly.

In the far left-hand corner of the chamber, next to a gated delivery ramp, a heavy reinforced-steel double trapdoor is set askance into the concrete floor. Multicoloured graffiti obscure the original words painted on it, and Jacob is mouthing something under his breath.

'What does it say?' asks Harry.

'It's just children messing around,' mutters Jacob.

'Bullshit. Tell me what it says.'

Jacob's finger traces the largest of the scrawls, daubed in bold white letters. 'It translates from Xhosa as, "Four little pigs rest in hell".'

'Bastards,' growls Harry, then points. 'Look at this.' He fingers the bent and broken padlock meant to secure the trapdoor's metal cover.

'*Aiee*,' exclaims Jacob, shaking his head in disgust. 'They've never even made sure it stayed locked.'

Jacob grunts under the strain of pulling the two halves open, one after the other. They creak loudly on their hinges, then clank over onto the concrete, the sound echoing loudly through the silent storage area. He peers down into a dark stairwell as a cold, moist draught wafts over him.

Doubtful, he turns to his colleague. 'Are you sure Msimang was suggesting he hides somewhere down here?'

'He said something along those lines,' confirms Harry.

Jacob's groping hand finds a light switch and clicks it. A few seconds later, a row of fluorescent tubes flicker on consecutively, revealing yet more concrete steps descending. Dust particles drift slowly under the invading light, tinted an eerie olive green by the surrounding walls.

Harry cocks an ear suddenly. 'Did you hear that?' he hisses.

'What?' asks Jacob, looking up sharply.

Harry holds a finger to his lips. He brings up his weapon and retreats a few steps back towards the door they came in by. He strains his ears again but hears nothing amiss.

'What?' urges Jacob, getting ready to descend the stairs.

Throwing another glance over his shoulder, Harry returns to Jacob's side. 'Just nerves, I guess.'

Without another word, Tshabalala disappears down the steps.

Harry is about to follow him when he again hears a faint clattering sound. His stomach clenching, he hastens back towards the service door, from which the latest sound definitely originated.

He is about to put his ear to it, when it bursts open with tremendous force. As it smashes into his head the detective grunts in pain and staggers backwards disorientated, desperately blinking away white stars. He looks up to see the largest man he has ever seen step through the doorway, a contemptuous smile across his scarred face. Even as Harry realizes who he is, Taiwo Ejiofer raises his assault rifle, and five other men charge past him to secure the storage room. Without taking his eyes off the police officer, Ejiofer barks orders at them in Zulu.

He then addresses Harry in English. 'Drop your weapon, my friend.'

Harry's gun is still lowered after the severe jolt he suffered, but Taiwo's is ready and aimed. It would be a simple thing for Harry to flick his pistol up and take a wild shot, which might or might not hit the Nigerian in time. Harry slowly begins to lift his weapon.

Taiwo raises an eyebrow in mock surprise. 'I said *drop* the weapon.'

Shots suddenly crack from the mouth of the trapdoor, but Ejiofer seems not distracted in the least.

'Harry?' Jacob's anxious voice calls up to him from far below.

Silence momentarily blankets the scene. Then two more shots ring out – a scream – another burst of fire – a howl of pain – then panicked shouting and more gunfire.

Again abrupt silence.

Neither Harry nor Taiwo moves, both men standing tense as tripwires.

Another single shot rings out, with an air of finality. Harry's eyes widen slightly, while the Nigerian's smile grows even more satisfied.

'Where are my wife and child?' growls Harry.

'If you don't drop that weapon immediately, you'll never find out.'

'A police raid is being mounted. It's all over for you,' retaliates the detective.

'Let them come. I have nothing to fear from them.'

Harry swallows hard and yells, 'Jacob! Let me know you're all right, mate.'

There is no answer.

'Jakes?'

Except for his own rough breathing, there is only silence amid the cloying smell of Ejiofer's expensive cologne.

Harry grips his gun even tighter.

'If I drop this, will you take me to my family?'

The confident leer has not left the Nigerian's dark face. 'Either you drop the weapon or I shoot you. Simple choice. Your last chance, my friend.'

Harry listens intently for a moment, then realizes it

does not matter whether his friend survived the firefight. Ejiofer still has him fixed dead in his sights.

'Take it,' hisses Harry in disgust, abruptly tossing his weapon at Taiwo's feet. 'Just take it – and take me to my family.'

The huge Nigerian moves forward with almost arachnoid speed. He is already swinging the butt of his rifle. It connects with Harry's forehead, rupturing his recent wound from the day before. As the detective topples backwards, the big man kicks him viciously in the stomach. Harry drops to the floor in a bundle of pain.

81

There is a loud electrical hum in this enclosed space shaped like a cross, where two bisecting corridors allow access to vast panels of circuitry, arrays of switches, red and green displays and numerous levers. The hair on Jacob's nape begins to crawl.

He already fears the worst for Harry. Was he killed in that hail of bullets that suddenly clattered down the stairwell?

'Where is he?' Jacob hears a voice nearby as someone whispers in Sotho.

There is no reply.

Jacob peers around the corner to his right and glimpses figures slowly creeping towards him. Looking in the opposite direction, he notices a fire door leading out of the chamber he is trapped in. It is his only means of escape, but also in full view of the oncoming gunmen.

Jacob closes his eyes and tries to calm his breathing. How many of them are there? He cannot tell for sure.

They will surely gun him down once he breaks cover for the emergency door. And even if he reaches it, there is no guarantee of an escape route beyond. So what to do? He needs to do something soon.

He leaps out into the corridor and fires off twice. There are two moist thuds as the surprised point man takes it in the thigh and left shoulder. Jacob immediately ducks on, into the other half of the bisecting corridor, reaching cover just before a piercing scream bursts from the wounded man's lips.

Without giving them any chance to react, Jacob flicks around the corner and fires again. One round shatters another man's jaw. Further bullets cause the others to scramble aside from the exposed corridor. Panicked return fire crackles around Jacob as the detective launches himself towards the emergency exit. Chips of concrete spit all around him as he slams into the door, pulls the lever and throws himself down the staircase beyond – down into the third basement, where those four policemen disappeared.

Here he finds himself in absolute darkness, and this time the moist quality of the air reminds him of a cave. Stopping at the bottom of the short flight, Jacob senses that this chamber is really massive in its black abandonment. He feels along the walls nearest to him, but finds no switches.

His heart is drumming frantically in his ears and his eyes are gaping with fear. He raises a quick, grateful prayer to God for his escape so far, before he starts fumbling for another ammunition clip. Someone abruptly crashes into the door above him, and Jacob slips to one side just as the door is thrown violently open.

For a split second the scene remains quiet, while a gunman contemplates the darkness below. It is now infused with a pale greenish light filtering down the stairs from behind him, silhouetting him conveniently in the open doorway. Thick grey dust coats the floor, like the surface of the moon. The albino's henchman reaches out and locates the light switch that Jacob missed in his headlong tumble down the stairs. It clicks once, twice, without result.

In one flowing movement, the detective slides out of the corner, bracing an outstretched arm against the wall, and quickly fires off one round.

His successful head shot slices through the silence, and the man above him crumples in the doorway. The door swings shut again to the echo of the gunshot, but gets stuck halfway against the dead man's recumbent body. A variety of shouts and yells jounce down the stairs towards Jacob, who is already retreating into the enveloping darkness.

He does not hear Harry's frantic yell over the chaos he has caused.

82

'You whore's cunt!' screams a young voice down the stairs. 'We've got your *baas* up here. If you don't come out, I'll kill him myself.' Sixteen-year-old Nyameko clasps the inscribed bullet the albino once gave him, which dangles from his necklace, and waits tensely for an answer from the darkness. A minute passes, but none is forthcoming.

The boy turns around to face a purple-shirted man significantly older than himself, who is cowering well away from the half-open doorway. 'Mondli, go call the boss. Tell him to bring over the cop. I'll stay here.'

Mondli nods vigorously, glad to leave this boy with the shiny insectile eyes. The man hurries past his fallen comrades slumped in the power-room corridor. Both men are clearly either dead or unconscious.

'Come, let's go over and see what's happened to your friend.' Taiwo prods Harry with his toe, having already tucked the fallen police officer's gun safely into his belt. Harry drags himself up from the floor.

'Take me to my family, you bastard,' he splutters.

'I'll do what I want and when I'm ready,' growls Taiwo, his previously jovial tone now evaporated. He peers across the huge floor area towards the entrance to the power room with a growing sense of unease.

Harry staggers groggily forward, Ejiofer jabbing him in the back with his rifle. At the mouth of the trapdoor staircase, down which Jacob disappeared, a man in a purple shirt suddenly emerges, gesticulating and jabbering wildly. As he is nudged into following this man below, Harry registers the two bodies lying in the corridor beyond him and allows himself a malicious smile. 'Trouble?' he inquires casually, wiping blood from his forehead.

'Let's move.' Taiwo shoves Harry forward.

The detective is herded towards a door standing ajar at the far end of the noisy power room. A third body is wedged in the doorway. A teenager stands glued to the adjacent wall, urgently waving them on. Harry finds the boy's features bizarre: his head is strangely elongated and seems too large for his skinny neck, while his eyes are disconcertingly bulbous. He clasps an oversized .44, which looks cumbersome and awkward in his youthful hands. Beyond the door Harry can see only darkness.

A rapid-fire discussion erupts between the three black

men in a language Harry cannot even identify. All he can make out is the one word, 'Tshabalala'. Ejiofer abruptly tosses his rifle to the man in the purple shirt and draws Harry's pistol from his belt. He grabs the detective by the back of his neck and violently shoves him through the opening. More incomprehensible words are shouted, although Harry can now perfectly interpret the situation he is in: if Jacob does not surrender, Ejiofer will shoot Harry.

'Jacob,' calls out Harry, 'don't oblige them, mate.'

'Shut up!' roars Taiwo. 'Tshabalala, what do you say? Do I kill him or are you coming out?'

There is no answer.

'Speak to me or I shoot your friend right now.'

When there is still no answer, Ejiofer suddenly yanks Harry backwards and throws him to the ground. 'Give me my rifle,' he barks in Zulu. 'You two, guard him. I'll deal with this myself.'

Taiwo retrieves his rifle from purple shirt, as the boy waves his .44 warningly in Harry's face.

Taiwo rolls up his sleeves and turns back to the floored detective. 'Now I show you how a *real* warrior hunts. You learn a few things when you're fighting in the bush, and when you wear these – ' Taiwo traces the intricate scars up one bulging arm – 'you get to enjoy the danger.'

The boy nods his approval, as if he knows exactly what the enforcer is talking about.

Taiwo assures himself that the wall switches are indeed not working, before descending into the gloom.

'What you look at?' Nyameko again shoves the pistol in Harry's face.

'Nothing,' mutters Harry, averting his eyes from the weapon.

The boy reacts to Harry's calm with further threats in broken English, while the man called Mondli buries his face in his hands, standing over the sprawled body of his fellow gunman.

Harry clears his throat. 'Mind if I take a light?'

'What?' The boy suspiciously pokes Harry's chest with the barrel of his .44.

Harry shrugs. 'Just want a cigarette, mate. You want one? It's Luckys.'

Both men stare at him, then at each other, and nod reluctantly. Harry notices how they are both sweating profusely. He reaches for his pocket, which draws a sharp hiss from the boy.

'Relax,' says Harry. 'I've been searched already.'

The detective pulls out his packet of cigarettes and offers it to his captors before extracting one himself. He chuckles softly as he sticks a Lucky Strike into his mouth, but does not light it. 'Looks like nothing worked out for any of us, eh?'

'What you mean?' asks the boy.

'Well, *I* thought I'd catch you off your guard here. And *you* – well, maybe you thought you were invincible.'

'What does dat word mean?'

'It means you believed no one could touch you.'

Mondli titters. 'Of course no one can touch the albino.'

'It's not quite the case, though, is it?' Harry turns around to indicate the carnage behind him. 'That's quite a mess there. Did *they* have his protection, too?'

'Shut up!' snarls Nyameko.

Harry looks at the ground in mock submission. After

fiddling with his unlit cigarette for a minute, all of them listening hard for any sound from the darkness below, the detective looks up again. 'Do you really think he can protect you all once the police and the army come crashing in here? All *he* has to do is turn and run, like the cowardly witch he is.'

'You don't know what you're talking about,' growls Mondli, one eyelid twitching, before returning his gaze to the door. 'He's a powerful *sangoma*. We took our oaths to him, so he'll help us escape.'

Harry's next question seems to punch Mondli in the stomach. 'All this blood and death is more than you ever wanted, though, isn't it?' He gestures at the three corpses. 'Is this sort of mess really what you've swapped your soul for?' Harry does not wait for the man to answer. 'I know plenty of *sangomas* and *nyangas* ready to burn your boss as a *baloyi*.'

'What you know?' scoffs the boy.

Harry finally lights up with forced casualness. 'It's got to do with my partner – the one down there in the dark. You see, he's a very special kind of police officer. He spends all his time hunting people like your boss – like *baloyi* and *umthakhati*, and whatever else you call them. He *always* finds them in the end, because he himself comes from a powerful *sangoma* family. And when he finds them – ' Harry pulls a disgusted face – 'it's a very ugly thing that he does to witches and the people working for them. It really scares me.'

This revelation produces the effect Harry wants. The boy glances over his shoulder towards Mondli, while the older man twitches and stares at Harry with frightened eyes.

'You *lie*,' spits Nyameko, the .44 now back on Harry.

'A whitey like me isn't going to know about these things, unless a Bantu tells me.'

'But our leader is not a *baloyi*,' insists Mondli.

Harry sighs appreciatively. 'Maybe *you* think so, but this Tshabalala, he wouldn't have been able to kill your friends here if they had been blessed by *good* means. A man as powerful as him can kill only those who receive favours from someone evil.'

Nyameko's eyes wander over to his partner again. This time Harry strikes. He smacks the boy's armed fist aside with one hand, at the same time bringing his other hand up to grasp Nyameko's wrist. The boy gasps in pain, and the pistol drops to the floor. Mondli turns around from the door in surprise, just as Harry shoves the youth violently into him. Before either can recover, Harry is crouching with the gun in both fists. 'Now put your hands up – *quietly*.'

The albino's two followers stare helplessly down the barrel of the .44, then Mondli lets Harry's own gun clatter to the floor.

'Lift your shirts and turn around.'

Harry is shocked when Mondli reveals a lacy red bra beneath. 'What the hell is that?'

'For protection,' mumbles the man, sounding almost offended.

'*Ssht!*' hisses Harry. 'Now pull up your trouser legs, let me see your socks. No girly stockings, then? Take these – ' Harry throws them a pair of handcuffs – 'and lock yourselves together through the handle of the door.'

Harry waits until he hears both cuffs click firmly in place. 'Now, kick me over my gun.' Looking terrified, Mondli obeys without hesitation.

A look of malice spreads over Harry's face as he stoops

to pick up the second weapon. 'Now, you two arseholes listen to me carefully. I'm going after the big man down below, and after that I'm going after your big boss. Then, if I find *anything* bad has happened to my family, I'm coming back for you both, understand?' As Harry's lip curls murderously, the two prisoners nod vehemently.

Harry eyes the dark void beyond them, then turns his attention back to his two prisoners.

'Where is your boss, the albino *baloyi*?'

A loud splashing noise comes from the darkness below, then automatic gunfire rings out. The unexpected din startles both gunmen. When they all hear Taiwo suddenly curse in frustrated pain, Harry smiles a deadly smile.

'So, tell me where the albino is and maybe I'll get my vicious partner to spare you. I'm sure you know what he'll do to you if I allow him.'

Mondli is visibly trembling, clearly not having been selected for the rougher side of the albino's business.

'He's upstairs,' blurts Mondli. 'Top-floor penthouse suite.' Nyameko swears at his comrade in Sotho.

'You *sure* he isn't down below?'

'What?' Mondli looks genuinely surprised. 'No, no, he's upstairs. What would he be doing down here?'

Nyameko has meanwhile hung his head in angry defeat. And down below them, silence has fallen once more.

'Is that right?' Harry turns to Nyameko. When the boy spits wordlessly at his feet, Harry takes this as confirmation. 'That's all I need to know.'

Retreating a short way back towards the electrical panels humming behind them, he locates an emergency tool rack. Pulling out a dusty torch, he is surprised by the strength of its light-beam. When he makes his way back to the two men handcuffed to the door, he discovers the eighteen-year-old hissing urgently into the darkness beyond it, doubtless trying to attract Ejiofer's attention. Harry moves quickly, pistol-whipping the youth around the head, as the other man squeals and ducks aside. The detective shoves the pistol barrel into his nostril. '*Shut up.*'

With the gun still pressed to Mondli's face, Harry listens intently, but hears nothing further from below. Slowly he begins to descend the stairs.

At the bottom, he switches the torch back on and steps carefully into the gloom of the cavernous chamber. Though Harry has light, he realizes he has also made himself an easy target.

83

Not knowing for sure how many men had followed him into the darkness, Jacob decided to follow the first service tunnel, which he located by groping along the wall. Minutes into this tunnel, he heard the worrying sound of automatic gunfire exploding somewhere behind him. Shortly, he reached a position where the air smelled fresher and a strong draught began playing over his shoulders. Testing the darkness with his hands once more, he discovered a maintenance shaft of some sort: a service ladder, plumbing pipes and electrical cables, most likely supplying the apartments directly above. Without hesitation, he pulled himself up into the steel cage of the service ladder, climbing hesitantly at first and speeding up once he noticed a faint hint of light far above him.

*

Harry's anxious breathing and careful footsteps sound deafening to him in the abandoned silence. Sweat trickles down his face and his shirt clings to his back. The stark torchlight reveals a newer series of footprints amid other, much older, tracks faint with age. The detective lets the torch beam rove over floor, walls and a dozen massive concrete pillars which support the whole structure above him. Occasionally he catches glimpses of industrial junk and urban decay, of thick twists of wiring criss-crossing the walls and ceiling like vines. Leaking pipes have left stains of white and brown; some even exhibit slimy stalactites. Massive steel girders can be seen piled in one corner, as if the original builders of Ponte had rushed to finish the job and to leave the site as quickly as possible.

A sharp smell of cordite cuts through the foul air, mingling with the swampy stench of foul water.

The detective comes to an abrupt halt as his torchlight creeps towards the centre of the chamber. There, in front of him, lie the legendary four wells filled with putrid water. The four square pits, set fairly close together, each extend roughly four feet across. In three of them the water glitters with an eerie greenish black light, a layer of scum on their motionless surface. The fourth well's surface has recently been disturbed; some of the water has been splashed over the sides. A thick cloud of cordite still hangs nearby and Harry searches the dusty floor for clues to what happened. He discovers a dripping trail, leading from the pit towards a large machine some distance away, which stands against one of the walls and resembles an outdated drycleaner.

'Come out of there, Ejiofer!' yells Harry, guessing what has happened. Then, 'Jacob, where are you?'

No one answers him.

He takes a deep breath and advances towards the big machine.

'Get your soggy arse out here where I can see you,' yells Harry, but instead of heading directly towards the machine, he circles to the left, around it.

That is when he spots something that chills him to the bone. '*Shit!*' he curses out loud.

Unsure how many storeys he has climbed, Jacob is now paused on a rung in the maintenance shaft, feeling along the edges of the grate above him, which is blocking his exit. From beyond this metal barrier an orange glow falls onto his face from what looks like a bathroom window situated higher up. The grate, as far as he can tell, is situated close up against Ponte's inner wall, while a stench like he has never experienced assaults his nose. This can mean only one thing: he has reached the bottom of the building's inner light well. His prying fingers do not find any fixtures or hinges along the sides of the grate, but some disgusting black muck is dislodged and falls directly onto his face. Jacob shifts position and smashes his shoulder desperately against the grating. With a repulsive sucking sound, the heavy steel comes unstuck from the grimy concrete, budging ever so slightly on his fourth attempt. Grasping the highest rung more firmly with both hands, Jacob presses his bruised back against the grate and heaves with all his strength. A few tense seconds pass before the cover is worked completely loose and slides off his back, clanging to one side.

Pulling himself through and out, Jacob discovers the source of the stench: a giant pyramidal mound of squalor in the middle of the building's hollow core reaching for the sky. Broken television sets, discarded furniture, fridges, washing machines and waste bags full of age-old kitchen garbage all haphazardly cling to each other to form this precarious tower. When his breathing calms down somewhat, he can hear the countless rats burrowing through this hellish mess.

Burying his face deep in his sleeve, Jacob climbs over the worst of the garbage lining the circumference. It takes just a short while to find a locked service door leading back into the building. Pulling his pistol, Jacob shoots the lock out, yanks the door open and staggers into what seems the freshest lungful of air he can ever remember.

After quickly wiping off his filthy hands he pulls out his mobile and tries his partner's number. The phone rings for a while without connecting before switching over to voicemail. Jacob leaves a short, anxious message, then tries the station. He is quickly patched through to an irate Superintendent Niehaus.

'For God's sake, Tshabalala, where are you two? You're *blerrie* investigative officers in this case, and you aren't even here!'

'We're already in Ponte,' admits Jacob. As he rounds a corner, a gang of dodgy-looking kids, smoking in the gently curving passageway, take one look at him, flick their cigarettes onto the carpet and hurry away.

'*What?*'

'They're still here, but they've now got Harry's wife and child, too. We need back-up *immediately.*'

Jacob hurriedly relates what has happened so far, and then listens patiently while Niehaus admonishes him harshly before proceeding to bark commands at the men he has already assembled at the station.

Niehaus turns his attention back to Jacob. 'I want you

to stay put, Tshabalala! I don't want to see another officer down.'

'Sorry, superintendent, but I've got to find Harry, if he's still alive. I don't think we have much time.' Jacob hangs up.

Finding a functioning lift, Jacob presses the call button repeatedly. On the indicator, he is watching it rising slowly from some parking basement when his phone suddenly trills.

An animal roar erupts just a few yards to Harry's right, and the officer realizes he has fallen into a trap. He swings around, bringing his torch up to reveal a glistening expanse of naked ebony flesh as Ejiofer streaks towards him. The enforcer's body is entirely covered in horrific scars. Harry fires instantly, and two blinding orange flashes dazzle his retinas in the surrounding near darkness. One round misses its target completely, the other impacts with a thud just before a giant shoulder crashes into Harry. The detective is raised clean off his feet and sent flying. As he crashes to the floor, his head cracks against the concrete, and the torch is sent spinning from his hand. Dazed, he instinctively tries to roll aside and get up, but a heavy mass lands on his stomach. The .44 is wrestled from his hand before a fist like a sledgehammer smacks into his face.

'You thought you could kill *me*?' Taiwo roars triumphantly. The injured man is actually laughing as both his fists rain down on his victim. 'You damn stupid cop!'

Harry manages to bring up both arms to cover his face, but the barrage is then shifted to his chest and stomach. The Nigerian switches to Yoruba as he continues to yell a stream of words at the uncomprehending man pinned beneath him. Harry drops one arm and begins feeling along his waist. A fist instantly finds the gap in his defences and two powerful blows rock his head back against the concrete. The detective gasps in agony, and fights not to black out. His hand finally locates his service pistol. Tearing it from his belt, he aims roughly upwards and pulls the trigger.

He flinches as a liquid mess splatters his face. The enforcer's massive body goes suddenly limp, then flops over to one side.

The detective groans in pain, curling himself into a foetal position. His nose feels as if it must be broken and one eyebrow is split.

'Jacob!' he croaks, his battered ribs unwilling to expand to their full capacity. The detective coughs to clear his bruised throat. 'Jacob!' he manages, a bit clearer this time. 'Where the fuck are you?'

A loud clattering of feet echoes through the chamber's black void, which is illuminated only by the white beam of Harry's fallen torch. From where he is now lying, Harry can see the damp clothing Ejiofer shed behind the unidentified machine to provide a false trail for his pursuer.

'Sneaky bastard,' growls Harry to the body lying next to him. Staggering painfully to his feet, he heads back towards the fire door. Only once he gropes his way to the top of the stairs does he realize that the two handcuffed underlings have broken free and fled.

Jacob answers his phone.

'Jakes, it's me—'

'Harry? God be praised! Where are you?' Jacob cuts him short. He moves away from the lift door, intent on keeping the phone connection with his partner.

'Doesn't matter now,' the voice groans. 'Two of them

still on the loose . . . think I know where they'll be heading. Albino lives on fifty-first floor . . . a penthouse. Amy must be up there, too.'

Behind Jacob, the lift pings open to receive him. When he does not step into it, it continues on its way up.

Harry continues, 'The direct lift is probably guarded. I reckon we take the two remaining lifts to the fiftieth floor, then take the stairs the rest of the way and converge on them from two sides.'

'Right,' agrees Jacob, 'but where are you now?'

'Reception lobby by the parking lot, where we started.'

'I'm up on the seventh floor already, the lowest floor of the residential complex. Call me when you get to the fiftieth.' Jacob disconnects and switches his phone to silent, then studies the building plan displayed in the lift foyer. The lift would be the quickest way up to the albino's lair, but, locating the course that both of them just agreed, Jacob turns and sprints down the corridor curving off to the left.

84

Periodic red light from the large advertisement strip just above the albino's apartment illuminates the people gathered in the boss man's study. Adusa just cannot believe that Taiwo is dead, yet the two men now standing before the albino would not lie about the cop being the survivor of their struggle. He bites his tongue as their furious leader picks up his ritual knife from the desk.

'You told him *that*?' he thunders at Mondli, after Nyameko reveals that the policeman now knows where the albino can be found.

Mondli begins a tremulous explanation, but it turns into a wet gurgle after the knife flashes. A thin spray of blood spatters the albino's chest as the other man reels back frantically clutching at his throat. Nyameko exclaims in horror and tries to duck out of the way, but the handcuff still binding him to Mondli holds him fast.

A yelp is heard from underneath the albino's desk, but no one in the room pays it any attention.

'You are a worthless idiot, that's what you are!'

Mondli drops to the floor, his arm jerking violently in the handcuff connecting him to Nyameko. With a roar of unrestrained rage, the albino turns and sweeps the ritual objects from his desk. The lion's skull shatters against the wall before he gives the heavy desk itself a shove. There is a child's scream from underneath the rocking furniture, and Jeanie crawls out to seek safety in a corner by the window. Barely noticing the child, the albino is now ranting away in his own language. Then, as quickly as his outburst erupted, he falls quiet again.

Adusa watches him impassively, mulling over his own future and how best he can escape any danger to himself. It seems high time to strike out on his own again, since this debacle has gone on too long for his liking.

The albino turns back to face the terrified youth. Plucking his spectacles from his nose and wiping at his eyes, he whispers in Yoruba, 'What is to be done?' He continues mumbling, all the time staring fixedly at a point just above Nyameko's head. The uncomprehending boy bites his lip, terrified of looking up to discover what exactly might be hovering above him, and with which the albino is now communicating.

The albino lowers his angry gaze back to the youth. 'You are absolutely sure that Taiwo must be dead?'

'We . . . we heard it all, Wise One.'

'I will have Moloto's head for this,' the boss mutters. He turns to Adusa. 'We're leaving. We cannot risk getting cornered here. You, Godfrey and Collin will accompany me and the child in one car. The rest will take the woman in another.'

'How about I take the woman?' counters Adusa.

The albino raises a questioning eyebrow, while Nyameko's eyes flicker between the two Nigerians and the body of Mondli, looking for clues as to his own fate.

'You disagree with me?'

'I just think it's best that I distract the police from you and the child, White One,' lies Adusa. 'I will make sure no one follows you. We will guarantee your escape.'

'All right, then.' The albino nods hesitantly. 'We'll do it your way.'

With these words he stoops to wipe his knife on Mondli's purple shirt before sheathing it in his belt.

'Get up. Come here!' the *baloyi* barks at the little girl still huddled in a corner behind his desk. Jeanie's face is puffy with all the tears she has already wept. She shakes her head defiantly at the monstrous man now looming over her.

Scowling, the albino grabs her cruelly by the arm and, lifting her completely off her feet, hoists her to his shoulder. His expression indicates no animosity or hatred. In his eyes she is just a creature like any other animal.

'We go now,' he grunts to Adusa. 'Forget the rest of the packing and leave everything else here.'

'What about me?' squeals Nyameko, rattling the hand-cuff still binding him to the corpse's limp arm.

The albino turns slowly to stare at him. 'I have no use for any bearer of bad news. Surely you know the history of our African tribes? The bearer of ill fortune was always killed instantly. Be glad I'm not doing the same to you.' Turning away from the quivering teenager, he storms through into the living room and there barks commands at the few followers he has left. Pausing at the doorway to the albino's study, Adusa looks back at the strange-headed boy, whose eyes are wild with panic. Casting a quick glance at his departing master, Adusa says, 'There is a machete in his cabinet somewhere. Try to cut through the other's wrist – that's best.' He turns and closes the study door behind him.

85

The lift slows to a crawl, then stops with a gasp on the fiftieth floor. Its steel doors drag open, and Jacob glances at his gun's safety catch before stepping into the empty corridor. He decides to press on up the stairs without waiting for Harry's phone call. Pausing in front of the fire door, he holds his breath and puts an ear to it. No disturbing sounds reach him, so he pulls it open slowly and peers out into the corridor. The penthouse level has the atmosphere of an abandoned warehouse. Its flock walls and thick carpets are better preserved than on the lower floor and help absorb the sound of his footfalls as he steadily advances into the corridor, listening for the sound of voices. Opting to head right, the detective crosses over to the corridor's left-hand wall, so that the gentle curve of the cylindrical building will offer him some cover.

Jacob's senses are prickling at random details. Above him an air vent whispers like reeds chafing against reeds.

The air has a sharp smell that makes his nose itch. A large cockroach, barely visible, is pottering along the brown carpet several feet ahead of him, a fat egg sac protruding grotesquely from its abdomen.

Suddenly Jacob hears an urgent muttering somewhere ahead of him, then a door slamming, an angry voice. A young, maybe female, voice is whimpering.

People are now heading towards him. At the same instant, his mobile vibrates to an incoming call.

Jacob retreats along the curved corridor, answering its buzz in an urgent whisper. 'Harry, they're heading towards me now.'

'Where exactly are you?'

'On the fifty-first floor already.'

'I've just reached the other side of the building.' The phone goes dead.

At that very moment, Jacob finally lays eyes on the albino *baloyi*. The man coming into view is speaking on a mobile phone. Dressed in a smart gold-green tunic, he is striding ahead of two of his henchmen. One of them is a corpulent young man, who appears armed only with a carving knife. The other, a grey-bearded man in his forties, is clutching a 9 mm pistol in one hand and carrying Harry's terrified daughter in his other arm.

Spotting the policeman with his back pasted to the corridor wall, the witch stops in angry surprise. For the briefest moment, only he and Jacob are aware of each other.

The albino's eyes widen and his body tenses – just as the man called Collin notices the cop. The henchman yells out, and shoots without warning.

*

Harry bursts through the fire door, shedding any caution as he sprints down the left-hand corridor. His breath erupts in thick rasps; his gun is clasped tightly in his hand.

Apartment numbers fly past him. He passes a lift lobby, its indicator lights out cold, then another series of empty apartments. Seconds pass as Harry runs, then suddenly two shots echo down the corridor. It spurs him on. An unexpected image of that young girl executed yesterday runs through his mind.

Harry presses on harder, arms and legs pumping faster.

Into view comes a group of men bundling together in front of a lift door some twelve yards ahead. Their attention is distracted by something happening further down the same gently curving corridor. Harry immediately distinguishes his wife's anguished cries among their babble.

'Amy?' bellows Harry.

She looks around, hope spreading instantly over her frightened, haggard face. As the albino's thugs also turn in his direction, weapons come up and gunfire rips through the silence, like sudden thunder tearing through storm clouds. Harry flattens his back against the protection of the curved wall as bullets zip past him and burrow into carpeting and wooden panelling.

A bell pings, with the sound of doors sliding open. Harry hazards a quick glance along the corridor, in time to see Adusa bundling his wife roughly into the lift.

'Harry,' screams Amy, 'he's got Jeanie. Help us!'

More cover fire crackles, and Harry is forced to duck back. He hears his wife yelp in pain as the elevator doors close.

Harry turns and smacks the wall in frustration, before darting back in the direction he came from. His only hope of giving chase is to find another operational elevator. A few seconds later, further gunfire makes him flinch. He can only hope that Jacob is having more luck in finding Harry's daughter.

The albino's group has retreated from their encounter with Jacob back to the lift lobby beyond his apartment. They find themselves too late to join Adusa and his men in the alternative lift so instead they plunge down the staircase, with the cop somewhere behind them.

Having not so far been trusted with any weapons, Godfrey feels more than helpless with the carving knife he has hastily retrieved from the albino's kitchen. His right hand clutches the banister as he hurries down the staircase, moving ahead of Collin, whose progress is slowed by having to carry the child.

'Hurry,' hisses the albino, a few paces ahead of them.

The little girl is crying again, the sound of it clawing at Godfrey's conscience. He hears the pursuing cop's feet closing in on them down the concrete staircase.

As the albino reaches the next level down, Godfrey suddenly hears a voice behind them demand loudly, 'Stop, or I shoot!'

The young man stops immediately and looks up. A brief flash of relief washes over his face, before Collin crashes into him, sending him tumbling down the stairs. The fire door on the level below clanks shut after the albino escapes through it.

Jacob repeats his demand on seeing Collin still bent on making a getaway. Collin stops and stares coldly back at the policeman. 'Shoot me?' He laughs. 'You wouldn't do that with the girl in my arms.'

A little further down the stairwell Godfrey groans as he staggers upright, just out of Jacob's view. The young man stoops and picks up the kitchen blade he dropped.

Jacob's hand holding the gun rests comfortably on the banister rail overlooking the lower flights. 'Jeanie, your father and I are coming to fetch you and your mother, OK?'

'Where's my Duddy?' asks Jeanie, trying to push herself loose from the man who is clutching her painfully around the waist.

'He'll be here now.'

Godfrey stares up at Collin's back, debating what to do next, then he glances briefly over his shoulder at the emergency door a few steps below him. The albino seems to have vanished without trace.

Collin levels his pistol straight at Jeanie's face. 'You can shoot me if you like, but I guarantee you'll be killing her, too. You'd better know I'm not afraid of you. If this body dies, I'll already be somewhere else. You do whatever you want; my soul is safe.'

Jacob licks his lips uncertainly. 'You'll still pay for the things you've done to those children.'

'Do you honestly think I'd have done everything I have done for the White One if I still had any soul left in this body?' Collin chuckles. 'Of course not! I am a father myself; I have a son whose belly is full, and I know he's happy in school. This physical form of mine is unclean, yes, but my soul is not. You see, the albino and I have hidden it away where no one can find it.' Collin takes a hesitant step down. Noticing Jacob's pistol wavering, he breaks into a big grin and descends another three quick steps to disappear from Jacob's line of sight.

Abruptly, Jacob hears a painful sob, just before Jeanie emits a piercing scream.

Jacob curses and hurls himself down the lower flight's remaining steps. There he finds the albino's two henchmen confronting each other, but Harry's bawling daughter is now in the younger one's arms. The youngster's face seems contorted with despair, while the older man's face is frozen with surprise. Jacob then notices the knife buried deep in Collin's back.

Stepping back, Godfrey yells defiantly, 'You killed *my* brother! I watched you shoot him while he was begging on his knees!'

'You little shit,' gasps Collin, bringing up his pistol.

'No!' yells Jacob. Leaping from where he is standing, he smashes into the armed man. But he is too late, as a deafening roar reverberates within the confined space.

The stabbed man's head cracks heavily against the wall and his pistol clatters down the stairs. Jacob pulls himself free, as Collin finally crumples unconscious to the floor, but he stares in dismay as the younger man also sways. Godfrey's hands and chest are now covered in blood, his horrified eyes fixed on Jeanie who, also blood-smeared, lies prone on the steps between them.

An accelerating City Golf screeches around the corner from Klein into Smit Street and drifts across two lanes, leaving a trail of rubber. The vehicle hits the opposite kerb before Niehaus manages to regain control.

Cursing in Afrikaans he turns to Bobby Gous, who is holding on tight to the dashboard, looking very pale, 'I don't mind Molethe – he's a good man – but he's a fucking snail when it comes to getting things organized.'

Niehaus stamps on the brakes as a big woman steps out into the road without looking. He swerves neatly around her, before dropping the car into second, extracting a protesting scream from the engine. Bobby eyes the speedometer and winces.

'What the hell those two palookas were thinking of, I don't know,' complains Kobus.

'I would've done the same,' grunts Bobby.

'What the hell do *you* know?' bellows Niehaus. After a few seconds he says, 'Oh, fuck, you're probably right.'

The car seems briefly airborne as it screams down Saratoga's steep incline. When it settles again, both officers' heads smack against the roof of the cramped interior. Seconds later, they clip past a broken gate and enter the lower-level parking lot.

'I thought Uys said this area was locked up, for sure,' mutters Gous.

'Look, there's Mason's car,' says Niehaus.

'Where to now?'

'Fuck knows,' answers Niehaus grimly, surveying the dark basement area extending around them.

86

Jacob scrambles over to where Jeanie is lying, picks her up and hugs her limp body tightly.

'I . . . I'm so . . . sorry,' whimpers Godfrey, shock blanching his face as he begins to stagger backwards down the stairs. 'I didn't mean for this.'

A couple of steps down, he trips on Collin's pistol and tumbles down the rest of the flight, thudding resoundingly into the emergency door on the landing.

Only then does Jacob see clearly the ragged hole in the boy's side.

Jacob quickly runs his hands over Jeanie's body and discovers only a swelling on the back of her head, where it must have connected with the edge of a step. He kisses Harry's daughter on the forehead, giving silent thanks to God, before laying her down on the stairhead nearby

While he is handcuffing the stabbed and unconscious henchman to the railing, Jacob suddenly hears the door below creak. Immediately reaching for his weapon, he peers down the stairwell. The emergency door stands ajar, Godfrey's weight still slumped against it.

Jacob stands up and moves carefully down towards it. When Jeanie groans softly behind him, he glances back to see her stir and open her eyes.

Jacob progresses swiftly down the remaining steps, listening intently before crouching down next to the body of the younger man. He feels carefully for Godfrey's pulse, but finds none. Sadly patting the young man on the shoulder, Jacob gets up and carefully pushes the door fully open.

He sees nothing in the passage to his right. But, swinging his pistol to the left, he is just in time to glimpse the distinctive form of the albino about to disappear further around the gently curving corridor. He must have been hanging about waiting for the outcome of the conflict.

'*Stop!*' yells Jacob futilely.

The witch does pause briefly and turn around. Jacob senses a slow, arrogant smile spreading over that hideous face, and for the briefest moment he even imagines the *baloyi* is winking at him.

'Damn you!' hisses Jacob through gritted teeth.

Abruptly something grabs at the back of Jacob's leg.

He looks down into Jeanie's large frightened eyes. When he glances up again, the corridor is completely empty. His prey has disappeared.

To Harry's intense annoyance, the descending elevator halts on the fifth floor. The door slides open to reveal a waiting clergyman and his wife, who register Harry's bloody appearance and gasp in unison.

'Out of my way!' he bellows, pushing roughly past them. He does not have a moment to lose and cannot endure waiting for his lift to resume its downward journey. He sprints down the corridor towards the other elevator, the one that Adusa and his men have used to make their escape with Amy. Reaching the lobby, he butts open the fire door to the staircase, after noting that the lift has halted at the sixth parking basement below him.

Harry again bursts through a fire door, his chest heaving for breath, and desperately fumbles for the pistol in its holster. He wipes sweat from his eyes and surveys his dark surroundings. The parking lot looks cool and empty – nothing to see except for a few cars ticking as they cool down. He takes the few steps over towards the lift and anxiously studies the blinking floor numbers. The lift is already ascending again. So how long ago did it stop here?

His own car is parked one floor further down, on the level most accessible from Saratoga Avenue.

Suddenly the roar of an engine starting up reaches Harry's ears. A split second later the sound of gunfire being traded on a massive scale throws him into action. Car tyres squeal as he runs further out into the parking lot, attempting to distinguish the source of the noise. Over the tops of stationary vehicles, Harry sights a silver Ford

Cortina speeding down the incline before it disappears from view behind the lines of parked cars.

Harry weaves his way between the parked lines to reach the exit route. Spotting the Cortina racing directly towards him, he ducks back between two vehicles and brings up his gun.

The bullet-scarred car shoots past and Harry stares after it aghast. For the briefest of moments his own eyes met Amy's staring out at him bewildered through the car window.

Harry dodges back between an old Fiat and a white Nissan Sentra, as a skull-capped man sitting in the back seat of the Cortina thrusts a weapon out the window and fires off a burst at him.

Without pause, Harry rounds the Fiat and heads back the way he came. He has no idea how he is going to stop them, but he knows he has one last chance before they reach the thoroughfare outside.

Weaving between the parked cars, he sprints like he has never done in his life, driven by sheer desperation. He reaches the staircase, leaps down the two interceding flights of stairs and bolts out into the lower level. He is in time to see the Ford streak past four rows of cars, break sharply into a ninety-degree turn and enter the exit lane closest to him. Without hesitation, Harry runs out into its path and raises his gun.

'Stop, you son of a bitch!' he roars impotently.

He can see Amy with her hands pressed against the windshield, screaming his name and shaking her head in warning. Instead of slowing, Adusa drops the vehicle into a lower gear and stamps on the accelerator. The car's body lifts as the V6 engine charges. It thunders towards Harry, but he dares not shoot for fear of harming his wife. As if from far away, he hears someone yell his name. Turning his head slowly, as if in a dream, he never gets to see who it is.

A violent force hits him sideways, sending him flying straight into the back of a parked Cressida. The air is driven from his lungs, and behind him he hears shrieking tyres, a desperate scream – before a massive explosion of crunching metal drowns out everything else.

Harry sags to the floor and blacks out.

A rough hand is slapping at his face. 'Harry? . . . *Wake up*, Harry!'

Harry grimaces and opens his eyes, trying to sit upright. He grunts in pain, realizing some of his ribs may be broken. He slumps back to the ground, partly propped up against some car's bumper. He is vaguely aware of a distant voice apologizing, begging his forgiveness . . . then everything suddenly comes into sharp focus again, as Harry recalls where he is and recognizes who is speaking to him. It is his colleague Bobby Gous.

'Jesus, we didn't see her, Harry. We just saw them all climb into the car, so we opened fire. We never saw her.'

What's he on about? wonders Harry. He shakes his head and manages to straighten up further. Bobby's face comes back into view. Harry blinks rapidly and wills away the nausea overwhelming him. The air is thick with burnt rubber, and smoke is stinging his eyes. The smell of brake fluid combined with petrol is noxious. But Harry gradually differentiates another sound, one that cuts through his heart. Nearby a man is weeping in unrestrained grief.

'Amy?' whispers Harry. He tries to struggle to his feet.

Bobby Gous grabs him roughly by the shirt to restrain him. He is trying desperately to block Harry's vision.

'*Amy!*' screams Harry, struggling weakly against Gous's restraining hand. 'Let go of me, you little fucker!'

Harry tears himself free, then manages to turn around.

One of the stationary cars has been hit so hard it now lies tilted on its side, crushed hard against a concrete pillar marked with an orange 'A1'. A blue Opel has been rammed forwards into the two cars facing it. The Cortina itself is now a mangled mess of rent steel, its windshield scattered like a thousand diamonds all over the remains of the bonnet and the ground beneath. Large quantities of liquid are dripping from underneath the vehicle, slowly flowing along the exit lane. What used to be Adusa Okechukwu protrudes grotesquely from the driver's side.

Niehaus stands with his head buried deeply between crossed arms resting on the roof of the Ford, his shoulders hitching violently.

Harry moves forward, but Bobby tries to hold him back. 'Harry, trust me, you *don't* want to see this.'

Mason grimaces and weakly swings a fist. 'God *damn* it, that's my *wife* in there!'

He tears free from Gous and stumbles round to the side of the vehicle where Amy had been sitting. One look confirms his worst fears. He slumps to his knees, grabs one of her bloodied hands and fights for breath before a long, low wail finally escapes his throat.

Niehaus backs away hastily as Harry drops his head into his dead wife's lap.

There are police sirens everywhere, and Harry vaguely hears car doors slamming, commands being shouted, but none of it means anything to him – it is all too distant, all too alien. All he can feel is Amy's warmth slowly ebbing from her broken body. He grips her hand tighter, and tighter again, as if he can prevent what little life she still exudes escaping. Nothing exists for him any more except her still form before him.

A firm hand eventually grips his shoulder, but Harry does not want to hear what its owner is saying. Gradually, its persistence breaks through to him.

'Harry . . . Harry . . .?' It is Jacob's voice. 'Harry, listen to me.'

'Bugger off. Leave me alone with her!'

'Harry, someone else needs you. I'm sorry, Harry, but Jeanie needs you, too.'

Jeanie?

'Where?' gasps Harry, wiping away tears.

'Come,' whispers Jacob, holding out his hand for Harry to grasp.

As Harry pulls himself up, he immediately spots his little daughter standing with one tiny hand clasped in Niehaus's fist.

He staggers towards her, she breaks away from Kobus – and father and daughter hug each other harder than they ever have before.

87

It is seven o'clock on a Saturday morning when Jacob and Nomsa pull in at Johannesburg International Airport. Stepping out of his little Nissan Champ, Jacob looks up into a crisp blue sky and inhales a big lungful of morning air, while listening to the roar from a landing Boeing. They have never been to this place together, and it is Nomsa's first time at the airport.

'You don't have to come in, if you don't want to,' says Jacob, noticing his girlfriend's wary expression.

Nomsa smiles coyly at him over the roof of his red vehicle. 'It's not *this* that I'm worried about.'

Jacob knows full well what she is talking about. This day is going to be eventful, indeed. After the imminent meeting, they will be mounting a two-hour drive in the direction of the Magaliesberg mountain range, for the purpose of visiting Jacob's father, whom Jacob has not seen in eighteen years.

'I know.' He smiles reassuringly.

Turning towards the building, which Jacob has always thought of as grotesque with its horn-like spires, Nomsa grabs hold of his hand. 'Can I ask you something?'

'Sure,' he replies.

'I'm just anxious, understand?' she begins uncertainly.

'Of course, I understand.' Jacob turns so that he is facing her completely and takes hold of her other hand, too.

'We . . . we met through the church, and we have done so many things together as two . . . well, I don't want to say *religious* people, but as two Christians. Now, we both know you've changed, you've experienced things I can't yet fully come to terms with: and I'm not saying I'm holding it against you. It's just . . . I'm afraid, with you going home to see your father, and you talking so readily about your grandfather again, that we will somehow drift apart.'

Jacob lets go of one hand and gently lays a palm on one of Nomsa's cheeks. 'I won't deny that I've been thinking heavily about my grandfather's teachings. And I'll also not deny that I'm going home to rediscover my family

– and my past, because it is in my past that my grandfather lives on. But don't worry, I may seem a sort of prodigal son returning home, but I'm not turning my back on you, or on God. It's just that I realize this is the only way I can get close to my family again, and to my grandfather. If I never went back to them, life would have a lot less meaning for me.' He pecks her softly on the forehead. 'Hmm?'

With a nod, Nomsa lets go of his hand and hugs him tightly. 'I understand.'

Nina absently taps her pen against one tooth while she eagerly studies the arrivals information lighting up in neon green on the electronic boards. The vast hall is milling with people at this time when overnight flights from Europe are arriving every fifteen minutes.

Listening to an electronic voice making an announcement, she is briefly reminded of the time she spent in hospital, wallowing in feelings of guilt and failure. The deaths of those children in the shack under the M1 overpass will perhaps make her question for the rest of her life her decisions as a journalist. It is a shadow that will hang over her head forever – but at least she feels it will somehow give her work a more conscientious direction in future.

For the moment she has cropped her hair again, and she is wearing tight-fitting designer jeans and a black mandarin-collar blouse, while deftly applied make-up conceals the remnants of her bruises.

'Will you just calm down?' says the man standing next to her. He is in his early forties. Thick spectacles magnify the laughter always glittering in his eyes, while a thick brown beard nearly covers his smiling mouth. A Sony video camera is perched on his right shoulder. 'You're behaving like someone's about to ask you out on a date.'

'This is it, Oliver. Here they come!' Nina waves enthusiastically at the three people now emerging through the arrivals exit, pushing a trolley laden with their baggage. Between the sad-looking elderly couple Tumi looks fresh and composed in a lovely navy blue summer dress. Some paces behind them walks a stern-looking, long-nosed man with a heavy coat slung over one arm. Nina recognizes Chief Inspector William Ackroyd from Scotland Yard.

When she spots Nina, Tumi's face breaks out in a happy smile and she waves. Nina instantly waves back in response.

'Excellent shot, Nina, most excellent,' mumbles Oliver Rankin, the freelance journalist Nina's editor in London had wanted her to contact in the first place. Ironically, they have been getting on well from the moment they met.

'Is he really dead?' whispers Tumi, as she hugs Nina fiercely.

'Your uncle finally got what he deserved,' Nina replies evasively.

The last time they met, Tumi's face had been a picture of total defeat. Nina gently pushes her back and studies her changed expression. Overlaying the suffering she has experienced are now hope and expectation, visible in her shining eyes and beaming smile.

'Are you ready to see your parents again?'

Tumi nods vigorously.

With a knot growing in her throat, Nina greets Tumi's two guardians, Mr and Mrs Holmes, both of whom are clearly struggling with their emotions.

'We want to thank you for all you've done,' begins Tabitha Holmes, as her husband is giving Nina a mighty handshake.

'Nina!' a voice calls from the milling crowds around them.

She turns and spots Jacob, and her eyes light up. 'How great of you to come. Here, meet the girl who made it all happen. No . . . stand still a moment, smile for the camera. Tumi, this is Detective Inspector Jacob Tshabalala. He's the one who helped track down your family.'

Tumi greets him hesitantly in Zulu, and then Jacob is overwhelmed by the number of other people whose hands he has to shake. Before he knows it, everyone is moving towards a coffee shop at one end of the concourse to get better acquainted. He glances apologetically at Nomsa, sitting next to Tumi, but as their eyes meet briefly, hers are glittering at him with immense pride.

Jacob leans over to Nina, who is describing animatedly the documentary she is currently compiling. 'Nina, I have to go,' he apologizes.

'So soon?'

'We have a long drive ahead of us.'

Nina glances briefly at the rest of the group. 'I'll walk out with you.'

As they head towards the car, Nina lets a hand rest on his shoulder.

'So how is he doing?'

'The funeral takes place this coming Tuesday,' replies Jacob. 'I don't know . . . if he didn't have Jeanie to look after, things might be far worse.'

Nina nods sadly. 'It's a dreadful mess, that's what it is. And you?'

Jacob glances at Nomsa and considers the monumental

task immediately ahead of him. 'I should be absolutely fine the minute certain journalists stop plaguing me with questions.'

Nina laughs loudly. 'You should be so lucky. Any luck yet in tracing the albino?'

Jacob pauses and stares down at his feet. 'No, and I don't think we'll hear from him again any time soon. He's . . . he's a tricky one.'

For a moment Jacob wants to bare his heart to Nina. He wants to tell her that, now more than ever, he fears the albino might be a real witch after all. How often is Jacob now startled awake at night by howling dogs? Then, lying sleepless, staring at the dark ceiling, he becomes convinced that his nemesis is more than the clever charlatan the media describe. The dreams he has of the *baloyi* playing with him are deeply disturbing. He wonders what she would say if he told her all that. No, he cannot share his distress with her, or even with Nomsa. Not yet anyway.

They say their goodbyes at the exit to the car park and Nina is left to finally reunite Tumi Maduna with her anxious family waiting in Cullinan.

Coming out of the Christof Van Wyk building, where the young Inspector Mason spent a good portion of his career as a detective with the Murder and Robbery Unit, Harry stops momentarily at the head of the steps and soaks up the unattractive view of Biccard Street, crammed with cars and teeming with people. He exhales with an air of finality. It has been done – Chief Molethe has received his resignation. The chief did not press him too much about reconsidering this final decision, certainly not after Harry made it clear that his daughter is now his priority. This Molethe understood wholeheartedly, or so it seemed.

443

Over the last week Harry has come to face a truth that Amy urged him to confront all along: working in homicide was never going to help him to exorcize the demons of his own past. Rather, it kept his boyhood friend Roger's death alive in his mind, buried deep but always ready to resurge and possess him all over again. All he wants to be now is a regular guy, and above all else a regular father.

A sudden knot of emotion in his throat forces Harry to swallow hard. He fumbles in his pockets for a fresh pack of Lucky Strikes. Tearing off the cellophane with a shaky hand, he thinks back to the funeral yesterday, recalling how Jeanie reacted. Everybody commented on what a beautiful, peaceful funeral it was. He cannot understand what could be so beautiful and peaceful about listening to clods of soil hitting his young wife's coffin, especially when she is dead because of his career. As he threw red carnations on her casket the immense guilt he felt was overwhelming. He will have to come to terms with that guilt somehow, the same way he has to come to terms with other things going back to his blighted childhood.

He stops picking at the foil protecting the tobacco and studies the packet of cigarettes in his hand. Then, abruptly, he throws it to one side.

She hated these things, too.

The glass door behind him opens. 'What are you doing, standing out here in the open?' asks Jacob.

'Nothing.'

Jacob grunts in disbelief.

'Oh, shut up and let's go.' Harry smiles thinly. 'I promised you lunch, didn't I?'

Thus it is that Harry finally gets to tell his own childhood story to his friend. Jacob listens intently and nods occasionally, as if Harry is confirming something Jacob knew all along.

As they are leaving the restaurant, Jacob suddenly grasps Harry's hand firmly and stares him in the eye. 'Fate and destiny are complex things we shouldn't try to understand, my friend. God has a purpose for you, and it's up to *you* to discover what it is.'

Harry nods. 'Thanks for all the support you've given us. Things have been tough, and I know Jeanie has appreciated it a lot.'

'How is she now?' asks Jacob.

'She spends a lot of time with her grandparents these days, but she's doing much better.' Harry blinks rapidly, then smiles. 'You know she thinks you're a bloody hero?'

'Me?' asks Jacob and, smiling shyly, shakes his head.

'I want you to come over and visit us sometime, you and Nomsa, like we talked about.'

'We'll come, I promise. But first I want you to meet my father.'

'Oh?' says Harry, not having expected that.

'I want you to learn what it is to be a Zulu – ' Jacob laughs mischievously – 'like we talked about.'

After arrangements are made, the two former colleagues depart, Jacob returning to the office, Harry going back to an empty house, and still without any idea of what to do next with his life.

A knock at his door wakes Golden Boy with a start. He slips his hand underneath his pillow and grabs hold of his gun, rising from his bed just as another sequence of persistent knocking disturbs the dead of night. Dressed only in his red silk boxer shorts, Boy cocks his pistol and carefully approaches the front door. With Duff and Rhaj arrested in London three days ago, he has been expecting the police.

He peers through the spyhole set in the thin wooden door. Even though his back is turned to the door, Golden Boy immediately recognizes his old business associate. Rather than opening up, Boy carefully places the nozzle of his gun against the door, in line with the albino's back. It would be so easy to rid himself of this man who has cost him so dearly over the last few days.

Abruptly the albino, now dressed in jeans and a *Topsport* tracksuit top, turns around. Instead of banging again on the door he puts his eye up close to the spyhole and whispers, 'Open up.'

Golden Boy steps back from the door and clasps the gun with both hands. He gulps audibly, wondering how the albino tracked him down.

'Open up,' comes the whisper again, more urgent this time.

Not knowing how long the albino is willing to stand out there in the corridor and risk drawing attention, Boy pulls back the bolts, though he leaves the security chain in place. He opens the door barely a slit and peers out.

'What do you want?' he whispers.

The albino smiles at him, flashing his unusually large white teeth. 'The only thing you can give me now is safe passage out of the country.'

'Are you insane? They're onto me because of you.'

The albino shakes his head in patronizing disbelief. 'Don't you ever read the newspapers? They are onto you because of those Brits you had dealings with. That's right – Maduna's niece escaped because *your* people screwed up, not mine. So, I should say you owe *me* a favour.'

'I can't afford dealing with you right now,' replies Golden Boy out loud.

'All I want is safe passage out of this country – and the chance to speak with you about an idea I have,' whispers the albino. He folds his arms across his chest and positions himself squarely in the doorway, as if willing to wait there until the end of time.

Boy flicks a nervous thumb over his nose and tries to peer up and down the corridor over the chain. Perhaps listening to the albino would not be such a bad thing, after all.

'Are you alone?'

'Of course,' replies the albino.

'What's happened to Sibongile?'

'She packed up her things and disappeared with her family. No one knows where she's gone. Come now, open this door.' The albino impatiently grabs hold of the handle.

Golden Boy pulls the chain free and opens up the door. Smiling at him, the albino rubs his hands together and steps into the apartment.

Six weeks after the fateful events in Ponte City, Harry finds himself driving along the R27 on the way to a farm owned by the Goosen family, where Jacob's own family has lived and worked for four generations. In the back seat Jeanie is happily prattling to Nomsa, telling her about some television show she watched the night before, while Jacob relates to Harry Superintendent Bornman's latest discoveries. It was while he was digging deep into the past histories of those three executed club owners that the superintendent unexpectedly unravelled the mystery of the heroin tip-off SANAB received that led to Ngubane Maduna's arrest.

The three victims, later identified as ex-Narcotics detectives, found themselves in trouble financially when the ecstasy trade became swamped with more and more opportunists. Suddenly their club was not earning money, and all the kids began looking for heroin instead. Desperately needing to find a cheap source of H, these ex-cops and their old-time buddy André Viljoen, the only one of the tight-knit group still in the force, hooked up with a Nigerian who seemed to have ample supplies. The Nigerian was called Oba, and the ex-SANAB detectives began buying from him at ridiculously cheap prices, not realizing that the Nigerian was skimming off a much bigger man's pile. Before they knew it, they had all of them attracted the wrath of an organization much larger and more dangerous than they had imagined.

'And what about the girl?' asks Harry.

'There is still no positive identification of the body, although the albino's sidekicks gradually helped us piece together the story of her murder. No one seems to know how she arrived in Newtown, although we now know that this Sibongile woman was partly responsible for luring children off the street for the albino's purposes. I suppose only she will know her victim's name and where she originally came from.'

The two men sit quietly for a while and watch the green bushveld sliding past while listening to the car radio. The heat mirage that is the road stretches into the distance.

'You've gone to visit your father every weekend since Ponte,' observes Harry solemnly. 'Has that got anything to do with our run-in with the witch doctor?'

'No,' answers Jacob, although this is not entirely true. 'My father's dying. He keeps holding on, I think, until he is satisfied that I will fend properly for my family – which is ridiculous, because they mean *everything* to me. *He* is the one who . . .' Jacob pauses, then waves a dismissive hand. 'We are coming to terms with each other, slowly.'

In the rear-view mirror Harry catches sight of Nomsa, listening attentively. 'You two really hated each other that much?'

'The dispute wasn't just about us: it encompassed the entire family – past, present and future generations.'

'So what brought you back together?'

'My father had a vision,' says Jacob matter-of-factly, 'which caused him to see things in a different light.'

'What was it, this vision?'

'You want to hear it?' asks Jacob, genuinely surprised.

'Of course, I want to hear it.' Harry turns the radio off.

Jacob relates him a tale that, as far as Harry can tell, only the son of a *sangoma* could come by. After his friend finishes, Harry looks at him and laughs abruptly. 'It seems you Zulus certainly have a long-winded way of asking for forgiveness.'

Jacob frowns humorously at Harry. 'And it seems you whites don't have any appreciation for a good story.'

Harry pulls his vehicle up beside the largest paperbark thorn tree he has ever seen, which casts its shade over an earthen yard surrounded by a modest collection of mud-constructed huts with corrugated iron roofs. He turns to peek into the back seat and smiles at the way Jeanie is ogling this strange environment.

Out of nowhere, Harry asks Jacob, 'Doesn't your father have a problem with Nomsa being Christian?'

Jacob smiles sadly at Harry. 'I think the imminence of his own death has taught him a lot more about the value of life itself and how precious little time we have to worry about such differences.'

As they climb out, they are immediately greeted by a stream of children gushing out of the various huts or from the nearby undergrowth, where they had been playing. In no time, Jeanie is surrounded by children levelling questions at her in Zulu, which she, unfazed by the incomprehensible but apparently friendly barrage, answers with questions of her own in English. With great gusts of laughter, the white girl is swept away to play in the lush surrounding greenery.

Jacob laughs. 'Your little one's going to be filthy by the end of today. They've just decided to teach her how to make clay figurines down on the river bank.'

Harry looks after his daughter, and a swell of silent panic washes over him.

'Don't worry.' Jacob grabs his shoulder. 'She'll be fine. She's got a whole flock of *piccanins* to look after her.'

Jacob's mother, Martha, comes to a doorway, followed by Grace, her sister-in-law, and they wave greeting to the new arrivals. Martha is a large woman, ageing gracefully, with hair greying at the temples. From behind them, the cooking smells of lamb and sweetcorn drift out into the yard.

Harry is guided to a building set slightly apart from the rest of the compound. Fresh mud has been applied to its exterior, repairing the damage done by recent thunderstorms. Inside it is cool and dark, smelling of old age mixed with the various odours of *sangoma* medicines. Five men are seated on the floor in a large circle, desultorily chatting in the presence of a man looking so wasted by his tuberculosis that Harry is surprised he can still sit upright in his cot. Harry is introduced to the younger men, Jacob's three cousins and his father's current students, before he is invited to take a seat amongst them.

Surveying the room, he is interested to observe that it is not adorned like the muti shops he has seen in Diagonal Street. Sure, there is what looks like an altar standing over in one corner, and there are a number of shelves heaped with highly decorated blankets, but here there are no dried animals suspended from hooks. Instead, some AIDS awareness posters have been fixed on the walls, along with a couple of educational charts depicting the ecosystem and various indigenous trees and animals.

The hoary *sangoma* sucks in a few stuttering breaths before he whispers, 'It is good to meet you, the friend of my son.'

'It's an honour to meet you, too,' replies Harry, bowing his head clumsily.

The conversation continues in Zulu, with Harry alternately eyeing the room and these rural farm-workers, who can barely speak either English or Afrikaans. At first he is nervous, having never before experienced this kind of social situation, but, as jokes are exchanged and Jacob leans across to translate them for him, Harry gradually finds himself relaxing.

A while later, in an astonishingly strong voice, the venerable *sangoma* suddenly announces, 'Harry Mason, I will throw the *amathambo* for you.'

From a cracked leather pouch, the withered old man reverentially pulls out his bones, incanting over them for a while before throwing them onto the sacred mat that lies central in the room. Everyone leans forward eagerly to study the distribution of the shells, stones, bones and an old fifty-cent coin. One or two heads nod, but no one dares speak. Finally the *sangoma* himself cackles loudly.

He whispers something to Jacob, then points a finger at Harry.

The guest, feeling like they have discovered his high-school love letters, turns questioning eyes on Jacob. 'What does it say?' he hisses.

'My father says you suffer from a sickness of the spirit.'

'Meaning?'

'You are not cursed after all, my friend. You've merely chosen the wrong path in life. You have what the Zulus call *ukuthwasa*. You have been deaf to the demands of your ancestors.'

'My *ancestors*?'

All the men in the room laugh at Harry's astonished face. The old one mutters further.

Jacob nods. 'My father says there is much they want to teach you. They want you to open your mind to them and *listen*.'

The conversation veers away from Harry again, leaving him to mull over what has been said. Some time later, however, the talking begins to quieten down, and a dark cloud of expectation can be felt gradually building up in the room.

'Ask him,' says the *sangoma*, when Harry snaps out of his reverie.

Jacob licks his lips and turns to his friend. 'Remember how you refused to visit a *sangoma* when I thought you were cursed by that evil fetish we found with that girl's corpse?'

'I don't really want to talk about that case,' interrupts Harry, painful emotions stirring deep inside him.

'I know, and I understand that,' replies Jacob, looking at the others. 'But this is important, Harry. It concerns your daughter.'

'What about my daughter?' asks Harry quickly.

'Will you trust me – *us* – with what I have to say?' queries Jacob.

'What exactly are you driving at?'

Jacob glances furtively at his father, who merely closes his tired eyes and nods. 'When witches get hold of a child, they generally try to pollute or curse it as soon as possible.' Jacob waits a second, letting his words sink in, before continuing. 'They try to connect the child with themselves, so to speak, because of the child's great worth to them in effecting their evil deeds. So even when a child is rescued, it may still be tainted with a witch's evil.'

Harry shudders. 'What are you saying?' He stares around at the rest of the men in the room. 'Has Jeanie been poisoned or something?'

'Did he make her *eat* anything? Did he *pour* anything into her ear, did he *cut* her?'

'Hell, I don't know.' Harry's voice climbs several notches.

'Has she told you about anything of the sort happening?'

'No!' Harry insists emphatically.

'Will you allow my father to examine her?'

Harry narrows his eyes. 'In what way?'

'I . . . we, just want to be sure, for your own sake.'

Harry lets his eyes roam over this small group of men who have dedicated themselves to becoming healers of afflictions which for the most part Westerners cannot see or understand. They all look so serious and sincere about their intentions. Thinking about the things that have happened to himself and his family over the last month, Harry lowers his head, and repeats, 'In what way do you want to examine her?'

Jacob tells him and, after a moment's hesitation, Harry consents.

It is Martha who brings Jeanie to the door. The little girl, now covered from head to toe in red clay, picks up on the sombre mood inside the hut and becomes instantly serious herself. She enters the room, her eyes cast down and her hands clasped behind her back. Everyone except for Jacob, the *sangoma* and Harry files out the room, leaving Jeanie standing near her father.

'Come here, child,' whispers Jacob's father.

Jeanie looks at Harry apprehensively. He nods to her. 'Go on.'

His daughter proceeds slowly towards the old *sangoma*, who tries, without success, to give her a reassuring smile. 'Give me your hands,' he commands.

She holds out both her hands, with the palms facing up. The *sangoma* grasps her by both wrists, rubbing each of them with his thumbs. Next, he runs his gnarled fingers up her forearms to her elbows, rubbing them gently, then turns her arms so that he can study them from all angles. Lastly, he closes his eyes and puts a hand to her forehead. All the while, Jeanie stares at him with a strange expression: part concentration, part fearfulness, part reluctance.

The *sangoma* opens his eyes and looks at Harry.

'Is there anything wrong with her?' Harry blurts.

The *sangoma* briefly shuts his eyes, then reopens them with a relieved sigh. 'No.'

'You sure?' presses Harry.

Jacob laughs suddenly. 'Harry! What kind of a question is that for a white man to ask a *sangoma*? Of course, he's sure.'

Harry meets Jacob's gaze, before Jeanie distracts him. 'Can I go play again?'

'Yes, love.' He brushes a strand of her hair from his daughter's forehead and smiles. 'Go play.'

BLOODY HARVESTS

For a long time after that Jacob's father refuses to meet his eye.

Late the same afternoon, with the sound of herd boys rounding up cattle in the distance, and a blood-red sunset washing over the bright green of the bushveld, Harry stands leaning against the paperbark tree, watching eight girls braiding Jeanie's hair, all of them chattering to her as if she can understand them. Comparing her experience with his own discomfort on their arrival here, he is impressed by how easy it has been for his daughter to adapt. Now she is smiling again, enjoying herself again – how carefree she seems.

He sighs, turning to look at the sinking sun. He misses Amy so much. He desperately clings to his already fading memories of her voice, her scent, the softness of her hair, the taste of her lips. What is there for him to do next, without Amy? What could he ever want to do without being able to share it with her? This loneliness is a terrible thing to behold, but perhaps Jacob's father is right: Amy may be much nearer, much more involved in their lives, than he realizes.

Jeanie's sudden squeal of delight – 'Look Daddy!' – draws Harry's attention back to her. The angelic grin spread across her face cuts instantly through much of the darkness that has been hanging over him these last few weeks. Her father waves to her in return, as a cold breeze plays over the back of his neck like a ghostly kiss.

Perhaps there is hope after all.

March 2002 to February 2004
London and Pretoria